Contents

For all who long for a different way to live, let the abundance born of love be the song of our souls and the legacy of our lives.

*For a seed to achieve its greatest expression, it must come complete-
ly undone. The shell cracks, its insides come out, and everything
changes. To someone who doesn't understand growth, it would look
like complete destruction.*

– Cynthia Occelli

Trigger Warnings

This book is about traumatic events happening to a fictional character and how she works to recover from those events that shaped her life. She uses various healthy and unhealthy methods and coping skills, which are articulated. However, to protect your mental health, here is a list of potential triggers that might be hard for some readers.

- Allusions to sex (closed door);

- Sexual Assault (on the page);

- Group Rape (referenced);

- Gun Violence and physical violence between characters (on the page);

- Suicide Bombings and aftermath;

- Discussions of divorce and infidelity;

- Implied matricide;

- Inferred mild stalking;

- Alcoholism and addictive behavior;

- Use of offensive language;

- Bullying;

- Dysfunctional family system;

- Religious themes from Christianity and Matriarchial systems;

Please take care of yourself, and if you experience anxiety or a traumatic response while reading, evaluate if you should continue reading and make plans to check in with a licensed mental health care professional.

Introduction

How do you see the world?

Do you see it in black and white or in color?

When you wake up, what is the first thing you think of?

Is it what you have to do, what scares you, or do you wonder if there is something more out there for you?

Do you live with eyes that see the least, the most, or somewhere in between?

We are the people who see the in-between; the more out there that is possible. We have since the dawn of Creation. We would *like* to see the most in what is. That's what we've been taught to do. When we look out into the world, we see the potential of what could be for ourselves and others, the energy and flow of life in and through everyone.

Yet, for the most part, the last six thousand years have been about violence, domination, and scarcity. Our human history is littered with bodies of humans and civilizations. We have denied essential parts of ourselves and our experience, seeming to gain what we want only to lose what we need. Most human minds are not trained to start with and end in abundance. Our default mold or "natural" tendency begins with seeing all we don't have.

Our world, our place in the world, is different, as is our mindset. We aim to be the people who, like those Spanish-speaking toddlers yelling to their Mamas in the store – "MIRA!" LOOK! SEE! We are tasked with seeing the could-be and teaching others how to. Our mission is to show everyone's lack is not where we start. That natural tendency to reach for what's missing is not how we were created to exist. Just seeing those toddlers screeching for more proves it. We learn scarcity. We aren't born into it.

We start there, but there is more. We were created with souls that long for transformation and freedom. The world spins on towards that end. If we lift our eyes past the fear of lack, an incredible life is waiting. A life full of hope, promise, healing, and redemption. Living with abundance shimmering on the edges of our vision is possible. We don't have to start with only seeing what is wrong but to begin to work together for what is right.

If you look deep inside yourself, you will see that desire at the center of your divinely human soul, longing to belong and find purpose. It is the longing that is human and the sense that is Divine.

We've experienced, lived, and taught this for generations since the start of it all. It may surprise you that for tens of thousands of years, our way of being was the norm. We naturally lived together in the cradle of civilization through abundance, collaboration, and equality. But that isn't our world anymore and hasn't been for a while.

We are still here, though, with eyes wide open, and others still come to us to find out how to unlearn lack and live into wholeness. But when bloodshed and violence rule the world, it is nearly impossible to stay alive without closing your eyes sometimes. Closing them to the screaming and suffering that dominate our global senses is the only way to adapt in seasons, so we have.

It's only a means of survival, not a long-term strategy.

Survival mode never leads us to what we were intended for. When the immortal hands crafted us from stardust, we were fashioned with eternity in our center. We can still access it, even as I am a realist and know that even stardust is still just dust. I know it looks and feels like dirt that turns into mud when mixed with blood and water.

Still, that mud we've lived in for thousands of years holds our intrinsic knowing, yearning for more. Survival may be where we start, but it is only the place to start. Thriving is what we are meant for. This is the magic we seek to wield, the wonder of what is possible when humanity reaches its fullest potential.

Only cooperation, not competition, fosters it. Only that is what our society – in Teleosis – holds the key and promise to teach humanity to grow back into our creation molds. Our High Priestess embodied that promise, that it is never only for the individual but for the whole. It is the possibility born out of this stardust, rooted and grounded in the earth's dirt, that we can all thrive and this world can be better than it is.

This is the vision we cast. This is the goal we seek. We wage This war with soft, open hands against fear and scarcity. And we've done it since the first man and woman walked the earth with the Creator – the God, the Goddess, and the Spirit. We know what is possible and what still is available. It requires new eyes to see.

Sounds too good to be true?

Yes, it almost is. There have been many, many ages when we've had to hide ourselves from the world to sprout again when the chaos dies. There have been times when we've been killed for this "radical" idea of more. We've been killed off so thoroughly that only the barest of remnants are left. That group of revenants emerged again when it was safer or less dangerous. Sometimes, only one or two of us could hang in our space to our sacred texts and then share them generations after we rebuilt our people and places worldwide.

We were strong, but now we have been forgotten. Not everyone wants to see this vision reborn. Instead, They would use the secrets we wield for their power-hungry plans. They would keep the world's eyes shut,

This is where we find ourselves against those who prefer everyone's eyes closed. As in the typical way of the world, there are those whose desire for power eclipses anything else. It costs them their soul, and they take the souls of others as they work tragically hard to close everyone's eyes.

Soon, our eyes wide shut will come to an end. We have been on the descent, but soon, there will be one to remember Herself. She will enable our ascension again. She will witness all that could be and plant the seed that will grow into a flower in the desert, a miracle for all to admire. This will be Teleosis again.

We will not stop in our pursuit to show people what could be if they were open to it and set people free from the tyranny of lack. We want all people to be the "MIRA!" people, for us all to be the ones who are fulfilled and fulfilling their meaning and purpose. Some call this perfection, yet we think of it more as progress, intelligently planned and directed through the application of abundance and potential within human DNA to craft the world into a Garden rather than a wasteland.

This remains the question: how do you see the world?

And do you want to see it differently?

Prologue

"**O**pen your eyes, sweetheart. Tell me what you see."

The little girl didn't want to wake up. She was sleepy and didn't want to stand in the dark, facing the sunrise before it even appeared. She did not want to go through the morning religious exercises her mother insisted they do each day. It was training disguised as worship. She was glad to be with her mother, though sometimes she wished it was just for fun. Her mother was warm against her back, keeping away the chill. She held the little girl close into the softness of her body as they stood facing east in the pre-light of day.

"I don't want to."

Her mother softly chuckled. "I know, darling. Would you like to hear what I saw when I opened my eyes this morning?"

It had been like this every day since the little girl could remember. Her mother, the High Priestess, instructing her each moment, in their faith, in what would eventually be her job. She had to know what the FourFold God was like to help and teach others.

The little girl knew she had to learn what it meant to serve The FourFold God if Their presence was to be felt in the world. This was a God like no other. They were four-fold, in the image of unity: Father and Son, Mother and Daughter. This was the God she and her ancestors had served since the beginning when the Divine and humans sang the Song of Creation – together.

This was the practice her mother was teaching her, to open her heart to learn to sing.

Yet, she wondered if The FourFold God, Who had once walked with humanity but long since left our presence really cared what she saw every morning. Were They that picky that they needed her up every day at pre-dawn? Was it necessary to learn how to sing? And did it matter if what she saw was real or pretend?

The little girl mumbled something into her mother's midsection. Her mother gently turned her around to face the coming dawn. Her proud mother sighed – a signal of her expectation. This wasn't a chore for her to perform yet. There was still magic to the silence and deep stirring connection.

"*Ahava*, I remember being your age. I remember thinking It didn't seem like The FourFold God would care whether I did these spiritual practices. But now I know They do – and these practices are just as important for us to remember our origin, story, and mission."

Her mother paused, breathing in deeply. There wasn't any tension in her body, not like later. There was only a peaceful energy thrumming through her. The little girl could hear that energy vibration just as she could hear her mother's heart beating.

"*Ahava*, Noni, we have to remind ourselves each morning that healing rises on the wings of the dawn."

The little girl didn't respond to her nickname. It was more familiar than her name. Her family had called her that since her birth eight years ago. She'd only heard her full name used when she was in trouble. She would hear *Inira Inanna Boehme* and know she was done for.

Here in the half-light, she stifled a yawn and responded, "I don't see much right now except stars. They look like our solar lights when running out of juice."

She could hear the smile in her mother's voice as she replied, "Good, very good. Light to find our way. The stars are the light of endings, meant to guide us into the new beginning. The stars show us this, their light coming from old, faraway places while we stand among the new worlds. It is all a cycle. We stand here to practice our true sight, which will reveal to us that the new will come in the dark but guided by the light. Our people have known that since the days of our First Mother and Father. The new beginning comes in the dark guided by the light of the ending."

The little girl felt her mother's voice resound through her. She wondered what would come next. This was a strange power she had then to weave and craft a story. To make meaning out of seemingly nothing. Every morning was always similar but never the same.

"My *hamuda*, sweetheart, hear me." Her voice took on a reverent tone, softer than when she was leading services but still tinged with power, "What I see in this morning, as the inky dark blue of night fades into pinks and oranges, is possibility. There is always the possibility of something changing or someone coming into the world today that will lead to more of the abundance The FourFold God means for all humanity to live in. There is always a chance in each sunrise to see the revelation of who They are. This is why we are here and have lasted so long as a civilization. This is the change the world has needed, and we get to be the ones who carry that message. We will be the stars that light the way for others. Can you see it?"

"Not really."

Her mother's chuckle was a little loud in the quiet. "That's ok, *hamuda*. I know one day you will. It is your inheritance and your purpose. Learn all you can, and experience everything possible because one day, you will be the mother who teaches the daughter what it means to hold onto our faith and remind her of The Four-Fold God - that They are still here. Now, you see the sun breaking just over the wall? That means it is time to say our morning prayer."

The mother moved the little girl to stand by her side. They held hands and raised their others to the dawn, repeating, "We thank You, Our FourFold God, for the rest You have given us through the night and for the breath that renews our bodies and spirits. May You renew our souls with faith in You, the Source of all Healing, as You rise on the wings of the dawn. Blessed are You, FourFold God, Ruler of the All, as You renew the work of all Creation daily. We bless Your Name as the Peacemaker and Peace Bringer. Teach and enable us today to walk out the possibilities of peace for us, our people, and all humanity. It is so, by the Hand of the Father, the Strength of the Son, the Wisdom of the Mother, and the Love of the Daughter."

Chapter 1

I nira sat up so suddenly. She was startled by the clarity of the dream, so intense it was like she had traveled back through time to those idyllic childhood days when her mother was still soft, not the relentless taskmaster she had become. Between the hangover from their Friday night dinner out with friends, in which Inira drank more than she ate, and the intensity of the dream, Inira's head was pounding. Her husband Francis reached out in his sleep for her, but she slid out of bed. She didn't want his comfort. She longed for the comfort of the one she'd lost.

It was not long after she lost him – lost everything– she stopped saying that sunrise prayer. She hadn't said it in decades. She could feel the emotion welling and wanted to be alone with it. The result of all that wine wasn't helping her to forget him like it used to. She rose silently from the bed and put on her robe. She stopped in the bathroom to drink a full glass of water with four ibuprofen and settled in the living room's big, comfy chair.

It was then she let the tears fall. She tried to stop the hiccuping sobs that followed; the palpable grief felt like a pain in her chest. The hole would never be filled because she knew where she was and not where she felt she was supposed to be. The dream was a memory that felt like someone else's life. Someone with dreams, true love, and eternal, forward-moving purpose.

Her reality fell on her. It wasn't bad; it only felt so much less than what it could have been. Her marriage was decent by Western standards, and her work satisfying enough to keep her going, just not as important and impactful as it was meant to be. The more she dwelled in this emotional cul-de-sac, the more tears fell. The more tears that fell, the quicker the descent into the pit of longing, which represented all she felt was missing from her life.

All that had been taken from her, not just by her enemies but also by the ones she'd loved the most.

Her dream – or memory - was a remnant from when she'd lived in the heart of the Garden, the compound the High Priestess and her family inhabited, in the heart of Tov, the capital city of Teleoisis. It was all before her father was killed, and her mother changed "to get serious about Inira's training." Those days, before Father's death, her sister was her best friend, and Tomas was their constant playmate. They would slowly grow in love as they grew, along with the planned partnership arranged by her mother.

Inira had been meant to take her mother's place, a High Priestess not just of religion but as head of State. Tomas was to be the Consort by her side.

These memories of "what should have been" were all-encompassing. She wondered if any Baileys were in the house to add to her coffee or if she'd finished it earlier in the week. It was her go-to morning mood stabilizer, and she used it more and more.

Inira was stuck in this thought spiral even as she could feel the warmth of her mother's body radiating into hers. She clung to the warmth as memories of her mother like this, living her life in joy rather than from pain because they were few and far between. This was when she'd made training her for her future role as leader and visionary fun. This warmth was like coming back into the sun after a long time in a dark, cold room. It slowed her tears and calmed her breathing.

The pain reliever also kicked in, saving her from head and body aches. Now, the pain was only her soul.

She was no longer the Chosen One among the Chosen people, kept alive and thriving by the FourFold God Teleosians had worshipped since their creation. They were the original people of that ancient cradle of civilization, taking their knowledge, culture, and vision to an island off the coast of Greece in the Aegean when the Indo-European invaders from the North ran out the Goddess-worshipping cultures in the Near and Middle East around six thousand BC. That thought turned her stomach sour.

At this moment, Inira's eyes caught movement in the hallway. A small form crept towards her, silent and careful. She smiled.

The sunshine of her life, who made up for all she'd lost and what was missing in her present, stopped in front of her chair. Inira, now smiling broadly, held her arms open for the little girl, almost nine years old, with dark, thick curls even tighter than hers. The scent of a sleepy child enveloped Inira as her daughter, Emerie, crawled into her lap.

After she got settled, Inira whispered, "Good Morning, my *Ahava Shalom.*"

The little girl mumbled something unintelligible, so Inira leaned down to hear her better. She tilted her head and was rewarded with the strong scent of morning breath, which made her chuckle even as she wrinkled her nose. "What did you say, darling?"

The little girl repeated what she said, barely above a whisper, "Why were you crying, Mama?"

Inira sighed. What do you tell your child of the life you've lost? How could she make her understand? Inira took a deep breath and replied, "I was thinking of a friend I lost a long time ago, and I miss him. I miss my home."

It was all true, even as she boiled it down so her daughter could process, at her age, witnessing her mother cry. She didn't yet grasp that the people of Teleosis had been kept alive by the Four-Fold God for eons to ensure the world knew the original design for humanity. They had been delivered from the hands of those who would steal, kill, and destroy the unity of masculine and feminine they represented. Inira and her Consort would have led the Counsel of Wisdom to show a different way of wholeness to those other cultures steeped in patriarchal oppression.

Teleosis was not just a movement, an idea, or a religious practice. It was the most technologically advanced nation on the planet, where everyone only knew abundance. Scarcity and poverty didn't exist. The inhabitants of their island were allowed to develop their Divinely inspired gifts, talents, and passions without worrying about food, safety, or shelter. It was a model for global economic, political, and humane activism.

Until it wasn't. Until the gods of greed, power, and corruption of the human heart had defeated the FourFold God at long last.

Snuggled up into her mother's neck, Emerie asked a favorite, almost daily question: "Mama, will you tell me a story of your home?"

Inira smiled. She knew the one her daughter craved. The stories she told Emerie were about how she kept Teleosis alive when it had all been scattered to the ends of the earth fifteen years ago, when Tov was blown up on September 10th, 2000. Then, they were forgotten when the rest of the world joined in the experience of terrorist-level destruction for itself on September 11th, 2001, and, of course, the violent ambition of the subsequent Second Gulf War.

So, Inira began just where Emerie liked her to start.

"My daughter, my *Ahava Shalom*, hear me. As we learn from the sacred text, Our First Mother and Father were given the Earth to steward. Sophia and Adan lived in the Garden of Creation with the FourFold God. They had many children, but their first two changed everything." Inira began to recite the ancient poem, the first she ever memorized at four, just as her mother had taught her, just as each Teleosian child was instructed, and just as she had begun to teach Emerie, ever precocious when she could sit still long enough to listen.

The FourFold God blessed the union of Sophia and Adan for their faithfulness. They were blessed with twins – boys meant to take wives and continue to build. Zayin and Sha'ar were the sons of promise. Zayin chose to reject the promise, taking what he wanted for himself. His mind, twisted and warped, believed Sha'ar was favored. A black spot on his soul grew to overtake all that he was. Until one day, he ended both lines of promise with his very own hands.

Inira paused and waited for the question, "Mama, what was the black spot on Zayin's soul?"

Inira smiled, proud her daughter remembered the back-and-forth way of teaching children to look at every facet of a text. "Well, it was jealousy – the first harm done to his brother and his parents. He mistakenly thought Sophia preferred his brother because the little boys were running back together one day for supper, and Sha'ar tripped. Sophia ran to him and hugged him tight, only holding Zayin to her side after. It took just that one extra moment, given to another who was hurting, for the seed of jealousy to take root. It grew, and it grew and..."

"It grew," Emerie said in response to Inira's pause.

"Yes, very good. It grew into such poisonous fruit that, when eaten, it changed the fate of the whole world. What happened, *Ahava?*"

"When they grew up to be men, Zayin killed Sha'ar with his bare hands, choking the life out of him. Violence and domination, which this world was never meant for, then entered Creation through the hands of the Son of Promise." The little girl's recitation was serious.

"Yes, it was tragic. Adan and Sophia pleaded for mercy to the FourFold God, for Them to reconcile and set right what had gone wrong in Zayin's heart. The FourFold God invited Zayin to walk in the Garden, and he did. But he could never again grasp the love They offered. He could no longer accept the truth and purpose of the FourFold Way. He clung to his childish fantasy of being second place, and no amount of wisdom or comfort would change his mind."

Emerie whispered, "He was lost and didn't want to be found."

Inira shook her head. "No, he didn't, and it began to drive him mad, so His Mother and Father had to send him away for the community's safety. The FourFold God went with him, visited him in dreams, and even gave him his family. The Divine had a hand on him until he was again dust."

"From flesh and bone and bone into dust," the sweet child's voice intoned.

Inira nodded. "Yet the madness continued, of the self-will run riot. Zayin's children used their FourFold God-given gifts to serve themselves instead of others. They became greedy and corrupt and have inflicted much pain on this world. Women and children suffer at the hands of men still. Can we change it, darling?"

The little girl hesitated, overcome with the moment's seriousness, seeming to ponder if humanity could be redeemed. When she finally spoke, Inira got chills.

"Through love, all things are possible."

That wasn't part of the script they usually played out. To Inira, this felt like a prophetic utterance that must be documented. Much like that day long ago when a former Teleosian resident testified to who she was when she arrived on the shores of America, bereft of home, land, and husband. That husband had betrayed her, betrayed them all. She had loved the sleeper cell who took it all away from her, and she still did.

She still hoped for the redemption of his story, but it seemed it was as likely as her ever returning to the land of her birth. So, her reply to her daughter was only one word. "Indeed."

They sat together in comfortable, warm silence, Inira thinking perhaps her one and only daughter had fallen back asleep. She took a deep breath, the warmth of the dream long since faded with the rush of remembering why she was where she was today. As she breathed mournfully, Emerie popped her head up and looked into her eyes, the milk chocolate orbs round, meeting her dark ones.

"Don't be sad, Mama. You'll see your home again."

As she stared into those eyes that mirrored hers, Inira felt a firey hot sensation, like lightning, crawl down her spine and settle into her womb space. It was like the words of her precious child had been planted directly into her soul. If they were still in Teleosis, there would be no question in Emerie's path to becoming Heir, even if she was Inira's only daughter.

The prayer from her earlier dream surfaced, and she could have said it. She just felt like there was no point. The Fourfold God of her understanding was no more, and she was trying to find her way without Them: no Father, no Mother, no Son, and no Daughter. It would take divine intervention to prove Their existence to her when there was nothing left to return to.

She did the next best thing she could think of and kissed her wonderful girl on the lips, silently blessing her voice to remain powerful and for her vision to always be this clear. Then she said, "C'mon, my little love. Let's go make pancakes."

Chapter 2

N*ine years later...*

It *all still hurts*, she thought. Her memories, now so much clearer because she'd gotten sober, were still painful, and she sighed in frustration. It was no longer the sharp pain that had driven her to drink but a dull ache. Maybe it was getting sober that brought the reality of who she is now and what her life was like to the forefront of her conscious mind.

She wasn't performing the early morning ritual but was still up before the sun. She had exactly thirty minutes before needing to drive Emerie to swim practice. It was her turn today, thanks to their one-car lifestyle. Teleosis had been at the forefront of climate care, but she could only do what she could here in the States. On other days, she rode the train into the center of town, where her building was. She tried to use that downtime to center herself, using affirmations and quietness, but it was anything but an official prayer.

She heard her daughter moving as they both got ready. Emerie was on the second floor of their brownstone. Her husband of nineteen years, Francis, was still asleep. He'd kept his sound sleeping ability through all the stages of Emerie's childhood. He had just gotten used to Inira taking care of everything. Years later, Inira wakes up early, no matter what. Hangovers never changed that. Emerie was eighteen and a senior in high school, keeping her schedule as she had for years. The one thing Inira still did for her every morning was make her lunch. She only had another few months to do it, as Emerie would go to college. Inira held onto this small act of service as a conscious choice to do things differently than her mother. Inira and her sister had been left to their own devices young when their mother emotionally abandoned them after their father's assassination.

Inira sighed as she now understood trauma in a way she hadn't as a child. It gave her a new level of empathy for her mother. She was working through her resentments, so it was a crap shoot on whether she was in the mood to reject the past or overcome it. A lot depended on how she felt about her mother that day, but it usually boiled down to this: if it were the opposite of her mother's behavior, Inira would do it.

She finished Emerie's lunch and got herself dressed for work. With a quick kiss on the top of his head, avoiding his morning breath, she said, "See you later. Hectic today, so I might need you to cook dinner." Francis grunted his assent with a yawning, "OK, bye." Inira had felt something shifting in her towards Francis, a very safe choice to marry after the chaos of her arrival in the States. They married just over a year after her arrival. She wondered if she would have chosen him if she'd been sober. Several women in her home group had told her, when she first started going to the meeting, that a marriage could change radically for the better – or worse – when one partner gets sober. She was now beginning to see the truth in her heart. She was walking the line, trying to decide if it would get better or worse. Complacency had bred apathy, with little passion existing between them. They were both comfortable. Or Francis was, but Inira was finding she was not.

Inira was busy enough that healing her emotional wounds was an arduously slow process, as was pressing into sobriety. She went to AA meetings as often as she could, but it never ended up being more than once a week. She had her home life – which included most of the domestic work. That fell to her because of patterns set years ago in her efforts to play the part of the perfect wife and to hide her drinking. Her work was generally fulfilling, with a major presentation looming. She hadn't had much in the way of dreams lately, and she thought, gratefully, that maybe things were starting to settle, and she was getting used to her brain functioning more like a normal person's. She contemplated this as she drove into work and promptly forgot about it as the numbers on the spreadsheet went black.

Just after lunch, she suddenly felt like she'd been hit with a two-by-four in the back of the head when the scent of vanilla and lavender struck her full in the face. She was instantly confused and paralyzed. She had the brain-scrambling sensation that she was being ripped through space and time, landing on the spot of the counter in her grandmother's kitchen, which she always occupied. She could see her grandmother making biscuits, bread, or any other baked goods she felt like.

They would recite the ancient texts or stories her mother wouldn't dare tell her. Inira nearly felt the weight of her little legs swinging back and forth as she soaked in the dark and forbidden history of the world and how the High Priestesses became Warrior-Queens to bring forth the light. She could almost reach out her hand and touch the copious amounts of Mediterranean lavender growing in the garden outside. She could taste the pure vanilla extract her grandmother made herself and used as a perfume. She could see the woman who was the center of her life reaching forward to touch her nose with a floured-covered finger during one of the juicier parts of a story.

Those two scents swirled around her, draping her in warmth like a parka on the coldest day of the year. She hadn't smelled that combination since the Darkest Day attacks. That realization was like a bucket of ice water over her head. The momentary experience of pure love at the memory of her grandmother was replaced with full awareness of that black hole in her mind like she was staring into the dripping maw of her fear.

Her fingers itched for a shot glass. A quick swallow of the throat-burning liquid courage would chase away these intense feelings.

In a herculean effort of will, Inira wrenched her consciousness back, away from the fear and memory sensation. Returning to the present, she caught the date on the calendar out of the corner of her eye. The realization of what would happen in a week – the presentation for the highest-profile foundation they've ever had

– slammed into her. The annual report on the progress of their investments on behalf of the non-profit arm of the Nahas International Conglomerate to the entire board is due to be completed tomorrow.

Finally, she clawed enough brain space to move again. She knew she needed something strong to fight the sluggishness of the emotional roller coaster her body had just gone through, to cancel wherever that lavender and vanilla scent came from hopefully. Only espresso will do the trick.

Slowly pushing herself away from her desk, Inira moved to stand as she heard, "Inira! Hello Inira! Are you ok?"

The large, green-flecked brown eyes of her top client advisor, Charlotte, come into view.

"You've been sitting there for six minutes staring at your screen and not moving. Are you alright? Is it the stress of this presentation getting to you?"

"Uh, yes, I think so. Were you timing me?" Inira asks quizzically, the conversation helping to recover her sanity again.

Charlotte smiles softly, "Well, it was so weird and sudden; I thought maybe you having some kind of seizure or stroke."

Shaking her head and arms, Inira responds, "Well, no, not a seizure, but maybe a stress-induced panic attack because we've got a week left before we fly out. But thankfully, I've got you and want your help preparing the financial reporting slides."

She didn't trust herself to see the numbers on the screen for a while correctly. She needed some time to recover from that memory-conjured hallucination. Looking directly into Charlotte's eyes and channeling 'boss mode,' she tried to project confidence by saying, "This is a huge deal to this foundation board, so we need to be 1000% accurate. You've always been great with numbers, so come here and prove my work."

Charlotte was still looking at Inira as if she had three heads as she stood to walk over to Inira's desk. Inira breathed a long, slow breath to ensure she was steady as she entered their offices' modern, efficient kitchen workroom. The stakes of this meeting are large. Well, not for Inira but for her boss, Stanley. As the President of Triune, playing on this level of field would ensure his legacy to his family is complete. He still has a few more years in him before he retires, she thinks hopefully, and whether his sons sell the company or keep it going, there will be plenty to go around. Enough to buy a small island for each one.

As high-profile as meeting with Nahas International is, it is nothing compared to what she would have handled as High Priestess and even as Heir. A ten-second scan of the headlines could tell her all she needed to know about the world every morning. It was usually another version of the same old story. She spoke and wrote with easy eloquence and could handle contracts, negotiations, and the egos in any room. She was an expert at building connections and relationships. She could do all the things a C-level officer in a mul-ti-million-dollar corporation could do because she was supposed to take over running a country and a religious movement at the age of twenty-one.

This job was a cakewalk, and with this account, for the first time in twenty years, Inira felt like she had a challenge in front of her worthy of her attention. She had helped Stanley build Triune De-velopment. He recruited her for the role, allowing her to get a visa. The organization specialized in managing business development services for non-profits. Their clients outsourced critical tasks like fundraising, donor relations, and volunteer recruitment to Inira and her team. Even though she already ran the company, she wanted to do something different after this.

It seems sobriety was shifting a lot of things internally.

The newly formed Nahas Helps was a coup for her boss and Tri-une's board. It was now the largest non-profit in the world, with tons of money to burn. Whenever the Board Chairman raved about it, Inira had to manage her face. She had to bury a hundred retorts about how Nahas Helps doesn't even scratch the surface of what Teleosis did for the world over thousands of years. Nor did she bring up that it was done without having to clean up the messes Nahas Global made in the first place.

Nahas Helps was much more of a PR move born out of needing to deflect attention away from the other parts of Nahas that were morally questionable, if not outright reprehensible. They were using blood money to help stitch the wounds their business practices created in the first place. Her pride and ego wanted to scream about it. There had been a place where good was done without any toxic side effects. But she kept her mouth shut like she was expected to do in a man's world. She kept her head down. She let the board take credit for her team's work because she knew more than anyone what would be at risk if she started telling people the truth about Nahas. It would only reveal who she was; she didn't want that.

Since they wanted "the best" on this account, to make sure Nahas felt coddled and secure, she was running point and leading the presentation. She would rather be training Charlotte to do it, but a mandate from the boss is still a mandate, regardless of whether that boss is the President, her mother, or the Counsel. Stanely was wonderful to work for, but he reported to guys who loved the reputation of being 'warriors for justice' without ever having to get their hands dirty.

Usually, the clients come to the Triune offices for the reporting, but this is not any usual client. Everyone was traveling to Nahas' London offices for the meeting. It would include a full three days of eating, drinking and schmoozing. She was not anxious about the temptation to drink, just anxious about the stress of the whole experience. Nahas Helps is getting the full dog and pony show she hated. It reminded her of all the ceremonies and meetings she had to preside over in Teleosis as Heir. Even though she never took the mantle of High Priestess, she'd had enough to do. She liked leading, and despite that small part of her that still craved attention, she felt like she now preferred leading from behind the scenes, out of the public eye.

After inhaling from the small coffee cup, the lavender intrusion finally vanished. Charlotte completed her review, giving her a thumbs up, and the espresso gave Inira the energy to keep plowing ahead for the next three hours straight. Glancing at the clock, she realized it was time to head home, trading her metaphorical Boss hat for her Mom-and-Wife hat. The Mom hat was her favorite. She adored hearing about Emerie's day and, if allowed, giving her some undercover training on dealing with people and situations. High School relationships were just as slippery to manage as anything in global geopolitics. It was an excellent training ground for whatever Emerie did next.

Inira pulled up to Emerie's school and made the transition to Mom complete, just as her daughter got in the car with a huff and announced, "Guess what happened in Economics today?" Inira smiles the whole way home.

<h1 style="text-align:center">Chapter 3</h1>

The days leading up to the departure to London were a seeming repeat of the day before, regardless of whether or not it was the weekend.

Wake. Prep for the Day. Drop Off. Work. Pick Up. Dinner. Homework (for work and for school as needed). Bedtime.

This wasn't a shocking departure from the normal routine, except that work never switched off. It was a lamp fueled by midnight oil that just kept burning. Somehow, Inira had to find a way to keep it lit through the next seven days. Once on the plane, there would be no breaks, no decompression time, just the marathon of corporate life and the one she had been trained for.

Inira didn't make any AA meetings before the London trip. AA Meetings were the medicine, the infusion of chemotherapy against the cancer of alcoholism. She no longer had the desire to drink, but her mind was unlearning all the crazy, insane ways those with addictions expressed themselves in her life. Workaholism was a close second.

She thought she had a good reason to have been drinking all those years. The loss of everything and everyone she knew and loved seemed like an excellent reason to stay drunk most of the time. But it wasn't working for her anymore and had eroded who she knew herself to be. On the outside, it hadn't affected her life, not in an obvious way. For the first six months, she'd been on the "pink cloud," as they called it. She learned a sober life had a different kind of magic to it. Yet, it wasn't consistent, and the pink cloud feeling had faded since the acquisition of Nahas Helps and working ramping up.

Without the fellowship she found in the meetings to calm and center her, she felt restless, irritable, and uneasy. With her mind constantly stimulated by work, she couldn't settle. Her sleep was fitful. Her sponsor told her she would grow out of this phase; it had a shelf-life while her brain was still healing. She just tried to keep going, even faking it until she could. Unfortunately, the closer she got to leaving for London, the snappier she became with those closest to her.

"Why don't you go for a walk to soothe your nerves?"

Francis approached her from behind and touched her shoulders as she poured over the presentation again. This was about thirty minutes after she'd lectured her daughter about the importance of college admission grades, which made dinner unreasonably tense.

She answered, just a little testily, "I'm fine. I need to review the reports and tweak the presentation again, and then I can relax."

Inira knew she was on dangerous ground. She knew Francis was probably thinking of what was best for her, even if his helpful suggestions always hinted at invalidating what she knew she needed in favor of what he wanted her to do. She knew she was stressed out and frazzled, but what was missing in their relationship was Francis, after being told so many times over the year, doing anything to help her. His expectations were that the burden of the family, keeping everyone happy, should be her responsibility no matter what.

He didn't see her need to succeed, even in the shadows. He sometimes resented her working late, especially when his schedule was thrown out of balance. Theirs was a good partnership, especially when it came to Emerie. Yet, lately, it had been unfulfilling. It wasn't only the more roommate-like status they had reached but his lack of awareness concerning the changes coming for their family. He was happy to keep doing as they had been for the last twenty years. He probably wouldn't have had a problem if she never had stopped drinking, even if it was killing her. He was relatively happy as long as she kept up her end of things: the homefront and then her job.

But if he wasn't happy, he didn't talk about it. So, at this moment in time, making what he thought was a helpful suggestion, in that she take a break and pay attention to him, struck a nerve. It had always been a source of contention in their marriage. Francis, being an American man, was raised on the American dream. It put them on uneven footing, especially when Inira felt like she had to choose between her beliefs and his comfort.

She knew when she'd married Francis, he was safe. He was good and worked well, but comfort and security were his main goals. He always started out soft in his requests, but she knew where this would lead – her either shutting him out and him pouting, then to a knockdown drag-out fight. When he wanted attention, he could eventually get very pushy about it. He was what she needed when they met, but she was pretty sure she didn't need him now. She didn't know what to do about that. And work was a great substitute. She was fully in her boss bitch mode but was in too deep tonight to admit that she was running on fear and adrenaline.

Francis began to wind up into his pattern of pouting. She could feel his energy escalate as he made another suggestion to pull her away from what she was focused on and into his orbit. "What about a nice hot shower? Or maybe you and I could spend some time together tonight."

He waggled his eyebrows at her and smiled.

Ah, so that's it, she thought. He wanted sex.

She didn't smile back because the art of seduction only became Francis's go-to when he wanted it to be. She knew his cues, even after being numb and going with the flow for so long. When he wanted something, he started with sweetness to try and get it.

Her first husband, Tomas, had known how to hold her emotions and still be dominant, even in a very quiet way. Their attraction was palpable. And their sex was passionate. In their three years of betrothal and one year of marriage, they had spent many hours learning how to please each other. Their sexual union was sacred.

It was for pleasure and procreation, yes, but also for communi-cating with the Divine. It was part of the Teleosian religion, with the High Priestess learning the art of pleasure to connect to the spiritual world.

Tomas had been an exceptionally good partner in bed and life until he changed. He had a force of presence about him that she still craved. Francis was much more equality-oriented, more neutral, and was scandalized when Inira explained how sex reflected the very force of life itself. Over the years, she had tried to show rather than tell him, but he was always uncomfortable with the vulnera-bility and openness required to reach new levels of pleasure and connection.

Their sex life was adequate but not fulfilling.

Plus, she couldn't think about sex with the pressure so high around this meeting. A romantic evening with Francis was not on the agenda. She was annoyed he'd suggested it, especially when she knew he was more or less scratching an itch. When he had a big trial he was gearing up for; she went to bed alone often. She'd learned to leave him alone, but he thought he knew better when it came to her. She pinned him with a hard stare that wiped the smile from his face. His face hardened, and she knew a fight was coming.

She did keep her tone soft even if her eyes were flint. "I think I'm going to need some space tonight, honestly. I must be ready for these meetings, which take all my energy."

He replied tersely, "You must make time for me eventually, Inira. We are married, after all. Some even consider it part of your wifely duties."

She raised one eyebrow at him, and he turned on his heel in a huff, leaving the room without a word.

She was so far down the road that she decided to commit fully. An apology would not help things, or so she told herself. The best thing to do was to stuff it down into the box in her mind called "Francis and his issues," making the excuse to herself that it was him and not her. She had an important job, and while he meant well, she didn't need his advice and certainly didn't have time to take a break. She thought she could justifiably resent him for getting in the way of what she needed to do.

A small voice inside her head whispered, "You've done this before, and look how it worked out." It was a raspy, dangerous voice. She didn't like this voice. This voice felt an awful lot like her nanny's voice. Judah was a harsh woman. She was tasked with ensuring the future heir of Teleosis could meet the impossibly high expectations of the country and history. Between her mother and Judah, Inira had all the proper training. While Inira had excelled, it had come at a steep price. The grueling pace and schedule had taken her identity and any security within herself. This voice crept in at times like this when Inira knew she was isolating herself. She knew that her current path was leading to a breakdown.

It was what her mother, Eliana, always wanted to happen, to break her down. That was how her mother taught. It wasn't always this way. Inira knew it because her mother and grandmother often argued about how she should be taught. Her mother completely changed following her father's death. She wanted to regain Teleosian influence and power and do it quickly. And the way things had always been, with the High Priestess being installed at twenty-one, was going to be enough.

Gone were the days of the Healer-Priestesses, the women who owned their power, sexuality, and intelligence. Now, it was time to take the world on, take it by storm. Her mother wanted to usher in an agenda that ensured Teleosis was in control of its destiny. And who better to do that than her mother and the Counsel?

Her grandmother wanted to mold her, to shape her gifts to become what she was always meant for. Her mother wanted to mold and shape her into her own image and use her gifts to dominate. There was a new era on the horizon for Teleosis, with Eliana at the helm, born out of grief and a need for vengeance. She wanted to make the world pay for the loss of her husband, and the best way to do that was to play the game by their rules.

She'd only just begun to unpack this insidious thought cycle in therapy.

The parts and pieces were there, but she'd never been given an instruction manual to assemble it.

Breaking out of her reverie, she decided she could make it up to Francis when this work meeting was over. In less than ten days, she could return to the calm, approachable, even fun Inira she'd remembered herself to be. She could rekindle their romance. This was just one little hiccup, and she held onto that thought like it was a life preserver that would keep her from drowning in self-pity, guilt, and shame.

She spent the rest of the night practicing her speech, which would happen on the first full day of business meetings. She knew this had to be perfect. She reviewed the dossiers on Nahas' leadership, spending extra time on Mattias Nahas, the CEO of the conglomerate. She wasn't sure if he would be there, even if he were on the attendees' list. This was the first year of Triune's partnership, and Nahas Industries was well known for their attention to detail in every arm and department. Some might call it extreme micro-management, but this was the company culture so Mattias would be there. Everyone would be there.

This was an excellent reason for Inira's level of anxiety to be high. It didn't feel like a regular meeting. It felt like it would be make or break. Everyone on her team was acting like it. This was how Nahas wanted the world to view them as benevolent despite how they made their money. They could change their reputation by looking like they did great in the world.

Inira wasn't in a position to tell someone else, like Mattias Nahas, how to run his corporate empire, even if she could. Her job was only to direct the funds to maximize the most good. There was no picture of Mattias Nahas in the dossier, which was strange. There were no pictures of Mattias Nahas to be found anywhere that showed his appearance. Any images on Google showed him wearing sunglasses or getting out of a car from behind or side profile. It seemed odd that he was so private, almost reclusive. His social media accounts were sparse, and there weren't even any pictures of him from his university days.

Even from these glimpses, she thought he did look familiar. But it was a vague sort of association. Something about his profile snagged at the corner of her memory. Perhaps she'd seen him at a conference, but she doubted it. A wealthy and powerful man didn't move in the same circles she did.

She was aware she was nervous about meeting him. It almost felt like an audience with royalty, even if she had been considered that herself at one point in time. There were protocols to learn. The women on the team were encouraged to soften their "feminine attitude," which was an androcratic code for holding back on expressing thoughts aloud. Having grown up in a culture that celebrated and elevated all forms of feminine expression, this was a huge challenge for Inira. In the United States, when she had to operate in male-dominated spaces, she felt like she was, in effect, pulling a veil over her face – hiding her true self. It was frustrating and just as limiting as if she had a real veil over her head.

Holding back what she had to contribute, swallowing what was often called "her pride," left her drained. She knew now there was a different level of repression at the high levels of power in Teleosis, but the culture itself was centered on free expression. Divine-given intelligence, grit, and thoughtfulness were expected to be on display, not hidden. Gender bias had never been a part of the atmosphere in Teleosis. The equality of humanity was not just an ideal in Teleosis; it was the water everyone swam in.

So, for Inira to walk into a space that leaned so heavily on men who didn't want to collaborate left her on edge. Life in the greater world beyond her home was founded upon imperialism and a mindset of dominance, and she had ways to deal with it. The main one was no longer available to her, to numb it with alcohol at the end of the day. Finding new ways to deal with life on life's terms was difficult.

She was concerned that being in such an oppressive space, with men quite used to being in power and control, would set her off. And these memories and flashbacks she started having weren't helping her concerns.

Just after midnight, she crawled in bed next to Francis. He was sound asleep, their tiffs over the years never keeping him up at night. She knew she was pushing herself and had slipped into an old pattern of thinking that if she could please the most important person in the room, everything would be alright. It had been drilled into her, and under stress, that's what was coming out. She had to find a way to rise above it, to become the person she was meant to be.

Yet, right now, she was woefully low on the willingness to rise above.

She heard the thoughts of her therapist echo in her mind again.

Perfection won't save you.

With those words in her mind, she fell into a fitful sleep, ready for the alarm to go off at any moment.

Chapter 4

On this day, twenty-five years ago, Inira heard these words:

"*Hamuda, arise.*"

The sunlight streamed through the stained-glass ceiling of the Temple. It was so bright she could barely see. She had to shield her eyes from the riot of colors. It was meant to remind the worshippers and penitents of the glorious nature of the Four-Fold God, how everything given by Them was multi-faceted, multi-colored, and complex, to represent Their piercing beauty. There was order in the initial confusion; the pattern of the prism was chosen specifically because the seeker had to learn and look for the order behind the chaos.

Right at this moment, Inira didn't think or care about any of that. She was trying to open her eyes to see during this rite of passage that would make her formally the Heir of the High Priestess. She had been from birth but only in name. Now, it would be made manifest. She'd been training for this moment for months if not years. For a culture so bent on giving everyone freedom of choice, the magnificent irony of this day was that she had never chosen this path. It was what she'd been born to be and what had always been done.

She was eighteen today, the day she came into her birthright, whether she wanted to or not.

She'd been kneeling for nearly an hour, so her irritation was high. As the ritual liturgy was performed, others stood and knelt repeatedly, but she stayed on her knees. The visual was that she was quiet and submissive to the Counsel before her. She might be the one to lead, but the image presented in this service was that it was truly the Counsel in charge of the FourFold God's vast influence.

That irritation and lack of agency felt like a popcorn kernel stuck in her gum. It felt like a part of her soul was inflamed, the discontent simmering low in her belly. Tomas was behind her, on a bench, a soothing presence. He couldn't touch her, even as he had already been named her Consort. They would be married in a year's time, with two years to train together before she became High Priestess.

Tomas, already 20, was strikingly handsome with green eyes, dark hair, and a dulce de leche complexion. His South American heritage showed, even if he'd lived his whole life in Teleosis. Thinking of him, tall with a strong, muscled build, Inira could shift her concentration away from the discontent to the heat forming in her lower belly. She was desperate for him again, even as any time she shifted, she felt the soreness in her core.

Their decision to come together last night had been mutual and a long time in the works. They were promised to each other, betrothed already. While they hadn't chosen each other for marriage, they would have if the decision had been left up to them. They were deeply and soundly in love and had dragged on not sharing their bodies with each other for too long.

They'd decided to claim each other, not waiting for any official sanction. Pre-marital sex wasn't frowned upon in Teleosis. If the hearts and bodies were aligned for intimate communion, it was encouraged. The hold-up was that the complex Inira lived in didn't make it easy to get away with. It had taken considerable time and effort for them to figure out a way for Tomas to sneak into her room. Her going to him would have never happened. They'd found secret places to share kisses and hot, hungry touches, but they both wanted this to be an experience that couldn't be interrupted.

He'd appeared in her doorway just before midnight, taking up all the space and air in the room. Thinking of the tender yet strong way he led her into shared bliss, both their first time, did a good job distracting Inira from the discomfort of kneeling and her frustration. She remembered the second round they'd enjoyed a few hours before daybreak.

At the thought of that, she had to hide the wicked little grin behind her hands as the High Counselman glanced down at her between stanzas of the never-ending poem he was reading.

Inira had loved Tomas since they'd met, her first day at primary school at six. It had grown from puppy love into a much more mature feeling. To have fallen in love with the person she'd been told to marry seemed like proof of the blessing on their union by the FourFold God – Father and Mother blessing them as Son and Daughter. Inira had an irrational fear he would be taken away from her like her father was. It was a deeply rooted fear because Tomas seemed to be the only person who truly knew her as herself – not by some title or role or proximity to power – which was how she remembered her Papa had treated her before he was killed.

She felt like she knew herself when Tomas was around. She wasn't sure she would be complete without him by her side. It was easy to get lost in the thought of everything they'd whispered in secret while they lay bare before one another. Last night felt sacred, maybe even more so than today, with its rigid formality and high liturgical style. Consummating their relationship felt holy and reverent. It gave Inira the rare sense of the Presence of the FourFold God, and together they would benefit the whole world.

So lost in her thoughts about Tomas, especially given how close he was, Inira almost didn't hear them call her forward. Her mother and the Elder Counselor beckoned her forward to don the mantle of Heir she would wear until her mother retired and she was installed as High Priestess. She was startled, hearing her formal name but staying on her knees. She made eye contact with her mother, who narrowed her eyes.

She probably thought I fell asleep.

It wasn't a bad assumption since Inira and her sister had nearly perfected sleeping with their eyes open over the long years of ceremonies they had to attend as The High Priestess' daughters. She would have paid any amount of money to see the look on her mother's face if she really knew what she'd been thinking about. She even had the platinum band he'd given her tucked into her undergarments, as she knew he had the one she'd given him in his pocket.

She knew where he kept the ring because they'd dressed each other before parting ways. It was another sacred act establishing their union – a symbol of their love and service. They couldn't wear the bands till they were officially wed, but they pledged always to have them on their persons. The act of dressing each other was the first of many in days to come when they would serve each other as husband and wife, now, to her, a reality even though she had to wait for the official sanction of The Counsel.

Her mother made a nearly invisible hand motion Inira knew meant to hurry up. Years of being in public spaces with her mother, she knew what she was saying just by the tilt of her head. She tried to shuffle faster. This was how she was supposed to appear, but it felt like she was groveling, begging for acknowledgment. She felt humiliated and wondered for the millionth time if this was what the FourFold God wanted for her.

With that one little order from her mother that no one else could see, the dreamy warmth of Tomas' body on hers and sweet promises for their future were gone. Like plunging into an ice bath, Inira was fully in the moment of her life, which never seemed to be her own the older she got. Having given birth to two daughters, her mother had the chance to extend her rule, with two seats granted on the Counsel of Wisdom. Inira was named as the Heir, eventually the High Priestess. Her older sister, Samira, was named High Counselor. Already married and with her first child on the way, Samira had followed the rules perfectly. She was ordered and measured in her thinking. She was born for her role as the Counsel.

Inira, however, always felt like a mess in comparison. Slow to mature, physically and emotionally, and quite stubborn, her mother told her she was "the bane of her existence."

"Why didn't the FourFold God give me a dutiful, pliant daughter for an Heir? I hope you have a daughter just like you!" It seemed her unquestioning obedience was all her mother wanted, and Inira could never give it. She wanted freedom, and her life was the opposite of it. This ceremony was a huge reminder that her life was not her own. She kept shuffling forward, and a nagging little voice asked again, "And what would you do if you got your freedom?"

She'd never had an answer. She could never imagine her life as anything but a series of ceremonies, meetings, and dutiful obedience. Except with Tomas, everything else was laid out before. She knew she'd gotten lucky that they chose him for her. Tomas was still not a choice she'd made for herself until last night. In the darkness, between their shared touches and caresses, Tomas had asked her a striking question,

"Do you think The FourFold God is still guiding Teleosis? Have They truly been behind all of this since the Creation and development of humanity?"

Inira remembered this as she got close to her mother. He had always struggled with their religion. Denying the selfishness of greed, power, and all the trappings of self-centered violence, Telesosis promoted wholeness. Across the world, there were outposts and outreach centers that did so much good. But Tomas had begun asking questions two years ago. He said he'd received a letter from someone who lived far away, a distant family member. He didn't tell her who it was or show her the letters, but his discontent was palpable. His questions fueled her hopelessness at being forced into a role she didn't feel qualified for. It made the last argument with her mother two nights ago epic. She dared to say she didn't want to go through with this ceremony, and her mother responded with an explosive strike. Inira could still feel the slap stinging across her cheek.

It was the last time she and her mother had spoken. With her mother's handprint still on her face, she said she would go through with the ceremony but would redefine her role afterward. She was about to be 18, so her mother needed to treat her like an adult, not a child. Her mother laughed and said,

"You still are a child, *Hamuda*. Only the ignorance of youth tells you otherwise. This selfish behavior reflects the darkness in you. It must be purged from your soul, or you will never be High Priestess."

Little did her mother know maybe that's exactly what she wanted.

"Daughter of the Light, arise!"

The command shocked her back into the present, and she finally made it forward. Seemingly obedient enough, she was called to stand. She could feel the irritation radiating from her mother like burning sunlight. She helped Inira stand with a vise grip on her upper arm, much more forceful than needed. It would probably bruise. She stood to her full height and looked down into her mother's face. Inira was a head taller than her mother; their height difference was due to latent genes on her father's side.

But even towering over her mother, she felt small.

"*Hamuda*, bow now." Her mother whispered so low only Inira heard. Annoyance flashed on her face because Inira knew the routine. The use of her nickname didn't help either. She might be the Daughter of the Light to the rest of the universe, but she would always be the childish "sweetie" to her mother. Inira had asked her mother many times since the announcement she would be Heir to stop calling her "*Hamuda*," but Eliana didn't seem to care. She kept using it to put her in her place, and to do it now grated on Inira's nerves.

She loved her mother, but the combination of her control over her life, all the expectations she never seemed to live up to, and the straight-out emotional abandonment following her father's death had created a chasm she wondered if they would ever bridge. Her mother seemed to see her as a little girl instead of the woman she'd become. Her mother led a religion designed to draw out purpose and maturity from everyone but still treated her youngest daughter like she was seven.

Inira bowed so that her mother, the small slip of a woman, could reach to put the veil on her head. It sat like a headband crown, falling in brilliant periwinkle blue around her face and shoulders. Catholics would think it looks like a communion headdress. Most people would think of a bridal veil. It didn't share the color, but the effect was similar. She was to be married to Teleosis first. Then Eliana removed the pendant that hung around her neck and placed it over Inira's head. Inira straightened to her full height, the pendant resting right between her breasts, right above her heart. It was an emerald meant to symbolize the rebirth of life Teleosis would give to the world.

Where men had failed and tainted so much of the Divine's vision for Creation, Teleosis anointed a woman to bring forth lift and light.

"Eliana, present your Heir."

The High Counselor, Patrician Savoy, boomed the command across the holy space. He'd always been kind to Inira, but she suspected it was due less to his inherent fondness for her and more because of her proximity to power. He was a replacement, after all. He entered the High Counselor role when her uncle died, trying to save her father, the last Consort. The successful assassination attempt shadowed their family's existence. He was killed as a warning that the world powers had grown more aggressive in their desire to gain the power Teleosis had held for so long. It was the ability to create and all the wealth that went with it.

Inira's mother's fingernails bit into her shoulders as she turned Inira to face the room. This was a dreaded moment, the public presentation. Yet the first pair of eyes she looked for were his, and Tomas did not disappoint. Her heart's true love was looking directly at her, taking it all in. He smiled brightly, delighted that she was his bride. She'd never felt anything less from him. Then, she found her sister staring at her, too, in love and support. It was what she should do, and Samira would never go against what she was supposed to do. At least Inira could count on her consistency.

Patrician Savoy droned on,

"Today, we again present the line of continuation to the world. Let it be known that the FourFold God has again blessed us with a Heir who will serve this realm and the world faithfully and without hesitation. She has been adorned with the humble markings of her office until such a day when she inherits her duties from her mother, who has served excellently despite the grief she has endured. Today, Mother elevates Daughter into the Light. Let all of Creation rejoice!"

Everyone in the room stood and cheered. Inira relaxed her shoulders a bit, not realizing how tense she had been and how rigid her posture was. It was over, and now she would go to the reception and then could retire to her rooms. Before she could start down the steps from the raised altar, her mother grasped her hand and held their hands bound together aloft as if in victory.

The only victory was her mother's. She'd just gained more power. Her mother had indeed won. Her mother was the only girl in her family, which meant her brother was her High Counselor. Now, with two seats filled by her children, her mother would keep her voice after she'd retired. Inira was fulfilling her destiny under her mother's thumb. The triumph on her mother's face gave her pause, and she unlocked their clasped hands and followed the procession out. She snuck one last look at Tomas as she passed by his row, and he blew her a kiss. After the reception, he would be waiting for her in her chambers.

Other words he had whispered into her neck last night came back to her as she walked down the aisle to the reception hall just outside the Temple space.

"I will keep all the promises I've made you, but I don't know if I can keep all my promises to Teleosis."

She hadn't gotten the chance to ask him about it right then. She'd just giggled and sighed as he kissed his way down to the apex of her thighs. Then she forgot about everything but him. Now, as she watched the rainbow colors of the prism of the ceiling's glass play off the front walls, she wondered what he meant. With that thought echoing in her mind, instead of feeling the heat from the sun as the Daughter of the Light and relishing it, she shivered.

Chapter 5

Inira woke up to prepare for her flight; nothing was in her mind until it hit her. Like a brick wall crashing down on her chest, she realized today was her forty-first birthday. In the craziness of the preparation – in the middle of their hectic life in general, she'd forgotten her birthday. She had mixed feelings on the heels of that realization because of all the memories of what would have been happening on this day twenty years ago. Every year, she had this reaction to her birthday. It was not a happy day for her. Her twenty-first was almost the one that didn't happen. She'd spent the day sifting through the ruins and helping recovery efforts. There were so many people to dig out from the rubble, some alive but most of the dead.

It was always this memory that flooded her every September 10th.

She lay in bed with her hand on her chest, breathing heavily. The pressure on the inside of her chest threatened to swallow her. What if the bombings had never happened? This would have been the day she would have anointed her daughter as Heir if she and Tomas had one. What kind of mother would she have been? Would they have had more kids? Would they have been happy if everything hadn't ended so horrifically?

It took her a long time to work through the panic, just under the surface on this day. Francis was already up, making coffee and humming. It had soothed her in the past, but it worsened the feeling today. When they first met, she found his attempts to change the narrative around her birthday thoughtful and sweet, but he never understood her response to her birthday. Year after year, he tried to make it a joyous occasion.

Despite many years of trying to communicate what she needed, which was to pick any other day to celebrate, he doggedly kept trying to "make the best of it." She knew it was how he was raised, and he would always try to help. And this year was tough. She was sober, questioning her future, and had to perform hugely. She knew she hadn't healed enough to feel happy and wondered if she would ever be okay with her birthday being celebrated.

The dream, vision, and potential for her life on the world's stage were dust. She fisted the sheets, trying to breathe deeply and get her bearings. She took her hands and pushed her palms into her eye sockets. The darkness comforted her. She no longer saw the staccato flashes of light from the day the terrorist attacks ended her world. What was also true is that she had a new life. She had rebuilt herself in a new world. She felt that she was on the precipice of something new. It was tiny compared to the overwhelming feeling of panic.

She walked through some affirmations she and her therapist put together in their last session. She was alive. She had a purpose. She had gifts. She had a family. She was not alone. She was hopeful that she could handle what was to come in strength. She was sober. She repeated them five times before she felt calm enough to rise. She took three more deep breaths and felt a few tears escaping before she made herself unlock her hands from the vise grip she had on the bed and sat up. She needs to say goodbye to Emerie and make it through the celebration she knew was coming. The faster she could get gone, the quicker she could return to Emerie, and hopefully, things would be clearer on where she and Francis stood.

She opened the door and braced herself, plastering on a wide smile that didn't match her eyes.

As she pulled her suitcase out of the bedroom, she was greeted with singing. Francis and Emerie stood there, singing "Happy Birthday," Stevie Wonder style. She tried hard to let this moment chase away the gloom. Waking up sober and being present with her family was a gift, even as she had to take another deep breath against the anxiety. That anxiety wouldn't win right now, and she knew she deserved this joy. She kissed them both. He was still cautious because of her rejection last night, but he looked like he was trying to make the best of it.

They presented her with a delicious tiramisu, which was set to perfection. She asked him, "How did you sneak all this past my notice?"

He grinned at her, proud of himself. He responded with, "Well, it wasn't that hard. You've been pretty preoccupied."

Her stomach burned, even as she hoped he didn't mean it the way she took it. He was right about it; she had upset their normal routine, letting Francis carry the evening load for the last few nights. She knew he didn't like that. He looked like the cat that ate the canary, so pleased with himself and maybe even pleased with showing her he could care for her when she wasn't caring for him. She decided it was better to pause and not respond and let the joy continue to buoy her weary soul even if she had to force it.

They gave her their gifts, and she was struck by how thoughtful they were. Her gift basket from Emerie was all for her trip and included a neck pillow, noise-canceling headphones, a water bottle, and a small bag of snacks that could go in her purse. Francis's gift did bring tears to her eyes: A pair of white gold hoops and a white gold pendant with the Teleosisan crest on it. He went to pull her into an embrace, and she let him. He wasn't perfect, and she was questioning their path forward, but there were times when he was thoughtful and sincere.

He whispered against the shell of her ear, sending shivers down her spine, "I know you are dealing with your past, with all that happened on your birthday. I know you are in pain. Yet, it is still a part of you. Don't forget it. It was not happy circumstances that brought you to me, but I'm grateful it happened. And the memory of Teleosis can remind you that your purpose is alive and well. Your FourFold God is with you, my love."

She was full sobbing against him now – ugly cry. His sweet words made her feel bad for stonewalling him. The last year had been such a monumental change for all of them, and she tried to remember he was adjusting too. For him to show such kindness to her when they weren't in the best place was genuinely humbling. It reminded her she was not what she lost. She was a gift. It was a needed reminder.

He let her cry on his shoulder for a few minutes, then gently pulled her to stand upright. Emerie came over to give her a hug. It would be a long day for all of them. Francis gently lifted her chin with his fingers to meet her eyes and kissed her softly even though her face was a snotty, tear-soaked mess. He whispered sweetly, "Happy birthday to our *Ahava*. Now let's get you to the airport. The sooner you go, the sooner you will return to us!"

Francis held her hand for a good portion of the ride to the airport. It was a comfortable silence. She was surprised by the warmth she felt. She was not big on gifts, but this was so thoughtful. She decided she would have to try harder with him when she returned. They could make this work. She hoped they could. He caught her hand as she stroked his face and brought it down to the armrest.

Then he said, "Inira, I know this isn't the best time to say this, but I need to. While you are gone, please think about us seeing a marriage counselor. Your sobriety has been a big change, and I'm concerned about how distant we've become over these last few weeks. I think you – I mean we – could do better."

She was stunned. It was the wrong time, and it shattered the happiness she had moments before. "Francis, this is a brutal way to bring up your unhappiness. I feel baffled and hurt by this. I'm floored."

He winced.

She looked at him when she knew he wouldn't meet her eye, "Why did you decide to tell me this now?"

He sighed and said, "You know how unhappy I've been. Things have changed, and I want us to understand what our lives will look like from now on."

She was still looking at him. "What was all that when you gave me the necklace then?"

He did look at her then, "I meant what I said. I may be concerned about us, but I know you still have a purpose and that your past impacts you for better or worse. I want us to be together. That's why I want to go to counseling. I know things have changed, and you aren't hearing what I need. So we can work out our future when it's just the two of us in the house. Promise me you'll think about us in London, and we can talk more when you get home."

She sighed and shook her head with her eyebrows, hitting her hairline at his statement. She spoke the only truth she knew at the moment. "I will be thinking about our future, Francis. And I do appreciate the life we've had together. It may look different from now on, but I hope we can find a way to work it out."

He nodded. He seemed satisfied with her response, even if he should have listened for the deeper meaning. They were close to the departure drop-off point. On the heels of her birthday, this conversation made her feel the need to get out. She was glad she was leaving. The car ride had indeed moved her forward in her thought process about her marriage, even as no definitive plan had formed in her mind as of yet.

Francis got out and put her bag on the sidewalk, then pulled her in for a hug. She hugged him back, although not quite as fiercely. She kissed him robotically on the cheek and then said goodbye. She felt the anxiety return as she walked to the flight check-in kiosk. Given the rollercoaster of emotions she had just gone through, she wondered if there were any chance she would sleep on the plane. She thought that she would come down and feel so drained she would drop off into unconsciousness at some point during the six-hour flight.

She was dressed comfortably but still stylish. They would arrive late evening; the whole team was traveling together. She sighed at that thought, feeling like a teacher on an elementary school field trip. Despite all these people being adults, she knew there would be many questions, and several of her team members had never experienced the dubious joy of jet lag. She checked in, dropped off her bag, shouldered her carry-on, and that was when she heard her name being called.

She turned to look. Charlotte was even more put together than Inira, which was not surprising. The woman, being of Creole heritage, was so striking. Her skin was a different shade than Inira's, more rich café au lait, to Inira's darker olive. Inira wondered for the hundredth time how many heads this woman would turn while they were in the meeting. Their clients might be patriarchal, but they were still men and probably would make their interest in Charlotte obvious.

Inira was Charlotte's biggest fan, not jealous in the least. She loved that they were on the same team and did not see her as a competition. She hoped Charlotte would excel to greater heights than Inira. In her culture, women were meant to lift each other. She smiled at her and said, "Hey Sweet Charlotte. How do you look so fantastic before 7 a.m.?"

Charlotte winked, then said, "It's a talent and a gift. Are you ready for this trip?"

Inira's long-suffering sigh was her only response for a moment before she said, "Ready as I'll ever be. I know it will be success-ful. We've put in the hard work, you more than anyone. I know these types of men. They won't make it easy on us. They are still getting to know our organization, and they have a reputation as being bastards to deal with. Mattias Nahas more than anyone. Since he will be there, I expect rough treatment. Billionaires are not like other people. Fortunately, we know what we are doing, don't we?"

Charlotte nodded her assent gravely, her southern roots com-ing through in her answer. "Yes, ma'am, we surely do. I appre-ciate this opportunity."

Inira looked at her straight-faced, "Charlotte, it should be you running this presentation. I hope this will open the door for you to step into more of the responsibility I know you can handle. Not just because that means I have less to do." She smiled a sheepish grin at her second.

Grinning gleefully, Charlotte led the way to the security check-point. They paused conversation as they shuffled bags and iden-tification for the roving eyes of the TSA. While walking to the gate, Inira confided something to Charlotte, something she'd been holding in but felt the urge to share with her now.

"Charlotte, I have to say, not being heard or listened to is one of the most frustrating parts of working in the Western world. Where I'm from, the collaboration between the genders made everything better. It was focused on the good for all, not just the few. It's why I like working at Triune and working with you. I hope we can shift the narrative, even in a small way."

Charlotte nodded and asked, "Inira, what happened to your coun-try? I know you were important; Stanley has hinted at that a lot. You had a lot of clout, so what caused things to go south?"

Inira wasn't in a place to share the whole story and said as much, but she did promise Charlotte she would explain it all one day soon. "I will tell you the full story; you deserve that. It's more than we have time for, and today, I'm not prepared to tell it."

She paused, collecting herself as Charlotte stepped closer and squeezed her arm. Inira pulled the tears back and let out a shaky breath before she said, "In the end, the dream of Teleosis died because of greed. The desire for power was the Trojan Horse that took it all down. Like it does every empire, it wasn't just one day but the last hundred years. The heart of it was eaten like a worm eats an apple till it rots from the inside out."

They arrived at their gate. She stopped and turned at Charlotte before finishing, "Yet, I do have hope and believe that love, real love, covers a multitude of sins. That's not from my Scriptures, but it applies." Charlotte nodded and smiled as they sat down amidst the rest of the team, anxiously awaiting the signal to board. "Thanks for taking me back to church, Boss."

Chapter 6

More than six hours after residing in her business class seat, Inira felt dim when she exited the plane. It wasn't as long as a trip to Teleosis from the U.S., a total of fourteen hours- but it was a long time to be in one spot. She hadn't fallen asleep for more than twenty minutes, so she would need to be more caffeinated than usual.

Exiting the plane, she was flagged down by an older man. Her heart warmed when she saw him. He was dashing with much more salt than pepper in his hair. Her boss, Stanley Holland, was a white man in his sixties. He'd grown up in privilege on Long Island, definitely the old money, but acted anything like it. He was raised to keep his eye on opportunities for the most unfortunate. His father started Triune after World War II, seeing the desperate needs from the effects of war. In his youth, his father sent Stanley to spend several summers in Teleosis.

This was how, when her country and life collapsed, Stanley brought Inira to the United States. He was less a knight in shining armor and more a mother hen gathering in a lost chick. She lived with him and his family for almost a year until she and Francis married. Stanley walked her down the aisle. That was not how they did it in Teleosis, but Francis' mother insisted, and she was in no shape to argue. The weather wouldn't have cooperated for an outdoor wedding like she would have had in Tov anyway.

Despite the current instability in her marriage, those were still happy memories. Stanley had always been a stabilizing presence, including being a character witness in their immigration issues to prove her and Francis' marriage was a love match and not for the goal of getting a visa. She was grateful to walk with him into these meetings and on her birthday. Which he remembered like the right, proper gentleman he was.

"Happy Birthday, Daughter of Light! How was your flight?" he said, offering her his arm.

Stanley asked this question with a smile on his face. His mouth was usually upturned when he spoke to her. It was almost as if they shared a secret, and his use of her now-defunct title felt like an inside joke. It was one of her favorite things about him. He was disarming, downright charming when he meant to be. He made her feel seen for what she could do for him and for who she was deep inside. She wasn't sure if it was the influence of Teleosis or just who he was.

He offered to carry her bag, but she declined. She did take his arm, squeezing it warmly, and they began a stroll to baggage claim.

"Stanley, I'm not such a feminist that I wouldn't let you pull my bag, but I'd rather walk with you than give you more than your hands can carry!" He grinned, and they continued at their leisurely pace. She also knew she was stronger than he was. Even though most people didn't notice because he was still in good shape, he was getting frail, but she saw the changes. His walk was more of a shuffle, like he was tired and had recently been out for many doctor's appointments. She asked him how he was feeling, and he waved her off, returning the conversation to her. He valued privacy, so she gave it to him. She knew when he wanted to let her know what was going on with his health, he would.

She looked at him as she adjusted her pace again to match his slower one, "It was eight hours in one spot. I got a lot of work done?"

Stanley chuckled and spoke loud enough for her to hear him over the press of terminal traffic. "You've had this presentation ready for weeks. I can't believe you are still working on it. I know this is a huge opportunity for the firm, but I hope you are taking care of yourself."

Stanley was the only one at Triune who knew her about her struggle with alcoholism. He was the one who got her into rehab and allowed her to take the time off she needed. Inira owed him a lot, so she was pressured to perform this week. She didn't want to let him down. This account would be his legacy to pass on.

She nodded and then changed the subject. "Your granddaughter still wants to intern this summer?" Inira knew she wanted to move on when Stanley retired because it wouldn't be the same without him there. She didn't know where or to do what. With her rocky home situation, she felt the tightness in her chest return. There was always the possibility that he would sell the company or his sons would when he passed away, but if Stanely wasn't there, Triune wasn't home.

This week was a big part of that story. He nodded, and they fell into a companionable silence till they reached their baggage claim carousel. When they separated, she turned to him, still standing close, and said, "As always, I am grateful for your trust and confidence to see it through."

Stanley smiled even brighter and reached up to hug her around the shoulders before he said, "Just remember how far the Four-Fold God has gotten you. And how much farther do you have to go? It's not all work and no play. I'd like us to ride the Eye together sometime this week." He winked mischievously at her.

After everyone cleared immigration, a man approached Stanley just before they got outside the airport, letting him know he was their driver and would take them to the hotel Nahas had secured for them. The company owned the whole thing. They could rest up before dinner with the Nahas reps later that evening. She arrived at the hotel ready to nap and encouraged everyone else to do the same. She and Charlotte had connecting rooms, making their morning prep easier logistically. The whole staff was on the same floor, so Stanley stopped her as they peeled off to their rooms.

"Inira, why don't you and I have a drink after our dinner? The club soda will be on me."

Inira gave him a tilted head smile as she teased, "Stanley, are you trying to wine and dine me? I thought we would save that for the clients?"

Stanley laughed aloud at her joke, "In my prime, I might have tried to win over the Heir of Teleosis, but as of today, I don't have the arrogance. I know she is way out of my league."

Inira's heart did a little twist. She replied, "Well if I can get a nap in, let's make sure to have a few stolen moments together before we part ways for the evening." She winked. Not all older men in a position of power were like Stanley. She knew she could trust him, and he trusted her, so their informality was sweet rather than creating a power dynamic. He waved her off with another beaming smile, and they both went to their rooms for rest.

Chapter 7

Two hours later, following a longer nap than anticipated, Inira felt rushed and anxious. This was a formal dinner with the Nahas Helps Executive team. There were fifteen of them to Triune's 10. They were outnumbered, which told Inira Nahas wanted to show them who was in charge. Usually, in client presentations, Triune held most of the chairs in the room. Now, it looked to be like their entire week here would be all in front of not just an audience but a large one. This dinner was formal, so everyone was dressed to the hilt.

Charlotte looked regal in her emerald, green flowing gown, with cap sleeves and a high neck. If she'd had a tiara, that would have completed her queenly appearance. Her hair was natural, curly, and long, and she'd styled it to the side, draping over one shoulder. The cut of her dress made it so it moved with her. It tastefully showed off her toned form.

All of the women had to downplay their bodies. Nahas employed people from many different religions, but many of the executive staff were Muslim or followers of the Nahas' funded religion. This separatist faction seemed to be a conglomerate version of the most conservative aspects of all the major world religions. It had a lot of Christian theology but was focused on the elevation and manifestation of a man's wants and dreams.

It was considered a cult because they didn't publicize their worship services. It was by invitation only. Their doctrine left little room for anyone but cis-gendered men to be in power, and it made Inira – and the other women on the team – uneasy.

Inira had chosen a black velvet wrap-style dress, which was loose enough to be modest but still striking. Her bodice was also modest, a simple V that dipped just below her collarbones. She paired it with her dark brown, wavy hair half up, with the Teleosis pendant and new earrings. Simple but classy, the pendant rested on her heart beneath the neckline. The thin gold chain was barely seen, almost blending in with her skin.

She also chose to wear her engagement ring fitted next to her wedding ring. She usually only wore the wedding ring, but this was a formal event. The whole week was formal so she wouldn't be taking it off. She felt funny about it, knowing her heart was leaning towards separation, especially after the conversation in the car. She didn't want to be mad at the bad guy in therapy, and she didn't feel like it was just her who needed to do better. Still, she didn't want anything misconstrued around a lot of men.

She wanted to operate in the truth of herself, as this last year had taught her more and more what that meant for her personally and practically.

They were transported to their dinner location by limousine. Inira expected nothing less, even if she felt the need to flaunt wealth was overdone. She'd been taught wealth and power were rooted in what was given, not what was taken. Once at the restaurant, they were ushered back to a private room with one long table. She was seated at a table with Stanely, Charlotte, and Giselle, the non-profit's best research analyst and grant writer. It struck her that all the women were together with the junior executives on one side. Charlotte caught her eye and raised a sculpted brow.

Surprisingly, one significant power player- Mattias Nahas- was missing from the dinner. When Inira inquired if he would be joining them, she got a response from a man at the head of the table in a black-on-black suit that matched his ebony beard and eyes.

"Deitas Nahas will join us tomorrow. He had other commitments this evening." He dipped his head in reverence to her, but some-thing about his eyes made her wary. She felt like there was something familiar about him. Yet, her mind got stuck on the title he used for Mattias Nahas.

Deitas? What the heck was that title? She wondered and even mouthed the word to Charlotte, who gave her a minute shrug as she'd never heard of it.

As they ate their delicious seven-course dinner, she listened to Nahas executives wax philosophically about their impact on the world and tell each other they were probably the masters of the universe. They leaned back in their chairs, laughed loudly, and several of them even belched. Many of them had several bourbon, whiskey, or scotch glasses, adding to the air of male superiority.

She distracted herself with thoughts of how her stomach felt in light of the shapewear beneath her dress. It was doing an excellent job of holding her food consumption in check. Dinner was great, but there was a lot of it. She was still in good shape and had dropped fifteen to twenty pounds since she stopped drinking. She reasoned that would only help her now that she was in her fourth decade of life. Sitting next to Charlotte reminded her how tall she was. Inira had broad shoulders, long arms, and muscular thighs. She silently prayed thanks for learning to embrace herself at each age and stage. Worshipping the Mother meant moving from the Maiden, the Mother, and what is known in the broader world as the Crone. The Maiden embraces the flush of youth, the Mother is the creator of life in her womb, and the Crone is a woman in the later stages.

This way of viewing the stages of a woman's body made much more sense to Inira than the constant striving she experienced in the West to hang onto her youth. Francis had hinted at her "middle softness" a few times, which incensed her. They'd had fights about it because he desired her to maintain an "image" that was acceptable, just like his friends' wives had. Their culture clashes were getting more pronounced. Inira knew she was beautiful and resented having to prove it to her husband. Image was not everything for her, and she felt like she was preparing a case against him in court.

It wasn't a great feeling. She knew she had to deal with her building resentments, or she would act out somehow. Thankfully, a new voice shook her out of her thought spiral.

"Mrs. Boehme?"

She blinked and made eye contact with the person addressing her. A surprisingly young man with dark hair and green eyes sat across the table and looked at her expectantly. For a second, she couldn't place where she was. Looking at him reminded her very much of the way Tomas would look at her when he'd caught her in the middle of a daydream.

She shook herself and replied, "I'm sorry, I must have missed the question."

The young man smiled, and it was so much like Tomas's. Inira felt her breath leave her chest in a whoosh.

"I asked if you are looking forward to presenting tomorrow?"

Inira recovered quickly, hoping he hadn't noticed her reaction to him. She'd been sitting across from him this whole time, so caught up in her head. How had she not noticed him? She shook herself, mentally scolding herself before responding, "Oh yes, yes, of course. I'm proud of what we've accomplished and what we see as the future for Nahas Helps. I'm sorry, I've been distracted. What was your name again?"

The young man grinned at her with all his teeth this time, and Inira's head swam with déjà vu. He looked like he was cut from the same gene pool as Tomas, except his coloring was lighter, and his eyes were rounder and turned up in the corners. She figured he had some Asian parentage. Her guess was Korean.

"Yes, I noticed you were deep in thought." He chuckled, deep and melodic. It made her shiver. "It happens to the best of us. My name is Lukas Nahas, and I am the Executive Director for Nahas Helps."

She could not get over the cunning in his eyes. He was so young. The longer she looked at him, the more the connection between him and Tomas shifted like Lukas could have been Tomas's son.

"Nahas is your last name? Are you related to Matti – I'm sorry – Deitas Nahas?"

His smile dipped, the glow on his face darkening as his lips tightened. She'd never seen that expression on Tomas' face. She inhaled, bracing for something she couldn't name.

"Yes, I'm his son. He wanted me to find a place where my skills would be most helpful. I started in the main corporation, overseeing several divisions. Those we call "Research and Development." It was stressful work that didn't suit my goals in life. So, when my father changed the company's direction, he appointed me to work under Chief Director Ahmadi to learn the ropes. I hope I can take over the entire foundation after a few years. I want to do good in this world and leave a legacy for my family."

His face relaxed as he talked. It was interesting to watch the change. Inira knew how to read people. Body language gives you more information than words ever could. She gave him a big grin and turned on a little of her charm as she replied, "That sounds excellent! That's my same goal in life. I look forward to working with you." She gave him a conspiratorial wink, taking a chance on his youth, allowing for a little more freedom in their speech versus what she could tell would be stilted and stodgy with his elders. She was rewarded with a wink back, but his face turned serious.

"Yes, assuming your work pleases my Father."

She inwardly groaned and noticed he lowered his eyes to his plate as he said, "Father." Inira couldn't stop herself before asking,

"Do you look like him? Your father, I mean."

She held her breath as he raised his eyes to meet hers again.

"People say I look like him, especially my eyes. My mother is Korean, so I'm built more like her and her family. My father once told me if I'd put a little meat on my bones, I would look just like his twin brother."

Blinking in confusion, she spoke automatically, "Your father has a twin? I apologize for not knowing; it wasn't in my research." Inira was beginning to think their research was not thorough enough.

A tiny seed of worry began to creep into her mind. Maybe they weren't as prepared for this week as she thought. Pausing before speaking more quietly, Lukas replied, "It isn't widely known. His brother died in a horrible accident many years ago. My father doesn't like to talk about it."

Inira nodded solemnly and changed the subject. She sensed that if she pried anymore, it would come off as just that – prying. She went to a line of questioning that usually made everyone happy, especially men. She quizzed him about himself, and he happily obliged her. It seemed to Inira that this young man wanted someone to talk to, yet she could tell he was still guarded like an animal was prowling under the surface.

Questions that seemed harmless were Inira's specialty, and she could keep the conversation going for hours while sharing very little of herself. After almost two more hours, the dinner was finally concluded, and they were brought back to the hotel. Stanley caught her arm before they stepped into the elevator and asked, "You still up for our drink?"

She nodded and then looked at Charlotte. Charlotte and Giselle had both been bored out of their skulls at dinner, plastering on pleasant, passive smiles with vacant eyes. Charlotte looked worn out, and Giselle looked about to fall asleep, standing up in her dark fushia dress and matching heels.

Pitying them, she said, "Charlotte, if you think there is anything I need to know before tomorrow that you gleaned from your conversations tonight, write up some bullet points for me in an email before you go to bed. We have an early start and can go over them at breakfast."

Nodding in relief, she took Giselle by the arm. Once they were on the elevator, Inira turned to Stanley to set some expectations. "Hopefully, this will be a quick drink. I'm not sure I can put anything more in my stomach before I explode."

Stanley chuckled and winked, as he usually did with her. "I unbuttoned my pants at the start of the meal!"

Inira laughed as Stanley shifted on a dime. He said, "Let's just quickly debrief. Did you hear anything tonight that demands we change our approach?"

The Deitas comment came to the forefront of her mind, as well as Mattias Nahas having a twin brother. She shared this with Stanley, and they both agreed they didn't know if that information added any new variables to how they would approach the week. Their focus needed to continue to be concerned about whether or not their vision aligned with Triune's going forward.

Stanely replied, "I saw you spoke with Lukas Nahas quite a bit tonight."

Inira started a bit, knowing that if Stanely noticed, so had others. Indeed, the whole experience had the vibe she was being watched. "Yes, but it didn't look bad, did it?"

Stanley knew what she meant: "No, nothing like that. I was entertaining the Chief Director, and since Lukas is his second, it is only natural you both engaged, and that is probably why you were sitting across from each other."

Inira sighed, relieved, but said, "You knew his son was part of this team?"

Stanley shook his head again. "No, it was Ahmadi who told me who he was. Does that change anything for us?"

Again, Inira didn't think so, but that tiny seed of doubt grew. She shared that thought with Stanley. Then, she put a hand on his arm and looked down into his face, "Stanley, what do you make of them calling Mattias Nahas Deitas? I have never heard that title used before. I know what it means definition-wise, but do you know what it means in terms of what they believe about him?"

Stanley's face grew dim. "This is why I wanted you on this presentation. Mattias Nahas isn't just the Chief of anything for Nahas International. You know how far and wide their reach goes. I think it extends to funding governments and influencing policy around the world. He knows how Teleosis did things and wants Nahas Helps to provide a front of goodness and mercy while continuing to expand their power around the world. I suspect they may want something from you, Inira."

She suddenly felt cold. She knew all of this, and while the opportunity with Nahas Helps was massive for Triune, she'd often had to fight her way through her discomfort at working with them because of the possibility of her invisibility cloak being ripped off. She didn't want to be used for her birthright, and what Nahas Helps was trying to do felt like they were part of an effort to put lipstick on a pig. Or, more accurately, a thinly veiled wolf disguised in sheep's clothing.

Stanley drew in a breath and continued. "I know you know all of this and suspect their intentions. I only warn you because it is possible because of your involvement; they know who you are and what you bring. It might be a good front, but it could also be considered a front for something darker. We will get out if it is, but it won't be easy."

She smiled at her old friend. She and Stanley had this discussion many times. She knew where some of their clients' money came from – dark deeds that now funded the light. They also both knew her cover, so to speak, could be blown. She'd made her peace with that. She knew nothing was as pure as their work through Teleosis – not even Teleosis. "I know, Stanley. I'm comfortable with our role here and will ensure not to get swept up into anything that puts Triune – or me – at risk. You know I know how to play this game."

He leveled her a look. The sharp look in his eye was telling. Then he dropped a bomb on her that might have kept her up at night.

"Well, then let me answer your question then. Inira, Mattias Nahas may have designs on this world that surpasses what anyone has ever been able to accomplish before. There is a reason why they call him 'Deitas.' Surely, you know it is an allusion to the word 'deity.' They call him this title because they think of him as a god."

Chapter 8

Shivering with foreboding to her bed that night, Inira couldn't stop wondering what undercurrents were at play. She had managed to maintain her anonymity for so long, including in a public community like AA. She knew she wasn't like the rest of her compatriots in the trenches of recovery. Her losses were more significant than an average person's, personally and culturally. It was why she had sought the help of a trauma-informed therapist and did the deep work, as uncomfortable as it was.

The theory of Nahas selecting Triune because of her involvement set her on edge. Usually, when people got too close to finding out who she was, she would retreat, often with a drink. She would pull back from friendships, or Stanley would take her off a project. She'd created contingency plans for being found out, even as she knew a part of her desperately longed to be known for who she would have been, not just for her own selfish ends but to restore the good name and work of Teleosis so that this world could be a better place, rather than continuing to watch it get worse from the sidelines.

She didn't know how to process that Mattias Nahas was considered a god. She was used to having virtual royal status in Teleosis, but divinity was at another level. The High Priestess was a vessel for the Divine but always careful never to claim equality with it. It made them different from monarchies – they kept their purpose in view rather than leverage it for their gain.

She contemplated the vast differences between the Teleosian religion and most other major world religions – at least the way the few used them to elevate themselves above the rest of humanity. Mattias Nahas was just a man and had the traits and faults of any other man. Like many other powerful men, she wondered about his lengths to hide those. Or did he have the drive to convert the masses to his religion? Was he a zealot or just swept up in the glamour of it all?

She didn't know, but she knew she would find out, and it gave her goosebumps, which she had until an hour after she crawled beneath the covers. She meant to look at her email and the presentation, taking in Charlotte's notes. But after Stanley's revelation, she couldn't shake the dread.

She had never met anyone who considered himself a god before. After grounding herself, she said the Serenity prayer and the "before slumber" Teleosian prayer for the first time in years. It floated to the surface of her mind and steadied her in ways it hadn't in years.

I accept myself just as I am. I am safe in my body. I am safe in this place. As I rest, Father, protect me. Mother, guide me. Son, enlighten me. Daughter, inspire me. It is so.

As she started drifting off, the conversation with Lukas Nahas returned to her and how much he looked like Tomas. It was thoughts of him that must have inspired the dream.

She dreamed of the beginning...

All she knew was softness under her feet. It was lush, blue-green grass that reflected a pristine sky. She could hear a river that flowed out into the world not far from here. That one river became the four that gave the world life, supplying the handiwork of the FourFold God with the sustenance it needed to thrive. No thorns, poisonous insects, or animals to fear – just peace and tranquility. Everything was in harmony, from the sky to deep under her feet.

She heard singing, low and pleasant. She followed the sound, having to travel a long way but not getting tired. As she walked, she saw wonders of all living things, perfection and beauty personified. There was nothing amiss, nothing that had been lost. She did not know pain or trouble as if negative or shadow emotions didn't exist. She was ultimately at peace within herself.

As she neared the source of the singing, she heard it more clearly. It wasn't getting louder, but it resonated deeper in her soul. Her sense of serenity deepened. Her heart began to beat in time with the pulses of the voices. As she approached the structure at the center of this place, which felt like the center of the universe, she could see the light pouring out.

It was this light and sound that gave birth to all life. As she got closer, her feet splashed through the trickle of the river as if it were born from the light. After climbing steps that did not tire her, she stepped up and into the structure through a wide arched entryway. She entered the structure's heart, pulsed with light, vibrating with anchoring, powerful energy. It was the origin of life, and everything began with singing.

She could feel the warmth drawing her in, close. She saw various beings standing around a large oval-shaped table. Their attention was drawn and fixated on the source of the light, warmth, and sound. They swayed slightly, their gaze never turning from the center, which pulled her in as if she were on a string.

Next to her, she felt a different kind of warmth. A beautiful male, also full of light, had come to stand next to her. She knew him as she knew herself as if they were one in two different bodies. Together, their halves were whole in an intimate communion.

She could feel the warmth of his skin as his arm brushed hers. His skin was light, whereas hers was dark. His hair was dark, cascading down his strong, muscular shoulders. He reached up to touch the small of her back, tucking his hand under her long, fair hair. He reached for her other hand to lead her closer into the circle but stopped and faced her before they arrived. As their hands met before them, she noticed they were forming their small circle, just the two. Her dark eyes met his, a shock of green. She could feel the energy arcing between them like the circuit was now complete with their hands joined. She was entirely at peace, clothed in only light, sound, and the warmth of his body close to hers.

She kept her eyes on the male, and they both opened their mouths and began singing. She felt power flow into her as their voices joined in harmony. She could see her skin lighting up like a spotlight radiated from her heart. She saw the male's eyes shine and his skin take on a different hue. They were a pair, a team. As they sang their combined song, a new world began to form, new possibilities started to emerge, and new timelines branched off to bring about the best possible outcomes.

They sang the Song of Creation together, and Inira never felt so alive and capable of doing anything she wanted. She wanted to heal, restore, and recreate this world into the image she knew was reflected at the heart of the FourFold God. They were with her, filling her up, uniting her with the man.

They were one, and in her heart, Inira knew this was exactly as it had always been meant to be.

Chapter 9

I nira woke up dazed, not knowing where she was and not caring.

Inira could feel the song's resonance in her soul, but it began to fade from her mind as she became more and more conscious. As she remained wrapped in the blankets, she could feel the warmth of the light, the feeling of safety, and the strength of the man's hands in hers. She could feel the power they contained and redirected together. This was how it was always supposed to be, in sacred union, their energy swirling and combining to create, recreate, and bring about the manifestation of the life the Fourfold God meant for humanity.

For the first time, Inira felt supernatural strength, which came from inside her, dwelling in her bones and blood. This was the birthright and promise of her ascension into High Priestess if it had only happened. But strangely, the bitterness of her lack didn't flood her like usual. What remained with her was the residual potential of that power that lay dormant within her.

The pre-dawn light was barely showing behind the blackout curtains. It was just before 5 a.m., London time. Their first meeting didn't begin till 9:30 a.m., so there would be plenty of time to start slow and meet Charlotte and the rest of the team. She didn't have to jump out of bed and hit the ground running. Her only wish was to return to the dream, to that place of serenity, to feel the power instilled within her.

For the first time in many years, she had felt at home, where true peace was found, and more alive than she ever thought possible. In the aftermath of the dream, she felt fully herself, connected with everything and everyone around her. The unity she had with the man, the beings, and herself was complete, lacking nothing. She couldn't form the words to describe how her body, soul, and mind felt the abundance of the Divine flowing in and through her into the past, present, and future.

Bits and pieces began to return to her in waking consciousness. She and the man were naked. She furrowed her brow as she knew it was her, but she simultaneously looked different, younger, and more ancient. There was no shame in their nudity because they were meant to be exactly that way. She was shocked when she realized the man had the same eyes as Tomas. The same eyes that had looked at her from the face of Lukas Nahas. The look in those jade green eyes felt like she'd known him her whole life and any life she may have lived before or would since. There was an essence to the man she would know in anyone.

Those eyes unsettled her. She still thought of Tomas often, but it was nothing like in the first five years after she lost him, often hiding it from Francis, who longed for her to move on even as it was so fresh. Early on, she saw those green eyes everywhere, in every painting, billboard, even a blade of grass. It was a big reason she started drinking as much as she did, to take the edge off that overwhelming grief of losing him. It was also why she married Francis so quickly.

Inira sat on her bed with the shades drawn for ten minutes without moving, reliving the power of the dream and letting all the thoughts swirl in her mind. She continually tried to return to the peace, even as it leaked out of her. She knew she would, for a long time, try to feel the tug of the bond to the beings, to hear the melody they sang, the wholeness she felt standing in the light, and the powerful energy they channeled. It was so different than what she often felt on the inside.

But the experience did fade, so Inira decided to make herself some coffee. For the first time in several weeks, she walked through her morning prayers with more than just dutiful obedience. She prayed several AA prayers, and it even felt right to add in the Teleosian morning prayer:

Mother, you've woken me from slumber; nurse me at your breast. Father, you've given me another breath; give me strength to pass any test. Son, allow me to serve the lost, the least, staying before you on my knees. Daughter, connect me to my heart as I rise again to start.

Her presence in a program like Alcoholics Anonymous, which was spiritually based but tied to no specific dogma or doctrine, had begun to repair the damage to her faith by discovering how much money the Counsel had been embezzling and the attacks. After the dream, she felt that the spiritual place inside her was now a door blown open wide after being sealed shut for too long. To prolong the feeling, she opened her curtains, watching the sunrise. She felt like today held a new beginning.

Halfway through her second cup of coffee, she heard a knock on the door that joined hers to Charlotte's. Inira sighed and silently asked The FourFold God to let her at least stay connected to this feeling when things began to get stressful. She didn't believe her God listened anymore or maybe didn't exist, but she asked for Their help in this small thing.

Perhaps this dream was sent by The Fourfold God to rekindle her faith.

Charlotte was wearing workout gear and had spent time in the hotel gym. She was annoyingly chipper as she walked through their shared door with her laptop.

"Good morning, Boss! I hope you slept well."

As the image of fit, Charlotte's dancer physique had allowed her to bounce back into her pre-baby shape with ease. She brought Inira to Pilates with her, and Inira got hooked. She admired Charlotte's energy and enthusiasm, even with a three-year-old son at home.

Their age differences were noticeable, with Inira having ten years on Charlotte. Where Charlotte was classically beautiful, Inira was striking, with dark hazel eyes shaped like almonds and dark wavy hair falling over her shoulders to the middle of her back. It was still a messy bedhead, and Charlotte's tresses were secured in a bun at the top of her head. With the dream's power still beckoning her, Inira could only smile and appreciate the younger woman.

There was no sense of competition between them because Inira knew she wouldn't be able to be here and be so well prepared without Charlotte. While the last few years had been bumpy in her personal life, she felt tethered to this work and the goodness of it nearly every day, with the younger woman's passion and drive refreshing her. This trip was essential to the transition that Inira felt would be coming soon. Stanely wasn't getting any younger. Inira didn't know what she wanted to do next, but she knew that choice would present itself quickly.

She shook off the last of the dreamy feeling and switched to Boss Mode.

"Charlotte, with the whole team being there today, we will need to ensure we address all the key players, but our primary focus will be on the top three: Mattias Nahas, his second, Chief Director Ahmadi, and Lukas."

As Charlotte grabbed her coffee cup, Inira continued, "I continue to be impressed. You were quite thorough. I appreciate you including your spot research on Lukas Nahas. I spent some time talking to him at dinner, so this fills out his background quite nicely. He will be essential to have on our team, so we must ensure we are in his good graces. He is the heir apparent, if not the lynchpin for our relationship with Nahas International."

Inira had a sneaking suspicion that while Lukas was important, he was still under his father's thumb. With Mattias Nahas having so much going on elsewhere, she knew he would want things squared away in his absence. Stanley's words last night echoed back to her: *He is practically a god to them.* Inira wondered if Lukas was being groomed to inhabit the role when Mattias was done.

She shivered again at the thought of meeting someone like Mattias today. Lukas may be necessary for Triune's future, but Mattias held all the strings.

Charlotte looked at her laptop, combing through her notes. "Let's talk about Chief Direction Amin Ahmadi because I believe he has great influence and sway over Nahas." She flipped the screen around, and Inira recognized the Arabian-looking version of Johnny Cash, who had called Nahas "Deitas" last night. To Inira's shock, he was Persian. He had grown up in Iran, his parents being part of the elite forced to flee when the revolution happened. Ahmadi had gone to boarding school in Europe but returned to live and work in Iran after graduating. He'd been a Shi'a Muslim before converting to this new corporate-sponsored cult, which took shape in the early days of forming the conglomerate. Since the beginning, he had been there and always connected to Mattias Nahas.

Inira wondered, for the second time, why he seemed so familiar to her.

"Charlotte, maybe Giselle can do some more research on Ahmadi. I'd like to know more about him, in general, and it would help me try to make some connection with him."

Inira paused, and Charlotte quirked up a brow. She was so sharp; she never missed a thing.

"What are you thinking, Boss?"

Inira looked down and tapped a finger to her lips. "I wonder if they have a long personal history together beyond business associates. I'm willing to bet they met in school. Nahas seems to be the kind of guy that would keep his friends close; he is certainly a fan of an all-boys club, which probably helped with Ahmadi's conversion from Islam."

As the two women and two women of color at that, their radar was always up. The supremacy of one person based on their skin color or gender over another was still such a foreign concept to her, given how she'd been raised. Yet, she'd figured out how to work this system, even as it grated against her soul.

Inira asked her second, "Charlotte, what else do you think we need to cover before meeting with Stanley for breakfast?"

Charlotte flipped to her notes on her laptop, reviewing anything left unchecked. She looked at the presentation one more time, making a few suggestions. They wrapped up their coffee talk and got ready to meet Stanley and the team for breakfast at 7 a.m.

Every moment in a highly conservative patriarchal environment required these ladies to be on point. They were dressed to go to war. Inira would wear the most professional business outfits, a full pantsuit with a vest. Charlotte would wear a suit with a feminine skirt yet exuded business style. Giselle had to draw the least amount of attention. It was an effort to stack the deck so the women would not be seen as women but as equals. It might not change any minds, but it would at least help them get into the right mindset.

Stanley was wearing a three-piece blue pinstriped suit with classic wingtips. He looked like he stepped off straight out of the catalog of Stuarts on Uxbridge Street. The other team members were men, and they were also in suits, having been instructed to wear the best they had and have different options for the office and the dinners later.

As they loaded up after breakfast to go to the offices and prepare for the first day, Inira said the Serenity Prayer several times. She tried to calm herself by remembering the song from her dream. She tried to tap into the peaceful feeling, but nerves quickly devoured access to that restful place inside her. Her butterflies were much more like piranhas as they were escorted through security and to the largest, most richly decorated conference room she'd ever seen.

As they walked into the conference room, she felt the back of her neck prickle in warning. She'd first felt it weeks ago when she started researching the man behind the company. It had returned to her several times, like a memory of déjà vu she couldn't place. As she took a step into the conference room, the split second she looked up to greet the Nahas team, that sense of foreboding flooded her system.

It was only when she realized who was already in the room that all her careful planning and appearances went straight out the window.

Mattias Nahas sat at the head of the table. Her knees began to buckle when she saw him, and she had to catch herself on the edge. It wasn't his tall frame, handsome face, or immaculate black suit with a blue shirt and paisley tie that made her feel this way. It wasn't how he was framed in the view of the complete London skyline in the floor-to-ceiling windows. Nor was it the set of perfect white teeth grinning warmly with a massive hand reaching for hers. She felt herself recoil and forced herself to take his hand physically.

She felt her mind spinning and spinning into nothingness. The peace and power from the earlier dream were long gone like they never existed. Meeting Mattias Nahas for the first time, and he was smiling like he had been waiting his whole life for it, was world-breaking.

She was ready to faint, but it wasn't because of how gorgeous he was or how powerful he seemed. It wasn't because he was her big fish client. It wasn't because he was a billionaire; Inira had been around the powerful and influential all her life.

No, Inira Kleo Boehme wasn't ready to faint because of any of these things. She was utterly untethered from herself at that moment because she was staring into the jade-green eyes of her first love and husband, Tomas.

This man before her was the replica of her beloved, who had killed himself, her mother, her sister, and every member of the Counsel of Wisdom with a suicide bomb strapped to his chest when he walked into the Temple on the Highest Holy Day in Teleosis. It was called the Day of Making, but it became her unmaking when Tomas pressed the detonator, blowing up her entire world.

Chapter 10

To say Inira was triggered was the grossest of understatements. It couldn't begin to touch the well of chaos she felt inside. She started shaking. But just as suddenly as it began, the shaking stopped. She went numb, as if her system could take no more input, and had completely shut down.

A subtle roaring began in her ears. She was moving but like a robot. His face was before her, but it started to blur as she shook his hand, the light from the enormous windows obscuring his face. She suddenly flashed back to the windows in the Temple, how much light they let in to fill the worshippers with the expanse of the FourFold God. She got to her seat, standing behind her chair. The meeting began as Mattias took his seat, and the introductions continued. She was rooted to the spot, only vaguely realizing Charlotte was tugging on her arm, almost like a young child pulling on her mother's sleeve, encouraging her to sit.

The roaring in her ears continued to build. She ended up plopping down in a chair but had to move as it was wrong. She felt like the middle of her chest had opened up into a bottomless abyss, like a black hole that sought to devour her entirely.

"Inira, what's happening? You look like you are going to be sick!" Charlotte whispered in her ear from her left as they settled beside each other. Stanley was to her right. The rest of the team was stretched out on her side of the table. Nahas Helps, on the other. If that wasn't a clear visual for sides being picked with a battle about to begin, Inira, even in her haze, didn't know what was.

She spluttered her response with a nod, that yes, she was alright, even though she was not at all. She couldn't bring her eyes up to the head of the table where Mattias Nahas sat. All the light coming in from the huge windows shadowed his face, but she could see the green of his eyes in her peripheral vision. She would have seen it even if her eyes were closed. That green was permanently scorched on her mind's eye and heart.

She made the mistake of looking across the table, meeting the green eyes of Lukas Nahas. Before she closed her eyes to salvage her sanity, he locked onto hers and gave her a slight nod and a small smile as if he knew what meeting his father could do to people.

He had no idea that she was meeting the twin of her dead husband, the one who had been the spark that led to the whole powder keg of her existence being blown to smithereens. How could he? Her mind raced to settle on one thought that made sense. Mattias Nahas wasn't just intimidating; he was her trauma and her greatest love personified.

She had to get her racing thoughts in line. She was trained from birth to lead in the most stressful of situations. She'd also worked too hard in therapy to give this man power over her life. She didn't know how she was still conscious, moving, talking, but she was. She felt dizzy, and the pull to faint was strong. Everything was riding on this moment, and she couldn't dissociate now. She teetered on the edge of surrender until Charlotte reached under the table and found her hand. She gave it a painfully tight squeeze, grating the bones of her left hand back and forth in her right.

The pain helped. It grounded her to reality, which helped stop her emotional and physiological freefall. Inira practiced breathing in for four counts, holding her breath for four, then breathing out for four counts. It was a technique called "box breathing" her therapist had taught her, and it got oxygen to her brain and slowed her heart rate. Charlotte's touch was a wake-up call to the parasympathetic nervous system, breaking through the adrenal spiral.

Her sister Samira would grab her hand sometimes when their mother would give them a look or comment during Temple services, a site visit to an outpost, or just when they were at home. The tone of her mother's voice was always pitched. It seemed her bitterness and grief after her father's murder permanently made her vocal cords grate together. After the Heir Naming ceremony, Samira was almost permanently holding her hand because Inira's anxiety would surface almost daily, triggered so thoroughly by her mother's vitriolic animosity towards her.

Inira never seemed to grasp why her mother targeted her after her father's death. Maybe it was because she looked like him, or perhaps because she was the Heir. Either way, Samira helped Inira more than she realized by this simple act of stability of physical touch. They both felt the pain of their mother's change, but she seemed to instinctually know that her job was to prop Inira up so she wouldn't falter. Samira was the epitome of kindness, which was their grandmother's legacy. Her father's mother always made sure the girls knew they were loved, and Samira took on that mantle after her death.

Inira spent the next ten minutes box breathing, trying not to be obvious about it. She felt like she'd had too much coffee. She stared through those giant windows, naming them as another grounding technique, using the London skyline for something to look at. She mentally named the Eye, Big Ben, and Parliament as she began to feel herself in her body again. The adrenal spiral left her exhausted, but she had a job to do. Stanley was finishing his piece and going through the agenda for the rest of the meetings. Before he turned it over to her, she walked through the Serenity Prayer. Memorizing prayers came naturally to her. It was her turn to present, so it was time to perform.

She took a moment to visualize her strong self, dressed in a flowing periwinkle robe, the color of the winter sky just before sunrise, like on the first day the world was created. Underneath the robes was a shirt of ultra-light, blindingly white chain mail. She had a circlet of platinum on her head, with an opal resting in the center of her forehead. Matching platinum bracelets on her wrists, with a slight breeze but no weaponry. It was an image she'd seen in one of the history books, an illustration of one of the Warrior High Priestess from around the time of the Crusades. She had imagined herself in that picture, and it made her feel strong enough. She didn't need weapons. She was secure in herself.

She knew she could keep herself level if she didn't look at Mattias Nahas. They'd already discussed who each speaker would focus on, and hers was Ahmadi. So, she took her final moments to observe him, finding she was stable enough to look down at the table.

As Stanley said his final words, Lukas caught her eye. He didn't smile again. It was enough of a connection, a low spark that gave her enough energy to stand. She gave Charlotte's hand one last squeeze, sharing a brief, grateful glance with her, and let go. She put her clammy palms on the top of the table, feeling the cool of the oak. Then, she began to wonder if the wood was oak. She spent a few seconds debating on what kind of tree the table was made of and sighed with relief. She was returning to herself.

When her mind started to ask questions, engaging in a dialogue rather than the screaming monologue of a panic attack, she knew she was coming out of a spiral. She put her hand to her sternum and rested it there, comforting herself after such an intense experience. She noticed how her back and hips felt in the chair, slightly uncomfortable, but was glad for it.

She pressed her feet into the floor, feeling the soles of her wedges, wiggling her toes as much as she could in the restrictive dress shoes, and sought out the feeling of the material of her dress suit pants whispering against her legs. Her mind cleared. She was alive; she survived, standing at the edge of the dark abyss. She didn't want or need a drink, even as she contemplated what would happen if she let herself go there. No, the craving wasn't there. She was okay right now.

Then Mattias spoke just after Stanley introduced her.

At first, it was a whisper on her skin, like he was at her shoulder, his breath on the shell of her ear. She shivered, her body reacting to the memories of Tomas's whispered secrets in the dead of night. Mattias' voice increased in volume, and the heat of those long dormant, dust-covered memories rose to the surface like a volcano contemplating eruption. She was lost to the song of his voice that clanged like a gong through her.

Until she realized he was speaking to her.

"Ms. Boehme, would you like some water before you begin?"

She blinked. Had he addressed her directly in the middle of the meeting? He was so informal like it was just the two in the room. It was odd to feel so familiar with someone she'd never met. She recalled all the mornings Tomas brought her a glass of water after they woke up while she stretched in bed. She felt she would break apart if she met his gaze, maybe do something stupid like throw herself into his arms and sob.

He is not Tomas! She mentally screamed at herself.

She didn't look at him directly, more in his general direction, managing to stand up and then turning her focus on the screen. "Thank you, Mr. Nahas; I would like some water before I begin."

"Ms. Boehme, I know you are unfamiliar with our culture, but allow me to educate you. His title is Deitas, so please address him as such." Ahmadi spoke so smoothly that Inira felt lit like slime over her arms. He didn't speak loudly; he didn't have to. He more or less purred, but she felt the intention of his comment. He was putting her in her place in the most acceptable of ways. She felt like a mouse in the paws of a panther, and indeed, there was a predatory glint in his eyes. A not-so-small part of Inira wanted to reach across the table and give him a solid punch to the throat for the exertion of authority, but that wasn't her style, especially here.

"Amin, you do not need to correct Ms. Boehme. She is our guest. Inira, let me assure you that you can call me Mr. Nahas or even Mattias. It is what makes you comfortable. We are equals here." Nahas looked at Ahmadi, and the other man met his eyes, cocked a brow before he bowed his head in deference. Inira watched the short interaction with fascination. These men were not of equal status, but both seemed to emanate a kind of power. Mattias was straightforward control, whereas Ahmadi exuded the skills of a puppetmaster. She would need to keep her wits about dealing with both; that was clear. Before she began again, she met Ahmadi's eyes. He gave her a serpentine smile, and she recognized what it was. It was clarity. He knew who she was. He also felt so familiar to her; she couldn't place him.

"May I call you by your first name?" Again, Nahas' question felt like a whisper, seductive. It startled her back into the present, and her agreement rose almost like a compulsion, pressing through her body onto the tip of her tongue. He looked at her as if the rest of the room had disappeared, and only the two of them were together. She shivered again. The heat in her caused by hearing his voice flamed her cheeks, even if she still didn't fully face him. "Yes, of course. Mattias."

It was beginning to dawn on her that there were other motives for their visit, and right before she started her presentation, a nagging thought whispered.

How much of this visit is about a business relationship, and how much of it is about me?

She could tell Mattias' face was locked on hers; the light behind him continued to cast him in shadow. He nodded and said, "Then, let's begin. I've been looking forward to hearing you speak since we set up this meeting."

She didn't have any idea if he was sincere or not. She decided to err on the side that he was trying to intimidate her to keep the balance of power with himself. That was the easier option to deal with. So much of her training to be High Priestess was in dealing with the power-hungry, especially men. She pulled on every one of those strengths now.

She put on a beaming smile and looked around the table, meeting each person's eyes as she firmly stood her ground. Lingering slightly longer in meeting Lukas and Ahmadi's eyes, she finally came to face Mattias fully. Now that she was standing, she could see him better. Holy hell, he was tall. She could tell this even though he was sitting.

Putting on the High Priestess mask, she began giving the most excellent Ted Talk version of the potential of the partnership of Triune and Nahas Helps of her life. It was stunning. She held the room enraptured, weaving a spell with her words. Something loosened and flowed from within her as she continued to speak. This was a deep magic that came from her comfort level with the material and her belief in her vision for a better world. She had always been good at speaking in public, especially when the message meant something to her. The power of the redemption story possible with this man's investment and resources was captivating.

Everyone, including her team, was leaning in. She noticed tears in Giselle and Charlotte's eyes. This is why they worked for her – her ability to tell a story was entirely on display like they had never seen. She could inspire and motivate with words she knew. She'd only used this level of gifting on rare occasions like it was her superpower, but it had never failed her when she did. Where the FourFold God may have forgotten to give her so many other things, They hadn't failed in this.

Looking down to her right at Stanley, she saw him radiating pride. She put her hand on his shoulder, and the support she felt from those she valued the most fueled her passion, giving her the power to bring her storytelling to its brilliant conclusion. She led them down a path to see what their investment would do, the people it would help, and the change it would inspire worldwide.

The message was only two points: the present and the future. The contrast between the two was compelling, and she knew, with her passion and energy behind it, along with the well-researched facts provided by her team, it was a slam dunk presentation. No one could deny what Nahas Helps was doing now and what was possible, mainly when they targeted their investment in three areas. She encouraged them to invest in finding a cure for blood-borne diseases, setting up reliable supply lines to clinics and hospitals in the poorest of areas around the world, and building up emergency response infrastructure with local governments so help could arrive much faster when disasters struck. These were enormous goals, but with the financial resources of this global conglomerate and leveraging the logistical operations they already had in place, it was a long-term project that could be acted on immediately.

The return on investment she proposed was simple and profound. They would see the plan would work with only six months of data. It was brilliant and spoke at a corporate and humane level. It was quickly the most aggressive yet doable plan she'd ever proposed, and it was all modeled on what her agenda would have been had she taken over as High Priestess. Once upon a time, these goals were at the heart of how Inira wanted to change the world for the better. Now, she hoped Mattias and his team would see this vision she cast and run with it.

As she sat down, the room remained silent for a beat. It was as if those listening had a spiritual experience and needed a moment to process their wonder and awe. She'd always had the same feeling at the end of one of her father's speeches. Then Mattias Nahas began clapping. It was so loud it hurt her ears. The force of the sound waves between his palms physically made her eardrums vibrate. She had the urge to giggle like a little girl. His approval might be part of his game, but it stoked the fire within her to explosive proportions. That long dormant volcano of desire and need for Tomas' recognition and love awoke with a vengeance.

She heard his whisper from long ago, *Good Girl. Such a brilliant girl. My wife and healer. So perfect.*

Everyone else joined in, but she kept her eyes on Mattias. His look held her in a vice grip. There was something between them that felt like electricity crackling between them. She licked her suddenly parched lips, and he tracked the movement.

As if her hand was possessed and without thought, she reached up and pulled the Teleosis pendant from under her shirt. The cool metal in her palm helped cool the heat of her blood. He noticed it and went still. He stopped clapping, and the rest of the response quieted down as if the rest of his team had to mimic him. Suddenly, it was like he was somewhere else, someone else. A hard look came into his eyes, and he spoke.

"Ms. Boehme, Inira. Thank you, that was excellent. My team has much to learn from your example, both in presentation style and content delivery. Truly, truly excellent. This has been a most enlightening morning. Let's break for lunch, and we will hear the rest of your team present this afternoon."

He stood up swiftly to walk out of the room. He paused as he moved past everyone. "Amin, make sure Ms. Boehme is seated next to me, at my right hand, for the duration of her visit."

He spoke as if no one else was there. Inira turned and quirked an eyebrow at Stanley. He shrugged and said lowly, "We knew you would make an impression."

Inira wasn't sure what that impression would mean for her. She felt off-kilter, both from the panic attack she'd endured as well as the letdown from speaking. She could also feel another energy's undercurrent–as if another agenda was in motion. It was visceral and sharp. Her team gathered around her and spoke their praise and excitement in hurried whispers. She took a deep breath and reminded them they each had a job to do this week to bring this vision and guide it into a real, living, breathing action plan. The rest of this week's success was up to them.

She wondered if that was true or if their experience with Mattias Nahas and his team hadn't started yet.

Chapter 11

Their lunch was in a private dining room on the conference area floor. They were surrounded by the same floor-to-ceiling windows, continuing to give them a spectacular view of London. The food was a delicious feast of Persian delicacies. It was food Inira enjoyed, but she didn't have much appetite. She was drained and exhausted from earlier. She found solace in the cup of Persian coffee. She ate enough to fuel her for the afternoon, drank her coffee, and let her mind rest.

It wasn't hard to do. Despite his insistence that she sit next to him, Mattias didn't speak to her or even look at her. It was the strangest sensation. She knew he was aware of her; she could practically feel his body heat, but he acted as if she didn't exist. There was a secret connection only they were aware of, which heightened her emotions. It thrummed between them, and she felt it in every fiber of her being. She felt the notice of Amin Ahmadi as well. He spent most of the gazing at her every chance he got as if he was trying to pick her apart. She wondered if he had expected someone different. She felt an ominous energy coming from him; even when their gazes connected, he wore an amiable smile. Her intuition told her not to trust him, yet she was still curious. She couldn't shake that feeling they'd met before.

She was set apart from the rest of her team, and since Mattias was not engaging her in conversation, she had the time to contemplate his striking resemblance to Tomas. Beyond their secret connection, it looked like Tomas made him a magnet for her gaze. Tomas was the love of her life, and he had killed himself and everyone she loved. Despite being the trigger man for the terrorist organization he'd secretly joined not long after her coronation as Heir, Inira never stopped longing for what they had before, during the happier times. The CIA told her later, in her political asylum debriefing, that Tomas had been approached, recruited, and radicalized by a group called the Serpents. She knew all about the Serpents. They were the ancient enemy who had made it their mission to take down Teleosis and take over the world. They wanted nothing to do with everyone thriving. They wanted all the power, all the wealth, everything under their control. With Tomas on board, the Serpents had found a way into the inner circle.

They used and exploited him, which allowed her to let go of her fury towards Tomas. She had known Tomas was unhappy. She knew, in the days leading up to the attack, his discontent with the whole ruling Counsel was coming to a head. She would never have imagined it would take such an extreme form. It wasn't till after the attacks she learned how corrupt the foundation of Teleosis was and her mother's part in it. Embezzling massive amounts of funds wasn't only a sin committed in the West, no matter the justification.

She had spent years trying to deduce his motivations. She knew he had loved her, so the unanswered question of why he went to this extreme plagued her. It was yet another reason to black out drink, ensuring she could stop the whirling dervish of her mind, trying to rationalize and figure out the unimaginable.

She never blamed Tomas for getting caught up, even as she should have. He was a grown man who'd made his own choices. They were choices she could never understand, and maybe her wounding led her to blame the organization he became a part of. Her mind told her he was at fault, but her heart could never get there. The cognitive dissonance was only quieted through alcohol, and she loved that feeling of numbness and silence in her mind. She knew they could have changed things together if he'd been completely honest with her. It seemed everyone in Teleosis around her had secrets. Secrets always lead to death, but for some reason, she was still alive.

Now, she was in a room with all her secrets on display.

Maybe she could never hate or blame Tomas because he was the reason she was still alive. He was the reason she was in her apartments the morning of the bombings. He'd turned off her alarm, going so far as to lock her in her room. Otherwise, her last view of this life would have been him with the bombs strapped to his chest. The last thing she would have heard was him screaming the Serpents' battle cry, *"Uno mismo es la única manera!"*

Self is the only way.

Now, she was sitting next to his carbon copy. Looking so much like Tomas, just two decades older, Mattias created a swarm of desire, attraction, and longing with a bone-deep sense of betrayal and devastation. She'd never been angry at Tomas. She knew from therapy that was a problem. She'd never fully come to grips with what he had done – the magnitude of what he had caused. She knew she should have laid it all at his feet, yet she never could get there in her heart. The enemy that had shared her bed never got what was coming to him. Now she wondered if she were sitting at the right hand of someone just as dangerous once again.

She took covert chances to study Mattias and look for the differences between the two men. Where Tomas had soft features, Mattias was hard. It was as if the years he'd lived had turned him into stone. There was a pinching around his eyes, several shades darker than she remembered Tomas' eyes. He had silver at his temples. Tomas had been in the prime of his youth. While Mattias had maintained his muscular, athletic physique, he wasn't young. Somehow, to Inira, that added to the fascination.

Mattias was a vision of what she would have experienced had the bombings never happened. Mattias was Tomas of her present and future. She couldn't deny that this man was gorgeous just on his own. He was exactly the type she liked, and while Francis fit most of that bill, Mattias had an air of danger to him. Francis never would. Francis was safe, a little softer, and a much less dominant energy. She thought Francis being the opposite of Tomas was the answer. Now, she knew her choices had resulted from trying to cope with what she'd been through.

Being next to Mattias felt like she was too close to an electric fence. She could hear the hum of it in her veins, the call to get closer, only a siren's song of pain and suffering waiting to happen. She wondered if she could turn away.

With lunch ended, they returned to the conference room. The afternoon was a small group break-out time to tackle the specific direction of how Nahas Helps would execute the plan Inira presented under the guidance of the Triune team. Charlotte was the lead. She was more than ready for the task and excited to get started. While neither Stanley nor Inira was surprised when Ahmadi announced Mattias and himself would excuse themselves from the afternoon, for a split second, Charlotte's face turned sour before she got it back under control.

The most powerful in the room never stayed for the nitty gritty details. That was Lukas' job and his middle management. Inira gave Charlotte a one-shoulder shrug and a small smile. She had warned Charlotte this was the way of things. This was Lukas' project to manage, and they would give him enough rope to hang himself with. She felt Mattias Nahas had ulterior motives for this foundation and meeting. She knew he would make his wishes known when he chose to. She was grateful they had made it this far with no pushback. That in and of itself was an excellent sign.

Having returned to the conference room, with everyone a little happier thanks to full bellies, Inira was startled when Mattias spoke directly to her.

"Inira, may I speak with you in my office?"

Inira looked up sharply from her laptop screen to see Mattias standing in the doorway. Ahmadi had a disdainful look before his mask shifted back to neutrality, but Inira caught it. He leaned in to whisper to Mattias. She wasn't sure if he was reproaching his boss, but by the look on Mattias' face, he didn't like what he was hearing. She was sure the "Deitas" Ahmadi wanted her to use was for effect. She didn't buy into their cobbled-together religious posturing. It was too much like all of the ultra-conservative sects of every major world religion. It made goosebumps creep along her arms to think about a worldview where men and only men mattered.

She got up, and Stanley gave her a nod and a smile to go ahead. She allowed him to be who he was in this meeting. She paid him the respect he deserved as her boss and the company president. She walked out and followed a step behind Mattias to the other side of the building to a private elevator. Ahmadi was walking on the other side from Mattias when Nahas addressed him.

"Thank you, Amin. You are dismissed. I know you have important work on our other priority project to accomplish and need all the time you can get."

Ahmadi's face darkened a shade, but the mask didn't slip. Inira could read him, though, and he didn't like being dismissed for a woman. He bowed so reverentially it made Inira want to roll her eyes as he said, "Yes, Deitas, I will see you at dinner." He didn't even look at Inira when he turned to go.

"Amin, stop. Please turn around and politely take your leave from our guest."

Inira felt the slightest prickle of warning at Mattias' tone, and it unsettled her. This was the alpha addressing his beta – a power dynamic she had seen at work. The FourFold God knew she experienced it often enough with her mother and the Elder Counsel members. She hated it, but simultaneously, when it came to Amin Ahmadi, she would take all the help she could get in dealing with his slippery self.

Misogyny took lots of forms, and Amin Ahamadi was a complex and subtle dealer of it. His version was more like Death by a Thousand Cuts. It might only feel like a bit of pain here and there, but you eventually bled out.

He bowed at the waist, not profoundly but enough that she heard Mattias grunt in approval before he spoke, "Forgive, Ms. Boehme. I will take my leave now to work on a top priority for Deitas and Nahas International. I will see you the next time." It was formal, stilted, and full of his self-importance. As he stood up fully, Inira realized she had a few inches on him, but he had appeared taller. She smiled and gave him a regal nod. He was gone before her head returned to the center, and she was alone with Mattias Nahas.

They got into the elevator, and she was suddenly aware she and Mattias were alone. Her mind started spinning and was strangely blank at the same time. She couldn't form any words to make small talk with the man who looked similar to her first husband and was so clearly not. They emerged from the elevator a short ride later into what was a smaller, top-floor private space. Inira could tell this was a suite with several rooms and wondered if it doubled as an apartment for Mattias. She complimented the décor and said,

"This is a stunning view, Mr. Nahas. I can only imagine how it impresses all who come here."

"It's Mattias, please. I don't bring anyone up here. This is my private, personal office. A sacred space, if you will, so only a chosen few ever see it."

The back of her neck prickled, and she felt rooted. Why had he brought her here then? She shivered slightly and continued to look around, hoping it would give her a clue about what to do. She didn't feel like she was in danger but wasn't dumb enough to feel safe. She knew her physical responses to the man were dangerous enough because she felt warm when they got in the elevator together.

"Would you like some tea? Please have a seat. I'll be right back."

He invited her to sit on a plush couch and disappeared behind a nearby door. She heard some rustling and realized he was preparing the tea service for them. She was thrown for a loop. He was going to serve her tea? This small gesture was entirely at odds with what she knew or expected from him. He came back shortly with tea and a small serving of biscuits. She nearly jumped over the back of the couch when she saw them. They were her favorite – Mandelbrot. It was like biscotti but from Israel, and Inira wondered how the hell he knew what her favorite kind of biscuit was.

She pressed her sweaty palms into her pants, her suit vest suddenly making breathing hard. She would have loved to unbutton it, but she thought that would give him the wrong idea. She took out her pendant and held it tightly in her palm. Mattias noticed the movement. His eyes narrowed for a split second before he said,

"You take any cream or sugar in your tea, Inira?"

The way he said her name felt like a gentle caress on her cheek. She could feel the heat build in her chest and cursed herself for being unable to keep her body in check around this man. But suddenly, a thought occurred to her that gave her some grounding. Wouldn't he know how she took her tea if he knew her favorite teatime treats? She decided to test this theory, not let him dictate their interaction.

"Please excuse the informality of my question, but I would think you already know how I take it?"

Nahas gave her a broad smile, which reminded her so much of Tomas she thought she may have had a stroke. She wondered if she could get his upper hand with that face.

"Indeed, I do, Inira. One lump it is. I have done my research, as I'm sure you have on me."

She huffed. "My spies never told me how you take your tea."

He smiled even broader at her again as he handed her the cup and a saucer with a slice of Madelbrodt. The warmth from his eyes made her feel slightly dizzy.

"You need better spies. I'm afraid we share a secret, do we not?"

She was so distracted by his smile that she didn't realize he had asked her this question for a second.

"I'm sorry, what did you say?"

He kept his eyes on hers, not saying anything for a moment. He looked into her eyes and spoke quietly, "*We share secrets, don't we, Inira?*"

Inira was taken aback. She was not prepared for this in the least. Yet she knew she had to get a handle on herself, so she used a usually highly effective tool – a question for a question.

"I know many secrets about you, but I wonder how much you know about me?"

They felt loaded as soon as she said the words as if she was daring him to bear his soul to her. Or perhaps reveal her soul to him. She wasn't sure where this conversation was going or why she was in his private space, but she thought she wouldn't like the outcome. She braced herself for the worst, but he surprised her with his answer.

"I know that you are brilliant. Not just from what I saw earlier but from all the information my team gave me on you. You are quite accomplished. Not only that, but you are also a wife and a mother. You have built a life for yourself, a career that makes a huge difference in the world. You are the entire package: brains and beauty. No wonder Triune had been such a success since Stanley brought you on board."

She was not expecting a compliment, and certainly not one that covered her entire life. Had he also just called her beautiful? Inira mentally slapped herself. She had to maintain control despite this chaotic feeling inside of her. Yet again today, she was grateful for her mother drilling into her the importance of maintaining her composure, no matter what.

"Thank you, Mr. Nahas. Mattias, I mean. Yes, I have worked extremely hard and have reaped many blessings because of it. Extraordinarily, little has been due to my outward appearance, though."

He grinned. "Yes, I didn't mean to imply anything other than I didn't expect you to be so striking. I've seen your social media and knew you to be attractive, but in person, you are quite dazzling, especially when speaking. Your ability to hold a room in a spell is remarkable. I was enthralled."

Before Inira could interject, he continued.

"Seeing you present today made me realize there could be possibilities for you here, at Nahas International, to run Nahas Helps, the largest non-profit organization in the world."

Inira gut turned sour. This is why he called her up here? To try and pick her off because he liked what he saw today? She looked at him hard.

"Mattias, I appreciate your interest, but I have a home at Triune. They are my second family. I am sure your offer would be appealing to someone else, but I'm happy where I am. Plus, you intend to make your son Lukas the heir apparent. Nahas Helps, it seems like his game to win."

He chuckled. "I don't mean to offend you in the least. My way of doing business usually leads me to make offers when I see something I want. I should have known you would have more integrity than to jump. I was only thinking my son could use the mentoring of someone who is so clearly talented and able to impact this world. He is young and impressionable. He would have the right balance with a person like you guiding him."

She quirked her eyebrow. "I'm sure you provide plenty of balance for Lukas. He is a bright and passionate young man, ready to make his way for good."

He waved his hand dismissively. "Yes, yes, Lukas is primed and ready. His mother feels sure of that. She has been ready for him to be at my side but often overestimates that his youth needs to be tempered."

Inira heard what he was saying on the surface, but she saw the emotion lurking under his words. There was something where he and his ex-wife were at odds concerning Lukas' abilities. She couldn't explore this because he preempted her next question with what he said next.

"I brought you up here hoping to steal you away from everyone, of course. I love a prize, and you certainly are one in every way." He smiled a self-deprecating smile. "I do, however, want you to know I am very interested."

That gave her pause. "Interested in what?"

"In you and your abilities. You are a remarkable woman. It might have been too forward for me to think I could lure you away with an offer."

Inira looked at him, "Perhaps more than a trifle arrogant too."

He chuffed, "Yes, I'm sure your spies told you that about me. I didn't get where I am without my ego." He continued, "Meeting you in person today and bringing you up here was more selfish than that, though."

Inira tilted her head, breath catching slightly. She felt like he was on the cusp of revealing something. One part of her was excited to find out, but another part screamed in warning. She decided to listen to the part that wanted to keep herself safe. She had plenty of experience with men who excited her and left her in shambles.

"Mattias, you don't need to say anymore. I appreciate the opportunity to work with your team and cultivate the opportunity to use the wealth and influence of Nahas International for the betterment of the world."

He looked at her for a long time before he said anything.

"That's exactly why I'm interested in you, Inira. You have a vision. You know how you see the world. You see it in color, not just black and white, and with wide-open eyes. I know the first thing you think of in the morning is how to make a difference and make goodness a reality on the earth. You have concrete, actionable ideas on how to do it. Perhaps it might scare you, but you have eyes that want to see the most and not the least. You are a rare woman, a rare person. You've been through so much, Inira. I want the chance to get to know you better. For the sake of the secret that we share."

Oh no, she thought. She could feel in her gut he had been buttering her up. She knew the pretty words had duped her, and the alarm bells were now like cathedral bells in her ears. This was all too familiar a narrative. It meant he knew who she was, but that realization did nothing to prepare her for what he said next. The secret she'd carried for years and had known the moment she saw him.

"The secret we share, Inira, is Tomas. And I want us to share his vision – my twin brother's life's work- together."

Chapter 12

Her vision went black as she dropped the teacup and saucer, splashing tea all over her shoes. The roaring returned to her ears.

In that one moment, Mattias had ripped open a decade of work by admitting he not only knew her past, but he knew Tomas. No one had ever said his name outside of her therapist, sponsor, and the CIA. They only knew him because of what she'd told them and government intelligence. Francis knew of him, but she'd long agreed not to bring him up. It made Francis uncomfortable, and she wouldn't share that part of herself with anyone. She wanted to keep that part of her still in love with Tomas tucked away, safe inside. She didn't want to have anyone weigh in an opinion on him and what he did. She might have admitted she had a problem with alcohol, but she never admitted she was still in love with the man who murdered everyone around her. She knew it was twisted, but she wanted to keep Tomas all to herself, her one true love, her secret fantasy, even as it was killing her. She tried to drink him away, and when that didn't work, she stuffed him so far down into her heart no one could find him. No one would know about him.

Everyone else had almost everything of her. Tomas was hers to keep and dream about. They'd kept his name out of the press as the original triggerman. No one knew he existed because no one knew to look for him. He was just assumed dead, and he was, but no one knew why.

Now, Mattias was admitting to not only knowing him but being his brother, for Christ's sake. She never knew Tomas had a brother. Knowing everything she'd kept so closely guarded, Mattias blew the safe place within her wide open.

They had that in common, blowing up things, she thought darkly. She wasn't sure if she was relieved or enraged. She didn't know if she wanted to kiss Mattias for freeing her or slap him for the way he did it.

She was also aware he had another agenda. He had to have one. She didn't know what game he was playing, but she was sure now it was a game. She was just a pawn in it. Yet, the pull to talk about Tomas was as strong as her revulsion to be used.

She didn't want Tomas to be unknown or to have never existed, especially after discovering why he'd be a part of such atrocities. She would never agree with the brutality and level of sheer violence of the attacks he led. Still, knowing the corruption he had discovered, that her own family had profited from it, she had come to understand he thought what he did was right.

As the blackness cleared from her vision and she started to hear sounds again, she was startled. Mattias was kneeling in front of her, saying her name. His eyes were a wash of concern and panic. He had not expected her to react this way. She swayed where she sat and struggled to breathe normally, not just from the rush of emotions and memories but also because of his proximity.

"Inira, Inira, I'm so sorry. Talk to me, please. Please, Noni, please talk to me."

That use of Tomas's nickname for her was too much. As he reached for her hands, she bolted upright.

"No. Do.Not.Touch.Me! How dare you? I don't know what you are trying to do, but DO NOT TOUCH ME. You do not have my consent to be this familiar with me."

She slapped his hands away and rushed towards the elevator.

"Noni, please, wait!"

She was livid now, and the emotional whiplash might do her in. Still, anger gave her power and energy. She spun on him, consumed by wrath, and yelled, "DO NOT CALL ME THAT! The man who called me by that name is dead. I don't care if he was your twin or you are him resurrected. How dare you?? HOW DARE YOU!! Using my past against me and setting me up?? I'm finished. Go to hell, Mattias. It's where Tomas is, and you belong with him."

Mattias Nahas looked as if she'd slapped him. She wished she had. Whatever his motivations for doing this, she knew they were not in her best interest. She knew that a man like Mattias Nahas would use whatever he needed to get what he wanted. She'd learned that much about him, and any man who had his subordinates call him the title of a god had too many issues. She could not deal with that or be around him a second longer.

As if he had read her mind, he said in a rush, "I'm sorry, Inira. My only intention was to share what I'd shared with no one else finally. It's not because Tomas was my brother and your husband. It's because only you could understand me. I've waited so long to contact you, reach out to you, and be in your presence. I wasted years blaming you for living, but now I see there was a greater work happening. I couldn't wait to share it with you, especially seeing how captivating you are. Tomas told me of your beauty and talent. He said you were luminous. He RAVED about you. He made sure you were not hurt that day. He wanted me to help you to continue the mission together. If Tomas couldn't be there for you, he wanted me to be."

She spun on her heel, marched right up to him, and this time, she slapped him hard. She left her handprint across his bronzed, muscled cheek. Any attraction to him withered in that moment of his confession. She let him have it.

"Tomas and the Serpents destroyed EVERYTHING I loved and cared about. EVERYTHING. HE KILLED MY ENTIRE FAMILY and everything Teleosis stood for. It is a PILE OF RUBBLE now because of what he - what YOU - orchestrated. Did you wait for me? You waited to tell me? You kept this inside for decades until you thought I would be ready? Well, I am NOT. I might not have agreed with everything about how Teleosis was being run, but I damn sure didn't agree with killing innocent people to get my way. That is the antithesis of what we believed in – what I STILL believe in. Mattias, you and whatever villainous plan you have can go straight to the seventh level of hell and rot there."

Mattias was staring at her. His eyes glittered like stones. He probably hadn't ever been struck by a woman, but at this moment, Inira couldn't care less. He had admitted to knowing everything about her and being a part of the group in charge of her destruction. Now he was coming for her? She was so angry, she was nearly foaming at the mouth, choking on the incredulity, and he had the NERVE to stare at her.

The tension between them grew the longer they stared at each other. Inira thought about slapping him again, but she started to be aware of how close they were. He was no more than a forearm's length away, and the air began to feel like it was shimmering between them. The longer the moment stretched out, the more she realized this anger wasn't dangerous only because of the chance of physical violence. His attraction to her was palpable. She became aware that he was looking at her mouth, and his hands were switching at his sides as if he wanted to reach up and grab her.

It set her on fire.

It had never been like this with Tomas. He was always sweet, gentle, and understanding. Francis had always been safe, funny, and true.

But Mattias Nahas was edgy and dark. It lit her up like a Christmas Tree. She could feel the rush back of all that desire that had just vanished a moment ago.

What the hell is wrong with me? She wondered.

She broke the stalemate by backing up, surrendering her hands, and saying to him, "I'm leaving. Please don't contact me again. I do not know how to deal with this, but you should know that everything about Teleosis is in the past for me. Tomas and his dreams – your dreams – are gone. It's dust. I have nothing for you, and you have nothing for me. Triune will work with you; Charlotte will be Lukas's lead and primary contact. If you try to contact me again, I will go to the authorities and have you arrested on outstanding terror charges. If you try to get anywhere near my family, especially my daughter, I will put a bullet in your brain."

Inira didn't believe in guns, and they certainly didn't own one. She was steeped in nonviolence, but what he'd confessed made her feel like she needed to draw a hard line. Yet, she knew at this moment she had to threaten him, or she would do something far worse – stay.

Mattias didn't reach for her, exactly. His hands kept twitching. Even as she said the words, she knew a man like Mattias wouldn't' stop. He'd never stopped before, and she doubted no one was still alive that stood in his way. She hoped to be the first. She backed up towards the elevator. She didn't turn her back on him, couldn't take her eyes off him. She pressed the button, and it opened immediately for her.

She stepped into the elevator, still facing him. Just as the doors began to close, she closed her eyes and took a deep breath, only to hold it as her eyes shot open when she heard his palm smack against the doors. He stood before her on the other side of the threshold, fear and desire waging war inside her, vying for dominance. There was nowhere for her to go if he stepped inside, and she had the distinct feeling if he did, she might be leaving the building in pieces. The violence on his face made it an unreadable mask—only the muscle under his right eye twitching.

He held the doors open for more than a few seconds. Panic was making Inira feel trapped, like a wounded animal.

"Let me go, Mattias." She tried to make the words sound commanding, but they came out just above a whisper.

"Never." He whispered back.

"Why are you doing this?" She could feel her eyes start to burn from the tears, but she would be damned if she cried in front of him. She would go to hell herself before she begged any man for anything. Looking her up and down one more time in a possessive, authoritarian way, he paused and then said,

"This was all supposed to be mine. You were supposed to be mine. And what belongs to me, I get, no matter what. We will build it all back together, Noni. You are the Daughter of the Light, and I will be your Consort. I am the Son of Promise since Tomas is no longer here. We will take what is ours. *Uno mismo es la única manera!*"

Self is the only way.

The Serpents declared their motto in whatever language was convenient, but this Spanish version must have been Mattias' mother tongue.

He reached out to touch her, but she flinched away. He withdrew his hand and held her gaze until the doors closed. When she got to the conference room floor, she ran straight to the restroom, locked the door, and threw up.

Chapter 13

What do we do when there is nowhere to go?

Where do we turn to when the world is so dark?

Where do we look when we can no longer see?

When our vision fades

When the darkness invades

How do we go on?

Only You, the FourFold God, can save us.

Only You, the Everlasting to Forever, can mold us.

Only You, the Knower of Light and Dark, can show us the way.

Show us the Way.

Show us the Way.

Show us the Way.

***

The prayer repeated over and repeatedly in her mind as Inira sat on the floor of the immaculate corporate bathroom, doubled over after hurling her guts out. It was a song in the Teleosian worship book she'd learned years ago. It came flooding back to her. She didn't have to wonder why she remembered it now. It was more of a chant with a steady drum beat usually played behind it, resembling the beat of a human heart.

Her heart was beating so erratically after her encounter with Mattias that she was grateful for the steady cadence of the song to slow it down.

At one time, she had over 200 hymns memorized. Her mother's favorite punishment was to make sure to memorize a hymn. She would have to sit there until she knew it by heart and could recite it thrice. This one, specifically led by the High Priestess, was one of the earliest she learned. It was written over a thousand years ago, during another time when the threat of destruction loomed large over Teleosis, during the 2nd Crusade. Inira had viscerally felt that same threat as the elevator doors closed on Mattias' thundercloud face.

The longer she sat there, the cool tile against her hands, her full consciousness returned. She began to take in where she was. It happened to be the most luxurious corporate bathroom she'd ever seen. The marble and gold on everything shimmered, making her feel dizzy. She had vomited several times, her body rejecting the physical intensity of the cocktail of emotions she'd felt that day. She thought about how nice it would be to get back to her hotel room and drain her mini bar. How easy it would be to lose herself in a blackout bender. It was a choice she wouldn't make. She wanted the promise of a life lived sober.

There was too much at stake for her to go out.

She started shivering as her body settled. She needed some water and probably something to eat. She couldn't go back to the conference room. She didn't want to risk throwing Charlotte and the team off with her appearance. Nor did she want to run into Mattias again so soon. She couldn't see that look on his face again, the sheer level of will to possess her.

Mattias had looked like he would devour her body and soul if he got the chance. She had never felt that level of fear from a single interaction with another person in her entire life. Yet, there was also a blooming desire with it. She had felt her body respond to his possessive words. Had she always longed to be dominated by a man like that? She didn't think so. She had known the overwhelming terror when the bombs started rocking the city all those years ago, but this was different.

This was an obsession.

A dark thought wriggled through her brain.

What would it be like to be possessed by him?

It couldn't have been what she had shared with Tomas because, though he was strong, he was always tender. Was it because Mattias looked nearly identical? Or was it something else?

Inira had always been pushed to the forefront and made to stand on her own. She would have been High Priestess, a recognized world leader. She had never been told anything but that she would stand by herself in a seat of power. Tomas knew his role by her side but was always meant to be a step behind. Now, Francis was successful in his own right, but he wanted a modern woman, a partner, an equal, and the American dream. He wanted a woman who would bring home the bacon, fry it up in a pan, and never let him forget he was a man. Lately, especially since she got sober, that had been a mask she was less and less willing to wear.

A small part of her that she always pushed into the shadows poked its head up. *Wouldn't it be nice for someone to want me that much? Wouldn't it be nice to have someone lead me rather than always having to be the one in front? What would it be like if someone wanted the same things as me and would do anything to get it?*

She sat there, with her back against the tiled walls, her head in her hands, and wondered if this was when she started to lose her grip on reality. They said sobriety in the first few years often made you feel crazy because you are learning to deal with everything in real time, with all the emotions being felt rather than numbed. She was grateful for her time in rehab, even as posh as it was, but she'd always thought she was in a class alone. Most people might have drama, but they didn't have her backstory or an alpha male offering to give her the world in exchange for her soul.

She couldn't understand her mind at this moment.

The villain had revealed himself, and while initially being wholly repulsed by his darkness and obsessive, no possessive, claiming of her, she grappled with being attracted to him. She was a married woman! Well, maybe not happily anymore, but she had to deal with that separately. She didn't need to mix anything.

Yet, she had never experienced attraction to someone on this level. It was cellular and almost paralyzing. While she was revolted at how he hinted at accomplishing his goals, she wanted to be craved that way. His whole person focused solely on her, taking care of everything and desiring nothing but her at his side as he conquered. Her body felt heady, even if it was morally, religiously, and ethically wrong. It made her want to return to him and to.... what, apologize, fall at his feet, surrender, and give herself body and soul to him?

Maybe slap the shit out of him again. She didn't know.

She sighed. She had to get out of the bathroom, out of the building. Just then, her phone buzzed.

You ok? You haven't checked in, so I'm just seeing how it's going. I hope you've had a chance to think about what we discussed in the car.

Reading the text from Francis made her laugh – a little hysterically. Even thousands of miles away and across an ocean, he would want to know how she felt about their relationship and going to therapy when she returned. It couldn't wait, especially as she warred with her emotions and debated whether throwing her life away was a good idea. She was most assuredly still on the fence regarding her marriage, but now there was a new complication. She had options that appealed to her darker nature. It was her darker nature that craved Mattias. She had always been a good girl. It was what she was born to be. She had perfected being the person everyone thought and needed her to be. It was only with Tomas and occasionally Samira that she was entirely herself.

She heard the shadow whisper, *what would it be like to be on the winning side, even if it meant going bad?*

She scrubbed her hand through her hair, a sweaty mess. She was so drained and yet exhilarated. She couldn't decide if it was the FourFold God who was offering her a new path or an evil force meant to steer her to destruction. Her past was merging with her present, which would most assuredly determine her future.

She pulled herself up to a stand, padded her face down with a damp, very expensive-looking hand towel, and looked at herself in the gilded mirror. She looked wrinkled, and her makeup had run from the vomit-induced tears. She worked on her hair and cleaned herself up to an acceptable level. She cupped water in her hands from the sink and drank greedily. It was cold, and it helped settle her mind. She looked at her reflection and said,

"Ok, Noni. Let's make it through this afternoon and get back to the hotel. Then we can decide on the next best thing to do. Don't follow those dark thoughts any farther." A self-pep talk didn't seem to do much, as her body still felt drained and alive when thinking about Mattias.

There was no official dinner like the one scheduled for the previous night. The Nahas team offered transportation to several high-end London restaurants, but no formal interaction was required. Which meant, Inira could beg off from dinner. She would love to work out, take a long soak in the tub, and talk to her family. She wasn't sure if she would get much sleep, but she could at least try.

As she returned to the conference room, she saw nothing was amiss. Stanley smiled and nodded at her, noticing her wan complexion and giving her a querying look. She smiled, gave him a thumbs-up sign, and resumed her seat. She kept her eyes on Charlotte, leading the group discussion portion. Lukas gave her a little wave. She nodded to him but didn't maintain eye contact. As they wrapped up for the afternoon and the team discussed where to go for dinner, Inira kept quiet. When they asked her about staying in, she said jet lag had gotten its hooks in her, and she needed the night to herself.

Lukas caught her arm as everyone filed out. After her interaction with his father, the last thing she wanted to do was be touched by another Nahas and stare into another pair of green eyes. She was relieved and almost thanked the FourFold God his mother was Korean.

With a heavy sigh, she turned to him, "Yes, Lukas? Can I do something for you?" She knew her tone was short, but she couldn't help it.

He paused and looked down, not shy but seeming to decide what to say. She might have thought the gesture endearing if she wasn't as exhausted from being around his father.

"Lukas, anything I can help with?" She asked him again, trying to keep her tone soft.

He lifted his head and straightened his shoulders, looking her directly in the eye, sharp, almost hawk-like, "Mrs. Boehmee, I want to tell you what a marvelous job your team, especially Charlotte, is doing."

She smiled and nodded at him, "Thank you so much, Lukas. They are exceptionally talented and hand-picked for their skill set." She tried to turn on her charm and give him a big smile, hoping her breath didn't smell like vomit.

He stared at her again, making her feel uneasy. She decided she needed to push him to move this interaction along. "Please, Lukas, tell me what you are thinking?"

He smiled, and a flush crept into his cheeks. "I just didn't know if it was appropriate to ask about her. She is mesmerizing. Is she single?"

Inira was perplexed for a second, but when the words made sense, she tried not to sigh. She was unsuccessful. Inira was not surprised. Charlotte was a bombshell, even as she was probably ten years older than Lukas and had just gotten out of a toxic relationship. They would probably be working closely together if this partnership hadn't been blown up by what occurred in his father's office.

"She is, but I would counsel you to keep this professional. Charlotte can also speak for herself about what she would want with you, but I don't know that making things complicated by becoming romantically involved would be a great idea. Plus, you live across the North Atlantic."

He smiled, but that sharpness that came into his face. He nodded as he said, "Oh, I figured it would probably be complicated. When I see something I want, I know I will do what it takes to make it work."

Inira felt his father's words echo back like an ice cube trailing down her spine. A *tilt to the obsessive runs in the family*, she thought.

Lukas' face shifted back to a less predatory look, and he asked, "How was your meeting with my father? Will this be a partnership that moves forward?"

Inira swallowed, her palms immediately getting sweaty. "We shall see Lukas. It was a very enlightening exchange. You can be a lot like him, I see."

Lukas then looked sad and said in his clean British accent. "Yes, sometimes I think, as they say, the apple doesn't fall far from the tree."

She said goodbye to Lukas, who looked like he wanted to learn more about their dinner plans, but she expertly extracted herself with a smile and a promise to talk more tomorrow. She nearly told herself she didn't need a drink, and when she finally got back to the hotel, she decided to run on the treadmill till her legs gave out and then order room service.

Chapter 14

S he stuck to her plan and ran for almost ninety minutes before she thought she would collapse. She hadn't run that long since she trained for her first half marathon, and she would definitely be sore tomorrow, the next day, and probably on the plane ride home. It was the only way she could feel right within her body. She had the forethought to have the mini bar removed from her room when she checked in, but she still had to keep her head down as she moved through the lobby, past the bars. Her team had long since left for dinner, so she wasn't worried about running into anyone while drenched in sweat.

She stopped dead in her tracks when she saw Lukas. He sat in the lobby in a plush, ornate chair like he owned the place. He had a tumbler of whiskey or scotch – maybe bourbon in his hand. She debated whether she should walk past him, but since her head was clear, she knew he had un-business-like intentions towards Charlotte, so she decided to investigate.

She put on a chipper voice and smiled as she said, "Oh! Good evening, Lukas! I'm so surprised to see you standing here."

He had the nerve to look shocked to see her. He stammered, "Yes, I decided I would wait to see if I could catch Charlotte to discuss some last-minute agenda changes for tomorrow."

Inira tilted her head, quirked an eyebrow, and smiled like she was the cat that caught the canary. She thought she was dealing with a boy in a man's clothing, but she wasn't so sure Lukas hadn't done this before. She had just found out his father had been stalking her his whole life, so why would Lukas be any different? Deciding to nip this in the bud but still be a diplomat, she said,

"Well, I'm sure she is tired after doing a splendid job leading the group discussions. When she returns from dinner, she will check her email. Why don't you send her your thoughts, and she can read them at her leisure?"

He looked slightly confused at her suggestion that he make this meeting an email, and Inira knew it was because he had no intention of discussing business with her. But he didn't miss a beat with his reply, "Well, I think she likes to work better in person. But thank you for the information; I'll consider that and not make this a long night."

Inira scoffed in her mind, and it probably showed on her face. She wanted to say, "No, I don't think it'll take you long at all, Lukas." But instead, she said, "If you are serious, Charlotte is in the room that connects to mine. You are more than welcome to wait in my room until she returns. I'll even ask her what their arrival time is."

She meant for the suggestion to sound awful. She wanted to scare him off, either by making him think she would be listening in or even the more disturbing thought that she was hitting on him.

As soon as he heard his options, his face paled. He put his drink on the small table next to his chair, stood up, now several inches taller than her, smoothed down his jacket, and replied, "I think that is a bit too forward a move, Ms. Boehme. I am only interested in Charlotte in a professional capacity, I assure you. Plus, we want to keep our working relationship on solid footing. It would not do for me to be seen in your or her room."

Inira giggled inside before she said with a smile, "No, Young Mr. Nahas, that would NOT do. We will see you in the morning then. "

If he was offended by the dismissal, he didn't look it. He nodded to her curtly before exiting to the valet. She watched him go. He glanced back once, and it wasn't the look she expected. It was more of curiosity rather than any malice. That made her pause and question her motives for sending him away.

She hoped Charlotte hadn't given him any encouragement. She knew she wasn't Charlotte's mother, but getting in bed with any Nahas in any way wasn't what they did at Triune. She ran an organization that was squeaky clean that she knew of. Of course, the Counsel had been that way once, too, only to find out too late that it could be like everything else.

Inira shook her head, planning to ask Charlotte about Lukas in the morning. She could feel the exhaustion from her run setting in and needed to get upstairs, shower, and get in bed quickly before she fell face-first onto the posh carpet of the lobby. She also managed to order room service and respond to several texts from Francis and Emerie, who had a rough day at school. She said she was ok, but as a mother, Inira was hyper-vigilant. She wanted Emerie to know she was loved and belonged. Emerie had struggled to find her place in high school. She had a couple of close friends and a boyfriend for about six months last year. Yet, Emerie still found it hard to relate to kids her age. She knew Emerie wanted to be with someone who understood her, a man who had life experience and would make the big gesture, choose her, and treat her as well – or better – than her parents did.

Inira didn't know who would fit that bill, but she prayed to the FourFold God the best man for the job would find Emerie.

Also, Emerie had a mother with a vastly different upbringing and outlook than most of her peers. The things weighed on her mind, and her peers couldn't connect to it, much less conceive of the wider world. Inira had told her all the stories – good, bad, and ugly – of the world, especially of Teleosis. Despite Francis's protestations, Inira had never sugarcoated life or how the world works for women to her daughter.

Inira put a lot of knowledge into her. It was what Inira felt like she lacked. With the burden of this knowledge and growing up in the West, her daughter was self-aware enough to realize she was different. Still, instead of feeling confident in her values and beliefs like she had through her elementary school years, Emerie's self-confidence had taken many hits from kids and adults alike. She was beginning to blossom into the incredible young woman she was created to be, but that hadn't come without much struggle.

So, Inira did her best, probably too much, to cushion the blow. More than she should have, and it was a constant topic of discussion in her therapy sessions as the family group therapy they attended once a month. Inira and Emerie had always been close, but therapy helped bridge their gaps. When Emerie did reach out to her to talk, Inira moved Heaven and Earth to be there and listen. This time, despite the incredibly stressful day and relentless run, Inira picked herself up and Facetimed Emerie. She was just out of school, and Inira hoped she was not too tired or hungry to talk.

"Hi, Mom." Emerie gave her a small smile as she answered. "How's London?"

Inira was multi-tasking this call – eating dinner and drinking a small cup of coffee to make it possible even to have this conversation. She gave Emerie a thumbs-up while she chewed. Emerie went on,

"Dad's taking me out for dinner tonight. We have been eating in, and it's been SO boring. When are you coming home again?"

Inira swallowed and said, "In two days. Well, three to you because I'll see you in the afternoon when I return."

Emerie sighed and rolled her eyes. "I hate it when you are gone."

Inira put on a concerned look, but inside, she was beaming. It helped her to know she was missed. She desperately missed seeing Emerie every day and hearing about her days. "So, what's going on at school that has you upset."

"Oh, I'm not upset; people are just stupid and ridiculous," Emerie told her about several girls on her soccer team who were living into their age as teenage girls. They were posting derogatory comments about their classmates, including targeting a girl recently diagnosed with being on the spectrum; she was their star forward and in line for a national Academic All-American recognition. Her discipline and focus were so far beyond what the other girls could do that they couldn't compete. She'd already accepted a full athletic and academic ride to Stanford.

However, instead of being celebrated, she was targeted. It was ugly and hard for Emerie to reconcile why girls her age could be so mean to someone so remarkable. Emerie might have been this girl's closest friend. Inira listened as she ate, enjoying the warmth of the coffee that perked her up enough. She went to the bathroom to wash her hair and skin before bed. She asked the bare minimum of questions because she had learned Emerie didn't need her to fight all her battles. She needed her mom to be a safe place and a sounding board. Those family therapy sessions were paying for themselves right now.

"Does the coach know? What about Ginny's mom?" She asked.

"Yes, the coach knows!" She said loudly and indignantly. "He said he would investigate the issue, even though Ginny gave him the screenshots of all the snaps. But you know the district tournament is coming up, so if anything happens – which I doubt it will – it won't be till after that. Ginny says her mom wants her to get through this season, focus on her grades, and then be mostly done with her senior year and able to put this behind her when she goes to Stanford." She paused before she said, "I can't wait to make my friends and my own family when the time comes. I want to be around people who want to make the world better, not make it worse!"

They'd learned the hard way on other occasions that unless you were threatened with going to the press, very little happened in the way of discipline at the high school, especially the private school Emerie attended. She went there because of how it looked like getting into college, but now Inira wondered if it had been worth it. Francis thought it was only kids being kids, but Inira knew what Emerie was experiencing would only be more of the same as she became a young adult in the West. There was the one-time Emerie had been targeted by bullies in middle school; he had pushed all the right buttons and made all the right threats. He went alpha male, which he so rarely did. It was a relief, but then he switched back to relaxed mode, and now she never saw him getting out of it.

Inira and Emerie talked for a bit longer. Emerie was at home by herself till Francis arrived from work, so she was going to get her homework done. Before they hung up, Emerie sighed and said, "How am I ever going to find someone to be a real partner for me, Mom? Even you and Dad seem to be struggling right now."

Inira swallowed nervously to give herself the space to think of something to say. Ultimately, she said nothing but, "It will be ok, sweetheart. It will all work out, and someone who is there for you will come into your life when you least expect him to." Emerie sighed, and then they said their usual nightly blessing, the Teleosian evening blessing Inira had taught her when she was a toddler.

Dark has now fallen. We can no longer see. We trust the FourFold God to save us from every enemy. They will see us through the long hours of the night. In the morning, when sight returns, We will know Them in whom we have faith.

Inira smiled after she hung up and laid down to read, which always helped her fall asleep. She didn't know how long she was reading until she felt the book hit her in the face. The hard binding on the top of the book hit her squarely on the bridge of her nose, and she was now painfully awake. She sighed and picked up her phone. She'd missed a text from Francis about something innocuous, which she quickly replied to and said goodnight.

There was one other text from a number she didn't recognize. She debated leaving it for the morning and turning off the light, but her curiosity got the better. Her stomach dropped in both excitement and dread as she read it.

Ms. Boehme. Inira. Please forgive me for my behavior today. Your respect and attention mean more than I could ever say, and I fear I've broken your trust. For far too long, I have wanted to be with you and see what we could become together. I let myself run out of control. You make me feel so much hope; you are the only one I can share anything with. Please respond - Mattias.

Her mouth was bone dry. She expected he would contact her again, but not this soon. She expected to get a terse, legal email or even be served a formal summons to appear before him again. Not something as intimate as this, what felt like a confession. She felt that shadowy, insane desire wind up in the pit of her core again. Lying in bed like this, it felt like he was whispering in her ear, with his head on the pillow. She could almost feel his breath on her face, looking into those green eyes.

Maybe it was the jet lag or the run, but suddenly, her mind was like scrambled eggs. Her sense was gone, and she was sure she was misreading the line "what we could become together." Then she remembered her anger from earlier, the sheer fury she'd felt when she slapped him until the memory of the heat between them surfaced. Someone like Mattias Nahas, someone this powerful being this vulnerable?

It was an aphrodisiac.

A small part of her sounded alarm bells. She knew he was probably manipulating her; that feeling of being a pawn in a game thudded dully in her mind. But her body had already leaped. It felt like she had finally found someone she could merge her two worlds – past and present. She could share her whole self with him, trust him with things she'd never told anyone else because he probably already knew.

It was a false sense of security but security, nonetheless. One of the most powerful men in the world, one she knew wanted to be THE most powerful man, trusted her with his secrets. It was intoxicating for a tired woman, a woman tired of fighting, tired of not being a priority, and tired of being the one who had endured so much trauma and how to recover from it.

She didn't mean to begin to fantasize about what it would be like to have let him pull her close to him. She didn't mean to remember what he smelled like, to see if it matched Tomas' or competed with Francis.' She got swept up in sheer make-believe of how he could save her and merge emotionally and physically.

A reply came to her mind, unbidden and unsought, and before she knew what her fingers were doing, she was texting him back.

Mattias, I can't repeat today, but as long as you know I want to share things with you, we will be okay. Maybe you can make me hope again, even though I didn't know I'd lost it.

It took less than twenty seconds of watching the three dots for her to see the reply to come back.

You don't know what it does to me to hear this. I fear I'll be dreaming about you again tonight. And for the first time, maybe my dreams will become reality.

Inira, a grown woman with a successful career, husband, family, and the kind of experience only global heads of state ever receive sighed. She felt the door that had been sealed shut for decades crack open to Mattias. It was the intoxicating "what-if " world mixed with "what-could-be." It was a dark place, painted with shadows and quite possibly the door to the stairway of hell itself.

She was also too early in her recovery to understand she was trading one addiction for another. Instead of wine or vodka, she was pouring herself a drink from the well of fantasy land. It was furnished with the dark thoughts of how Mattias looked at her, of what she could share with him. She hadn't felt this wanted and desired in a long time. She lay there consuming these stories and fantastic thoughts, and at the same time, they were feeding off her soul. By the time she fell asleep with her phone in her hand, she was consumed by what it might feel like to be with him in work and life. This addiction might not have been alcohol, but she had taken the first drink.

Any recovering alcoholic will tell you that it's the first drink that kills you.

Chapter 15

The following two days were a blur. She didn't see Mattias but felt his presence with her constantly, mainly because they were exchanging messages with ferocity, confessing their hearts and heads like lovers of old trading letters. Inira closed the week's final meeting, shaking hands with Lukas and the board—Ahamdi's dark, brooding presence overseeing all the proceedings, standing in for his Deitas. Inira smiled to herself, knowing she was beyond his reproach now. The Deitas was firmly hers. He had told her as much, and the looks Ahmadi gave her confirmed that truth. He wasn't happy sharing time with a woman. In his text about it, Mattias reported,

Amin has always been my right hand. He also has no imagination. He will not be a problem for you, Noni. I'm so grateful to have you in my life now. Inira, you bring light and possibility back into my bleak life.

They'd exchanged no inappropriate messages, but if anyone from the outside read them, they would have seen Inira well on her way to crossing many lines and crossing them often. It was happening fast, like she was being sucked into Mattias orbit, and she let it happen. The gateway drug was how much they had in common. Another was the sheer amount of attention and affection Mattias was showering her with, which made the texts from Francis pale in comparison.

For her part, Inira hadn't spared Francis too much time, short texts, and said they would talk when she got home. She was going to be straight with them, that she was unhappy and wasn't sure she wanted to continue the relationship as it was. She planned on seeing her therapist for sure but felt that perhaps the timing of couples therapy had passed. Still, she was looking forward to being home.

That hidden door to her secret heart was now blown wide open, and Inira, with every response, teasing comment, and seemingly insightful question, was taking one more step down that dark stairway. She was still unsure where it led – for better or worse. Charlotte had shaped and stewarded the Triune partnership plan with Nahas Helps. She'd been the true star, as Inira knew she would be. Charlotte even managed a coup in the form of a small smile from Ahmadi, who seemed as charmed as possible. That wasn't near the level of anyone else. Still, given his calm exterior, it didn't seem to give anything away except absolute obedience to the Deitas and his mission. Lukas looked at Charlotte with hungry eyes, like a wolf circling prey. Inira hadn't asked Charlotte about their relationship yet; she thought she could do that on the flight back.

They were leaving for the airport in the early afternoon, so they'd packed up and checked out before arriving at the offices that morning. She was packing up her computer at the close of the last meeting, after her final presentation that included each organization's next steps when Stanley moved next to her.

"It has been an extremely successful affair, hasn't it?"

A little startled by his choice of words, Inira recovered by replying, "Yes, Stanley, indeed. Better than we hoped, I think!"

He smiled, "It's true, but I knew it could be done. We have one more meeting to go, however."

She was curious and turned to face him, "Oh? What do you mean? I thought we were going to the airport?"

Stanley waved a hand, "Yes, Ahmadi assures me it will be quick. The Deitas wants to give his blessing and congratulations in person before we leave. He wants to express his hopes for a fruitful partnership in person."

Inira's stomach gave a flip; she had not expected this. She was a little nervous because their messaging had become something that had taken on a life of its own, like a new pet that required regular care and feeding. She didn't know what it would be like to be face-to-face with him with so much between them. Inira followed Stanley to the private elevator. She had to channel all of her professional exterior to keep the grin off her face.

Stanley asked, "You've seen his office before, correct?"

She nodded without betraying her giddiness at seeing him again. "Yes, that first day of meetings. It is similar to this whole place, with a lot of windows. Remember, they think of themselves as masters of the universe." She winked at Stanley.

He winked back. "Yes indeed, but if they only knew there was a better way. I guess that's what we get to show them, eh?"

Inira smiled broadly and thought that was exactly right. It was so perfect, and it canceled that little worm of guilt eating through the apple of her heart for the last two days of texting with Mattias. That's why she was doing this – like she'd always been taught. To show those in the grips of androcratic domination, there is a different, better vision for humanity. This was her purpose, and now it was one she could share with the kind of reach and resources Teleosis had only dreamed of.

Mattias met them at the elevator. He motioned Stanley ahead and waited for Inira, surreptitiously placing his hand on the small of her back. Electricity shot through her whole body at his touch. He didn't say anything, but the gentle pressure said enough. He moved them to the couches they'd been sitting on just two days prior. She looked around and realized this was a sitting room, and Mattias' office must be behind a door she'd never noticed before.

He addressed them both, "I know you don't have long before your flight, so I'll be quick. My team is beyond excited for our new endeavor, and I have not looked forward to a project like this in years." He looked away from Stanley and directly into Inira's eyes as he said, "Years."

Inira felt her world shift on its axis. She was swept up into the green eyes, the bronze skin, and the strong shoulders. Every thought was gone, like a teenager with her first crush. Fortunately, Stanley responded, "Yes, getting your vision back is invigorating. We appreciate your extensive hospitality for our accommodations and the sumptuous dinners and workspace this week."

Stanley showed his salesmanship abilities, which he had been laying on thick all week. To see him interact with Mattias, she fondly recalled how persuasive he was. It reminded her how easily she had said yes when he had asked her to work with him. Mattias' attention was not on Stanley, however. He glanced back at Stanley quickly before returning to rest his gaze again on Inira's face. She was a little nervous at how Mattias focused on her and licked her lips. Mattias caught the movement, and his stare became even more intense. The moment stretched too long before Inira found her voice.

She cleared her throat and said, "My team sees hope and potential in Lukas and his ambitions. We have a solid business approach and plan. I think Lukas will make you proud."

The corner of Mattias's eyes tightened at the mention of his son's name. She knew it was because Lukas had a history of inconsistent follow-through, usually due to pursuing a girl. Mattias was perhaps not trying to sound dismissive, yet it still carried that tone when he answered, "Yes, well, my son is an integral part of the plan going forward, so I am counting on him to follow your direction and heed your advice, Inira."

The way he said her name was delicious. She imagined his voice was like a streaming fountain, and she was dipping her head underneath to receive refreshment. She didn't think she even cared to come up for air. She had to get a hold of herself.

It was time to leave, so they all stood and returned to the elevator. She wondered why Mattias hadn't come to the conference room to say goodbye instead of having them come to him. But maybe that was a final play for dominance, letting them know who was in charge. Stanley stepped into the elevator, and Inira moved to join him when Mattias put a hand on her elbow, and she felt like she'd been hit by lightning. Her arm radiated with warmth, and she immediately turned to face him.

He looked at her but said to Stanley, "Ms. Boehme will be along in a moment. Since she will be in charge of our resources, I want to give her some final, specific instructions."

Stanley looked a little confused. Surely Nahas knew whatever he said to Inira, he could say in front of them both. But he followed the directions, nodding, and the doors slid shut.

It all happened before Inira knew it. She was pulled straight into Mattias' chest. He had wrapped his arms around her so fast her arms were trapped at her sides. She was tall, but he was taller, so when she turned her head to look up at him, she found that her nose was right at the junction of his arm and neck, where his scent was the strongest. She couldn't help herself. She inhaled him and nearly groaned in delight.

He smelled citrusy and spicy with just the barest hint of musk. She didn't expect him to smell so bright and clean yet masculine. She loved it. She stayed with her nose in his neck longer than she should have. He was breathing deeply, too, with his face in her hair. She could feel the rise and fall of his chest against hers. He held her tightly but loosened as he felt her move to look into his eyes. He stared down at her, and she realized it would take only the slightest move of his head for his lips to come in direct contact with hers.

As if alerted to their proximity, her phone buzzed, breaking the magic of their embrace, while at the same time, she felt the diamond from her engagement right press into her palm. Her ring had somehow twisted, souring the experience in her mind. *Nothing kills a moment like remembering you are married*, she thought.

They backed away from each other, about half an arm's length, and Mattias let his hands trail down her arms as they moved. She jointly shivered and blazed hot at his touch. He spoke low, "I won't apologize for holding you, Inira. I couldn't restrain myself any longer. Thoughts of you are the only ones I have now. I can't wait to dream more with you. I only wish we could continue to make plans together in person."

Inira, thanks to her reality check, was now in her right mind.

"Mattias, you know I'm married. As much as I have relished our communication, I don't know how much sense it makes to continue now that I am returning home."

He smiled at her. "Did it make sense to you before you were flying back?"

She furrowed her brows together. "Well, yes and no."

He quirked a brow, "Yes and no? Tell me more. I always want to hear your thoughts."

Inira took a deep breath, trying to control her excitement at his touch and the growing dread of returning home to have the conversation with Francis. "I will treasure making plans for Nahas Helps with you, but we must limit our personal sharing time. This must remain firmly a business relationship."

Mattias gazed at her, openly staring at her face, making her think he hadn't heard her or was maybe choosing to ignore their situation by not saying anything. The moment was stretched thin between them again—another buzz.

Mattias looked in her pocket. "Should you check that?"

Inira sighed and pulled the phone up. "The team is ready to depart. We will be late if we don't leave now."

She also had a text from Francis, letting her know he couldn't wait to see her and missed her incredibly. She frowned deeper, wondering how any of this could work. Suddenly, she felt Mattias' heat again, his fingers brushing gently on her face. He had stepped forward, his face close again, "This was never just about business for me, Noni. It was always about taking what has always been mine."

She stared into his face, whispering, "I was never yours, Mattias. Not then, not now. I am my own; please remember that. It is imperative for everyone's sake we keep this professional. I love what we've shared, but my marriage is on thin ice."

Mattias moved a hair's breadth closer, and she could feel his skin blazing. He was so close again; if he did lean down to kiss her, she couldn't stop him. She knew she wouldn't stop him. She wondered absent-mindedly if he was always this warm.

His voice was warm and musical, nearly in her ear, "Yes, I will be the consummate professional. Your integrity is at the forefront of my thoughts. I know you've always sought to stand on your own. I want you to remember how good it feels to stand next to someone who truly values you for who you are, not just what you will do for them."

She blinked slowly, and he took his hand off her face. After another long moment that seemed stretched to breaking, she exhaled, not realizing she'd been holding her breath. She could feel the passion between them, and it was explosive. It was the type of explosion she knew pretty well. It would destroy everything around them if it went off at the wrong time and in the wrong way.

As she stepped into the elevator, Mattias said, "I will say blessing over your travels, Noni. And I'll ensure you know I am with you the whole way."

Chapter 16

The team was tired but satisfied with a job well done. The ride to the airport was uneventful. Inira wasn't looking forward to an eight-hour flight in coach, but nothing could be done about it. She let the rest of the team check in ahead of her, lost in her thoughts about Mattias. That worm of guilt started chewing in her heart again. She began to worry, not about any inappropriate connection but about how she would continue to communicate with Mattias and be present with her family, especially with Francis pushing so hard for therapy.

Francis had sent her another text about how he missed her but also how this week apart made it clear to him how much work she, well, they, had to do. He'd added the 'they' in a follow-up message. She was offended for a few reasons, but mainly hurt and angry because he was using his prosecutorial skills against her like she had done something wrong. She wondered if this was a reflection of how he felt about himself since she'd gotten sober and if there was more to it than he was letting on. She knew they would have to talk about it when she got home. She tried not to stew in her anger but was only moderately successful.

The check-in agent startled her when she said, "Welcome, Ms. Boehme. It looks like your seat has been upgraded to First Class. I'm sure you will enjoy the ride home!"

She had no idea how this had happened. She and Francis shared a frequent flyer account but didn't think they had enough mileage for that upgrade. She decided not to say anything about it. She thought of a distinctly Western phrase about not looking a gifted horse in the mouth, in case you saw the teeth were rotten and the deal was bum. So she didn't think anything more of it. She accepted it for what it was. As they made their way onto the plane, she got a text from Mattias.

Enjoy your flight home. I wish I were sitting next to you, but instead, I can offer you the type of accommodation you deserve, and that will allow you to be fully rested when you see your family. I hope you will think of me while you are in the air.

Inira's head swam. This was probably crossing about a thousand lines, but at least she knew where the upgrade came from. How he did it, she didn't know but rich people can do things poor people couldn't dream. She took the offered hot towel and requested Perrier instead of an alcoholic starter. She made her inflight meal choice and rifled through her goodie bag. She'd only flown in First Class once. She'd accompanied her mother on a state visit to the White House right after she went through the Heir naming ceremony. It was a whirlwind trip, and it didn't occur to her to ask why the High Priestess of a religion, a movement, and a country that sought to raise people out of poverty spent first-class funds on a flight.

When she mentioned the upgrade to Tomas later, he was livid. That was when he told her about his suspicion regarding the High Counsel embezzling funds earmarked for the poorest facets of their outreach. She remembered him saying,

If you give just a little to those in dire straits but then take the rest, it will still look like you gave a lot. It is the perfect scheme.

Inira dwelled on that for a second and then smiled. She realized that maybe this was redemption because now it was Tomas' twin who bought and paid for it all. She took out her phone to text Mattias these thoughts, and he responded with,

There are no schemes between you and me. I only long to do for you what my brother always wished– to give you everything you are worth.

They were closing the doors, so she texted him back one last time.

I'll take everything you give me.

She then texted Francis, just the generic "OMW" with an airplane emoji, and he sent back a thumbs up and prayer hands.

She put her phone in airplane mode and the noise-canceling headphones Emerie had given her. She closed her eyes to daydream till dinner was served.

Chapter 17

Breathe In. Breathe Out. Breathe In. Breathe Out. Breathe Deeper into those places that feel bound up.

Breathe out the resistance. Breathe out the tightness and sink into your heart. Breathe In; let the breath carry you.

Breathe Out, and notice what is loosening. Breathe Into what is still tight. Breathe Out and notice something new.

Inira moved through the fifteen minutes of stretches to loosen up after getting home from the airport. She was ready to collapse. With Stanley's blessing, she had already given the team the rest of the week off to recoup. Jetlag wasn't going to help anyone do their best work.

She felt like a zombie. She barely slept on the return trip. Francis and Emerie both picked her up, and she was grateful. She had missed them and knew with Emerie in the car, Francis wouldn't bring up their relationship issues. With no time to adjust, her body was rapidly shutting down, and the stretching exercise was the last gasp before she collapsed. She knew this would be a challenging trip, but with the unexpected roller coaster Mattias Nahas, she felt like a wet rag wrung out.

She slept for about an hour but then made sure to wake up. If she could stay awake till bedtime, she would sleep all night and have a head start on recovery. Emerie laid down with her for a while, telling her mom more about her week at school and her college applications. She also checked in with Emerie about how she was feeling. Their cycles often synced since Emerie started menstruating at thirteen. It had given them a lot to connect over, with Inira making a point to ensure Emerie knew her cycle was blessed and sacred – not to be dismissed as so many did in the West. There were many holy uses for blood in ancient Teleosian ceremonies, but menstrual blood was at the top. When Emerie was younger, it was "gross," but as she'd matured, she'd begun to see the wisdom in her body and how it stored and shed physical and metaphysical energy—and then rebuilt itself over the weeks again. Inira knew she was much closer to the sunset of her body's cycles, but she looked forward to learning how to transmit that energy in new ways when her cycle ended.

Emerie often jokingly told her she was headed for "Old Crone status" while she was beginning the "Maiden."

They didn't talk for long before they fell into a comfortable silence. Inira relished the fact that they didn't have to talk. It was a blessing to be at this point in their relationship where Emerie knew her Mom needed rest, and her presence provided that.

Francis, on the other hand, was all hustle and bustle. He'd missed his wife in the house and wanted to hear about her trip. Inira sat up in bed and gave him an abridged version. She left out a lot of details since most of those involved Mattias. She told him enough that he was satisfied. They'd long been partners in Triune's work. Francis was the silent partner, the unofficial team member. His insight, from his extensive corporate legal career, always brought a needed perspective to their approach and execution. She had always valued his wisdom and insight and hoped that would continue regardless of where their relationship ended.

He made dinner, which he said he was glad to be handing back over to her after tonight. It was a simple meal of fish, veggies, and rice but a family favorite. It was delicious in its simplicity. Inira was grateful for it after days of airplane, hotel, and restaurant food. She wondered for the thousandth time what it would be like to be rich enough to have those duties at home taken off her plate so she could exclusively focus on being present for Emerie and her work. Teleosis had been a much more collaborative society, even at the individual level. Men and women were equal and took on equal shares of raising children and the labor inside and outside the home. It was also intergenerational, with grandparents living in the home or not far away. They were involved in raising the next generation. Inira couldn't remember when she didn't see her grandmother after school until she passed when Inira was thirteen. Right after that cannon event, she met Tomas; He had become her rock, replacing the stalwart presence of her grandmother.

Inira sighed, remembering what it was like before this women-can-do-it-all lifestyle took over. She wasn't in Teleosis anymore but in the United States and the patriarchal expectations that came with it. No matter how forward-thinking a man was, a man still ruled the roost. At least that was true in their house and in their generation.

"So, what's your next step with Nahas Helps, Mom?"

Emerie often took an interest in her mom's work, which secretly delighted Inira. She hoped there would be a chance to pass her work on to her daughter. She chewed a bite, then answered. "Well, Sweetheart, I must regroup with the team after the weekend. I'm sure Charlotte will have a project plan ready for us. She shined this week. And I'll be in touch with Lukas Nahas and his father."

Francis looked up at his wife sharply. "You will be in contact with Mattias Nahas?"

Inira caught his tone, took another bite, and chewed before she carefully answered. "Yes, he was there and wants to see his son succeed. He is asking for regular reports from me about the foundation's progress under Lukas' direction."

Inira knew she was treading a line, but she wasn't saying anything that wasn't true. Francis put a derisive sneer on his face as he scoffed, "After all the research you've done and the news reports about Mattias, I'm surprised you aren't spewing fire. That guy seems like a rat."

Inira stiffened but kept her face neutral. "As with most media attention on someone famous and powerful, the reports were grossly exaggerated."

Francis continued as if he didn't hear her. "Plus, with all the harm his empire has caused around the world, we are sure this Foundation is a cover-up, glorified money laundering and PR. That and nepotism at its finest."

Inira, feeling defensive, responded, "Well, I was highly impressed with Mattias' vision and Lukas's determination to make this work. Mattias is less Tony Stark or Mussolini and much more of a regular human being who wants to live a legacy for the better. "

Francis snorted. "C'mon, Hon. You know he wants to take over the world. I don't remember you swooning over the rich. You had too much practice seeing what assholes they can be."

Inira got goosebumps on her forearms. He was hitting a nerve and cracking open that fantasy she had been living in her head. She wasn't ready to let it go, though, and puffed up a little, irritation leaking into her tone, "You know, Francis, I'm allowed to change my opinions. As a grown woman, I can admit when I am wrong. He may seem tyrannical, but I think he is focused on what he can give back instead of what he can take from the world. He really isn't what you think he is."

Francis looked at her intently but backed down. "Ok, ok. I didn't mean to hit a nerve. I am only saying what you've thought about him before. An about-face regarding Mattias is a surprise. "

Inira looked at him for a long beat. She decided the last thing she needed right now was to pick a fight while under the influence of the travel hangover, and both of them were sensitive to the relational rocky ground they were navigating. She had been vocal at home before leaving in her opinions of what an asshole Mattias probably was. While she wasn't entirely sure she hadn't been correct, how he treated her gave her butterflies. She felt important and cherished in a way she hadn't in a long time. She and Francis worked well together as parents and partners, but it didn't leave much room for praise and passion without purposeful intention. They'd gotten comfortable and complacent, him the most.

She'd felt that passion and purpose now in spades with Mattias. It was a heady feeling.

Perhaps to break her parents' awkward silence, Emerie piped up again as Francis got up to clear the table.

"What's Lukas like? Is he cute?"

Inira laughed. It was on point for what an eighteen-year-old girl, budding into an exploration of her own sexuality and romantic life, would want to know.

"Yes, he is very handsome. His mother, he told me, was a Korean supermodel. So, that mixture with his Venezuelan father's looks makes for a lovely package. Never mind, I'm old enough myself to be his mother! He seems hungry for recognition and willing to work hard. He seems to have a lot of potential, but the first night we were at dinner, I felt he was still looking for somewhere to belong. "

Emerie blushed and giggled a little. "Well, I'm not your age! I googled him. He is so striking! Did he and Charlotte hit it off?"

Another one of Emerie's favorite things to gossip about was Charlotte. She adored Charlotte as much as Inira and looked up to her as a role model. This was a big reason why Inira worked so hard to train Charlotte. She was another excellent model for Emerie.

"Yes, I think they did. Lukas even came looking for her one night. He was waiting in the lobby bar for her. I don't know if it was a pre-arranged meeting or if he would surprise her. But he is interested. I talked to Charlotte a little bit about it on the ride to the airport. She was coy but said she hadn't given him her number. I'll see if he's moved on Monday to make the connection more personal and give her my thoughts."

Inira could handle this as a do-as-I-say-and-not-as-I-do type situation. She didn't want to see Charlotte hurt or embarrassed. It was always best to keep business and personal relationships separate. She'd learned from how closely the Counsel of Wisdom was practically all blood-related at the end. She knew she was treading the lines of hypocrisy. Still, her situation was more complex.

At least, that was what she was telling herself.

Francis piped in loudly from the kitchen, where he was putting away dinner, "Well, I think you both should stay the hell away from the Nahas boys. They are snakes in the grass."

Emerie rolled her eyes at her father. Inira was also annoyed because she could hear his slight twinge of jealousy. As a rule, there was little they kept secret; they were a very open family. Given Inira's experience with a family that kept secrets, she'd worked hard to set a tone of openness and honesty. She'd told Emerie long ago that whatever she asked, she would be truthful with her in an age-appropriate way. There had been a lot more sharing now that Inira could be honest with herself, working on her recovery program, and there had been a lot of uncovering long-buried truths when Emerie had begun asking her about her old life before she met her dad.

Just then, Inira's phone buzzed, and the one secret she was hiding popped its head up.

Good evening, Noni. I am checking in to make sure you made it home okay. Are you recovering from the jet lag? I know this week was probably hard on you. I am seeking God's restful hand upon you.

She stretched her arms, and her yawn was not faked. "I'm going to head to bed. Now, with my stomach full, I hope to be able to sleep all night and be ready for the weekend!"

She wanted to get into bed and some privacy to respond to Mattias. This was her thing, and based on what Francis had said, she was sure he would disapprove of one-on-one communication with Mattias. Emerie hugged her, and Inira gave her a quick peck on the cheek. She did the same to Francis, who told her he had a brief to work on, so he would be up for a while. He kissed her on the cheek and said they would talk about their future when she was rested. Sensing the dismissal, she went into the master bedroom. She found herself smiling at the thought of Mattias as she got ready for bed. She spent the next hour texting back and forth with him.

She fell asleep before Francis got into bed. Her cell phone was plugged in to charge but turned upside down on her nightstand. She ensured Mattias' contact name was "MN," in case anyone noticed her screen when a message came. He was not a complete secret, she told herself before drifting off to dreamless sleep, but she had to be careful so that she would be.

Chapter 18

T *wenty years ago....*

"Tomas, I don't see why you continue pushing this. It isn't what we've done in Teleosis since the civilization formed. What you are saying isn't what we stand for. I want you to see that we can be true partners in everything we do. We can identify where our mission work isn't being effective, where things seem to lag, and then regain the kind of influence and impact Teleosis had at its height and beyond. The world is hungry for our message! Our generation and our children's generation will change the world!"

Inira smiled a little at the thought of their children. She hadn't yet taken over for her mother, but she was only two years away from entering into the apprenticeship phase of her role as High Priestess, which included Tomas as her husband. She would be introduced to the world, accompanying her mother everywhere, and planned to bring Tomas. She was convinced the world would benefit most from seeing a male and female in sync with each other. She'd even planned to have Tomas named High Priest along with her once she ascended. She knew it was unprecedented and would get backlash. Still, everything in her, the places she knew she connected to the Divine, told her transparent, practical gender equality with a woman out front was the vision that would shift the game. The world needed an example of what men and women could do – in union and communion.

The world has been trained to be afraid of strong, powerful women, and in recent years, the pundits in the West called their culture "matriarchal zealotry." Plus, the real zealots – the ultra-conservatives from any religion, saw the Teleosian belief in the Mother, Father, Son, and Daughter as scandalous, even dangerous. There were always protests at her mother's appearances, wherever fear was whipped up beforehand. Oppression of women was at an all-time high. The fear wasn't because The High Priestess was the head of the largest church or state but because of the amount of financial and technological capital Teleosis had. Everyone wanted what they had; her mother was growing paranoid about it.

Inira planned to use all that power to shake things up. Deep in her soul, she knew it was time to do things differently than tradition dictated. Ascending Tomas to the role of the first High Priest by her side would send a clear, unadulterated message. She and Tomas would be anchored together in heart and work. This was what she knew the FourFold God wanted for humanity.

Tomas approached her, cupping her face, and said, "Noni, you cannot change things here; they will not let you. Your uncle will be the first on the Counsel to block you. Plus, I'm not sure this is the way to go. It seems to be born from emotion, and we must show strength. If it works around the world to have men more in charge, maybe Teleosis needs to adapt."

Inira felt like he'd slapped her. She jerked her face away from him, backing up a step. As she did, her gaze hardened, and she shot him a look of pure outrage. "Excuse me? Men in charge? What the fuck does that mean, Tomas?"

He held his hands like he was trying to calm a cornered beast. "Don't get upset. I know how you can get when you get upset."

He had been saying this a lot line lately, with the comment that a man *perhaps* needed to be in charge. Then, when she got mad, he would tell her she was upset and emotional. It was the worst thing to say because it invalidated her feelings. Yes, she was upset and emotional, but that had never phased him before. It was also an inborn strength of women. Her emotional state didn't negate her logic; she could hold both simultaneously.

Before the last few months, he had always made space for her feelings. This new habit of cutting her off made her deeply unsettled. She kept wondering if maybe he was on drugs. He was less comforting and less comfortable with sharing power and more patronizing of her.

She took a deep breath and decided to be curious rather than judgemental. "Tomas, what do you mean? You aren't making sense. You've never talked like this before; it was not how we were raised. After all the study of history and anthropology we had done together about the impact Teleosis had on the world before the Indo-Europeans brought in their toxic masculinity of domination, where does this change of thinking come from? You and I were of one mind. This is a chance for us to make inroads for real peace. This is the mission – to show the world what is possible when we follow the model of the FourFold God. For Christ's sake – literally – that is what Christianity is supposed to be about as well! Yet you mean to tell me that it comes down to, 'If you can't beat 'em, join 'em?'"

Tomas sighed loudly as if he was dealing with a petulant child. "No, I'm not saying the historical influence of Teleosis as an alternative narrative to the ways of living is bad. I'm saying that now, in this time, the groups that are making big change are the ones who focused on centralizing power, and men are the best at that."

Inira kept staring at him like he had three heads. He'd been staying up late at night, emailing the leader of a group one step above a terrorist organization. One that followed the tenets of everything opposite of Teleosis – a group called The Serpents. It was starting to be alarming, along with her mother wanting to ensure she was ready. She needed him, and right when she did, he was facing another direction, spiritually and emotionally.

"This is our chance, *Ahava Shomri*. Are you letting this new connection steer you off course?" She whispered to him as she came closer, kneeling before him. She looked at him directly in the eyes. He would not meet her gaze. The ridiculous part of this whole argument was Tomas *knew* better.

The Serpents wanted women "in their place," and everyone else should fall in line. Even their very name was hijacked from matriarchal beliefs from the past. They were also on many countries' watch lists and at the top of her mother's. This new theocratic belief system was headed up by a firebrand of a preacher named Billy Sweggert, a white American male from a prominent political family. Sweggert cherry-picked traditions and doctrines from many world religions to see if they fit the bill of the agenda he was pushing. It was such a hodgepodge that many men and those women who came along with them, disenchanted with the current religious practices, could convert and still be comfortable. They precisely wanted men to be comfortable and everyone else working to ensure they stayed that way.

It felt like a cult in the worst way, and Tomas seemed to be getting hooked. She could not wrap her mind around it.

Inira returned to curiosity, softly asking, "What about this movement truly appeals to you? I want to know because you've spent so much time researching it."

Tomas sighed in frustration. Glaring at her, he said, "I've told you. I see myself making more of an impact with them – or through how they do things – than here in Teleosis. This place is stuck in the past, and The Serpents are moving into the future."

Inira had to control her response. She didn't want to laugh in his face. Patriarchy and oppression only seemed visionary to those who'd forgotten how badly it always works out for the world. She was already close to him but scooted closer on her knees. She didn't know how close he would let her get in the middle of an argument. But she needed the closeness. They'd been fighting so much about this lately, and it rattled her. Tomas had been her rock from the time she was thirteen, after losing her grandmother and her father. He had wanted to make changes, and she wanted to follow in his footsteps.

She'd fallen in love with Tomas at first sight. She found a true partner in him, or she thought she had until recently. She knew he would come back around. She couldn't imagine loving or being with anyone else. He was her perfect complement, and he was so damn sexy in his reserved way. He was big but not imposing. He never used his size to intimidate her or anyone else. Even now, she knew he respected her and wanted her to feel safe, so his change in thinking made her head spin.

She came up to standing, facing him with the solar lights from the garden framing her from the back. Tomas was sitting on the chaise lounge in her room. It was late, and they'd circled this conflict for a while. She wanted, no, needed this night to end on a happy note. He did, too, because he pulled her onto his lap. She could still feel his tension, and she tried to absorb it as she melted into him. Her sitting on top of him did things to him he couldn't control, and he huffed out a laugh as she squirmed down into him.

He leaned down to whisper against the shell of her ear, "Are you trying to distract me with your feminine tricks and beauty? Trying to prove a point, my delicious *Ahava?*"

She giggled and sat up to look at him, making where their bodies connected even more pronounced. "Maybe, but only if it is working?"

He brought his hands up from off her hips to cup both sides of her face and looked into her eyes deeply. He whispered with his lips above hers, "I love you; nothing changes that. I adore you. I support you. I don't know if I support what the Counsel is doing anymore. It will be such an uphill battle for you to make change with them in control."

She tilted her head and quirked her eyebrow as she whispered back into his face, "Battle for me or us?"

Tomas sighed again, those deep green eyes shading with sadness. "Whatever happens, it will be you who is left standing. Your mission is to change the world and bring about the Four-Fold God's vision. It is you who will lead the way. I will be here if I can. But one day, Noni, you will make sure Teleosis still exists."

She started to tear up, with several escaping down her cheeks. "Please do not talk like that; it scares me so bad. I can't do any of this without you. I can't stand against my mother, the Counsel, or enemies outside our borders."

He caught the tears on his fingertips and brought them to his mouth. He pressed his forehead to hers and didn't speak for a long minute. Their breath synchronized as she stayed in his lap, arms around his neck, and his hands returned to her hips, his thumbs making small circles. It was calming but arousing at the same time. The heat built between them, and she felt him through his pants. She felt him tense to move, to stand them both up, still holding her. She prepared to wrap her legs around his waist, shifting again, causing him to breathe out again softly.

"Inira, we need to get some sleep. We will go together, but first, I want to show you again how much I admire you. It's near worship what I feel for you. Remember these times when you are facing situations you never thought you could handle. Remember, I knew you could. You are the only woman who can sustain Teleosis. I'm sorry if what I say makes you question that. Not every woman is like you. You are glorious, and I will never stop wanting to be with you in every way possible. From now and into eternity. Forever and ever, amen."

Then he kissed her with a little more force than usual. He stood up, supporting her weight and not having to open his eyes to know where the bed was. Inira lost herself to him as she always did. His words at this moment would only come back to her years later, in a dream several weeks after she met Mattias.

Chapter 19

Her dreams continued to escalate all weekend, and her memories continued to come back. Inira looked forward to the distraction of work, especially after the conversation Francis finally pursued on Sunday afternoon while Emerie was at a friend's house. As he walked into the room, she could feel his desire for her to capitulate, and she felt her own spirit buck up in response to the pressure. It was as if the barometric pressure of the room dropped before an impending storm broke open around them.

"Inira, can we talk?"

She tried not to sigh too loudly and set down the book she was reading in their sunroom. She'd been soaking in a puddle of light, wanting to feel its strength without the brisk air of late Autumn. "Yes, of course, Francis. What's on your mind, *Ahava*."

He didn't immediately answer, and she gave him the space for the words to come. He sat down on the couch near her, but they were still distant. When they did, she was surprised, if not shocked. "Noni, I think I've been too hard on you." She didn't respond, so he kept going. "I know you've been going through a lot with getting sober and all the work you've been doing. It's been a big change for our family, getting used to the new 'you.'" She bristled a little bit internally but remained still. She decided to let him say his peace and then respond.

"It's been such a radical change, and I see the good in it, for your example. You've also been pouring into your work. That's good, too. Everything you are doing is good. I'm struggling to figure out where I fit in with it all. You don't need me like you used to, and it's set me adrift emotionally. I wish I could read your mind, and then maybe I could understand better what you wanted and needed from me. I don't want to be forgotten in your quest to become all you were meant to be." His voice was getting tighter; she could tell this was hard for him, but he was also suppressing his emotions probably more than was healthy.

She sensed the opening for her to respond, so she scooted forward from the seat of the chair she was in to the end of the ottoman. It was an effort to close the distance between them as she knew her question would be difficult for him to answer. "Francis, why do you think I would leave you behind?"

He sighed. "I knew you would ask a question and anticipated this would be it. You were born with a high calling, a great purpose, a great calling. I don't know if I'm enough for that or if I can help you with that. I don't know that I want to help you with that."

The last sentence shook her. "What do you mean you don't know you want to 'help' me with that?" She could feel her ire rising and demonstrated it using air quotes around the word *help*.

Francis's mouth worked as if he was trying to regain some moisture. He never liked confrontation, especially not when she got angry. He never seemed to learn how to respond, so he avoided it. But she wouldn't let him avoid it now. She let her anger draw out like a blade between them, and in the silence, you could almost hear the whetstone grinding the edge. When he moved to stand up, she held out a hand, and he stilled.

"Francis, things have changed. I know I am different. I know that is uncomfortable, and while you say you see it as good, your behavior says the opposite. It hurts me that you would see my getting sober as a bad thing for our family when I'm so much more present with Emerie and fulfilled at work. Indeed, I have not been happy about carrying the load of all the domestic labor, but that has needed to change for a while. We both have jobs, and we can share the load at home."

He puffed up, "I've been doing much more around here since you've been so busy at work. It's not like I do nothing."

She held a hand again but spoke softly, as she'd been taught in conflict to do. "I am not trying to make this a competition of who does more. You are a great father and always put Emerie first. You are also an excellent provider for us financially. You work hard and do your good work. I've always admired that, and it's a big part of why we have the comfortable life we do."

She paused to take a breath before continuing, "I am saying that to have a true partnership, the expectations need to shift. I can no longer be the woman who does it all. I want to experience a fulfillment that includes rest. Are you capable of making that shift for me rather than expecting me to shift back to a pattern of behavior that was detrimental to my health and, ultimately, to my soul? Will you support my sobriety and do what is needed to grow your soul? If the answer is yes, then we can go to therapy and work on our relationship. I'm unsure where this leaves us if the answer is no."

He looked back at her, and she could tell he was unhappy with the turn things had taken. She hadn't expected to draw a line in the sand. She knew she was changing, and it had started long before she got sober or met Mattias. She was remembering who she was and what she was created to do. To pursue that would involve difficult choices.

She echoed his words from the ride to the airport back to him, "Francis, you don't have to answer me now. You can think about it. I have been thinking about our future as well. I want it to make sense for all of us and know, deep down, that resonates with you. Please say you will consider what I've said?"

She didn't plead with him, but she let her own emotion over what their relationship had become seep into her voice. She longed for more, and they would always be family. She silently prayed as he walked to his home office and shut the door so that they would understand how to be in each other's lives in the future. She was asking the FourFold God for the best possible outcome for her, Francis, and Emerie, even though she had no idea what that looked like.

The next day, she returned to the office and enjoyed the buzz. Everyone was excited, with Charlotte embracing her role as the team lead. She and Lukas had already made plans to communicate regularly via text and video chat. Inira was relieved. She had been in this role for over a decade. She was happy to see the light of the torch she was handing off. She could have some mental space to think about what was next. It was symbiotic, as leadership should be. As she empowered Charlotte to live into her dreams, gifts, and passions, it cleared space for Inira to rediscover her own.

With this attitude, Inira attended her first therapy session in a month. She'd scheduled it before going to London and had a lot to discuss, including what was happening with Francis. Her therapist had been essential to unlocking Inira's dormant trauma and moving it out of the way. She told her therapist, Lexi, about all that had transpired in the weeks since their last meeting. She wavered on the cusp of being rigorously honest about what had happened with Mattias in London. She didn't mention it, but Lexi knew her too well. She was like a bloodhound with secrets.

Lexi tucked her legs up underneath her in the fluffy chair in her homey office. Light came in from the windows, making the place feel warm, even maybe a little stuffy. Lexi didn't come at her directly, which was her specialty, and Inira never saw it coming. Instead, she asked, "Have you had any dreams lately?"

Inira blinked several times before answering. "Well, yes. I've been dreaming a lot about Teleosis, both my time there and the creation myth. Almost every night I was in London and a lot this weekend."

Lexi held her gaze, face impassive. "You have long found wisdom and insight in your dreams. Why don't you tell me about them, especially who you've been dreaming about?"

Lexi was a specialist in Jungian psychology, so dreams were important to her. She hadn't asked Inira about her dreams in a while, so Inira took her time telling Lexi about them. It ate up some minutes, and Inira was glad because suddenly she was not feeling as good as when she walked in the door. After finishing the last one about the argument with Tomas, Lexi took a deep breath and tilted her head.

Inira braced herself because she knew Lexi was onto something. Her therapist was superb at her job, so Inira kept coming back.

Lexi spoke for an unusually long time, "Inira, the fact that you are dreaming about Teleosis and Tomas means you are at a crucial time in your recovery and healing from this trauma. You are no longer in the dark, but it is still going to take you a while to put some things to rest. Tomas played such a central role in your early, formative life. He became a pseudo-father figure for you – a place of safety that all children and adolescents need to mature into healthy adults. And he betrayed you in the worst possible way. Add on the issues with your marriage, let me ask you. Why do you think your subconscious mind is picking now to process your relationship with him?"

Inira sat still for a long moment. She could feel the sweat building on her back, not just from the overly warm room. Her body knew the answer long before it reached her mind. She knew she was dreaming about Tomas as a precursor, a portent of the future. Dreaming about Tomas was the result of Mattias being in the picture. She didn't want to talk about Mattias. She felt like his coming into her life after losing Tomas was a reward for her hard work. She had reservations about him and where this might lead, but she couldn't imagine he would go against what he'd said. Maybe she was being naïve, but she'd been tricked enough; she was sure she could smell betrayal from a mile away.

Lexi looked at her again with a penetrating stare when Inira didn't immediately answer. It sometimes took Inira a few moments to process and put into words. It was common for all those with addiction because addiction thrives in isolation. But those addicted don't know what they don't know until those answers and feelings have time and space to surface.

To encourage her to break her silence, Lexi continued, "Do you remember the origin of the Greek word Teleosis?"

Inira smiled, "Of course. Practically since birth."

Lexi said, "OK then, tell me. "

Inira took a deep breath, like she was beginning a lecture, but suddenly asked, "Well, how many ways do you want me to parse the Greek and dissect the foundational words......"

Lexi laughed, "No, Professor, just tell me the word's meaning. I want you to remind yourself what the ancient movement was truly about."

Inira looked at her, a little shaken. It was easy to get intellectual about all of this. It was easy to stay in her brain. What her therapist was asking her to do was engage her heart. That was where she struggled. Blowing air up and out of her lungs, Inira began with a voice reedy with emotion. "The word *teleosis* means transformation. It means to become what we were created to be, to fulfill the purpose the FourFold God knew from the beginning, and to realize the potential you were born with."

Lexi nodded for her to continue.

"The best analogy is an acorn that eventually becomes an oak tree; all that is needed is already in that acorn. Teleosis is meant to show the world what was originally possible and why the world was created. To show the union of both halves of the Divine – masculine and feminine – working together in their strengths as a Family to channel the power of Creation. The movement was a song sung from the beginning that brought about all we see and know, but instead of being rooted in harm and violence, it is a system of living anchored in wholeness, beauty, and creativity. It became an alternative version to what mankind has done – a breaking wall of light against the darkness we create when left to our own choices and devices."

Inira finished and felt shaky. She felt that dynamic energy had just been channeled through her, like when she spoke during the presentation. Lexi smiled slowly. "Yes, this is what captivates me about you and the vision you think was killed on that day when the capital city was destroyed. You can't kill a vision like this. From the rubble and ruins is what hope is built upon. It is what your recovery is built upon. What your drinking did to your body, your mind, and your family can all be redeemed. It can all be restored, but it will look and feel different. Just like if Tov and Teleosis were to be rebuilt, it would have to be different – so will your life."

Inira sat riveted as she listened to what she felt was a message from an oracle, a prophetic word. What Lexi said next felt like it had the potential to change her life."Inira, what I want you to remember is where your power comes from. I suspect you are hiding something, not just from me but from yourself. You may not start drinking again, but other obsessions turn into addictions. You experienced that with Tomas. He became your reason for living, and if that isn't the behavior of an addict, I don't know what is. And he betrayed you. I do not want to see that happen to you again."

Inira realized her breathing was very shallow as Lexi continued, "I'm here to help you, but you must be honest with me – radically and rigorously. When life happens, whatever form it may take – happy or hurtful – it is how we respond to it that makes all the difference. You got played by Tomas, your family, and your leadership. Many people betrayed you, and we still have work to do. This is a critical juncture in your recovery. I want to start meeting again every two weeks. We need to process what we haven't before – Tomas."

They booked the next appointment, and she packed up to go and stood up. Lexi was slow to get up with her, but when she did, the older woman looked her in the eyes and said,

"Remember, whatever you decide about your marriage, you have come far. I'm very proud of the progress you've made. Whatever you face in the future, no matter how devastating it feels, you have the tools to come out of it."

Lexi then did something uncharacteristic; she took both Inira's hands in hers and left her with what felt like a call and a blessing, "Your power, Inira, comes from within you. It's in there, and you can choose how to use it. You get to choose how this vision comes to light. You were born to show the world this light so they could and would no longer have to live in darkness. Don't forget this, and don't get distracted."

As she left the small house-turned-office, Inira felt emotionally drained yet strangely full of energy. She returned to her car to go to the office for a few hours when her phone buzzed.

Good morning, Light Bringer. Or should I say Shining One? What about The One Who Brings Me Peace? Which do you prefer? I looked up your name in several languages and found it beautiful, just as you are. I dreamt about you again last night. We were together, happy, and building a new world together. You were full of light. It made me long to be with you.

Inira felt suddenly dizzy. Before she looked at her phone, she'd felt a growing, returning strength. Reading Mattias' words made her feel like the ground beneath her feet was moving. She knew she was careening towards a choice when it came to him - to keep walking towards him or walk away. Even with Lexi's words fading into the background, that long sealed door in her heart cracked open even further. She felt hungry and lonely for something much bigger. Despite the warning bells, she wondered if partnering with Mattias was the only way to do it. He had all the resources, and he wanted her. She wasn't enough on her own. She needed him.

And she responded to that need, texting him back.

What time is it where you are? I miss you too. I dreamed about Tomas last night. I long to build that vision again. When can we talk?

It only took a few seconds for the response to come through:

Let's make some plans to fly you back to London. I need to see you in person. I want to hold you close.

Chapter 20

A song of meditation by High Priestess Amalthea, circa 3000 BCE, for those searching for peace.

I long for understanding

I long for release

I long for wholeness

I long for my missing piece

To see the world restored again

Put to right and made new

I long to be anchored

I long to know peace

I long to know wonder

I long for my missing piece

To see the world as whole again

As it was from the first

I long to be connected

I long to find relief

I long to experience belonging

I long to find my missing piece

To see the vision of God come to life

To see the world to be redeemed

I long to have my halves made whole

I long to find what I seek

I long to feel put together

I long to find my missing piece

I long for you.

I long for me.

Chapter 21

Mattias couldn't stop thinking about her. He had thought about her for years, but meeting her in person was much different than he thought.

Knowing so much about Teleosis, their theology, and her history, he had expected the fight to have gone out of her long ago. He envisioned a settled, complacent, maybe even frumpy working Mom from the State. With his looks, money, charisma, power, and clout as the head of a new world religion, he knew it would be easy to seduce her. He felt discontent at going that route, knowing she was his brother's wife, but justified it as a means to an end.

Then he'd seen her. He should have known better than to underestimate the woman Tomas had begged the Serpents to save because of his love and her potential. He should have known his brother wouldn't have wasted his breath on someone who wasn't worth it all. Mattias was utterly gutted when he saw Inira for the first time.

She was luminous. She exuded an intoxicating energy. He could sense how sharp she was, but in an easy, gentle way as she smiled and talked with her team before she saw him. He hadn't dreamed a woman could be as captivating as she was, and this was all before he heard her say a word. If he hadn't already been ill at ease for some odd reason about his plans before he saw her, he was struck dumb by how his world shifted with a glimpse of her face.

Mattias had strategically positioned himself in the room so that she could see his face when standing but not when she sat down. He watched her as she wrestled with her trauma over seeing him, Tomas' carbon copy, for the first time. He saw her panic attack hit her squarely in the chest. He had watched as Charlotte grabbed onto her hand, and Inira had held it like a life preserver. He witnessed her inner strength as she overcame it in a few minutes. He was in awe of her then, making him question everything he'd done up to this point.

Then she spoke.

The second she uttered a word, he felt the magic of her purpose wash over him, and he was a goner. Her gift was undeniable. The Counsel, her mother, the pressure of leadership, and the years since had only honed her skills and presence. She commanded the room's attention with the lightest of touches. Even Ahmadi commented later on how impressed he was, which meant he finally saw that she would be useful to their plan.

Yes, Inira was beautiful, but it was so much more than her face or her body, which Mattias now craved like water. Her essence is what held him in thrall. She wove a spell with her vision, and not for the first time in recent months, Mattias Nahas entertained thoughts of more than just his personal glory. His son, difficult as he could be, was back in his life, and he wanted them to build something together. Mattias was struck by her telling the story of a better, more just world where all could thrive through shared abundance.

It was a visceral pull inside of him to be with her. Like they were fated to meet, to be one, he would find himself staring off into space, daydreaming, creating a vision in his head for when she was all his. He never realized he'd longed for someone like her. He wanted to possess her while knowing a woman like this would never allow herself to be owned by a man, a system, or even her predestined role. He needed her to become the world leader he was destined to be. He had the money and political support but never had the heart. He was ruthless in his onslaught to the top, with dirty hands and dirtier connections.

The questions in his soul hadn't surfaced until he saw her. Then he could sense a piece missing in him that only she could fill. She would add to his life in ways no other woman or human could. What they could do and be together was beyond his wildest dreams, even as he knew he had to keep her safe from the pit of vipers he lived in. Connection with Inira felt as if his heart of stone had been once again made of flesh.

Yet, the plan that had been in motion for years was coming to fruition. Mattias, even if he wanted to, couldn't stop it. The trickiest part of it was that they needed her daughter, too. From what he could tell from Inira's text conversations with Emerie, which Ahmadi had been monitoring for months, they had a close relationship. Mattias felt sure that if her mother needed her, Emerie would move heaven and earth to come to her.

Inira was an excellent mother, much better than her own, which inspired undying loyalty. He wished again they were young enough to have their children or that Tomas had gotten her pregnant like he was supposed to. Their line would have been cemented then. He had been irritated for years with his brother for protecting Inira. He'd followed almost every detail to perfection, but when it had come to his wife, he resisted every attempt to coerce or own her. Mattias now understood what a unique and precious gift she was and could no longer resent his brother for his devotion to her.

They had another option to see their plan through, the most obvious being Lukas and Emerie united. Lukas had fought it out of some inborn sense of nobility despite his womanizing ways until he saw Emerie's picture. That same spirit in Inira was passed down to her daughter. Lukas had agreed to the union with Emerie, to yoke them as the new High Priestess and Consort once they arrived on Teleosian soil, with conditions. Lukas's ability to be noble showed up unexpectedly when his father really needed him to act like the ruthless tyrant he was raised to be.

The sourness in his stomach at the game they were playing churned like acid in his gut.

It was a good thing Lukas had no genuine interest in the Charlotte woman. She was gorgeous and capable; maybe they would find a use for her, too. At the moment, though, she was the means to the end of getting Emerie to trust him. They needed both women to unlock the secret power of Teleosis – the Song of Creation. They needed the women to give freely of themselves so their joint power could unlock mysteries that would finally enable the Serpents to dominate the entire world.

For months, though, Mattias had a question that tormented him in the dead of night. *Was this the right way to go about it all?*

He wanted to let Inira in on his plans, but he still needed her to trust him more fully. He knew there would be some convincing to go with him. She would not take well to sleight of hand. She dwelt in the light, in honesty, in truth. That and Mattias didn't want her to sense any weakness in him. His whole life, he had thought women were created to be led by men. However, meeting Inira and conversing with her was shifting his whole worldview. Mattas was sure, though, that she needed a man more focused than her husband.

There was no room for error, not anymore. Inira Boehme was in his sights, and just as he'd told her by the elevator several weeks ago, she was his. He always got what was his. Mattias was pulled from his reverie by a throat clearing. He was in his office, supposedly going through the plans for the next phase of the Teleosian rebuild. He didn't have to manage the day-to-day operations of Nahas International anymore. He didn't have to be present at board meetings; Ahmadi quickly took over that role. His Machiavellian ways made sure everyone stayed in line. He had dirt on everyone and leveraged it as needed. Mattias was needed to ensure the optics looked good and the vision moved forward.

The vision had come to Ahmadi long before he had discovered the secret of Teleosian power – the Song of Creation. To turn the power to create worlds into a weapon was the vision that was always his to manifest. It was the core principle of his religious values and beliefs. It was what he'd gotten from his mentor and the ties to the Conservative Christian Religious Right in the West. That's what made his sect so powerful. His religion wasn't about a Savior who was weak but who ruled and reigned by any means necessary.

Mattias' god had given mankind the power to make anything happen if they believed enough and worked hard enough. The Song of Creation was the final piece of that puzzle, and one Ahmadi had dedicated years to researching and understanding. Mattias was the frontman, with Ahmadi orchestrating the backend. They were the perfect pair and had been since boarding school. Ahmadi maybe even knew the ins and outs of the Teleosian rituals better than Inira, through countless trips to the island the rest of the world had long forgotten existed.

"Amin, what is that you need?"

Mattias was intense but gentle with Inira, but with everyone else around him, Mattias was nothing short of an overbearing asshole.

Ahmadi never flinched, his voice flowing like syrup over Mattias to the same effect – sickening sweetness. "Forgive me for intruding, Deitas. I didn't mean to interrupt you."

Ahmadi knew better than to say daydreaming, but Amin had known him long enough to know that was precisely what Mattias was doing.

"Don't call me that in private. That's just for show. I'm planning our next move with the Boehme woman, Amin. What do you need?"

Amin's barely contained scoff nearly had Mattias lunging across the desk. Mattias was aware of his opinions on Inira and women in general. Mattias enjoyed women; he never wanted to share his power until now. For Amin, it didn't help that his mother abused him so obscenely that while on a holiday from school when he was fourteen, he'd shoved her out a window in a fit of panic. He'd been smart and rich enough to cover it up by blaming it on a servant. His mother and her death had shaped Ahmadi's view on women irrevocably. Mattias was the one who spent the rest of the semester putting Amin back together. What came from that bond was a brotherhood they were both missing. They'd joined up and became the fangs of the Serpents.

And fangs were always hidden until just before the strike. Mattias had often wondered if those fangs would sink into his flesh if he didn't play his part or if it served Ahmadi's ultimate goals.

In a syrupy voice and with an oblique smile, Ahmadi sat down across the desk, "Very well, *Mattias*, I'm here to update you on the progress of my particular action items. Clearing the Temple site in Tov is going according to schedule. We need to decide now when you will secure the Boehme women to join us onsite."

He knew Inira was looking forward to seeing him and that he could secure her. It was how they would get her to bring her daughter along; that was the piece they hadn't worked out. Mattias growled low under his breath again.

"What must we do to take care of the husband?"

Pouring on the thickness of his accent, Ahmadi kept going, "I am working through that plan as we speak. We need to ensure Mrs. Boehme is free of him, but not in a way that would shut her down with grief. We can't kill him just to get him out of the picture. With discreet planning and revelations of your relationship, I can make it easy to get her here. If he rejects her, she will come to you that much more easily."

Ahmadi excelled at this: the intrigue and underhanded way of getting what he wanted. Mattias was the machete, and Ahmadi was the surgical knife. Still, Mattias felt he had to send a strong message to his second. "Amin, I do not want any of this to blow back on her. Her husband can know – must know of our connection – so she will be released from him. But this can in no way get into the press at all. I will not stand for her to be maligned. This remains above board. Also, we will not be cutting the Boehme women loose after this. They are essential to the future."

Ahmadi stiffened, and his eyes narrowed even further, but he didn't respond. Mattias knew he didn't believe women were essential for anything beyond male pleasure and procreation, even as he never pursued either avenue. Ahmadi wasn't going to argue or make it obvious.

Mattias believed Amin would follow him anywhere. With Ahmadi doing what was necessary, Mattias' hands would remain clean. After a long pause, Ahmadi said, "Then, I will work on the adjustments."

Mattias nodded, receiving the answer he wanted.

Ever the logistics planner, Amin asked, "Is our timeline still the same?"

Mattias steepled his index fingers under his chin, thinking. "I need an extra month to ensure Inira is prepared to join me. I plan on having her in London again before we take her and her daughter, with Lukas, to Tov to perform the ritual."

Ahmadi nodded, but Mattias saw him tighten his fists at his side, frustration leaking out of his calm exterior.

"Ensure you handle yourself on the ground in Tov while she is here, so you don't give anything away with your animosity."

Ahmadi released his hands and let out a long, controlled breath. "Of course. The Boehme women are essential, as you said. I will make sure to maintain the utmost politeness. I am grateful you understand my feelings even as I'm not entirely sure about yours."

This was a bold statement. It was not often Ahmadi outright questioned Mattias' direction and leadership. He rose to the challenge and stood up. "Excuse me?"

Ahmadi stayed seated and held up both his hands in defense. "I apologize; I meant no offense. Surprisingly, you would have such a high opinion of this woman, especially when you've known about her for her entire life. You know where she comes from and what she stands for. She is nothing compared to you and what you will do for this world."

Mattias quickly stood before the other man, and Ahmadi swallowed audibly. Mattias leaned in, bracing his huge hands on either side of the chair, and whispered, "Amin, I don't need your opinion. As I said, I'm aware of your feelings. But if I ever hear you question me or what Inira brings to this plan, I will kill you with my own hands. She is far more important to my agenda than you are. Don't forget it."

Amin Ahmadi had learned how to play the game, so nothing showed on his face as Mattias stared him down. Mattias could smell his sweat, though. Ahmadi might be the fangs, but Mattias

was the head. He would direct the strike where it would go –
and when. He would be vicious if he had to be.

Inira calmed the restlessness that had been with him since he
was an orphaned child in Venezuela, running an underground
cock fighting ring. The Serpents found him after he took out
his competitors. They sent him to school. The rest was history
and his future set until things started becoming real.

The silence stretched between them until Mattias got his temper under control. "You may go, Amin. Keep the plan moving
forward. *Uno mismo es la única manera.*"

Amin bowed his head in reverence, "*Uno mismo es la única
manera*, my lord and my god."

When the door shut and Mattias knew he was alone again, he
picked up his phone. It was late in the evening for Inira, but
after his temper, he needed to connect with her.

> *Good evening, my Peace Giver. Do you have time to
> talk? Your voice soothes me, and it has been a stressful
> day.*

It took only a few moments for the response to come back.

> *Yes, of course. I will be available about an hour after I
> finish the evening with my family. I'm sorry today has
> been so stressful. I'm glad I can comfort you. I admit
> I can't wait to see you again in a week. The pace of
> time must go faster! I hope we can talk through those
> details. It must make sense why I'm returning to Lon-
> don without Charlotte since she is officially running
> the work with your foundation now.*

Mattias rubbed his forehead like he always did when something
annoyed him. He would not have made the call to promote
Charlotte, but since Stanley did, with Inira's full support, they
would have to live with it. It would have made things much
easier had Inira stayed point on the partnership.

> *Bring her then. I'm sure Lukas would be more than happy to keep her busy.*

There was a long pause.

> *I am concerned they might cross the line, Mattias. This is a professional relationship, and the last thing Charlotte needs is to get entangled with someone and cast a shadow over her career.*

Mattias rubbed his forehead again as he typed out,

> *I will talk with Lukas and make sure he knows how to handle himself. I want you to be comfortable and trust me. You are my priority.*

She didn't text back for ten minutes, which drove Mattias a little crazy. He tried to busy himself with the reports on the status of the Temple rebuild, but he kept looking at his phone screen until, finally, a message cleared.

> *The intensity of this scares me, Mattias. You know that. I know the future we can have together, but I must sacrifice so much of myself and what I've built. Can you promise me what I will have with you will be worth it?*

Mattias blew out a breath, typing.

> *I will make sure it is all worth it. If you have second thoughts, after all, we've shared everything we know about each other, what must I do to make you feel secure?*

Security was what she had always longed for. He knew enough about growing up disconnected like you didn't belong. The Serpents had recruited him, but he'd transformed them into a global superpower, backing the most influential people and governments. However, Inira's deep need to be cared for and to feel safe called to him like nothing else. It felt like a drug. He saw her response come through, and he smiled. He would give her what she needed, and everything would stay on track.

I need some more time. What you are asking puts me in danger of losing everything again. It is a huge risk, and I'm willing to take it, but I need to know I'm not the only one risking it all.

He knew what to say to ease her mind because he meant every word. He wasn't even manipulating her with some trumped-up version of the truth to get her back to Teleosis. He shared his heart for the first time in his adult life.

Trust me when I tell you everything is on the line for me – my future. What I've planned for my entire life hinges upon you. I want you to be comfortable. I want you to feel safe. I want you to know you are the most precious thing in the world to me. Whatever proof of my feelings you need, name it. I love you, Inira, more than I love anyone or anything else. Come to London and let me prove it. Bring Charlotte. Bring Emerie. You name the day and time, and my plane will await you. You are everything to me.

Chapter 22

The days sped up with the timeline of her return to London solidified. She and Francis had another difficult conversation, and he was furious she would be gone again. It led to one of the worst fights they'd ever have. He grew increasingly discontent, complaining she had changed – for the worse. It did not help her desire to stay with him even as she still wanted him a part of her life. She felt the incredible tug of war happening within her. She walked around with a pit in her stomach.

She knew what she shared with Mattias had moved into something more than a work or vision-casting partnership. She knew she was falling for him, might have been since the moment she laid eyes on him, the carbon copy of her first love. So, the energy of her love, attention, and affection was redirected. When she and Francis did talk, he was distant and sleeping on the couch in his home office. She would find him in there, on his phone, typing away. She didn't know who he was talking to but could feel things disintegrating rapidly.

In Teleosis, a woman chose the man she wanted to be with, made the proposal, and the legalities of the relationship and any children of the union took her name. Subsequently, when a woman was done with a relationship, she initiated it and could move on, ensuring the house was in order. The legacy of the family was carried on in her name. She was experiencing the threat of the opposite in the West, even as she'd kept her last name.

Now, she was returning to London in a few days to see Mattias. On the work front, Stanley only raised his eyebrows when she told him she would be flying on the private jet and staying in a penthouse Mattias owned, not far from the Nahas International building, saying Mattias didn't stay there but kept it in case it was needed. Stanely would not question her morals, only her intentions. She was skirting the line of integrity and knew these situations always had the potential to blow up. Every time Emerie brought up her trip, Francis bristled. He couldn't stand anything having to do with Mattias.

It was similar to what she'd felt for Tomas. Tomas was just hers; his thoughts, body, and soul were hers. For the longest time, she didn't think she had to share him with anyone. Until she found out differently because he had a separate life, this could be part of it with Mattias. She could fill in the puzzle pieces in her mind of what had happened to Tomas and what led him to such a tragic action. To understand where his mind was and why he'd been so adamant to protect her, even as he destroyed everything around her.

Of course, she knew it wasn't just Tomas who was on the path of destruction. The Counsel, she learned, had been corrupt for generations. They were siphoning off of the very funds that were meant to build a better world. One confrontation with her mother – while her sister stood by and said nothing – led to a screaming match. Her mother defended her income as the reward for all the hard work she'd done and having to raise her daughters on her own after her husband stupidly got himself killed.

Her mother's scream still echoed in her brain, "I am owed this much for all that I've poured into this mission!"

She felt Mattias could be the one she could genuinely unburden herself to. Despite his intensity, she felt safe to cry in front of him. She knew he wouldn't get upset if she got angry. They'd been down that road already, anyway. She could mourn all that was lost and have him catch her tears, holding them like precious jewels. Mattias could be the one that met her heart's desire. Francis loved her, but she felt like Mattias could understand her in ways Francis never could.

In the fantasy land of her mind, Inira didn't remember at this moment that Francis had held all her tears for decades. He did know her. He did know her pain. He had shouldered her burdens before and after sobriety. He had loved her all the way through. It was only because of sheer self-absorption that she didn't face the reality of what she had and what she would miss when her decisions to go in deep with Mattias came back to haunt her.

The day before she was to leave for London – a month after she returned – there were many meetings to make sure things were taken care of while she was absent. Stanley had again questioned why they needed to return, but he trusted her. He had also been distant, looking a little thinner each day. When he assured her he was fine whenever she asked, she thought about reaching out to his wife. That seemed disloyal, though, like going behind his back, so she resolved to wait until he was ready to tell her what was on his mind.

Charlotte, however, was full steam ahead. She expected nothing less from her focused and fiery second in command. She was proud of her, and this account management was an excellent experience. She hoped Charlotte would stick around to take over Triune, but she realized that was her plan and may not be Charlotte's, especially with the exposure of working with one of the world's biggest companies.

Inira's phone buzzed. It was Mattias. She quickly turned her phone back over, sheepishly hiding her screen from Charlotte's eyes. Charlotte seemed to miss nothing.

"Nahas checking in again, eh? I feel like you two are mothering hens, breathing down the necks of Lukas and I. We've discussed as much."

Inira looked at her with wide eyes in shock. "What do you mean, mothering hens?"

Charlotte waved her hand like it was not significant. "Oh, you know, just all the texting the two of you have been doing. I know this is a big deal for you to get me groomed and ready to take over. Which I am committed to, by the way, at least for a few years until I can get Giselle up to speed and move on to greener pastures."

Inira nodded slightly, now sure what Charlotte's plan was and a little relieved it matched hers.

Charlotte continued, "Lukas told me his father is on his back about ensuring this foundation is set up and moving forward without error. He is under a ton of pressure. This seems to be Mattias' major focus, ensuring this foundation can handle the kind of work he wants. Lukas says he keeps going on about 'the great vision' of remaking the world better than ever, with Mattias Nahas at the helm. He keeps telling Lukas they will be gaining access to the kind of technology that will be a game changer and will make sure Nahas can never be controlled by anyone but Mattias. It all sounds very cloak and dagger, a little shady. But at least we are focused on doing good in this world before he takes it over."

Inira froze. She couldn't quite process what Charlotte was saying. The young woman continued to talk, but Inira was stuck on the words 'gaining access to technology' and 'taking the world over.' She sat with her hand cupping her face, trying to understand what Charlotte was saying.

"Charlotte, are you saying Nahas Helps is a front for another agenda?"

Charlotte waved her hand above her head almost dismissively. "Look, Inira, I'll be straight with you. You know, plans and purposes are funneling this charity effort. Lukas hinted at as much. I don't know what makes you think Mattias Nahas could have changed to be 100% altruistic, but that would be naïve. You are not naïve enough to be snowed by him. If he is insistent on this foundation working, something else is going on. He has some other endgame in mind. I think that's why he is calling you back to London. Or is there another reason I don't know about?"

Inira sat still and tried to breathe through the panic rising in her chest. Was she that naïve to think this wasn't just all about her and Mattias? She was not a twenty-year-old girl anymore, blinded by her emotions. She was not going to get played again. She still loved Tomas with every fiber of her being, but this left her wondering if Mattias had more influence on his brother's actions – and hers – than she had been thinking.

"Inira, are you alright?"

Inira shook herself loose, trying to move past the feelings of tension she knew preceded a burst of adrenaline, pushing her into fight or flight. She needed a clear head. She needed space to work through this rushed feeling in her stomach to get to a calm place.

"Yes, yes, I'm alright. Just surprised to hear you and Lukas are on the same page with conspiracy theories about his father's intentions."

It was Charlotte's turn to look shocked. Inira wasn't in the habit of gaslighting her like this. She'd always been super supportive. This was an unwelcome retort from Inira, and her tone communicated that. "Well, I know what I'm observing, Inira. You don't have to make me feel like I don't know what I'm hearing or experiencing. That is not what you usually do, so I'll excuse it, but please be more respectful when you have questions about what is going on. You don't need to question my thoughts about it."

Inira let the bristling feeling of the younger woman's reprimand flow in and around her like she was a rock in a stream. She didn't have the time or the emotional capacity to get into an argument with Charlotte. Charlotte could bulldoze anyone but Inira, so she let it end in a stalemate.

"Charlotte, I apologize; that's not what I meant to do. I was caught off guard by how deep you both feel Mattias' actions go."

Charlotte visibly relaxed. "Yes, I have questioned whether or not it is good for the integrity of this firm to get involved with Nahas International on any level. But truthfully, it would put us on the map, raising our profile from a boutique firm to a real power player in the non-profit space. It would give us the kind of clout to make real change. I'm willing to take the risk, or I wouldn't be here – on this account, working with you or at this firm."

Charlotte was always so sure of what she did and what she thought. Inira smiled at her. This was why Emerie admired Charlotte so much. Her convictions were unshakeable. Charlotte would make change in this world. The world would bend itself to meet her desires; she was that remarkable a person. A true warrior to make things right and for the right reasons. Inira had been like that at one point in time. She'd lost that die-hard conviction when she saw them pull the bodies of her beloveds out from under the rubble.

"Charlotte, we are grateful to have you. Please let me know if your suspicions get any deeper. We all must strive to maintain integrity, and you help me keep focused on that goal." As she said the words, they soured in her mouth, knowing what she was about to say. "Now, if you will excuse me, I've got some calls to make before the day gets any later."

The buzz was still going in Inira's skull. She needed to get somewhere private. She needed to breathe. She needed to lower her heart rate and get back centered.

She needed to talk to Mattias.

Chapter 23

As she stepped out into the cold winter air, into the parking garage of her building, she wasn't sure how this conversation with Mattias would go. She needed the privacy, but she also needed a change of scenery. She had a restless, unsure feeling deep in her core. She knew her tendencies to sway others and make them comfortable; they were active right now. Her feelings for Mattias could be overwhelming. She could get swept out to sea in them. Even as she knew she had dependency issues, she was aware Mattias could hide things from her. She thought she knew him so well because of the way he talked to her and about their future. Yet, she was an intelligent woman who had survived horrific things brought on by his twin.

If Mattias wasn't sharing the full story and had a hidden agenda, there was much more at stake than just Inira's heart. She wanted to trust him, but had he earned her unflinching devotion? She didn't think so and needed to address it immediately. The thrumming inside her chest made her feel like a dam about to burst. She was activated, fully ready to fight or run. She decided that running would not be what happened. She would grab hold of the situation as much as possible. Unbidden, a voice she didn't quite recognize, an ancient one, floated into her mind. The voice began to soothe and calm her. It was quiet and slow, like honey or oil dripping after being spilled on the countertop.

It reminded her of her grandmother's voice when teaching her a prayer. It was a chant, and she used it when Inira and her sister were very small. It was her favorite weapon to avoid tantrums, which was how Inira felt right now. She might throw a screaming, demanding fit. It was like her soul was seeking a way to calm her physical body, to clear her head, and give her the emotional space to confront what she feared.

And what she feared more than anything was another betrayal.

She started to hum, trying to remember the cadence of the little poem. It was only four lines long, an ancient nursery rhyme. Her grandmother had sung it a few times, but usually, she had tapped it out on the first surface she could find – even the girl's little heads.

Great and Holy. God Almighty. You are True. God Inside Me.

Inira tapped it on her leg as she formed the words in her mind. Over and over again as she began to speak them out loud. The more she chanted, the calmer she felt. For so long, Inira felt disconnected from her past. Now, though, as the dreams came to her and she tried to remember, she found it wasn't all devastation, grief, and loss. She feared for so many years that was all it was – pain, but she was rediscovering there was goodness there, too. It restored her connection with the truth and that power in her that was contained in the songs and chants like this. As she chanted for a few more minutes, she began to wonder if it was possible – like her therapist claimed – to merge the two – her past and present- and live a whole life.

She knew she had to make this phone call, which could change so much. She felt at peace with whatever happened and hoped peace would last, even if her fears came true. As she walked to her car, she chanted again and, as she settled, said the Serenity Prayer. Then she hit the call button on Mattias' private number. It rang only two times before she heard his voice like silk sliding over her skin.

"My light and strength! To what do I owe this pleasure?"

Every time they talked, he had a new nickname for her. It was like he was testing them all out to see what stuck.

"Hi Mattias – I need to speak with you, and I fear this won't be easy. Can you talk now?"

Her old habit of prepping the other for bad news, both trying to be comforting and direct, kicked in.

"Light Bearer, yes, of course. Let me return to my office, and I'll call you back."

"Were you in a meeting?"

"Yes, I was having dinner with Amin, going over some reports, but I will get back to him after we speak."

She could hear the steel in his voice, which must have meant Ahmadi was right there. She wondered if there was anyone else there, like Lukas, perhaps. She knew Mattias was probably not very far from his office, which was much more like his living space. He rarely left. He had houses worldwide, but this tiny suite seemed best suited him. They'd texted about it once, and he had told her that because of his upbringing in such abject poverty in Caracas, he was more comfortable there. He said he would rather live tastefully than flaunt his wealth. He had plans for the money that didn't include treating himself like a king. It was one of the things that she admired about him. It was a kind of humility and focus on his goals.

Mattias was nothing if not driven.

After only a few moments, her phone vibrated in her hand. He was facetiming her, which meant he wanted to see her face as they talked. He'd repeatedly told her he wanted to look at her beautiful face and memorize her expressions. She was smart enough to know it was also because you could get a better read on someone in a conversation when you were looking at them and not just hearing their voice. Body language reveals more than words sometimes. For this conversation, she wanted to watch his reactions as well. She blew out a breath as her heartbeat ticked up. He was so damn gorgeous.

"Mattias, hi."

"Lovely Light, what a pleasant surprise. You look wonderful; you've been sleeping alright?"

Seeing the warmth radiating from his face, all for her was disarming. She knew it was genuine. She had a strong sense of when someone was being fake, and since that first encounter when he declared she was his, she had never felt he was being false. It made butterflies dance in her stomach.

Her cheeks colored as she said, "Yes, now that you've let me get a full eight hours again." She smiled at him.

He gave her a slow smile. "How can I help it if your hours are late at night or early in the morning? I want more than stolen moments with you, Light Bringer. I want you with me, at my side, every minute of the day. When I've set my mind to something, I do all I can to make it happen. You've changed so much for me."

Inira was quiet, staring into his eyes. Looking at him through the phone, she tried hard to see into his mind. She had such warring thoughts. She knew, without a doubt, that Mattias was telling the truth. At the same time, Charlotte's questions floated around her consciousness like ghosts disturbed in their rest. Her eyes burned with the intensity of her feelings.

"Inira, what is it? I can see you are upset. What has been said to you to make you feel this way?"

"Mattias, the way you say things...You know so much about me. I need to be clear with you before we move this forward. I've said this before – I am risking so much. I know my feelings for you are true, but if I come to London, it will mean I have to make major life changes quickly. I can't do that if it feels like something else is going on. I've heard that maybe there is more to your vision, and I need to hear it from you."

Mattias' eyes narrowed, then softened. He scrubbed his hand over his face and ran his fingers through his wavy, dark locks. Inira felt a rush of longing to have her hands in his hair. She inhaled and held it; she needed to stay focused. It was hard when he looked at her – even through the phone – with such desperation.

"I need you so much, Inira. You know that. I don't have all these pet names for you to trick you. I'm not in this to notch my belt. I could have any woman I want. You know that's the way the world works.

But I have waited for you. I didn't have any idea I needed you like I needed air. Yes, I have plans, a vision of what we could do together. I always have since I knew you made it out alive. I did not expect you to be someone I would want to build that vision around."

Inira prickled when he reminded her of his power and prestige. Indeed, for many women, it was the only aphrodisiac worth pursuing. She didn't need reminding of how women probably did look at him. Her irritation built, and her breathing got faster. Her temper was never far away. It was the reaction her mother tried the hardest to break her of and she was never successful.

"Mattias, I understand who you are and what you could offer someone. I am no small catch, either. I may not have billions, but I come with a legacy and level of experience no other woman in this world has."

He smiled crookedly. "Out of all I just said, what I just declared for you, you got stuck on the idea of another woman having me?"

Inira blew out a frustrated breath. "Yes, I did. You aren't even mine, and I know I have competition."

His smile faded. "Well, that's the part you didn't hear then. I am yours. You have no competition. You are right; no other woman could or would compare to you. No other woman can stand with me and rebuild what's been lost."

Inira tried to process his words and read into what he wasn't saying. She shook her head and tried to recenter. "Mattias, I want to hear more about your plans. That's actually what I called you about. I have concerns about what I don't know about."

He looked up, closed his eyes, and said, "I'll tell you everything, but I need something from you first. Tell me you are mine. I want your assurance that what I dream of will be our reality. This can't work any other way. We will be in a union."

This shook Inira. This is not why she'd called. He was asking her to commit to leaving her family, her life of twenty years. He was asking her to break up what she'd built. Could she do that? Hadn't she already started to tread that path, though? Wasn't she admitting to her feelings that were already there?

An insidious thought snuck in before she answered him. *How far was she willing to go to fulfill the destiny that had been stripped from her?*

Then, out of nowhere, she got mad. How could he push her like this?

A fire erupted in the pit of her stomach and made her head swim. She felt hot tears gather in the corner of her eyes. She shut them so tight, and her breathing started hitching. She gripped the phone so hard she thought she might break it. She slammed her other hand down into the meat of her thigh.

She spoke to him with her eyes closed and through clenched teeth, "Mattias, you have no right to give me an ultimatum until you tell me everything."

Chapter 24

When she opened her eyes again, Mattias looked at her with alarm. His eyes were so wide, his pupils almost blown out.

"Inira – what? What is it? I've never seen your face like this; what does it mean?"

There was panic in the edge of his voice. It was still silky, but this was an unexpected response. It was for her, too. She wasn't entirely sure where the anger came from since she'd calmed down. She took another long, slow breath before unloading on him.

"Mattias. I'm afraid. It makes me angry to think that you aren't completely honest with me. We both know I've been through that before and know I will not go through it again. Charlotte is suspicious, making me wonder if I'm also being manipulated. You experienced that the first time I came to your office. You are too intelligent to have forgotten it."

He looked confused at this. "Inira, Light Bringer, are you upset with me?"

She blew a frustrated breath and stared hard into the screen at him, even more angry now that he was not reading her emotions correctly. "No, Mattias, I am not 'upset' with you. Now I am enraged."

Her voice had lowered to barely audible. She had never been a yeller or a screamer. When she was furious, she got deadly quiet. It happened so rarely that she could probably list the times Francis and Emerie had seen her like this on one hand. But her anger was in full force now.

Mattias sat up straighter, clearly not prepared to deal with this emotion. "What has made you so angry, my darling girl?"

Her throat felt like gravel as she forced the words out of her tight throat in a sort of whisper shout. "First, *do not* call me a sweetling name right now. Second, NEVER call me a girl. I am a grown woman and will not let my feelings or questions go unheard."

Mattias looked bewildered. "I am hearing you. You are not hearing me."

Inira gaped at him. "Excuse me? I am not the one who just drew a line in the sand. You are trying to force me into a decision that will wreck my entire life, and I don't even have all the information. I am afraid that I'm already in love with you and not for the right reasons – and that I will be betrayed again. That possibility makes me so angry I can barely speak. That and your family do not have a good record regarding being completely honest with me. I want everything you've promised, but I know you have other plans. If I leave Francis for you, it will be a mess. I will be a mess. I cannot make this decision lightly and to make you feel better. I've brought this up because you keep brushing past it like it isn't a problem. Do you think it is easy to pick up and leave? I have built a life and a family before you ever came along. Perhaps you don't see things like I do, and because of that, you expect me to flip a switch to bend to your will? I don't work like that. I will never work like that. You need to get it through your thick skull that you are not the only one with plans here."

She felt like she had just sprinted a mile when she finished speaking. Her heart was hammering, and her breath was coming in gasps.

Mattias looked shocked. She again pushed back on him, something she knew no one ever did without consequences. Yet, she wasn't one of his lackeys. She was his equal and then some, and he better start realizing it. He looked so surprised that she would push back, so confused by her anger he had no response. His hesitation made her sure of one thing, and she called him out.

"Mattias, I am powerful. I have knowledge you do not, and I know you want that. You may want me, but you also know you want my knowledge about Teleosis. You want the secrets of how we stayed secure for so long. You want access to the technology - the magic – we were entrusted with. I can see how you would play my feelings for it, not because you want *me* to fulfill your vision but because of what I can *give* you. Do not try to play me. I am not a twenty-year-old girl anymore."

Inira never anticipated the conversation would have taken this turn. But once she got rolling, the pieces clicked in her mind, and her mouth followed it.

"You know what else I'm figuring out, Mattias? You didn't get to where you are now without a full-blown plan. Tomas gave you the keys to the kingdom. I was it, wasn't I? That's why you said I was always meant to be yours."

"Inira, stop." Mattias sounded pained, like she was physically hurting him.

She kept at him, going for the throat. "Was I always to be a pawn in your game? Your ideology would never let a *woman* stand beside you as an equal. I've read that much about your supposed religion. It's patriarchy and androcracy on steroids. It's all about the men. What the fuck was I thinking? I'm glad I figured this out before I ruined my life over a fantasy."

She rarely ever used curse words, but this seems like a very appropriate time for one. Mattias hadn't looked into the phone before. He had his head down. He had propped his phone up, and his head was on his crossed forearms. She barely heard his muffled response.

"Excuse me, what did you say, *Deitas*?"

She knew she was very close to the line that would set him off, but she needed to see how he would handle this. If he ended it, she would deal. She was prepared for that. However, she was unprepared for what he said when he picked up his head and looked back into the phone. His dejected expression was not forced. He was not using emotion to manipulate her. She could see the genuine pain in his eyes as he spoke,

"No, my light. You are my love. Yes, I had a plan, but I've changed everything since meeting you."

His sincerity took some wind out of her sails, but she still had enough in her response. "Bullshit. You are not the type of man that can change."

He was still looking at her, the pain radiating from his face. For a second, she got worried he might hurt himself, the look of agony there so acute. He whispered now, not out of anger like she was doing. Her words had been clipped, precise. His now came out in a stream, like a confession before a priest. His voice was all broken in desperation.

"What you say is true. I wasn't able to change. Yes, Tomas and I had a plan. He was destined to be the trigger man because of his access. I worked out the supplies and raised the funds in the background. And we got everything we needed. You do not know how many powerful people want access to Teleosis and the Song of Creation, the global crime syndicates, and governments. The whole world knew what kind of innovation happened in Teleosis. You shared it with everyone. You didn't sell it; you gave it away. Yet, the only thing you held back was the source of your goodness. They wanted to make a profit from what Teleosis created. You know this, too. I have always been in the background, pulling the strings and organizing the details. It is why I'm at the top of the food chain."

Inira sat rooted to her seat, frozen as she listened to him, her anger still simmering, but she was still listening.

His voice never changed; he only sounded more miserable with every dirty explanation. Still whispering, he continued, "Yes, the Serpents believed Teleosis needed to be conquered. We were taught that women were weak and needed men to rule over them. It is what our ancestors knew, what every major world religion has leveraged. Women must not have too much power. They can't handle it, even when history tells us otherwise, and the oldest civilization on earth right in our midst? Teleosis – you were the proof – that we were all wrong. I know how wrong I have been. It has become the shame of my life. And that is why I need you because I can't go on as the leader of a false ideology that will only hurt people."

She knew firsthand how jealous and dark the world was towards those, especially those who reflected the goodness of the Divine mandate through femininity and equanimity. The world, since the first twin murdered his brother, preferred dominance. The world, save for the tiny outpost of Teleosis, had been cast in that image. His confession didn't completely subdue her anger. She wouldn't let it. She had doubts about the sincerity of what he was saying. She wasn't going to take his word for it all. She had done that with Tomas and almost ended up dead. She wouldn't make that same mistake with this brother.

Mattias put his head back on his arms, not facing the camera and seemingly waiting for his fate in her final judgment. He was so still, barely breathing.

"Mattias, look at me."

It took him a long while to look up into the screen, his green eyes so much brighter now for the redness rimming them. He got up and took the phone with him into the bathroom. She realized he was getting a washcloth to wipe his face because he had no tissues. She waited until he was done composing himself and then said more gently this time to him.

"Mattias, look at me. Why are you telling me all this now?"

He sighed deeply and painfully. "Because I know I've broken any chance of being with you. This is the end, isn't it?"

She wasn't sure. She realized that his level of vulnerability with her right now was something he never shared with anyone. It would be too neat to forgive and forget. She couldn't risk it all again without being sure. She knew how strongly he believed in his convictions, and no one changed their core beliefs overnight, not when they'd been so ingrained. Mattias' whole life had been about reestablishing control he'd never had in his childhood.

She saw, like a movie in her mind, as he grew up through adolescence and into adulthood, taking every chance to be the smartest, most powerful one in the room. He had rarely been played. Lukas' mother was a rare exception. But he ended that marriage as quickly as it had started. It made her wonder why he was different with her.

"Mattias, have you ever loved someone before?"

He didn't hesitate in his answer. "My mother and then Tomas. Now, only you."

The admission didn't undo her, but her heart squeezed. The anger had drained from her like someone had pulled out the drain stopper in the bathtub.

"Yes, *Ahava*, I see that."

He snapped his head up. "What did you call me?"

"*Ahava*. Do you know what it means?"

He shook his head as he pulled the wet washcloth down over and off his face. He looked a little scared.

"It means 'Love' or 'Lover' and many variations. It's Hebrew. It's a nickname I give only to those who mean the most to me. It doesn't change everything, but I am not angry anymore."

"What does it change, Noni? And what doesn't it change?"

She sighed. "It changes that I now know you are willing to change. That you are changing. That my presence in your life is doing some good. I suppose if a man like you can see the purpose and glory of Teleosis, then there is reason to hope. I want to be with you, but that will need to come at the cost of your pride. You will have to do something for me to convince me of the truth of all this completely. You will have to answer all my questions. I can't do secrets. Secrets kill everything around them. You must share all your plans with me without reservation, Mattias. Then you will become my *Ahava*."

She watched him breathe in and shudder. It was such a violent tremble she worried if maybe this had pushed him too far. "I don't like it when you are angry with me. You are terrifying when you whisper like that. I'd prefer you slap me next time. I've never cared about a woman's feelings. This is all so new for me. I knew you were unlike anyone, and I will endeavor to earn that name you've bestowed on me."

She sighed, explaining, "Women are the Bringers of the Truth. We draw it out and inspire others to live in it. The Divine Feminine is calling you into your higher self, Mattias. 'Self is the only way' can no longer be your driving force. You must replace your hate and pride with love and humility to live into all you can become. You can have your heart's desires, but I can't let you have them at the expense of the world's people."

He nodded solemnly, "I want that. I don't know how to get it."

"Look at me, Mattias." When he did, she told him, "I will be your guide. I will show you how we can be partners together. It will be hard; you will have to face your fears. It will require you to live with a whole different ethos. You will have to make shifts, and they will be felt. It will be as big of a sacrifice as I am making. I am worth that cost?"

A few weeks of conversation was only the start. They stood a chance if they could be rigorously honest with each other. Even as she knew the rest of her life would fall apart, if she could count on Mattias being on the side of Truth and learning to Love instead of Hate, she thought she could bear it.

His big emerald eyes loomed large on the screen, and she noticed he had a tumbler on the table next to him. He wouldn't forgo the need for fortification after a conflict like this. He moved to the couch, the phone propped on the table next to him. He was stretched out; she wished she could see and touch every inch of him. She wanted, after all this surge of emotions, to take her time and feel his body on hers. God, he was magnificent.

"*Ahava.*"

He turned to look back at the screen, his face still blotchy, but it did nothing to lessen the strength of his features. She felt like she had a string tied to her middle, and he was tugging on it, pulling her closer.

"Yes, my love light."

"I will come to London."

He exhaled so forcefully and rubbed a hand down his face in relief. "I cannot tell you how happy that makes me. I promise to show you when you are here. I promise to share everything with you, to show you every plan we have. I will keep nothing from you from here on out. We will be partners in rebuilding Teleosis."

"Yes, Mattias, that's non-negotiable. We do things my way now. Equal partners for the betterment of the world."

"Equals. I will learn if you teach me."

"Ahava, I will."

"I wish you were here so I could show you what you mean to me. I am much better at showing how I feel." He winked at her then.

She laughed. "It will always be interesting with you. Won't it?"

"And fun, too, I hope." His voice was a little husky now and somehow had dropped to a register that sent chills down her spine.

They'd never talked about sex. They'd never discussed how or when that would happen. Inira knew he wanted to be with her. Her body responded to him like it never had for anyone, full of molten heat and driving need. But she wasn't ready for that yet. She had to tell Francis she was leaving, and things were changing. She had to do that before going to London.

"Yes, Mattias, I know when the timing is right, when I am free, we will have all the fun." She batted her eyes at him.

"When you are free, you won't be free for long. You'll be mine, and I will make sure everyone knows it."

She shivered a little at his returning intensity. No, things would never be boring with Mattias Nahas. Of that, Inira was sure.

"I need to go now, *Ahava*. I will text you later. Thank you for what you shared and for being willing to change for me. I know it isn't easy. We can be partners in this. I have thousands of years behind me to show you how much better it is when we do it together."

"No, love light. I hope to become the man you believe me to be and live up to this vision, which is so different than I ever dreamed. I was taught yours was a of living that was foolish. But I can see how wise it is when you are behind it. That was what you were born for, I think."

Inira turned the full force of her smile on him, and she heard his breath catch before he returned a smile just as broad.

"Yes, *Ahava*, I was always meant to do this. And we will do it together. Dream of me tonight."

"I have dreamed of you for years. I cannot wait to make that dream – and yours – come true."

Chapter 25

Ahymn of warning, written by the High Priestess Claudia, in 1526 A.D.

The riders come.

They come at last.

They've come again.

They come towards us so fast.

We've made our deals.

We've set our price.

Never to be bought.

Because again, we will rise.

The FourFold God knows our names.

They see our foes.

And They know our pain.

It is by Their Comfort we will endure again.

The fire will come.

The Flood will storm.

With Zayin's family,

This is but the norm.

Prepare to defend.

Prepare for the attack.

Prepare just in case,

We are stabbed in the back.

Prepare for the onslaught.

Be ready for defense.

We manifest holy treasures.

For which are broad and dense.

The Spear will come.

The generations will pour in.

We must rest and grow.

For always are the sins of men.

Chapter 26

After ending the call with Mattias, Inira returned to the office for a few hours with a smile. Charlotte and Giselle commented, wondering aloud if Francis had something planned for the two of them tonight. Inira didn't roll her eyes, but it had been many years since Francis had surprised her. Given their relationship in massive flux, she highly doubted that he would anytime soon. It was close to their anniversary, but he was a stickler for celebrating it on the day. And their twenty-first wedding anniversary would come while she was in London.

She didn't miss the irony or the feeling of freedom twinged with guilt.

As they walked out, Charlotte, caught up in relationship fantasy land that made Inira want to roll her eyes, continued fantasizing about Francis doing the unusual, even the unthinkable. "He loves you so much! I can't wait to hear about what you all do tonight. You have to know you are my relationship goals. To have a stable relationship with a man who grew up differently than you. It's a dream come true for this black girl! I'll need all my magic to make it happen."

Inira's cheeks heated. Race was a hot button for everyone around her. She'd had to get used to the invisible but obvious caste in America. Her skin tone got attention and caused the mothers at Emerie's prestigious school to treat her differently. Francis was white but had been raised by activist parents in the South. He didn't have the lived experience, but he had been in relationships with people of color his entire life. His friend group was like the United Nations, and he preferred it that way.

"Yes, Francis is a keeper, but no relationship is perfect; you know that Charlotte. Don't go off the deep end."

Charlotte looked at her and laughed as their elevator stopped at the bottom floor. "Trust me, Inira; I am aware no man is perfect. But you got someone pretty darn close. You better take care of him tonight!" She winked and suggestively shook her hips.

Now, Inira did roll her eyes and, in a mock scolding tone, said, "Charlotte! I think this broaches the boundaries of our professional relationship!" Her shoulders shook with silent laughter at the younger woman's antics. Charlotte tossed her beautiful micro braids over her shoulder as the elevator door opened and did her best to sashay out into the lobby, with Inira following from behind. Charlotte saw him first. She declared, "Well, look here! The man of the hour!"

Inira was confused until she saw her husband standing in the middle of the elevator bank of the high rise. His shoulders were tight; his hands were opening and closing at his sides. As he turned and met Inira's face, her stomach dropped. There was only one reason he would be here, waiting in her building lobby. Something was wrong. Inira's breath came short; she fully expected him to tell her something horrific had happened to Emerie. Charlotte didn't seem to notice as she moved to the parking garage. She said over her shoulder, "Have a great time tonight, you two!"

Francis turned to face Inira. She noticed he had tears in his eyes, but he looked like he was about to rip her head off. She'd never seen him wear such an expression, and it built the ice-cold terror in her gut. She reached out to him, but he jerked back, away from her.

"Francis, what are you doing here? Are you ok? What's going on? Where is Emerie? Is she okay?"

He seemed to struggle to catch his breath, finally letting out a slow, shaky one. "She is getting a ride home and will meet us there in time to say goodbye."

Inira knitted her brows together in complete confusion. "Say goodbye, what do you mean? Who is leaving? Francis, please tell me what's going on!"

"Not here. Is your office cleared out?"

"Yes, we can go upstairs, but why? What's going on?"

Suddenly, and so unlike him, he roughly grabbed her elbow and dragged her through an elevator door.

"Ow, Francis! What are you doing?"

"I'm not going to get into here in the elevator. Just keep your mouth shut until we are alone."

Inira opened her mouth to say something, but nothing came out. He was gripping her arm painfully. She looked at him with bugged-out eyes, his whole demeanor unfamiliar and scary. It was like he was a different person than the man she said goodbye to this morning as he shaved.

She tried to yank her arm out of his hand but couldn't. She knew her arm would bruise. She hissed at him in shocked anger, "This is so unlike you, Francis. Tell me what's going on! Right now!"

"I am not someone you can order around Inira. Something happened at work, and I will show you exactly what you've done when we are alone."

Inira felt a crawling sensation along her spine. The ice in her gut spread to her heart, and she felt it shudder. She started shaking and had to breathe through her nose and out her mouth, both to contain her fear and tamp down her anger at how ugly his tone was. They rode up to her offices in silence, and it seemed like an eternity as she unlocked the door and ushered him into the conference room. His eyes roamed everywhere. You can see her office from the conference room. He narrowed his eyes when they landed on the whiteboard with the Nahas Helps development plan mapped across it.

She first entered the conference room door and jumped when she heard the door slam and lock behind her. She turned to see Francis stalking forward in such a menacing way she backed up until her thighs hit the table. She held up her hands in a defensive position, her mind entirely befuddled by the actions of this man who looked like her husband yet who had never, not once in their twenty years together, acted this way before.

"Francis –" she started.

He raised his hand to backhand her. She blocked him and pushed him back with all her force.

"What the fuck is wrong with you, Francis? You have never treated me like this, ever!" She nearly screamed at him; she was so alarmed.

"You've never given me a reason to, 'High Priestess.'" He said the title so mockingly it made her nauseous. He kept going. "You don't get to say anything until I finish." He breathed deeply, exhaling so forcefully that her hair fluttered even from a distance. A part of her brain logged the smell of the mint gum he had been chewing. He was only an inch or two taller than her, but it was enough now. She was so shaken by the fury radiating off of him. She had no idea what was coming. She didn't know if she needed to fight, take flight, or freeze.

He pulled out his phone from his pants pocket. He opened the screen and shoved it at her. When she finally could make her hands work to take it, he snatched his hand back abruptly; it was like she was a snake, and he didn't want to get bit. It took her a long moment to comprehend what she was seeing. She scrolled and scrolled until reality sunk in. Her legs started to give out, and she had to brace herself on the table. She ended up sitting on the edge as the total weight of what was happening hit her.

The tears came unbidden and threatened to spill over until she looked up into Francis' face and whispered, "I'm so sorry you found out this way. Where did you get these?"

His face looked like a storm about to break. He was red from his scalp down to the neckline of his dress shirt, which he had unbuttoned at some point. His salt and pepper hair stood out starkly against the beet-red shade of his skin.

"What, you mean all the texts you've been sharing with Mattias Nahas for a month now, as you made plans to leave me? Tell me, Inira, did you fuck him in London? I know he looks exactly like Tomas, so I'm sure that got you wet and ready for him."

She stood to her full height at the insult and reached to slap him, but he caught her hand.

"No, absolutely not. You don't get to lash out at me when you've been having an affair and are MAKING FUCKING PLANS TO LEAVE ME FOR ANOTHER MAN!!"

He was yelling so loud, now right in her face. This had never happened in all their time together. Even if they were both in a mood while they were drinking, it never got confrontational or violent. It just wasn't who Francis was.

"Where did you get these?" Inira croaked out between her labored gasps for air.

"Someone sent them to my *work* email. It was a file that came through on the pretense of a potential case. I could be *disbarred* for this; you know that, right? Not only is my wife having an affair, making me look like a damn idiot, but all of my work emails can also be subpoenaed and used in court. Do you know how foolish you are, Inira? I never would have believed it, but your behavior these last few weeks makes perfect sense."

As her rage ramped up once again, her voice got lower. "Stop right there. I wanted to change the nature of our relationship well before Mattias was in the picture. Hell, Francis. On the way to the AIRPORT, you told me I needed 'to do better,' like a marriage is completely one-sided. This is supposed to be a partnership. Don't come at me either when you communicate with others or sleep in your office." She went to move past him, but he stood like an immovable wall. Her words didn't fall on deaf ears; his eyes looked pained because he knew he wasn't innocent.

She declared to him, "Get out of my way, Francis. You are way out of line, and I need some space from you." She moved to go around him again, and at first, he planted his feet. She decided not to play his little game, walked the other way around the table, and began to unlock the conference room door to put some much-needed physical space between them. She wanted to let her tears cascade out of her in a rush, but she wasn't sure if that would be a good idea. She wanted to curl up in a ball in the corner and never leave because she knew this was the end of her family.

But she was made for more than that. She was trained to deal with angry men; she had never expected it to be him. She hadn't yet thought through how to tell him, but it wouldn't be until after this trip to London next week. He walked up behind her and put his palm on the door above her head. He still looked like a cornered wolf, ready to tear and bite whatever he could get his hands on.

"Francis, you need to give me some space. This is volatile, and you are not in your right mind. I will talk with you when you are calmer."

That seemed only to push him further.

"Are you not even going to deny it?" His justifiable anger was back, the momentary prick of guilt done. He practically screamed at her. She wondered if she would have to knee him in the balls to get him away from the door. She didn't want this escalating like that, but he needed to back off.

She kept her voice calm. "I'm not going to, but it is not how I wanted you to find out."

Francis tipped his head back and laughed like a crazy man. "You didn't want me to find out this way? Tell me, dearest wife," he practically spat, "how *did* you want me to find out?"

Again, she knew honesty was the only way forward in this situation. She thought about saying, *Never* but thought that was probably not the best response given how unhinged he was starting to look. "I was going to tell you after this next trip to London. We are going to rebuild Teleosis."

He snapped his head down, "Oh yes, I know, *High Priestess*." He spat the title again with derision. "You get to have the unreachable dream handed to you on a silver platter by a billionaire. And one who looks exactly like your one true love, right? I always knew

I had to compete with Tomas. Do you know how hard it is to compete with a dead man? Even one who destroyed your life, you still idolized him. Your trauma makes you ridiculously blind."

She stiffened and made ready to defend herself but knew she wouldn't get a word in. Plus, as eloquent as she was, she was no match for him in wordplay. She'd witnessed him laying out the final defense hundreds of times, and she knew when he was circling his final moment, he would tear into her to rip any defense apart.

With him caging in her like this, her back literally against the door, she decided to stand there and take it. Then, she would decide what to do. There was no fighting this. She was guilty of crossing many lines, but no one deserves this treatment. If this is how he reacted in the face of a personal crisis, he was no longer the man she wanted to be with. She would never tolerate physical and emotional abuse because once she allowed him to treat her like that, he wouldn't stop. She was leaving him, and she would rebuild Teleosis. She braced herself for the final blow.

"I'm assuming you are drinking again, as well."

Her head rocked back like he'd slapped her, even expecting something ugly; she never thought he would go that low. "What? No, I haven't, not at all."

"Well, regardless, your sobriety means nothing when you are still acting like a drunk. It is fine. You can go to London. You can go to him. But you are not going to take Emerie and me down with you. We are going to go home. You will pack your bags, say goodbye to Emerie, and leave the house."

"Excuse me, you are kicking me out and taking my child from me?"

"Fuck yes I am. We aren't in your dreamland anymore. I'm the man, the husband, the father. In our society, it is my responsibility to be upstanding and true. You are a faithless wife and not in a culture where women can do whatever the hell they want. You broke our SACRED vows, and I'll ensure you pay for it. You have a billionaire on your side; I'm sure he will make up for what you will lose in the divorce."

She grabbed at her chest, "Divorce? Are you divorcing me? You've already made up your mind?"

"Shit, yes. I will not tolerate a woman who is unfaithful to me."

It was her turn to laugh then. She felt the response rise within her. She could take the truth, but Francis had crossed a line when he brought up losing Emerie and her sobriety. She looked him dead in the eye and said the only thing she could. "So, for all your profession of love for me throughout the years, it can turn to hate so easily. Never thought you were the type to get out when it gets hard, Francis."

He rocked back on his heels and shoved his hands in his pockets. "I don't hate you, Inira. My level of love for you tells me when to get out. I've read all these texts. I'm glad you left me out of them, but you are clearly in it with him. I'm not going to fight for you if you want to go. It's obvious you've decided to do just that, *Ahava*."

Her stomach turned at his use of the nickname, knowing he'd seen the most recent texts. That was fine if this was how Francis chose to end their marriage. She felt miserable, for sure, but she knew this had been inevitable. She shouldn't have expected a quiet and respectful end to their union, but this was utterly unacceptable.

"Francis, it didn't have to be like this, and I will not allow you to treat me this way in front of Emerie. Ground rules of respect and silence if you can't manage that. You hear me? Otherwise, I call the cops. I understand you are in pain, but your behavior is disgusting and so beneath you. Think about that when I'm gone."

A little fire left his eyes when the truth of her words found their mark. She wouldn't call him names and make it ugly like he had. This confrontation left her feeling like she was coated in slime. She felt it out of the office, down the elevator, and into the car in the parking garage.

It was a tortuous 45-minute drive in traffic. He drove aggressively and swore a lot at the other drivers. She didn't dare take out her phone, although she knew she had missed texts and maybe calls from Matthias. She didn't want to add any fuel to Francis's spiral, and her mind raced on how to tell Emerie. She was eighteen, so

Francis' threat to 'take her away' was an empty one. She wanted to have a chance to talk to her and not let Francis' narrative win the day.

In the end, Francis told Emerie that she was leaving tonight for London and didn't know when she would be coming back. He treated his wife like a client who'd just been found guilty of a felony. He only let Inira see her daughter after she packed her sizeable rolling suitcase with what she could think of to take with her. She trusted Mattias would get her what she needed, but she had no idea how she would get to him. She had her passport in her pocket and kept her hand on it.

As she faced her daughter, Francis, standing behind her and to her right, the tears couldn't be contained anymore. She didn't know how to explain it to her, her failure to do better than her mother did. In the end, she was leaving, just as her mother had emotionally abandoned her after her father was killed. Emerie went to embrace her, which Francis tried to stop, but she pulled out of his grip.

Then she whispered, "Mama, I know he isn't telling me everything because he wants to protect me. But I am an adult. I can handle it. I promise. Just call me later and tell me what Dad won't. I'll make sure I come to you wherever you are. We are a team, and nothing changes that." Emerie was crying now, too. She knew a break was happening, but despite her assertions that she was an adult, she still held onto her mother like she had when she was a small child. Inira held on just as tightly like Emerie was going to turn into a spirit who would slip right through her fingers.

Francis was stiff and formal. He carried her suitcase out the front door as she and Emerie continued to hug each other. Inira didn't think she could let go.

"Inira, your Uber is here. Go so you don't miss your flight." Francis wasn't above blatant lies, but it was still shocking, seeing as she had nowhere to go. She knew how hurt he was. His commentary was a firehose she had to endure, only pushing back when he went beyond the pale. She'd expected him to be angry when she told him, but his finding out this way made it much worse.

As she stood on the stoop of their brownstone, looking at Emerie's tear-streaked face and her moon eyes, she felt like she had once again lost everything. It had all blown up, except this time she was the triggerman—her relationship with Mattias, the bomb that had gone off unexpectedly.

"I know you don't want to hear this, Francis, but I am sorry. I do love you. I don't know how to correct this, but we knew this had to change. I'm just so sorry it came out this way. I hope that one day after you see Teleosis for yourself, you will understand why I am choosing this path. Emerie, I will see you soon. I love you more than life itself."

He stared hard at her but didn't say anything. He was holding onto Emerie, and Inira wasn't sure if it was to hold her up or keep her from coming with Inira. She felt like her chest was caving in and stumbled down the steps to the Uber. As the driver took her to a nearby hotel, she texted Mattias what happened. She told him to wait for her to call him when she could think straight. She needed to know he had nothing to do with this. They had talked about telling Francis, so she didn't think he had a hand in this, but it was suspicious. She had her idea of who would be the culprit, but there was too much swirling in her mind to focus on it.

She felt like her soul was splintering. She knew she was moving forward towards what was always meant for her, being drawn to it even. This was the most awful way for it to happen, but she now realized it had been inevitable. She and Francis had been over before she met Mattias, and now, she had a path to redemption.

She didn't know how to explain it all to Emerie or make amends with Francis, but she vowed to try.

Chapter 27

It took her two hours to call Mattias. She landed at a nice hotel near her office as there was some convention in town. She put her credit card down and finally made it to the room. The day had taken everything out of her, and while she wanted to talk to Mattias, she didn't know if she could answer all of his questions. She threw herself in the middle of the bed and finally let herself come unglued. She cried like her leg had been sawed off, and she was the one doing the amputation. She couldn't call Mattias until she could talk, after 10 pm, 4 am London time. She hit the Facetime button, and he picked it up immediately.

He looked like he had been lying down. "*Luz de Amor*, finally. I've been tossing and turning."

She was hiccuping from crying so hard, and she answered him in a voice that sounded like she was a wet rag wrung out. "I'm sorry, Mattias. I couldn't call you until I could think and breathe."

"Inira, my darling – your face! What's happened? Is Emerie ok?"

"Yes, well, no. Francis found out about us." She'd texted him that something had happened but had provided no details. She started crying again, even as no real tears came out. She didn't think she had any tears left.

"WHAT? HOW?" He spoke loudly in alarm and fury. He sounded as if he was about to rip someone's flesh from their bones.

When he realized she was crying, he started speaking in low murmurs, something soothing in Spanish. That wasn't one of the seven languages she knew, and she couldn't focus on the words. She wanted nothing more than for him to hold her, even though her spirit felt the knife of shame twist deep. She wasn't ashamed that she wanted to be with Mattias but of how everything had happened. She'd always been so careful and lived her life with integrity. She continued to cry, softer now. This wasn't the torrent from when she first got to the room. Mattias started to sing what sounded like a nursery song. It wasn't in Spanish. It shook her out of her emotion a bit.

She took a deep breath and asked him, "Mattias, how many languages do you speak?"

He smiled into the screen, "Maybe as many as you, *naui salang.*"

Her laugh was small, no more than a huff, "What is that one?"

"Korean. Which I do speak, mostly so Lukas wouldn't forget that part of his heritage. I may not like his mother, but I respect her culture. I have a pet project; do you want to hear about it?"

She looked at him through the screen and shrugged, too tired to do much else, but her interest was piqued.

"I've spent much time looking up the translations of 'my love' and 'love light' in as many languages as possible. I want to spend the rest of my days figuring out the ones you like best."

Tears pricked her eyes again; at the moment, she didn't feel like she deserved affectionate names. "Mattias, I would love to hear them all, but I am tired. I feel empty without my family. Francis was so angry. He nearly hit me before I blocked his arm. He has never done that. It was terrifying."

His face hardened, but he kept silent, listening and letting her get it all out.

Inira continued, "I don't know who sent him the transcription of our texts. Who has that kind of access? You told me your communications are encrypted, so I don't understand how he could have gotten them."

Still looking furious and frustrated, Mattias exhaled sharply before saying, "I don't know, but I swear I will find out. Whoever it was will pay dearly for the pain they've caused you. I, too, had hoped we could tell Francis together."

That surprised her. "You wanted to tell him together? That would probably have gone as badly or maybe worse. He isn't as big as you, Mattias, but I assure you, if his anger towards me is any indication, he would have taken you down."

Mattias chuckled smugly. "*Cherie*, he might have tried, but it wouldn't happen. And I wouldn't say I like hearing that he was aggressive with you. No one touches what is mine."

"You are such an alpha and have a weird sense of ownership since we are talking about the man I'm legally wed to."

"*Liebeslicht*, that is a technicality for a little while longer." His face softened as he looked at her. "I want to care for and protect you, even when you don't need it. I want to be there for you. Will you let me? Can I provide for you tonight?"

Her exhaustion made her brain muddle, so she couldn't process his meaning, "What do you mean? How can you help?"

"Let me fly you here tomorrow. Just leave it all behind. That's what Francis told Emerie anyway. I need to hold you in my arms, *ama la luce*."

Her weariness made her emotions swing on a wide pendulum, and she giggled at the thought of riding on his private jet, plus the idea of a list of nicknames he must have written down somewhere. "Ok, how many was that now? Four?"

He grinned. "Yes, I have a list on my phone. I still have a long way to go, though."

She sighed wearily. "Maybe just pick one that feels the most natural and go with it. That's why I use *Ahava*."

"In that case, I will call you *luz de amor* from my mother tongue, Espanol. It is the most beautiful language there is."

Inira was glad for the sweet talk; it lightened her heart. It also distracted her from the pain, but she realized she could barely keep her eyes open anymore.

"Luz – can I bring you home to me? Tell me before you fall asleep. I'll make all the arrangements; you can stay with me. I can finally show you where I dream about you. Say you will let me bring you home."

It was several long moments till she could answer, just before her eyes closed and her body took her into unconsciousness, when she whispered, "Yes, Mattias. Bring me home."

***

Waking up after the second worst day of her life, face down in the coverlet, in a strange bed, fully dressed, was disorienting. Inira's back was killing her as her legs, at the knees, were hanging off. Her eyes felt glued shut with sand, and her mouth was so dry that her tongue was stuck to the roof of her mouth. It felt like she was hungover from a bender, only this was an emotional one, not due to alcohol. She'd been clenching her jaw in her sleep because it ached and popped as she opened it. It took her more than a few moments to remember where she was and what had happened. Her shoulders were sore, and her neck was tight. She truly felt like she'd been run over by a truck. The muscles of her abdomen were on fire as she tried to move around.

There's nothing like the extreme workout of sobbing yourself to sleep. My abs should be cut now, she thought miserably to herself.

As she came fully into her body and consciousness, she didn't start crying again, which was surprising. When she arrived, she expected to lay in this hotel room for days as the misery of her life crashed in around her. She hadn't charged her phone; it was lying screen-down on the bed next to where she'd passed out. It was dead, so she plugged it into the wall and returned to the bathroom. She had no idea how long she'd been asleep, only that it was the result of pure physical exhaustion brought on by emotional and spiritual stress.

Her lower back was cramped as she moved around the room. She could feel the emotional pain beginning to work itself up towards her throat. Half bent over, she made herself a cup of coffee, and it took her a maddeningly long to do so. She was in agony all over – radiating from deep inside. She knew, though, that her mental state would improve somewhat with coffee in the works.

She shuffled into the shower. She hadn't even bothered to unpack her toiletries bag last night. She stood under the spray of the scalding hot water for a small eternity. She let soothe her tight back, shoulders, and soul, circling into the drain with the grit in her eyes. She used the hotel soap and washcloth and scrubbed her skin till it was beet red. She felt like she'd been assaulted, which nearly had happened, she thought with a grimace.

That train of thought brought back a memory of when she was assaulted after she'd first come to the States. In her ignorance, having always been treated with respect and dignity, she wasn't even remotely prepared when she let a young, attractive stranger walk her to her car after they had kissed at the bar.

She started to shake violently as the memory surfaced. She had been drunk, of course, at the start of her drinking career. She was drowning her emotions so that she could function as she waited out the political asylum process. No one knew who she was, which was a huge relief. She could do anything she wanted. She'd had some money in her name from her father, but the rest tied up in her mother's, which she wouldn't get access to for ten years. She knew where that money had come from, so she promptly gave ninety percent of it to charity, with the rest going into trust for Emerie.

Her night had started fun, and the stranger she remembered was named Ryan. He was tall, with dark black hair, almost blue, and dark brown eyes. He was so different than Tomas. He had tattoos up his arms and slick-backed hair. She thought he might be a little dangerous, and she liked it. She was stupid. He was dangerous in what she thought was a sexy way that promised rough sex that she needed to keep her mind off her circumstances. She didn't see the signs that there was a whole other level of predator. She could only hold him off because of her defensive training, taken as part of her fitness regime for most of her life.

She knew the rest of the world wasn't safe, but she hadn't truly understood what that looked like until the moment at her car when Ryan had grabbed her wrists and wrenched them behind her back, making her shoulders pop. He licked up her neck aggressively, which made her try to jerk away. He chuckled; he liked the struggle. He kept his tongue going all the way up and over the shell of her ear and hissed,

"C'mon baby, I know you want it. Quick and dirty, right here, and then I'll take you home and show you what a real night on the town should end like."

At the bar, she'd had every intention of taking him back to her motel room, where the office immigration department put her. Now, the sheer force of his show of dominance and the menace in his tone immediately sobered her up. She did not want this. It had never been like this with Tomas. She'd never felt unsafe. It terrified her. She felt like she was going to puke all over him, but she wasn't entirely sure that would stop him. She wiggled her hips against his crotch. She wasn't encouraging him. She remembered what she'd been taught even though she'd never expected to use it.

The distraction of her enthusiastic response lost his grip on one of her wrists. He held on to the other but let one arm slip free.

Even as she was in fight mode, she never remembered saying no. She was mute in the face of the impending attack that was coming against her body and soul. Her voice froze, but her body remembered. It reacted to the threat she hadn't expected, asked for, nor could comprehend. She reached down with her free hand and palmed him. He groaned in pleasure, and she kept sliding her hand down so he wouldn't realize what she was up to. She slid her hand down to where she could cup his balls through his tight pants. Then, she wrapped her hand around them, yanked them down, and twisted hard. He wasn't expecting it and immediately let her go. She shoved him away with her hands, but he was too big, so she had to bring up her left leg and kick him to the ground.

He lay there writhing and moaning. She was grateful for the pain she put him in. She got into her rental car. He cursed her as she closed the door, trying to crawl closer to her, screaming, "You tease! You teasing bitch! Come back here and finish what you started! I'm going to show you how girls like you should be handled. I'll put you in your place, you slut!"

She slammed her car door, revved the engine, and never looked back, with ice-cold sweat streaming down the channel of her spine, from her neck to the top of her ass. She'd thought she would feel like a hero if she ever had to defend herself. She knew from that moment that it was an empty victory.

She never went out by herself again, and when Emerie was old enough, she'd put her in Krav-Maga. She never wanted her daughter ever to feel defenseless like she had. She'd made it out with no further damage, but she knew she was the minority, especially when intoxicated. She knew she had been a victim that night, and there was no way a child of hers would ever feel that level of helplessness and not have any resources.

Now, in the shower so many years later, she let the memories of that long ago drunken night and the situation from the night before with Francis wash out of her. She'd done healing on this sexual assault as part of her early work in therapy. She didn't have to go into lockdown or drink – which she reminded herself as she grounded herself in hot water, the smell of the hotel shampoo, and the feeling of the washcloth raking her skin. She finished up in the shower and toweled off. She walked through the hotel room naked, letting the sensation of the cool air further soothe her fevered mind. Francis' behavior was his own, and she dialogued with herself to embrace that.

Yes, she had crossed a line with Mattias, but now, seeing what Francis could do, she firmly decided that she was done with her marriage. She did not deserve to be treated that way by anyone and wouldn't continue to be in a relationship with Francis now that he had shown himself capable of physically harming her. She had been through too much. She was too powerful, she now knew, within herself. She had been unhappy in the marriage, but his aggression put the final nail in the coffin.

She retrieved her kit from her suitcase and returned to the bathroom. She looked at herself in the mirror and assessed her middle-aged self. She was tall, with lovely light brown skin that varied in depth. She was not all one color, as the skin that hadn't seen the sun was much lighter. Her arms were strong, and her waist was tight. Her hips had a pleasant roundness to them. She smiled when she thought of the statues of the Mother throughout the ages. They were rounded in the hips to symbolize past, present, and future fertility. All the phases of a woman's body were venerated in Teleosis because each had a distinct creative power for different aspects of the human experience.

The phase of her body now communicated the power of carrying ancient wisdom into the world, and she had nothing to be ashamed of. Her stomach wasn't flat, and she loved her body. It was a living symbol of what she had been through – the highs and lows – more of which were to come. Despite recent events, Francis continually reinforced Inira's already ingrained self-confidence. He'd always spoken about her beauty, his love of her body, in the dark and the light. He'd been physically affectionate and matched his praise with his words.

Her heart constricted in her chest at the thought of him. She leaned forward, bracing her right hand on the counter, and her left hand tried to soothe the cavity in her chest where her heart was. She breathed through the panic. She knew it would pass, but it was hell until it did. Her physical response to her situation made so much sense, so she let it happen. After what felt like several of the most extended moments of her life, the panic did indeed pass. She was tired again and finished her skincare routine with her favorite products that continued to clear her mood—the act of taking care of herself and bringing her into a different frame of mind.

She heard a strange sound as she continued to examine her naked form in the mirror. It took her a few moments to realize it was her phone. It had been charging this whole time and finally came back on. She went over to it, seeing she had missed several texts from Emerie asking if she was okay and a Facetime call from Mattias ringing through.

Holding the phone up to her face, she answered.

Chapter 28

"Good morning, luz de amor, you.........." Mattias suddenly turned red, looked away, and started breathing hard.

Confused, she asked, "Mattias, can we make this quick? I don't feel like talking much, and I'm headed into the office."

It was after 9 am, which was much later than she usually went in. She'd had the mind to text Charlotte last night to tell her she would be late. Let the younger woman think what she would about her night. Charlotte would see her swollen face and know something was wrong when she went in.

When Mattias didn't look back into the screen or answer her, she asked, "What's wrong?"

She had no idea what could be bothering him, and given her exhausted mental state, her irritation spiked. This was not a moment she needed to tend to his emotions, precisely what she would have to do if she was on Facetime with Francis. But this wasn't Francis; this was Mattias Nahas, who spoke up about his issue quickly.

He coughed. "Light Bringer, could you make this an audio call or put the phone down?"

Now, she was thoroughly confused and asked, "Huh? Why?"

He cleared his throat and took a deep breath. "Inira, I'm trying to respect you, but you are making that very difficult right now."

Her frustration spiked. "Mattias, tell me right now what the hell you are talking about! I'm still in a rough emotional space, so we might have to talk later if you don't make things plain to me right now."

He locked his eyes on hers, and they narrowed, but then he started to chuckle. He could tell she was angry, but what in the world was he laughing at? She knew she was being bitchy because she was exhausted and hungry and needed a lot more coffee. He seemed to recognize her tone and kept chucking as he kept his eyes on hers while he said, "My darling light, did you answer the phone naked?"

She felt the blush crawl up her chest straight to her hairline. In her reverie, the privacy of being alone in the room, she'd forgotten to at least wrap a towel around herself before she answered. She'd never had any problem with nudity. In her addled state, she hadn't even thought about it and was now embarrassed. Her embarrassment soon turned to something entirely different when she realized what she was seeing on his face. It was hunger. That woke her up and settled a deep sense of satisfaction. She knew he wanted her, but that molten gaze, proof that he desired her, sent electricity into her at a cellular level.

Still, she didn't make a move to cover herself. She has nothing to be ashamed of or fear from Mattias. Her emotions might be careening all over the place, but this felt a whole lot better than the panic she had been feeling about her marriage. She decided to tell him the truth. She cleared her dry and scratchy throat.

She smiled at him and said, "Yes, but on accident. This wasn't an attempt at seduction, although that would have been much more fun."

He chuckled again and cleared his throat, then said in an incredibly low, husky voice, "Oh, it would be fun, and trust me when I say I've imagined it many times. If that's not what you intend, wear a shirt so I can talk to you. Right now, I can't think straight."

He'd kept his eyes up on her. The tension between them stretched out for a moment far longer than she'd experienced with him to date. She made no move to cover herself for another three breaths. Staring into his eyes, this vulnerable, and seeing him so unguarded in lust gave her a jolt of power she hadn't felt in a long time. Her mind wondered what would happen when she was in front of him again.

She finally broke the spell when she moved towards her suitcase and, as she walked, said in a breathy voice, "Hang on." She turned her camera off and slid on a T-shirt.

When she turned her camera back on, she saw he was smiling. It was a genuine smile, and she could see his perfect teeth. The skin around his eyes pulled together in a most heart-warming way. This was a rare smile. She hadn't seen him give it to anyone else but often saw it when they talked. She could hear it in his voice, too. It communicated something very deep. It made the dormant butterflies in her stomach resurrect in full force.

"Mattias, why are you smiling?"

He let go of a breath he had been holding onto and said, "*Dios esta vivo*. Please let me tell you that you are absolute perfection, any time of day, especially with no makeup and after a horrible night. You glow, *mi vida*. It makes me yearn for the mornings we will spend together."

She felt a little dizzy at the force of his compliment. She felt so unbalanced, so off-kilter. She knew she needed to eat and that he was speaking the truth. She knew what she felt for him and how strong his feelings for her ran. Yet, reality stared her in the face. She never, ever expected to have to betray her family to feel this force of passion again.

She inhaled sharply, trying to keep her wits about her, and replied, "Mattias, let us pause the conversation about our future right now. My present is a disaster. All I can focus on is doing the next right thing. Do you know who sent him the records of our texts?"

His smile dropped then. "Unfortunately, I do not. Whoever did this covered their tracks exceptionally well, using a professional hacker who came in from the outside. Only 3-4 people on the planet could do that, and we know all of them. I have Ahmadi rooting out the person with our security team. I will find out who compromised us because they wanted to hurt you. You do not deserve that, Light Bringer."

She knew he would find out. He would not stop until he did. He was skilled at pursuing a goal to the very end. She sighed and laid back on the bed, rolling onto her side and propping the camera up to face her. "I know you will, Mattias, thank you. I need to get dressed to go into the office. I'll live out of this hotel room until I see you next week."

He smiled again, this time in delight. "Oh, *Luz de amor*, you aren't coming next week."

She hadn't expected this response and asked, a little shell-shocked. "What? What do you mean?"

He scrubbed his hands through his hair, a sign of expelling stress, but stayed calm. "You told me last night to take care of you. To bring you home. So, I am coming to get you today."

She was stunned. "What do you mean?"

He knitted his brows. "Do you not remember last night? You asked me to bring you home, and I would never leave you distressed. I will always come for you. My jet is being fueled as we speak. We take off in an hour. I'll see you this evening. Ahmadi will email you how to get to the airport, where I'll be waiting."

She couldn't speak. She was floored. She clearly did not remember agreeing to go with Mattias. She remembered falling asleep, but not what they had discussed right before that. Inira had only been that exhausted one other time in her life.

It was her turn to run a hand through her hair. "But wait, this afternoon? I have to go into the office. I have to prepare Charlotte and get ready for our meeting."

"*Amor*, the meeting was only a pretense. We don't need it now. Lukas and Charlotte have been informed and will continue to work together. They have the project in hand after a month of your guidance. You have done very well, *Amor*. What matters now is that you are cared for, and no one better to do that than me. I want you with me and have the means. I'm not waiting a week."

She laughed softly, somewhat distractedly. "No, a man like you wouldn't, would he?"

He'd switched into business mode, taking charge and control. This is the kind of movement he excelled at – getting things done. It was one of the reasons she was attracted to him; he was so decisive. She felt a little hysterical like she was floating, like her soul had left her body and some strange possession had occurred. She would be leaving. Today, with Mattias, if she chose to. The resurgence of her will came back to her full force. That idea of choice grounded her back. She had learned to take it when she could because she'd only had the illusion of it for so long. Her head swam, and she knew she needed more coffee as she asked, "Wait, I don't get a say in this?"

Mattias sighed patiently, knowing she would wrangle with him and how tired she was once she woke up. "My darling, you agreed last night when you said you would let me take care of everything. And I will. We will be together, and we can begin our new life and see this vision through, starting today. I'm no longer waiting for you or what's to come."

In her overwrought emotional state last night, she'd given him leave to do just that. Whether it felt inconsequential, every decision came with a price tag. She was split now, between feeling embarrassed she had given in so quickly and relief she didn't have to decide anything. Her ride on her emotional roller coaster didn't seem to be ending any time soon.

Still floating, she felt the fight leave her. She knew she would fight Francis, and he'd already assumed she was with him, but that's not why she agreed. She didn't want to fight Mattias. She wanted someone strong to care for her. She wanted to see the vision come to pass, and Mattias was passionate and meant to do it with her. He wanted to do it exclusively with her.

She had her Consort she'd longed for after what felt like such a long time in the desert. The oasis would come to her.

"Alright Mattias. I'll see you soon. I need to touch you. I draw from your strength. I feel so tired, *Ahava*."

The look on his face radiated a strange sense of power that would move heaven and earth to achieve his desires. This is what he lived for and what she'd longed for, and it would start today. Her life had changed completely when those bombs went off and again when she came to the States. Now, it would take another radical turn, and it was all she could do to hang on for the ride.

"*Luz de amor*, when I get you in my arms this time, I will bring the stars down to you without ever letting you go. I told you that you were always meant to be mine, but I know now that I am yours. We will do this together or not at all. I will see you in a few hours; get some rest."

This must be what fate feels like, she thought as she ended the call, and then her body cratered again. She wanted this. She wanted him. She didn't know if that made her weak or strong. She didn't know how to explain it to anyone, so she decided to wait. She had always been available with answers for everyone else. So, for now, she wouldn't answer to anyone.

For just a little while, she would keep something for herself. She could let everyone know where she was in a few days once she felt more restored. It seemed selfish, but after last night, she knew she could let go of the compulsive need to make everyone else comfortable. She would stay in contact with Emerie but discard the false image of the perfect wife, mother, and caretaker to everyone else.

That false image was not what the High Priestess was born to do. The High Priestess was born to ensure the mission of Teleosis continued. That didn't always look pretty or fit into a neat box. High Priestesses of other eras had done what was necessary to keep the mission going. They had sung the Song of Creation without reservation or hesitation and in defense of the world's people, whether they knew it or not.

She had that power within her, too. She would learn to sing and teach the Song of Creation to Emerie. Some way, somehow, the vision of Teleosis would continue. It was now up to her to figure out what that meant and how to do it. She would. It may not be the way of the pious, the moralists. She even felt that by choosing to do this with her, Mattias was also choosing a different path. They were both about to start living in an alternate reality. They would be exercising a power no one had touched in generations.

She wondered if perhaps this was the path the FourFold God had been leading her down all along. Maybe the foundation of Teleosis had crumbled to be rebuilt on Truth and Love.

Every religion has martyrs, and perhaps I'm the last living one, she thought suddenly. She had been done with the FourFold God for so long that it felt random; something like that would come to her now. Now that she was on the brink of living into her calling in a radically different way than she had ever anticipated, This was like no other time in history, especially Teleosian history. Perhaps Teleosis needed a different kind of High Priestess. It was time for her to step out of the shadows and into the light, empowered by the Mother, the Father, the Daughter, and the Son. All combined and all together – as their vessels united to do the same.

An old prayer of release, a prayer for liberty, came to her.

Where can I feel from Your Presence? Where can I go from Your Spirit? If I go to the depths of hell, You are there.

If the old prayer were true, the FourFold God would meet her wherever she went – even to hell. They would help her usher in this new reality. She wouldn't hide. She wouldn't cower. She wouldn't numb. She would let herself be found. She felt anticipation for the first time in a long time, like a little girl watching the sunrise. She felt possibility. It was born out of something terrible, out of her desire to be loved the way she deserved to be and to grasp a future that had been ripped out of her hands. This anticipation didn't feel innocent or pure like it used to. This anticipation had a shadow side, one that could swallow her whole. Mattias called her Light Bringer. The truth of the light was that you could only truly see its brightness when the dark was its deepest.

Chapter 29

After taking a nap and eating, she called Stanley to let him know what was happening, but he didn't pick up. That was odd and concerned her a little bit. They had been partners at Triune for so long that he'd not picked up her call. She left a voicemail and knew she would call him again when she got to London. She opened her email app to send Charlotte a message, officially saying she would be away. Then, she reviewed the message from Ahmadi with Mattias' arrival schedule details.

She desperately hoped Ahmadi would not be traveling with Mattias. He didn't say he was, but his second was so slippery. If he found a reason to accompany his Deitas, he would. Ahmadi made her feel like her teeth were in pain, like she'd been sucking on sour grapes. She sensed something was wrong with him even as she was sure he kept his tracks squeaky clean. He had always been cordial and respectful, even though she felt he would prefer she didn't exist.

Just then, her phone pinged with a text from Mattias:

My love light, I'm about to take off. Take care today, rest up. I am coming out of my skin to get to you. I've already charged your room and anything else you want to my account. Also, use the account number, which is included, for everything. I am meant to provide for you. Amin sent everything you will need until I get you in my arms. Soy todo tuyo, luz de amor.

Inira sighed from deep in her soul. That she didn't have to charge anything to her credit card, which Francis would eventually see, made her relax. She could disappear. She could get lost in what they needed to do now. She could leave behind the person every-one thought she was supposed to be and decide who she would be going forward. It made her head swim. She then ordered half of the room service breakfast menu. As she waited, she got some more coffee and laid back down. Her body was still screaming at her from the assault of so much adrenaline. Her throat was raw. She got a washcloth, which she soaked in cold water to lay over her eyes.

Now that she had decided to pursue the resurrection of her cul-ture with Mattias at her side, she drifted off in that floating feeling again. The cold compress lulled her. She didn't think of anything; her mind didn't race. It was an unusual feeling, as usually, her thoughts went a million different directions, trying to keep all the trains of her life running on time. Now, she released herself into the feeling of nothing and no one.

She must have dozed off because the knock on the door startled her. She might need to sleep for a week after the events of the last twenty-four hours. She was so full after she finished, she decided to go downstairs and walk on the treadmill for a while. She popped her earbuds in and just walked, feeling the lactic acid move out of her muscles with each step. The movement of her feet made her mind wander, and her soul dreamed of what was to come – how she would finally fulfill her destiny.

Her hour on the treadmill left her feeling relieved. She stretched a bit, then went upstairs and took another shower, using all her personal products. When she got out, she went through her top-to-bottom routine and sorted through her suitcase. She went for comfort with a hint of style in her jeans and a white t-shirt. Later, she would finish the outfit with gold hoops and a jewel-tone light-weight jacket. This made the day pass quickly, and the time to leave to meet Mattias suddenly arrived.

As she was walking out the door, a glint of metal caught her eye – her white gold wedding band. She stared at it for a long time. It was a part of her, having worn it without ever taking it off for twenty years. Francis made it clear it was over, and she had made her choice. She would never let anyone treat her that way again. The silence stretched as she stared at it. She took it off and immediately put it back on. She put on hand cream, still staring at her hand. She couldn't take her eyes off of it. Her mind, so empty that just a few hours ago, swirled with words and ideas, bursting forth like Athena. Her chest felt tight and constricted her breath. She closed her eyes and worked through the rising tide of panic.

The panic ran through her without abating for an extended period. She finally came back to herself with the pounding of her heart. She was still staring at her hand. Her panic flowed out of her like run-off after a summer storm. She dragged her gaze away from the fourth finger on her left hand to look at her watch. It was time to check out and find her way to the airport where Mattias would land.

It was time to decide her future. At that moment, she knew the truth of what she'd already chosen, what she had been chosen for.

She breathed in.

She breathed out.

Without another questioning thought, she removed her wedding ring and left it on the nightstand in the hotel room. She turned towards the window, closing her eyes to try and absorb strength from the sunlight. It was weak, filtering through the thick hotel glass, but she felt a warm caress of the FourFold God on her skin. Turning away, she let herself move into action. She grabbed her bags, and as the hotel door snicked closed behind her, she felt lighter. It could have been in her imagination; the ring weighed only a few ounces. Yet emotions carried weight, too. Inira left the ring in that hotel room, moving into a future she'd chosen without the press of society and the expectations of others on her shoulders.

It felt like the first day of the rest of her life. The gaping wound the break with her family had caused wasn't bleeding anymore. Hopefully, it had begun to close up and heal on its own.

***

All he could think about was her. Knowing they had been compromised and how badly her husband had treated her infuriat-
ed him. He was going to her no matter what. She had become
his sole focus. Her gentle soul, combined with her strength like
steel, was showing him that all work and no play was not a
satisfying life. Her view of the world had been growing in him
steadily for the last month, and no one had ever had this effect
on him. It had been an obsession for so long, but it wasn't that
because obsessions are fantasy.

Mattias Nahas, the man who had everything, had something
real now. He wanted to taste and see the goodness in the world
like she could. It was an undeniable force that propelled her,
and if he could give her back what she'd lost, he would sell his
soul to do it. Beyond that, getting to her, wrapping her up in
his arms, and carrying her onto the plane was his sole focus.
Nothing else mattered right now. Because of him – and their
decision to partner – her life had blown up. Before he met her,
he knew there was a distinct possibility her life would have to
be blown up again to get her on board.

He hadn't cared at the time because he wouldn't have imagined
himself to be the trigger man this time around.

The original plan had radically altered. He was hopelessly in
love with her and wanted to make sure the vision of Teleosis
came to fruition once again. He was still reconciling his past
and how he had played such a significant part in the destruction
of her life. He would never stop trying to make up for it now
that he knew her. Now that he knew how off – how wrong- he
and the Serpents – had been all long.

He had adored his brother Tomas. When he found out about him,
he couldn't help himself from finding him and contacting him. He
knew about the greed that had infected the Counsel and High
Priestess role. It took many months of conversations – primarily
by email – to convince him to join their cause. Tomas was the
cool, logical, levelheaded one. He saw the need for change and
looked to Mattias to create the plan to make it happen. They hadn't
had much time together, only discovering each other late into

adolescence. Yet, they did; it was as if Mattias finally felt whole and now had a family in the Serpents.

Mattias was the true orphan, left on his own at the age of five when their mother died. She had given Tomas up at birth, leaving him to be adopted by a family in Teleosis. But she'd refused to give up both, even though it meant a life of squalor for him. He'd had no one till the day the Serpents found him. During that first phone call with Tomas, they were instantly bonded. They had looked into their parentage together, discovering they were the illegitimate sons of the mafia boss in Caracas. He'd come to their small town to escape his dirty dealings. Mattias' mother had been one of his servants – practically an economic slave, and their father had taken what he wanted.

His father had lived and died steeped in the folklore of the capitalistic myth. Mattias hadn't known him but had inherited his money-making gifts. Their father invested in the local chapter of the Serpents. Their aim, which went over well with the poor in Caracas, was 'take what you want and don't look back.' After growing up on the streets, Mattias immediately embraced that as his life's mission. The Serpents legitimized him, sending him to school in Europe, in large part thanks to his father's drug cartel money.

He'd gotten the best education because the Serpent leadership saw him as their best chance for public domination. Between his looks, charisma, and skills in Global Finance, they had no problem backing him when he started Nahas Industries. He was dedicated to the mission. They'd poured their resources in, and Mattias conquered territory no sovereign nation ever could. Every government on earth was in their pocket. Those politicians needed what Nahas had to continue to thrive: the material weapons and the economic ones. They used them as much against their people as they did against other foreign powers. Nahas specialized in keeping the caste system evolving so that the few that remained in power stayed there.

It was the way of the Serpent. *Self is the only way.*

Tomas wasn't thought of highly when he was recruited – through Mattias. Leadership had doubted him right up till he pressed the button. Tomas had loved the purity of the Teleosis mission. He had just hated how corrupt and hypocritical the ruling Counsel was. There was no prominent caste system, but Inira's mother – the Counsel – and their recent ancestors had squirreled enough financial and informational treasure away to compete and stay alive. Tomas believed that was what was wrong with Teleosis. It was why he agreed to betray everything he loved, including Inira. He thought she would be better off being out of that system.

Mattias was not so altruistic. He had wanted her for himself because he wanted to control the last living tie to the Teleosian way and their technology. He hadn't ever thought about a romantic connection with her, even if bedding her would seal her commitment. Since Lukas' mother, he'd only ever used women – and very infrequently – when his physical needs were overwhelming. Now, he wanted every piece of her – mind, body, and soul. She was everything he never knew he wanted in a woman, and because of her, everything he believed in and had fought for was shifting.

Everything he thought he stood for and fought for, he realized, had been shifting, and Inira was the glue to hold it all together.

Her softness, compassion, style, and heart for truth and goodness captivated him. He had been hooked since he first heard her speak. He'd known everything about her for years, every detail of her life. Yet, he did not know her, and when he did, he understood Tomas' deep commitment to keeping her safe. She was special, unique, and made to rule the world.

He would make sure she did, right by his side.

Ahmadi, ever his shadow, continued to talk to him, even as he knew Mattias wasn't listening; indeed, he hadn't been listening to him for days. Ahmadi's impatience and disdain for the shift in their plans began to show. He was talking about their itinerary for the coming weeks when they would go back to Tov to do a walkthrough of the progress on rebuilding and show Inira. Ahmadi only knew two options: coerce or force her to give them the Song of Creation.

Mattias knew differently now, and Ahmadi was still in disbelief that this was the best way.

Amin Ahmadi prattled on contracts, project statuses, and the installation date of the new stained-glass ceiling in the temple. He would occasionally pepper his work reports with subtle comments about the secrets they were trying to mine from the culture they had both had a hand in destroying. An idea hit Mattias suddenly, and it made him break his silence. "The stained glass goes in this week in the Temple, you say?"

Ahmadi looked startled by his boss' voice and question. He didn't think Mattias heard a word he said. "Yes, Deitas, that is what I reported. How can this information serve you?"

Whenever he noticed Amin saying 'Deitas' since he had met Inira, his voice had the barest hint of mockery. He had called him on it before, but the condescension was pouring from him now. He knew Ahmadi didn't like Inira, but he also knew this man to be spineless. He grew irritated at his subtle manipulations, all communicated by clearing a throat or a shift in his tone.

Mattias snapped at him, "Get that tone out of your voice, Amin. I'm sick of it. We might have known each other for over thirty years, but I am still your boss."

The smaller man dipped his head in reverence, sliding back into his subservient mask. He was the viper in a pit of snakes. Mattias continued, "Move the scheduled walkthrough up to the end of this week and put a rush on the Temple ceiling installation. I will join you when Inira and I are ready, but we will need time alone together so I can get her up to speed on the project."

This time, the barest flex of Ahmadi's jaw tipped Mattias off to his irritation. Mattias knew Amin thought Inira was just another woman. Their whole ideology was based on tiers of power; for Mattias to change things suddenly sent shockwaves through the Serpent leadership. Lukas had reported as much to his father. Amin hadn't said a word about any concerning unrest, but he knew the man's goal was to accomplish their plan above all else.

Mattias continued speaking, barreling ahead with Ahmadi taking notes, "This is just how it must be. She is crucial to our success in obtaining the technology. You know that as well as I do. You were there when Tomas revealed the source of their power. She has to give it and willingly is the goal. If she and I are together, that will likely happen."

The lie was sour in Mattias' mouth. He wouldn't be using Inira to do anything, but he hadn't yet figured out a way to extract himself from the Serpents that didn't put her at risk. Now, when the leak of their text conversations, he knew the mole was close.

Ahmadi stared at Mattias with unreadable eyes, even as his head nodded in agreement. "Yes, that is exactly the plan we need to have happen. I am glad we have found a way to get her consent. It's only the one issue, though, with Ms. Boehme."

Mattias gripped the arms of his plane seat and took a deep breath. "You mean the issue that she is a woman? Yes, I realize that is difficult for many to accept. Yet, times are changing, and we are close to our goal. She is an invaluable asset; everyone will see that in time."

Ahmadi acquiesced, but Mattias could feel the disagreement roll off of him. Ahmadi had made his way up on Mattias' coattails, and his apathy towards women made him seem invisible to most outside the organization. Mattias had never once seen him with anyone – man or woman. The ones who screamed in the streets got the notice, not the ones who spent their whole life in the shadows. When it came down to the structure of the Serpents, Mattias was the unchallenged and unquestionable leader. His word was law, so he would change their laws if he had come to a new understanding of the benefit of having Inira by his side and what they could accomplish together.

In the moment's silence, Mattias played his hand, "I am not making any changes regarding a woman's role in our plans overall. They are still, as a gender, not our equals. What I need you to grasp is that Inira is the one who stands out. I will make it if I have to adjust things to accommodate her – not all women – but her."

Mattias wasn't sure how his feelings about the capacity of all women had changed, but working with Inira had made the foundation of his convictions turn into quicksand. If things continued to trend, he would probably be wrestling with changes to his belief set for the rest of his life, gender roles being the tip of the iceberg.

Ahmadi looked at Mattias like he hadn't seen him before and was now getting a glimpse of something new. "I see this woman has had a remarkable effect on you in such a short period." Bowing his head in submission, again, he was like a dog showing his belly to his master. "I see now, Deitas. Yes, I will ensure our plans and the Serpents move forward." This was Ahmadi's way of calling out Mattias' feelings. It was the most direct he ever got. He thought he had caught something off about Ahmadi's response, like he was agreeing and playing his part, but there was more to it than that. The words Ahmadi used were right, but for the first time in their decades together, they sounded wrong coming out of Amin's mouth.

Mattias changed the subject as they were landing. He pointed at Ahmadi, "Find out who leaked the information about our texts to her husband, or your head will be on a spike if you don't know by the time I see you next." It might also be Inira's soon-to-be ex-husband's head on the spike for how he treated her. It made him want to use his fists to settle the score like he used to do on the streets of Caracas.

Amin would be departing to visit their US headquarters, and Mattias wanted him gone before Inira boarded. He had one flight attendant for this leg of the trip, but he wanted only the pilot and co-pilot once he was with her. He looked up to dismiss his second in command but saw the man had already disappeared like a ghost.

He could see the Rolls Royce she waited in on the runway from the window. A long-forgotten feeling came over him. He suddenly felt incredibly nervous. For a man who commanded a global empire and the fastest-growing religion in the West, that one woman could weaken him was a new feeling. As the plane made the short taxi, Inira got out. His breath left him. She was dressed casually, in jeans, a t-shirt, and a jacket. He couldn't see her eyes; she wore sunglasses against the glare. Her hair was blowing around wild;

she had left it natural, which meant soft, loose curls he couldn't wait to run his fingers through. He'd seen her on Facetime over the last few weeks, even late at night without makeup on, and he loved every second, but she was almost always sad. Looking at her now, her whole posture had changed. She looked at ease and ready. He did not think he could wait another second to go to her.

The second the stairs were lowered, Mattias practically jumped down. She smiled at him, wider and happier than he'd ever seen. And then she was in his arms, and he was lifting her against him. She was tall compared to other women, and he loved that she looked directly into his face. She fit perfectly with him like she was molded to fit precisely against him. He could hear her soft giggles and sighs as he buried his face in her hair and whispered soft words of love and adoration in Spanish against the breeze. He held her tight for a long time. He felt like he would never be able to let go. She squirmed a little, and Mattias pulled back and looked into her milk chocolate eyes. Her sunglasses had come off at some point during their extended embrace. He gently threaded his right hand through her curls, tilting her nose to meet his. He pressed his other hand into the small of her back so she was flush against him. They were closer than they'd ever been.

He didn't ask permission to kiss her, but he moved slowly enough for her to stop him. She didn't. Her mouth was eager and ready for his when he brought his lips down. They lost themselves as if no one else in the world existed. Mattias' mind was utterly blank, and all that existed was this moment with her. He had been longed for her for weeks, and now the deal was done. Her lips completed him.

She was perfection and had no idea how she'd captivated him. He would tell her how everything had changed. He could trust her. His true north had shifted. It was her. He knew he wasn't worthy of her, and as they broke their kiss and he looked again into her eyes, he said the words he would say to her with his dying breath.

"I will give it all back and more, Light Bringer. I will be worthy of you. I will do whatever it takes to have your trust and a place by your side." Her beaming smile lit up his heart, and then they were lost to another kiss for a long time.

Chapter 30

T here is no tomorrow. There is no yesterday. There is only this moment. And Love opens the way.

The childhood chant bubbled in her soul as she and Mattias boarded the plane. It made her giggle with unrestrained joy because it encompassed everything she felt. She couldn't stop smiling at the over-the-top romance of his greeting. He had jumped out of an airplane and swept her off her feet. The sweetness of their first kiss tempered the anguish of the last 24 hours.

Mattias was fully elemental, so different from his brother and her husband. It was in the way he acted and moved. He had changed. He used to stalk, and now he strode. He opened up to her because she had opened up to him. It was what was always preached in Teleosis – the red thread through all the sacred texts. Love will change the world. It was happening before her eyes, and even her doubts and disbelief began to disappear as she witnessed his transformation. All that fire and drive to own everything and everyone was morphing into devotion. Her love and femininity opened him up to who he was created to be.

With only the cockpit crew, Mattias prepared everything for them. He handed her a glass of her favorite type of sparkling water with a slice of strawberry. The food was all her Mediterranean favorites. He had thought of everything. And, of course, his plane was gorgeous. She'd never seen such luxury. The seats were the softest leather she'd ever touched. There was an uncomfortable moment when he gave her a plane tour, and they came to the bedroom. There was only one bed, of course.

He noticed she was shifting on her feet with uncertainty, so he quickly told her, "The room is yours, and I will sleep on the couch, my love. We do not have to rush. I want you for the rest of our lives together, so I will not pressure you. You know how much I want you, but I will not make you move faster than you are ready."

Inira reached up to put one hand on the side of his face, with the other stroking the back of his hair like he had done to her a few moments before on the tarmac. She looked full into his face, stretching up to press her lips to his in a soft gesture of gratitude. She didn't know when she would be ready to be intimate with him, but she was not ashamed of her desire for him. She knew it was her choice and that he was validating that made her feel that much safer. She knew their coming together was inevitable. She wanted to be in the headspace for it.

The High Priestess and her Consort opened spiritual portals of blessing and illumination with their sexual intimacy. It had helped guide them through the ages. Sex was sacred and holy, and when a woman chose to be with a man, it was meant to usher in a season of joy. Sex was meant for pleasure, fun, as well as growth in intimacy. It was given to humanity out of the FourFold God's delight, to reflect a greater expression of Love the FourFold God had for all of Creation.

Sex was taken seriously because of what it did between two people and how that rippled through the greater whole. It wasn't repressed or oppressed. Sexuality and a delightful sex life for both partners were taught as part of the education of children. It was a big perk with Tomas, but it had been so different when she came to the States. She was so much more experienced in the ways of bringing a man pleasure. She'd had to teach Francis much about her body and how to make it enjoyable. Inira looked forward to seeing how it would be with Mattias, as he was so focused on her happiness now.

"Where are we going, *Ahava otsar*?" She spoke softly while looking into his emerald ocean eyes.

They were still nose to nose. His hands were clasped behind her back, holding her to him. He radiated heat, and it warmed the ice that had stayed in the pit of her belly since Francis had confronted her.

He leaned down into her neck and inhaled deeply before he said, "That's a new name. Tell me what it means, and I'll tell you where we are going."

She smiled, with her cheek now pressed against his neck. She turned her head to breathe in his ear, "It means 'love treasure.' I thought if you were going to try and use different languages to find my nickname, I would do the same."

She could feel him smiling and continued to whisper into his ear. "You are a treasure, Mattias. Hidden from me for so long. I want to uncover more."

He shivered and looked into her eyes, saying, "I am laid bare and open before you, *luz de amor*. I cannot hide anything from you. We are going to Santorini for a few days, and then I will take you home."

"Santorini? We used to visit there on vacations when I was little, did you know that? It was so close to Teleosis, just a few nautical miles away. Thank you, *Ahava otsar*! It already feels like I am on my way home, even though I don't have a home to return to now." She smiled again, this time with tears in her eyes. The pilot interrupted their embrace, letting them know they were ready to take off and they would need to get strapped in.

Mattias took her hand as they turned back to the seating area. He paused as he rubbed his thumb over her ring finger. He stopped and looked at her face, questioning.

She answered his silent question, "I took it off, Mattias. I may not be legally free, but I am free in my heart. I still love Francis, and I always will. And I chose to come with you to make myself available to you without hindrance. It was my decision to make, so I did."

He looked down at the floor, and she realized he now had tears in her eyes. He didn't say anything as they sat down next to each other. He put her to his left, in the window seat. As the plane started to taxi out, they were holding hands – now her right and his left. She felt no need to say anything that would dispel the moment's magic. A verse from the Jewish scriptures came to her mind, and she closed her eyes with her head back on the soft headrest to revel in it.

Ani le do di ve do di li. After a moment, she whispered it out loud.

She felt him lean over, and his breath tickled her neck. "What does it mean, *querida?*"

She turned to face him, looking again into his eyes. She felt like those eyes had a gravitational force to them. She translated, "My beloved is mine, and I am his."

The plane's wheels left the earth then, and Inira felt her soul take flight. Their lips met in an open-mouth kiss. It wasn't urgent; it wasn't hurried. They stayed in that kiss for what felt like hours. Everything fell away, and it was only the two of them, even more so than on the tarmac. It was a transcendent experience, blessed by the Divine.

This was how she'd felt when she experienced the creation moment in that dream. Full of possibility, full of potential – full. Complete. Whole. She never thought she would feel that way after Tomas. Francis was close for a while, but this with Mattias even outstripped them both. It was grounded in a spiritual, charismatic experience that she wondered if this was what it felt like to be plugged in completely to the FourFold God.

Eventually, they broke the kiss to eat dinner, Mattias preparing it. After they ate, they settled down to read until she got sleepy. Mattias showed her to the bedroom and the custom pajama set he had made for her – with her initials above the left chest pocket. They weren't silk, but the softest fabric – maybe wool – she'd ever felt. They fit perfectly, and his smile broke his face when she exited the bathroom after getting ready for bed.

He was in his pair of sleep pants of the same material but dark gray, whereas hers were an amethyst color that set off her skin, hair, and eyes. He wore a dark gray T-shirt. She was glad he wasn't shirtless as much as she wanted to see him uncovered. She wasn't sure she wanted their first time on an airplane, but she wouldn't have been able to stop herself if he had been bare-chested.

"You are lovely, Inira. This may be my favorite way to see you, just for me. Are you ready to sleep? We still have about seven hours till we land."

"I was, but now I'm awake. How about we lie down and watch a movie? Is it too much for you to lie down with me till I fall asleep?"

He shook his hand no and said, "I just want to be close to you."

He crawled under the covers with her, and she fell asleep with her ear to his chest.

They slept, wrapped up in each other. She woke to the captain's voice on the intercom, alerting them to their descent. Her hip told her she'd been on it too long. Mattias's hand had found her way to the inside of her sleep shirt, one of the lower buttons undone. She smiled. She loved this feeling of waking up with him. Mattias woke up slowly; she hadn't realized how deeply he'd slept. She got up to get ready and gave him privacy to do so. It didn't take him long before he knocked on the bathroom door. She was already dressed, having changed into a casual tiered dress in navy with sandals and her hair up. She wore the same good hoops, her favorite, and chose blush and mascara.

He wore a white button-down dress shirt – no tie- and navy European cut pants with a brown suede belt and matching loafers. He looked like he'd stepped out of a magazine. She opened the door, and he looked her up and down. "Perfection, again. Here's your coffee." She sipped; it was espresso, just how she liked it. Scorching hot, dark, and it burned all the way down. She drank as they landed.

"Thank you, *otsar*, you seem to know everything about what I like. Will you teach me what you do?"

He offered her his arm and let him walk her through to the seating area, down the staircase into the gorgeous Santorini sunset, where a car awaited them. They took a ten-minute drive to the other side of the island to a private house on the beach. They were utterly secluded. Inira didn't know how long they would stay, but it would be heavenly while they did. As they drove, he began to tell her about his life. He didn't stop talking for hours, as if he had been waiting for someone to listen. So she did. Only later did she start asking questions. It turns out questions weren't something Mattias Nahas was used to answering.

***

Amin knew he had to take decisive action before all his work under the auspice of following Mattias Nahas to the top was undone. He had taken a few hours to think through how to adjust his plans to suit this new information while ensuring they seemed on the side of the Deitas. He didn't need to play his hand too soon.

As venerated as the Deitas was, he had become dangerously distracted. Dangerously so, by a woman no less. Women had their uses but were a means to an end, and the Boehme woman was no different. She was beautiful, kind, and a powerful speaker. These were all things that would help the Serpents continue in their quest to access the Song of Creation. Her use was for the Serpent's ascension to the top of the world's power games, not to recreate her civilization. Inira Boehme was the last piece of the decades-long puzzle he had been putting together, utilizing the might and money of Nahas Industries.

No one needed to fall in love with a Boehme, though.

Mattias clearly had. That was bad enough. Yet, there was still another Nahas man to meet a Boehme woman, and if she was at all like her mother, Lukas didn't stand a chance. That required making sure this boy was fortified. He needed a pep talk, and he needed it now. They were both in the States to execute what Lukas thought was his father's plan.

Ahmadi set a meeting with the younger man, making sure it was in Lukas' office. Ahmadi had to seem accommodating, and by coming to Lukas, which would help with the image he had cultivated for years – the fealty he had pledged to Mattias when they were boys was still in effect. Like the Boehme women, Lukas was only here because he was useful to Amin's plans. Ahmadi's challenge had always been to make the boy feel important. It was how he had won Mattias's trust by staying with the image of essentially Lukas's godfather. It ensured all plans moved forward as they should under Ahmadi's direction. Mattias Nahas may function as the literal representation of their god on earth, but Amin knew just how human he was. He and Inira couldn't have children. Mattias had gotten a vasectomy after the unexpected pregnancy that resulted in Lukas, and Inira was past her child-bearing years without heavy medical influence.

Mattias didn't know this, but Inira was only good for one thing.

It was Lukas and Emerie they needed now—the next generation to carry on the lineage and mission of the Serpents. Teleosis was long gone and would stay that way. The Song of Creation needed blood to be activated and a Heir to continue to work effectively. Lukas and Emerie were essential to the future.

Ahmadi, focused and driven, rapped softly on the door. "Good Afternoon, Lukas. May I come in?" Amin was shorter than the young man and tried to use that to his advantage. No one would suspect the kindly uncle figure.

Lukas looked up from his laptop and sighed. "Is this going to be a long conversation, Amin?"

Ahmadi stiffened slightly at the apparent disrespect but played it off as a bad back. He was not used to hearing such a dismissive tone from the boy. "I came by to see how you were faring with your plans. Is there anything I can do to help?"

Lukas looked at him, sitting against his chair and folding his arms over his chest. He was looking over Ahmadi in a way that made him want to shift on his feet. He didn't, of course. He had many hours of training in boarding school, standing still and always towards the back of the room, which had served him well over the years.

However, Ahmadi had lived so long in making sure people didn't notice him, so the intense gaze was unnerving. He took the time to look back at the boy, close to his mid-twenties now. He was tall and powerfully built like his father but with softer features from his Korean mother. He was handsome, and his gaze sharp. Ahmadi realized he should keep his eye on the boy. He seemed to be turning into a man who pays attention to what's happening around him.

After a few more long beats, Lukas replied, "My portion of the plan is coming together."

Ahmadi put his hands together in delight, "Excellent! I knew you were far more capable than your father let on. The Charlotte Woman is making introductions now that her mother is unavailable?"

Lukas didn't move a muscle but replied, "So, my potential love life is what you came to talk to me about?" He unfolded his arms and waved with one of his hands—that annoyed Ahmadi.

Well, then they would dispense with pleasantries and get down to business. "The timeline has sped up to obtain the Heir."

That seemed to light a fire under the boy, finally. Lukas pushed forward in his chair, elbows bracing on the desk. "What do you mean the timeline has sped up? When and who made this decision?"

Ahmadi tilted his head and looked at the younger man. "Godson, I would have expected you to have been briefed as I was."

This was Ahmadi's favorite game, to pit Lukas and Mattias against each other, keeping their relationship off balance so that they never entirely made peace or agreement. It was one more way he destabilized Mattias' regime so that Ahmadi could oust him and take over once the Song of Creation was firmly in grasp.

Lukas continued to push back, "Wait, I thought we had at least another month. My Father said there was no way the reconstruction efforts would be ready until then."

Ahmadi steepled his fingers under his chin. He had purposefully been lying to Lukas about the status of the rebuild. Lukas had been so preoccupied with trying to get on that Charlotte woman's good side, to get an introduction to Emerie Boehme, he hadn't questioned it. Ahmadi wondered if he also wasn't trying to get the woman into bed, but his sources said Lukas had been making very little headway on either front. "Things have been progressing faster than expected. The Temple is nearly rebuilt, and we will meet your father in Tov, on Teleosian soil, on Saturday, with all players in attendance."

Incredulous, Lukas stared. "Saturday? How am I supposed to talk the Heir into coming with me and flying halfway across the world in 72 hours? This is impossible! I knew you were a righteous bastard, but this seals the deal. You could have given me plenty of warnings about this, but you are a slippery bastard. Now, you expect me to backtrack. You expect me to pull off what is impossible."

Amin Ahmadi chuckled drily. "Not me, dear boy, but your father. He is with Inira Boehme at the Santorini house as we speak. Now, we need you to come through on your part. Secure Emerie Boehme by any means necessary and have her in Tov on Saturday."

He knew Lukas had suspicions about his intentions, which was more or less the purpose of this little office chat. He wouldn't let the mask of the kindly uncle slip, though. "Lukas, darling boy, you are the son of the Deitas. You are the second in line to the largest company in the world and the fastest-growing global religion. The Serpents look to you to be the reigns from your father. There were indeed seemingly impossible feats your father had to pull off to prove he was worthy of moving up the ranks. This is your chance to prove your commitment and dedication to the cause. You are so capable. She's just a girl, after all."

He knew this was a dangerous card to play as Lukas had always been on the fence, especially regarding their methods of achieving what they wanted. His generation also didn't necessarily share the views on women as their predecessors. They had grown up in a different world. But it didn't matter now. Lukas needed to do his job and knew he had to stay in his father's good graces. Or so he thought. Ahmadi couldn't remember the last time Mattias and Lukas had a conversation. He had to get the Heir to accompany him to Teleosis so Amin could ensure the ceremony happened before the Deitas could change more than he already had.

Lukas' face was bright red. "You always do this – question my loyalty. Like I haven't worked my entire life for my father's favor. Even now, I'm not sure this will get him to give it to me or make sure the Serpents follow me. For all I know, this could be your ploy – a coup to take over finally. You've probably smelled blood in the water. I see what's happening with my father and Inira. And if things have changed, I know it won't be you who tells me. You have an agenda that sometimes works with my father's and the Serpents but always hides your real intentions."

Amin Ahmadi smiled at that and started to head out the door. "It's always been that way, young pup. That is the essence of who we are, who I have always been. *Uno mismo es la única manera* after all. See you Saturday with Emerie."

It was always satisfying that his plans were moving forward, and he was able to add some misdirection to the mix. Keeping Lukas and Mattias at loggerheads made exerting his own will with the staff and underlings much easier. No one ever suspected a garden snake was a cobra till it raised its head and struck. When he returned to his office, Amin called the head of operations in Tov to get a daily update on their progress in clearing out the temple's ruins. It needed to be ready for the ceremony.

Chapter 31

The time with Mattias in Santorini was nothing short of magical.

He had told her they would make the most of their seventy-two hours here before their next destination. He kept saying home but was never specific about where that was. He said he wanted to surprise her. The first day, they did everything they wanted. Water, especially the ocean, had always restored Inira's spirits. It was being in the essence of the Mother's heart. It could be wild, untamable, and then calm and healing. The blue of the southern Aegean spoke serenity to Inira's weary heart and soul.

Mattias seemed to thrive here, although he said he never came here. They ate outside, inside, and even walked into the small-town center for a visit to the local market, Mattias in his bathing suit and Inira in her suit and coverup. Mattias' bare chest was indeed a work of art. It stoked the fire of her lust and desire to be filled by him. They were completely anonymous.

When they kissed, from the moment his lips and tongue touched hers, she felt like she would combust. She knew it was right to decide when they came together. She wasn't his or any man's property. Her thoughts, decisions, and actions were her own. If her therapist had reminded her of anything, it was undoubtedly this reality of how she grew up. After one passionate embrace on the balcony after dinner, Inira told Mattias she was ready for him to take her to bed.

"Mattias, I want to be with you." Her voice was low and husky, and she was being kissed thoroughly, senselessly. She was ready for what came next. She could feel his body calling to hers, and she responded organically, just like the FourFold God had designed.

He pulled back, looking unsure. "Are you sure, *quierda?*'

She nodded and said, "Yes, I am sure. Coming into union with you in mind, body, and soul is what the FourFold God made us for."

But he didn't move. Inira put her hands on his face, "*Ahava ostar,* what's wrong?"

This was a man of action, standing here, taking no action. Inira knew he wanted her, and now she was thoroughly confused. Mattias backed away from her. He was frustrated, and she wasn't sure why. She had felt him tense when she uttered the word "God." She watched as his face hardened, his jaw clenching and unclenching. Suddenly, he moved away from her, opened the door, and walked inside. He left the door open, and Inira was so stunned she stayed rooted to the spot where he had pressed her against the wall. She peeked around the corner and saw that he was wearing a hole in the carpet, walking back and forth.

This was a different kind of movement than what she had seen before. It was fury and tension, and it scared her a little. She had been experiencing his passion focused on her, and it was intoxicating. Even watching him pace, with his shoulders rippling under his shirt, made her want to get up and take him by the hand to the bedroom. But she determined that she would wait. She decided the best place for her was on the couch, where she could engage in breathing exercises, slowing her heart rate and adrenal response to his sudden ferocity. It scared her after his relaxed behavior with her for weeks now.

She gave him time to articulate his feelings, but she started getting anxious as time stretched out. The power in his body was mesmerizing. She could see how he made his way in the world and how intimidating that must be for most. Finally, he broke the tension. "I cannot believe in your god, Inira. You would have me switch allegiances, lose my position, and give up what I've known to be true my whole life? Are you manipulating me so I can be putty in your hands for your purposes?"

Inira felt like she'd been knocked back into the couch with a physical blow. That had been the farthest thing from her mind. She didn't know mentioning the FourFold God was a trigger. It isn't like they hadn't discussed orthodoxy and how that led to practicing their faith the last four weeks. Why it was bothering him now, she didn't know but wanted to find out. The school of thought she'd been trained in when dealing with highly volatile topics like politics or religion – anything that someone was fully vested in – was to do exactly what she attempted. Wait until things are calmer, initiate physical contact, speak softly, and be gentle. When someone was as upset as Mattias was right now, it was an act of kindness and compassion to be gentle. It further demonstrated a different way than to let things escalate into a screaming match.

She started to get up to go to him, but he held her off. Stunned again for the second time in a few short minutes, she sat back on the couch. He waved his hand for her to continue, which annoyed her, but she didn't let it show.

She maintained her composure, "No, *otsar*. Not at all. I want us to be together, and in my belief system, it is the highest form of worship to come together sexually. I'm ready to experience that with you. To open my heart to you and have you open your heart to me as we knit our physical bodies together. I'm not asking you to give up anything; open to me as I will to you. It was part of the beauty of the Song of Creation, as I understand it. It was how the High Priestess and her Consort helped lead the way, and then the rest of the community could do the same. And all of Teleosis could live into the joy of Sacred Union."

He stopped pacing and looked directly at her. A look came into his face she hadn't seen since their very first meeting in London. When he spoke, his tone dripped contempt. "Yes, we see how well that worked out for Teleosis."

Inira was rocked. Why was he fighting her about her motivation for sex? It was holy; did he not want to experience that with her? She didn't understand where this condescension was coming from at the core.

She put her hands up in a defensive posture as one would towards a caged animal. "Mattias, I think it is best we pause this conversation. It feels unsafe for me right now. I have long since moved past defending the actions or theology of my home. Especially when it comes to the better parts of it, I have never defended the actions of the ruling Council, but I will not argue about the high holy practices that lead to community growth and thriving. Arguing is another form of trying to conquer another person. Our way was always an effort to meet where we are similar and focus on that over our differences. If you don't want to treat me with the respect I deserve, especially about something so personal, we will pause until you can get your mind together."

Like the big bad wolf, he breathed in sharply as if preparing to blow her argument down.

She kept her hands up. "Again, I'm not getting into it until you calm down. I'm here with you now and want to build something together. I want to be intimate with you and experience that bliss as only we can. I'm going to go for a swim. We can talk again later if you are up for it."

He was so big, so imposing. His shadow seemed to have grown with his anger. She got off the couch but didn't turn her back to him. His green eyes were flashing with an almost maniacal light. She turned around when her ass hit the door handle. She opened it and felt the relief in her escape as soon as the door closed behind her, and he didn't charge after. She did exactly as she said, aware he could see her from the house. She wanted time, in the soothing water of the Mother Ocean, to calm so she could think straight.

Her mind whirled because, for the first time in his presence, she felt like she'd glimpsed the animal within. She'd seen in his eyes the place where all the passion, fire, and need to dominate lived. It reminded her of Francis' response to the text messages, how he had grown more aggressive than she'd ever seen him. She was a strong, proud woman, and she did not like to be made to feel small and helpless, especially by a man.

She checked in and realized it was her mind that felt unsafe, not her body. Her body was aroused by his display of power, more so than when they were making out. She'd envisioned many a time in the weeks prior what it would be like to be the sole focus of that passion, and now experiencing it, she wanted to fuck his brains out, to rip into each other like animals, not take it slow. Sacred Union would happen anyway, but she didn't want it to be just fucking for him. She wanted him to be ready for another level of experience, and if she'd stayed with him just now, she would have probably said something that would inhibit that from happening for a long time.

She waded in the water, forcing herself not to look up at the balcony to see if he was or wasn't there. She was facing the darkened horizon when, what felt like hours later, she felt the water stir behind her. She didn't have to look back. She could tell it was him as if her body knew he was near. He encircled her, wrapping his big, muscular arms around her torso. She didn't fight. She could tell all the fight had left him in her absence. He had come back to himself. His breath was warm and heavy on the bare shoulder of her swimsuit.

His lips touched the tip of her shoulder bone, and she knew it was an apology. She felt this was the best place he could start, letting the words come later. He began to trail his kisses up the side of her neck, gently sucking on several tender places. Every touch of his lips felt like amends, making up for the moments they'd been apart, healing the tear between them. She felt herself melting into him. Her heat matched his, swelling at her core as she felt him swell behind her. They stood in the water like this for an eternal moment, as only lovers experience. It was as if they were between worlds, in a liminal space only they'd occupied.

If this was how he started his apologies for the rest of their lives, she might be tempted to argue with him every day. She reached back to grab his head and turned hers to kiss him as one of his hands left her middle, pulling her against him. His desire was evident. He reached up his hand in a loose fist. She didn't startle as his wet knuckles dragged down her chin, down her neck, all the way down her arm till he entwined his fingers with hers.

Then he whispered, with eyes gazing into hers with such sadness, "Forgive me, darling light. That wasn't about you. I am so sorry if I scared you. I never want you to be afraid of me. You bring so much to my life. I never want to fight with you. Sex has always been an act to me, nothing truly intimate. The idea of sharing my heart with you in that way left me so off balance. I want it. I want you, but I don't deserve you, Inira. I am ashamed of my part in ruining your life, in destroying your home. I know now how wrong I was because of you. And I'm realizing I was so wrong about your god, too. They seem too good to be true."

He took a deep breath, which she could feel, with his chest pressed against her back. He continued, "I know I can make you happy physically. I'm struggling with how to be that vulnerable and open with you emotionally and spiritually. I grew up believing sex was just for procreation or a man's pleasure. Thanks to you, I know there is so much more to it than that. You are prepared to give yourself freely to me, and I want to be that free with you. Give me time to work through it, but I don't know where to start."

She turned around to stare into his eyes, reflecting off the water, looking into his face with love and forgiveness. She whispered, "I forgive you, Mattias. Trust me to show you the way to Love, as the FourFold God intended."

She kissed him, pulling him as their tongues danced ferociously. Her need consumed her with every second and raised the temperature, making her feel like they could boil the ocean around them. As their passion grew, he made a low noise in his throat, almost animalistic, like a growl. He looked behind him; there were plenty of lounge chairs. She could feel his desire for immediate action and privacy where he would have her all to himself. His hands roamed over her and hers over him. The feel of his muscular back intoxicated her. When he turned back, their lips again crashed like magnets pulling each other together. They continued to kiss deeply. Mattias enraptured her with his mouth. She liked that she could bring him back to her in this way.

Then she felt his hands land on the roundness of her ass. He gently kneaded, almost reverent, as if he'd been waiting to touch her his whole life. She wrapped her fingers up in his hair. He pulled her even closer and then lifted her. She wrapped her legs around his waist and spun them in the water. They continued to kiss, Mattias carrying her up the steps, past the infinity pool, and into their bedroom. He did not even bother closing the doors to the balcony, letting the sea breeze create a supernatural effect as their lovemaking took them into open-hearted bliss.

They didn't leave the bed till the following day. They ate dinner there, with only a break to explore each other in the shower. Then they returned to the bed, finally falling asleep after midnight, exhausted after the hours spent twisted up in the other. It was not till the next morning that Inira remembered her phone. Once she opened it and saw the messages from Francis, she knew that reality had burst their love bubble.

Chapter 32

E xcerpt from a letter to the Heir, Tulun, from her mother, the High Priestess, Tabitha, August 1937.

Precious One,

The dark is coming. Undoubtedly, you have heard the rumblings from Western Europe, about the trouble developing there. I am doing what I can to orchestrate peace, but the leadership of the League of Nations points at Hitler and Mussolini, but it is much bigger than that. I'm afraid that what Great Britain and the United States are saying isn't what they really mean. Their propaganda is tiresome, age-old, and wholly anchored in the impotent binary of good versus evil, wrong versus right.

Unfortunately, what we know to be true is when men are left to figure things out themselves, only violence and bloodshed on a massive scale will be the result, just like before, and just like always. They've never learned to balance the masculine urge to lead with the feminine urge to create.

My efforts here are soberingly futile, and my words to collaborate before it's too late fall on deaf ears. The window for reconciliation has passed because the bloodlust to avenge the overly harsh punishments of the past has escalated too high in Germany. They've been working hard for a decade to build themselves back to power with a singular focus. Hitler capitalized on it and gave them a vision of a new society. It is only a new caste system built on oppression and has the potential to harm the most vulnerable irreparably. The Third Reich is the latest manifestation of the symptoms of the disease of this outside world.

This is a perfect example of how powerful a vision that gives people hope can be. It also demonstrates how far the human soul will go to control its destiny. We trust differently. I've been pondering how Love, as we know to be the heart of the FourFold God, will go to save and keep us. I don't know yet, but Their Hand stretches across the ages to hold and guide us, especially when it is darkest before the dawn.

We need to be wise and prepare ourselves. We must prepare to receive all we can from those fleeing the coming war and start now. Tell the Counsel you lead this effort under my instruction and direction. The refugees will stream across the Aegean to us, and we must be ready. Enact the Catastrophe Protocol and tell the Counsel to prepare camps on the outpost islands. We will need every scrap of land for those coming for safe harbor. We will use our political connections to help those who want to permanently relocate to the Allied countries.

We will enact our defense systems now. We do not need to wait. Teleosis is in far greater danger than ever. They haven't caught up to our level of innovation, but their weapons are at a level of power that could destroy the earth itself. They will only continue the pursuit of world-ending strength until they have it in their hands, and not even the Song of Creation has the power to stop them.

Get ready, *Ahava*. We have been given this time to lead, and the Mother and Father above have provided us with all we need. We might wish to be agents of peace, but They have appointed us in a time such as this to be a haven for those with nowhere else to go. The Son and Daughter will hold our hands.

I will see you in two weeks and expect a report on the progress of preparations. I trust you to see it through. You are young, but you have energy and drive. Use it all to benefit those who are running for their lives. This is what you've been born for, raised for, and trained for. We are in this together, my treasure.

All my love and affection,

Mother

{signed with the signet seal of the High Priestess of Teleosis}

Chapter 33

Emerie wasn't expecting to see Charlotte at her front door when she opened it, nor was she prepared to meet the drop-dead gorgeous man standing next to her, especially since she was in her post-school comfy clothes.

Her mother often said, "Indeed, the wind can blow the boat of your life from safe harbor into a storm in a heartbeat." Emerie felt the truth of that statement now, deep in her bones.

Her dad wasn't home from work yet, and she'd finally heard back from her mom, who didn't say much about where she was; there wasn't a ton of reception. Emerie was relieved to know she was ok. Even though she was with Mattias, which made Emerie deeply uncomfortable, her mother was the most important person in the world to her. Knowing she was safe and well cared for balanced her fury about her choice to leave her dad for another man. Emerie knew life got complicated and marriages sometimes didn't last. Her mother's matrilineal teaching complicated her feelings. Emerie was born and raised in the West, so she struggled to understand it all for herself.

She wanted her mom and her whole, happy little family life back. She also wanted to bash both her parents' heads in. And yet, she knew it wouldn't ever be the same again. Something had broken in her parent's relationship, and she was desperate to do whatever she could to mend it. She couldn't find her dad passed out in a drug-induced sleep again, even if it was a prescription. She couldn't go much longer without seeing her mom. It was quite the roller coaster happening in her head and heart.

So, to add this surprise meeting on her front door stoop to the mix was disorienting. Being face-to-face with Charlotte and this male model, who she knew to be Lukas Nahas, made her queasy.

She kept it together long enough to ask, "Charlotte! What in the world are you doing here?"

She felt something pull from her middle so that her attention slid from Charlotte to the man beside her. She could feel herself turn a shade of pink that was mortifying. She had never been this close to someone this good-looking, and he wasn't that close. He stood at least six feet from her on their front door stoop.

"Emerie, I'm so sorry to bother you at home. Oh, and this is Lukas Nahas, Mattias' son. He and I have been working closely as he runs Nahas Helps. Your mother isn't at home, is she? I haven't heard from her at all this week. Lukas is also looking for his father."

Emerie was suspicious that they would show up unannounced, but she was sobered by the news of her mother being out of contact with Charlotte. Her eyes were still drawn to Lukas as she said, "Yes, I know exactly who you are." His green eyes got brighter and more interested, which she tried to dismiss but was unsuccessful. She turned to address Charlotte, drawing up the regal bearing she had seen her mother do in conflict innumerable times. She might be furious at her mother but still wanted to be like her.

"Umm, no. Why would she be here? She is definitely with Mattias, though. Do you know what's going on, Charlotte?"

Lukas shifted his body weight to the other foot, and her gaze instantly snapped back like a magnet attracted to its opposite pole. When he spoke, his honeyed, silken voice soothed something in her. "There is nothing to worry about, Emerie. You have no reason to be afraid. Your mother is with my father, and all is well."

The formality of his language and the way he said her name seemed a little off, like he was trying too hard. She liked his voice, but she didn't like that she liked it because this was the son of the man who had helped ruin her family. She also didn't know people had voices like that. She needed to stop being preoccupied with him and focus on what they were both doing here. It smelled fishy.

The swell of emotions made her irritable, so she focused on finding out what she could. "Charlotte, why are you here? You've never been to our house unless it was Christmas. My family has been upended, so don't fuck around with me."

Charlotte was startled at her use of profanity. Emerie didn't usually cuss unless she was with her friends, and then she could use all her words. Though this felt like an appropriate time to get Charlotte's attention, she saw it had. Charlotte started to fidget with her hands, communicating her nerves. "Well, we are here because we haven't heard from her. I can't reach Stanley either, and we have to make a few important decisions regarding the Nahas account. Lukas can make them, so he flew over to discuss them with Inira and me in person. And since she hasn't been in the office, we had to check here. It was the only logical place we could think of since she wasn't answering her phone."

Emerie could get sarcastic in a hurry. It was in her nature at nearly 19 years old. She was sick of feeling like their only intention of being here was not for her welfare but to see to their own agenda. "Charlotte, you and my mom are good friends. You are probably her best friend if she had close friends. I've only known her to be at work, school, and home unless we went on vacation as a family. So, between the two of us, you, more than me, would know where my Mom is. If she had a secret hideaway, *you would know about it before I did.*"

She was on the attack because of her intuition, which her mother told her was her greatest gift as a woman. Her gut told her something else was at play, and she didn't feel like playing their game. Charlotte also knew the details of their abrupt separation, which added embarrassment to the hot pot of her emotional soup and Emerie's frustration that Charlotte would show so little empathy. She hadn't asked her how she was doing, how her Dad was, nothing. Just where Inira was, she could have asked Emerie that over text. She was just here for the information, and Emerie knew it.

"Emerie, sweetheart, I didn't know the extent of your Mom's relationship with Mattias. She hid it very well. I – "

This was a moment Lukas decided to cut in, and it did nothing to improve Emerie's opinion of him, smoking hot as he was.

"Emerie, *mi amada*, we aren't trying to interrogate you. Let me ask, have you heard from your mother at all?" Lukas opened his hands invitingly, almost like he wanted to move forward and hug her. It creeped Emerie out and made her stomach twist oddly.

She decided to push back; she was already in a crap mood, so taking it out on a strange man seemed like the right thing to do. "I took Spanish, so I know what you just called me. I'm not 'my darling' to you. For Christ's sake, we just met, so just lay off the charm, ok? I'm stressed out enough as it is. My parents' marriage is failing; my Dad kicked my Mom out, and she is off in Greece while I'm trying to graduate and move on with my life by myself." She took a deep breath, feeling the activation in her nervous system that made her say much more than she meant to. It seemed to do nothing but encourage Lukas. He smiled again and nodded at her. She didn't like that she got a jolt from his approval.

She physically turned her body away from him, as she had unconsciously been turned towards him, and answered Charlotte, "As I said, I know she is ok and that she is with Mattias. I don't know when she will be back. They are in Greece, and that's all I can say. If she wants to be in contact, she will be. Same with your father, Lukas. Now, if that's all, I will go inside and eat. It's been a long day and a shit-storm of a week." She looked between them when she added, "As you can imagine."

Emerie had not been raised to be so rude. She was raised to speak her mind, but respectfully. She knew her strengths as a female and her gifts as a person. She didn't have her dad's mind for law or her mother's gift for public speaking, but she knew the fake from the real when she saw it. It was something she had never been able to deal with. She moved to turn to go back inside and shut the door, when she felt, more than saw, Lukas take a step towards her.

When she turned back, slightly alarmed that she may have been more than a little excited, Lukas gave her a smile she thought was genuine and dazzling. She had to close her eyes to avoid being pulled into his gravitational force. He whispered, "I like you. We will get along just fine. Yes, take care of yourself, *mi amada*." Charlotte gave him a look of annoyance, but Emerie noticed he hadn't even looked at Charlotte the whole time they'd been standing on her stoop.

Charlotte was about to speak again, but Lukas spoke first. He clapped his hands and said again with all traces of formality and insincerity vanished. "I think we are done here, Charlotte. Let's get an early dinner and talk through what we need to do, and you can check in with Emerie later by text to see if she's heard anything. That sounds like a good plan?" He turned the overwhelming smile on Charlotte now, and she blew out a frustrated breath and nodded curtly.

That man was going to trap hearts with that face. He would probably keep them all locked up for eternity if Emerie's suspicions were right. No girl would ever get hers back. She was glad he didn't have on a baseball cap and turned backward, or she would be in a heap of trouble. She fully expected never to see him again and was glad for it. Lukas Nahas was probably a mind-fuck.

Charlotte turned back again to Emerie, "I'm sorry we bothered you, darling. You mean the world to me. Please let me know if you want to talk about anything – or need anyone to show up for you at any time. You are like family to me, both you and your mom. I'm always here if you need anything at all."

Emerie sighed and thanked her, even as she was still annoyed at her using the visit for information versus checking on her. Lukas gave a final parting statement that slivered over her skin like a benediction, "Emerie, you may not trust me, but I hope you grow too. With my connection to your mother and the work we've been appointed to do together, we will be in each other's lives from now on."

Emerie scoffed. "I doubt it. You are far too old for me anyway. Best you stick with a pursuit of Charlotte."

Charlotte turned beet red, but Emerie was surprised when Lukas' pupils widened as he'd suddenly walked into a dark room. His low, sensual chuckle made her stomach flip funny. She felt a fine sheet of perspiration break out on the hairline at the back of her neck when he said, "Charlotte is indeed someone worth pursuing, but I'm afraid you have it wrong, *jag-eun byeol.* My pursuit started a long time ago, even before I was born. So did yours, and we will meet again somewhere in the middle of it all. I'll see you again before it is all over."

Emerie looked at him, bug-eyed. She was smart but had no clue what he was talking about. "What did you call me? And what do you mean?"

Lukas laughed again, tucking his massive hands into his hip pockets. Her traitorous eyes tracked the movement, then snapped back up to his eyes, now with skin crinkled around them as his smile grew. She was growing to hate her attraction to this guy. Underneath it all, he was probably an asshole because Charlotte was attracted to assholes. Emerie wanted someone like her father – solid and sane, at least she thought so. The fire in her belly from this interaction with Lukas told a different story. Plus, her father hasn't been acting very sane recently. So, she elevated her teenage indifference as she widened her best protective stance.

It was time to stand tall as her own woman, as inexperienced as she was. She was getting a crash course in the "how to" of everything.

"Ok, whatever, I'll figure it out. I don't think I'll see you again. My dad will have a fit when he hears about this."

Charlotte tensed, but Lukas seemed to relax even more as if the threat of a challenge loosened his bones.

"I'm not worried about your father, little star. See you soon."

Ah, so that was what he'd called her. She didn't know what language; she didn't have the mastery of as many as her mother, but it sounded like an Asian dialect. Obsessively, she would spend the rest of the night figuring out which language it was instead of doing her homework, which she could finish in class tomorrow anyway. She was graduating with the highest honors, so the senioritis was strong. She had offers from two Ivy League schools, so homework didn't matter. She had personal standards, even though four-plus years at a dusty college didn't sound nearly as exciting as the kind of life her mother had when she was Emerie's age. Emerie always preferred to be busy, on the move, and doing something good. She was built that way, her dad said. College was expected, but secretly, she wanted something different, unusual. Lukas Nahas was unobtainable and far too old for her, but he practically exuded excitement. She wasn't sure if there was more to him than that, but she would probably never find out.

She quipped back at him, "Again, arrogant man, whatever."

Her sassiness pleased him, even as Charlotte looked at her like they'd never met. Finally, Charlotte grabbed Lukas' arm, pulling him off the stoop. He kept that loose, relaxed stance. When they reached the waiting car, Charlotte called, "I'll text you later, and if you learn anything about where your mother is, please let me know immediately, Emerie."

She nodded and should have gone back inside the house. Instead, she stood there to make sure they got in the car. Lukas saw Charlotte and then turned back to her. He winked at her.

The flirty bastard winked at her!

She watched them drive off, then went inside, locking the door, leaning against it, and letting out a long, low whistle. She knew that man was trouble, so why did she feel like today started a whole new chapter in her life? She had the strangest sense she was in for his type of trouble.

Chapter 34

With her phone on "Do Not Disturb" since she left to meet Mattias at the airport, Inira never heard all the texts from Francis rolling in.

Monday, 11:37 pm.

> *Inira, it's been nearly three days since I last saw you. I'm miserable. I never once gave you the chance to explain what was happening. I took those texts as Gospel. I want you back. I'm so sorry. Nini, please forgive me.*

Tuesday, 1:20 am

> *Are you up? Where are you? It's not like you to not be available. I need to talk to you. I am barely able to function without you.*

Tuesday, 1:25 am

> *I can't eat or sleep without you here.*

Tuesday, 2:28 am

> *I keep going over and over in mind what happened. I need to know where I messed up what I did to make you want him.*

Tuesday, 3:07 am

> *Never mind, I don't want to know. I don't want to know what you are doing off with him. You probably are. You are probably fucking him right now. Don't respond. I can't handle knowing you are with him.*

Tuesday, 8:12 am.

> *I took an Ambien after my last text but didn't sleep much. I'm sorry for my last text. Emerie woke me up before she left for school. She is worried about me. Fucking hell, she is crushed about what's happening. We haven't talked about it much. She did say you texted her back to let her know you were ok, but that's about it. She is worried sick. Why have you done this to both of us? Why won't you respond to me?*

> *Fuck it, I need to go to work, to do something besides sit around here all day and think about the shithole my life is with or without you.*

Wednesday, 11:49 am.

> *Inira, please call me. I know this is such a mess. I need to hear your voice and know that you are ok.*

Wednesday, 11:59 am.

> *I can't take the silence from you. I need you back. I want you. I'm so sorry. This is torture. If you don't respond in the next 4 hours, I'm finding out where you are and coming to get you.*

***

From waves of seemingly never-ending pleasure with Mattias as they came together time after time in sacred union to the waves of sickening guilt crashing over Inira as she read through the manic texts from Francis. She was pinned to the side of the bed and tried to decide if she was going to throw up.

She and Mattias had awoken together. He'd gotten out of bed, and she'd stayed in it, reveling in the delicious soreness in all the right places. She grabbed his sleep shirt from the drawer to bathe in his scent. She'd grabbed her phone now that it was fully charged. It was Thursday morning, Wednesday night, back at home. She expected texts from Emerie, which she had, and she'd responded to. Then she answered Charlotte, letting her know she was okay but not telling her where she was. Her mind was still on Mattias on their night together. Mattias' stamina and dedication in getting to know what pleased her was a dream come true. They fit perfectly together, and she knew she pleased him just as much because he'd told her repeatedly. Their sex had been intense, just like Mattias. Yet, it was also sweet, intentional, and otherworldly. He had told her when he wasn't thinking about what came next for them, he'd spent most of their time apart envisioning what he would do with and to her in bed.

Now, reading the texts from Francis, the sweetness of the time with Mattias was replaced with shame, which made bile crawl up her throat. She might vomit if the weight of her situation didn't crush her first. She didn't believe what she and Mattias had done, and would likely do it again, as wrong or sinful as some would call it. What she hated was that Francis was suffering. Given how he had treated her, he probably deserved to feel the way he did, but she knew she still loved him. She truly hadn't wanted to hurt him and owned that she did. Her religious practice was meant to min-imize harm and eradicate injustice. She felt like she was cheating on those principles more than she was necessarily cheating on Francis.

Yes, she felt the guilt of hurting him and Emerie. Yes, she was going to be sick.

She ran for the bathroom and hurled up what was left in her stomach from last night's bedside picnic. She kept dry-heaving, and when that finally passed, she stayed crying into the toilet bowl until she felt warm hands on her shoulders. They slid underneath her arms and the backs of her legs to lift her. She was still sobbing as Mattias brought her, not back to the bed, but out into the kitchen area. He maneuvered her till he had her positioned in his lap on the couch.

He reached over, grabbed something, and placed it in her hand. It was a box of tissues. His hand found the small of her back, just like before. He traced his fingers up and down the channel of her spine and then reached through the neck hole to knead at the tense muscles of her shoulders and upper back. She had nothing on underneath the shirt, but he appreciated that she already felt exposed as he kept her covered. She cried for a while longer; all the while, he was silent. Letting her have all the time she needed to express her feelings.

When she was calm enough, she said, "I'm sorry."

"*Amor*, what would you have to be sorry for?"

She leaned forward, giving him more access to her back. "Crying into your shoulder, getting tears and snot on you, making you take care of me."

He huffed and began scratching her back. She let out a small involuntary moan of pleasure, and he spoke. "I see my love likes that. I told you I want to take care of you. That means in every situation, and especially when you are in pain. I know you are strong and independent, and I will let you be, but not when you are sick with emotion."

"You saw the texts, then?"

It was his turn to nod. He finished scratching her back and then began to rub his big hands over her. His touch wasn't sexual but comforting. It still sparked a desire in her that she was the sole focus of his attention. She'd never once seen him check his phone or computer. She didn't even know if he had one with him. A fresh wave of guilt hit her when she realized she'd betrayed their bubble here by checking her phone. She'd brought the outside world into their sacred space.

Tearing up, she looked at him, "I'm so sorry, Mattias."

"Shh, shh, shh." He whispered that into her ear, then spoke Spanish calmly and reassuringly. It wasn't her strongest language, but she caught enough to know he was telling her how he felt to settle her.

After a few moments, he switched to English, "Inira, my light, you have nothing to be sorry for. You have a family who cares for you. You have a daughter you need to check on. I am not surprised Francis is having such a hard time letting you go. I know I never could." A small spark appeared in his eyes, then it passed.

He continued, "I didn't read all the texts, but I saw enough. It is I who is sorry for you to be going through this."

She looked at him then, "We are both going through this. This is only the beginning if we are going to be together." Inira said a little more firmly than she meant. Her emotions were everywhere.

He nodded, still stroking her spine gently in an almost ticklish way. "Yes, that is true. We are in this together, in mind, body and soul. I am with you and only you as long as it takes for you to be mine in the eyes of everyone and to see our vision come to pass."

She looked away, out the big window towards the sea, drawing strength again from The Mother, "I don't know if I'm ready for talk of a third marriage with the implosion of my second one so recent."

He put his hands on her face and turned her to look directly at him. He leaned forward and kissed her cheeks, gently licking away the salt tracks and then swiping his thumbs across her cheekbones towards her ears.

He opened his eyes to meet hers, the green sparkling now, "I don't care if we ever formally marry. I would love to call you my wife, but I already think of you that way. You are mine, and I am yours. I have already started changing my important documents to reflect you as my beneficiary. No matter what happens, I will care for you in this life and the next."

Inira was stunned, speechless. He meant to leave her a fortune probably bigger than ten people could spend in their lifetimes and had already begun doing so.

"That's a huge step, Mattias."

He smiled at her. "I've been prepared to take it since I saw you in person." The ferocity of his smile then made her breath catch.

Something poked at her. "What did you think of me before we met?"

He looked away, uncomfortable now. He shifted a little, not moving her off of him but adjusting her weight as if she were suddenly heavier. He hesitated, and she asked him again, now concerned at what he would say.

"I thought of you as a means to an end, Inira. I didn't take you seriously. It never registered why Tomas would be so adamant about caring for you. I couldn't conceive of partnering, of being united with someone. It was against everything I knew. I knew all the details of your life. I had doubts about the Serpents' way of life, but I didn't take them seriously because I had no other options. But then I met you and saw with my own eyes how much light you bring into this world. That light in you is Love Personified, and it has changed everything."

She laughed then. It was loud and broke from her throat like the sun breaking through the clouds after a storm. Mattias was startled, and she hurriedly said, "Well, then I would say you are like most other men in the world, raised to ignore the obvious strengths and see only our weaknesses, how we need protection and not taking our gifts seriously."

He leaned forward to kiss her, and she deepened it. He pulled away with a deep breath and whispered, "Yes, *luz de amor*, I have been misinformed about many things. That's why everything of mine is yours. I will never stop trying to make up for my mistakes. I want to show you how sorry I am."

Her blood and core heated at the hooded look in his eyes. "What about breakfast?"

"I'll make it again." They didn't even make it off the couch this time. Inira's past was forgotten, just like her phone in the bedroom, as they lost themselves in each other.

Later, they talked about her response to Francis while they ate breakfast. She needed to respond; she owed him that much. Mattias seemed disconnected from it, like he was counseling her on a business deal. She wondered if that was a coping mechanism. He'd made it clear on the plane with his general response to the situation, how Francis handled the news, and how he felt about Francis at all. She knew he didn't think much more about him than Francis thought of him.

Once she was satisfied and had sent a text back to Francis, Mattias switched the subject, "*Amor*, remember what I said would happen after this time together here in Santorini?"

She nodded, chewing her crepe. Mattias was an excellent cook, and she made a mental note to ask him where he learned his skills.

She swallowed and answered, "Yes, you keep saying you will take me home. I assume that is one of your homes since I can't and don't want to return to mine, save to get my daughter. I'm very interested to hear your plan, *Ahava ostar*."

He had been eating his crepe and took a sip of espresso before responding, "Yes, I will take you home. But it isn't home to your family or one of my homes, although I want to take you to see those. I haven't wanted to mention it, but on Saturday, we leave here for our next destination. I am finally going to take you back to Teleosis."

Inira became utterly still, the world swimming before her eyes. "Excuse me?"

Chapter 35

Inira felt like the floor had dropped from beneath her feet. She swayed on the bar chair in front of the island where they'd been having breakfast. Her head suddenly felt empty, and stars started forming at the edges of her vision as she felt the blood drain from her face.

"*Amor de luz*, what is it? What's wrong?" The panic in Mattias' voice barely registered.

Inira felt the world tilt and had a sensation of falling before she realized that she was on her way down. Everything began to go black, but she felt the sensation of hitting the lush, carpeted floor. She wavered there, between consciousness and unconsciousness. It was more like an out-of-body experience where she knew what she was experiencing but had no control over her corporeal self. It barely registered as Mattias picked her up and hugged her to his body. He was speaking Spanish again, something she realized, disjointedly, he did when deeply emotional.

"!Uy, me asustaste! !Aye de mil! Inira, tu despiertas!"

She could tell he was shaking her a little bit, clutching her as he continued to speak rapid, panicked Spanish into her hair. She remained catatonic, like he had spoken a magic spell that put her into a trance when he spoke the name of her homeland. She wanted to stay there, in her paralyzed state. It was better than returning to reality suddenly crashing into her body like a tidal wave. Even in her foggy state, she thought this feeling was better than being drunk, with no effort required and certainly no hangover.

They stayed like that for a while, Inira floating blissfully between as her soul decided if it would inhabit her body again. Mattias was frantic, crying, clutching her like a favorite toy that had just been damaged, and praying to whatever god would listen and answer. She heard him say, "*Mama, Papi, ayudanos por favor,*" over and over again.

Finally, Inira began to feel the sensation return to her fingers and toes, like pins and needles. She felt herself rushing back into her body and felt warmth covering her. She took a large, loud intake of breath. Mattias pulled her back to look in her face.

"Inira! Dios mio! My love, what happened? Are you alright?" His eyes were wild, and she could feel the pulse of frenetic energy off of him, like radar waves trying to detect the source of her sudden condition. He was shifting beneath her, trying to make her or himself more comfortable. She put a hand up to his chest. Under her palm, his heart raced unnaturally fast, and she willed it to slow. She felt the heat build under her palm, looked him in the eyes, and said, "Breathe with me, Mattias. Only one of us needs to have a panic attack today."

"That was a panic attack? That's what happens when you panic?" He was breathing so hard he could barely get the words out.

Inira continued, "Shhhhh. Shhhh. Slowly now, breathe. Yes, that was a panic attack. I've only had a few before. They are unusual. I'm sorry I scared you. Breathe, *Ahava.* Breathe."

They slowly started to synchronize their breathing together. He pulled her against his chest, his tears spilling out, and she realized then her upper body was in his lap, and he was sitting on the floor. He must have come down beside her when she fell from the stool.

As they centered and settled, he pulled back, asking her, "Amor, are you hurt?" He started looking through her hair, turning her head to check for injury. He even opened the neck of her shirt. She laughed.

"I don't think my breasts sustained any damage, love."

He scowled at her. "I'm checking for bruising. How can you laugh at a time like this?"

"It was a physical response to stress. I told you it has happened before, and I have to go with it to let it pass. And it does. My body was overwhelmed, but don't worry, it doesn't happen often."

"It better not; I cannot deal with you like that again. It was like you were alive but just......." He struggled to find the words as he returned to look into her eyes. He shivered as he said, "Gone."

She raised her hand to cup his cheek. "I'm here. I'm here. I'm here with you."

They sat like that for a long time, just looking at each other. No thought, words, murmur, or tremble except for their matching breaths and heartbeats. It was a peace Inira was loathe to break.

But break it, she did. "Mattias, I can't go back to Tov. That part of my life, that part of my history, is dead and buried under rubble."

He took a big, bracing breath, shifting her again to between his legs. She faced him, her legs straddling his hips. They were chest to chest now. She didn't feel lightheaded but closed her eyes to gain her bearings. His hands remained on her arms, ready to catch her if she slipped away again as if he had the power to hold her to this earth, to him, by his will alone.

He spoke so quietly, "Luz, I know. I see how big of a shock it was, and I should have better prepared you. But it's planned. I must show you the progress we've made. I started the recovery, the restoration project five years ago, and it is finally a place where I can return you home."

Again, she was stunned into silence. She didn't feel overwhelmed, but this information was too much. He'd been planning this for five years? Was this why he was with her? And what else did he want?

In her silence, he said, "Inira, it was also my goal to bring you – the Heir of Light – the one who stands to usher the light into the world. I didn't know you would do that willingly. I told you how I viewed you before, but that has all changed. Now, I want to show you and walk in the streets of Teleosis with you. I want to see what I can.

I want to change the world with you, starting with disbanding the Serpents. Please show me your homeland. You've given me all the secrets, and I want this too."

She stayed silent for so long that he took her hands into his. When she finally raised her eyes to meet his gaze, she saw nothing but love shining through the emerald color of his beautiful eyes. There was an openness and a look of hope. Gone was the cold, unreachable man she'd first met. He had changed, and she wanted to believe it was being with her that had done it.

Yet, she knew there was more to it than this. She had been schooled more than once on putting her complete trust in another's open eyes, his vulnerable heart, and the security of his body. She'd learned that with Tomas, and like a glass of cold water, she realized Francis was learning that from her. The bitter tang of betrayal, even the suspicion of it, never allowed one to trust again fully.

"I have not given you everything, Mattias. And it matters what I want, too."

It was simple. There was one secret she still had – a non-secret. She knew the Song of Creation was hunted by their enemies. She knew that power was coveted once it became widely known that it was the source of Teleosian prestige. But she didn't know it. Save that one dream, the song had faded. It took two in union with the FourFold God to sing it. It took the High Priestess and the Consort. She had never become that, not officially, and Tomas was dead.

Mattias wanted to be the Consort, but she wasn't sure he could be if she had never ascended to her rightful place. Her mother had said she had worked around the elevation ceremony, which had been changed long ago because the High Priestess was required to nearly give her life to transfer the Song to her daughter and son-in-law. But it never happened.

She wondered, or maybe suspected, he couldn't or wouldn't answer. These last few days, he had become a fuller picture of himself to her. She could now paint the different color schemes of his mind and heart. But she knew that picture might never be complete. There would also be something or some part of himself he kept back; not hidden, exactly, but not fully revealed either. His plans and purposes were at the top of that list.

She looked at him and spoke softly, like he was a small child, "I know you have plans; you have told me as much before. I need to know their full extent, not an edited version. Did you bring me here to get me close to Teleosis? What do you want from me, Mattias?"

He looked at her with shiny eyes. She saw that he recognized this was a moment of truth, unvarnished, and had the potential to destroy these last few days. He began slowly and unfolded the plans and methods of the Serpents to her. She could sense he was still editing, holding back details. She cataloged every movement, every time he looked away when his breathing changed. She was the lie detector, and Mattias was her subject.

When he finished, she responded immediately, already in her mind, "What I hear you saying, Mattias, is that the Serpents intend to use me as the way to unlock the power of Teleosis. They think it is in a vault in Tov that would allow them to be the most powerful force on Earth. Between the offensive weapons and the advanced innovations only ever realized in Teleosis, the Serpents could dominate the world. That's what you want?"

He looked down, for the first time, ashamed. "It is not what I want anymore. I only want you. I know things must change, and I intend to ensure they do. I will change all the rules. I will convince them to let us leave together."

She barked out a sardonic laugh. "Mattias, you are the Deitas! They will NEVER let you leave."

He crooked a half smile. "Well, that's the thing. I make the law when it comes to the Serpents. I can hand over the vision and ensure we are protected from retaliation."

"And who would you hand it over to, pray tell?"

"Lukas."

Inira felt dumbstruck; why hadn't she seen this? She'd been so naïve! Of course, his son was involved.

"Ahmadi has always been his advisor and would stay in that role. Ahmadi knows more of the inner workings of the Serpents than anyone. He has all the contacts and access to everything. Lukas will need his help if you will be with me and we exit. My personal fortune will allow us to fund Teleosis's work again."

This was too much to take in. First, the thought of returning to Teleosis and helping the Serpents gain access to the technology that will allow them to dominate the world?

She said as much to him. "This is too much, Mattias. I never signed up for this. I came to be with *you*, not part of a master-minded plan for world domination. Plus, I don't even know how to access the technology. My mother never got the chance to pass that knowledge on to me."

He reached for her, but she pulled back out of his grasp. She stood up, and he followed. He looked shocked, then wounded. "Don't say that, Light Bringer. I know now just how much I need you and how this is so much more than the plan of the Serpents. We will figure it out and leave it all behind. Just go with me, and I swear on my mother's life, I won't make you do anything. I will not force you, Inira. I adore you. I respect you. I will not force you."

"You brought me because you think you need the blood of the Heir to access the codes to get into the secret vaults."

That revelation landed with a thud in the room like she had punched Mattias in the throat. "What do you mean I need your blood?"

She threw her head back and laughed. "After five years of planning and research, you didn't still think it was simple codes or locks that kept the secrets of Teleosis, did you?" He shook his head like he was trying to clear water from his ears.

"Mattias, that's the joke. Yes, some locks only open with a drop of blood for the Heir or High Priestess. The Counsel squirreled away much ancient wisdom and knowledge, priceless artifacts behind locked doors. They are locked behind the specific chromosomal patterns in my DNA and the bloodline of a High Priestess. It's a very advanced science, which you and your team no doubt suspected."

She continued, "But that's not the real prize, all those hidden treasures. The real prize is the Song of Creation. You know this because we've talked about it. We have used it in times of great need and threat, and only then because of the cost to the Ones Who Sing. I would have to slit my forearms open, bleeding out near the point of death, to prove to the ancients that you were worthy of the power of the Song. It's why, for all her issues, I'm glad my mother died in an explosion rather than be forced to commit suicide to wield that power."

He looked stricken and pale. Yet, Inira remained calm and relaxed. She was confounded by the reality the Serpents didn't know this but also secretly pleased her ancestors were wiser than their enemies, at least in this respect. That Mattias didn't realize this gave her pause. He wasn't stupid and was at the top of the food chain of their organization. She felt a crawling sensation in her belly. It made its way across her skin before she said. "Mattias, if you didn't know, someone in your organization does and is keeping it from you."

He was still for so long that she began to wonder if he was now having a catatonic panic attack. Then he exploded out of his chair and into action. He got out his phone and yanked his computer from his bag he hadn't touched all week, and that was it. Mattias went to work.

Inira watched it all unfold with a sad, sinking sensation for him and her. She knew the visit he'd planned out for her and potentially the progress they were making towards an alternative to the violence and domination of the Serpents and their religious autocracy was being strangled. Her sense of uncertainty increased tenfold as she saw that mask of power and control slip over his features, so different from the softness she'd witnessed. The only one he wasn't able to reach was Ahmadi. Lukas would call him back, but she could tell Mattias was suspicious of his activity. Lukas said enough to make his father feel comfortable, as did all of those under Mattias, but Mattias was on edge without Ahmadi's soothing presence. Ahmadi had been his right hand for decades. That dependence didn't dissipate in just a few days. Watching the anxiety ratchet up Mattias' spine made that stone in the pit of her stomach get larger.

She felt sick with the confirmation that Mattias had indeed moved forward in his plan. She knew his plan had changed, but was it too late to stop the juggernaut that was the Serpent's final bid for ownership of all Teleosis had to offer?

She eventually got out her phone as well. She texted Emerie, Charlotte, and Stanley. Charlotte immediately responded, and Emerie a little later. Still no word from Stanley, and that little worm of worry grew as she thought about her boss and friend. He'd never been this absent from her life. She texted her therapist and her sponsor, just for good measure. The only one she didn't connect with was Francis. She'd responded to him and needed to leave it there while she thought about the next steps.

It didn't help that Francis' vitriol against Mattias returned like a ghost whispering in her ear. It felt a lot like the oily residue of shame on her soul. Instead of letting it fester, Inira took the opportunity to think and plan. She didn't know what the next few days held, but she knew she needed to be ready to respond, not as a victim and not out of resentment, as her disease of alcoholism encouraged her to do. More profound groundwork was laid into her being, of strength and identity rooted in dignity. The feelings of betrayal were there, but instead of lashing out, Inira did her best to center herself. She had serenity. She also knew Mattias loved her. Would it be enough to change the course of these events?

They would find out soon enough and have to fight in a different way than they were used to. They would have to fight together.

Chapter 36

A short poem written by the High Priestess, Eliana, mother of the Heir Inira, right before her husband was assassinated in an attempt funded by the Serpents when blackmail attempts failed.

When the dogs surround us.

When we feel the hot breath of our adversaries on our necks.

When our vision gets small, and all feels lost.

We must cry out to the FourFold.

When there is nothing left to hold onto.

When all of our plans and purposes are turning to dust.

When there is nothing but pain.

We must return to the FourFold.

When what is precious is destroyed.

When we've lost all access to peace.

When chaos reigns in our hearts and world again.

We must seek out The FourFold.

When the pain is too heavy a burden to bear.

When our hearts are smashed to bits.

When our families and mission are ripped to shreds.

The FourFold will be there.

The Mother to comfort and inspire.

The Father to protect and require.

The Son to save and redeem.

The Daughter to make things plain to receive.

The FourFold will be there.

Chapter 37

It was a long day. Mattias barely took a break from contacting his people, figuring out who kept secrets, and then strategizing with this latest information about the locks and the Song. He took a short break for dinner, and he tried to switch his mental gears to assure Inira she was in no danger. She could hear the gears grinding in his mind.

"I will not let any harm come to you. Nothing has changed. You are my destiny, my *amor de luz*. I will not let anyone touch you or force you to do anything. This would only be a visit to show you our progress in restoring the Old City and the Temple."

Mentioning the Temple made a sensation shoot down Inira's spine like someone had dropped a hot rock down her shirt.

"Were you hoping that if I saw 'the good work,'" here she used her fingers for air quotes, "that I would share what I know? Mattias, I don't know how to wield the Song of Creation. Of course, I've read about it, but they discontinued the ceremony because it was so dangerous. Often, the High Priestess died from blood loss. This can be so different and so good. You know that now, and I think you see the possibility of a reality that isn't based on bloodshed."

He put his head in his hands. "I've been working towards this my whole life. You've derailed everything."

Inira croaked out a laugh. She could be offended by his comment, but she knew this was much more about his internal struggle. It pricked at her ego, so she kept her eyes on what was now her reality – reminding Mattias he had already experienced another way to live.

"I don't think you believe that. This shift in you started before me. You've questioned this path. You told me that yourself, in the infinity pool two days ago. Everything we've shared, how we've connected, let it lead you, *Ahava*."

She felt him coil up in frustration before he stood and started to pack his things aggressively. "I need some space," he barked out roughly.

That action and statement pissed her off, but she kept her mouth shut. Diplomacy was needed; there was too much at stake for both of them. She knew he was worried and wanted to assure her, but there were machinations at work he didn't realize he couldn't stop. It finally dawned on her that she couldn't talk Mattias out of the path he was on. His determination to see his agenda through initially turned her off from him; when pointed in her direction, it had become an aphrodisiac. Alpha male that he was, it was intoxicating and reality-numbing when pointed in her direction. This revelation of the return to Teleosis and the plan behind the scenes to use her for their ends was finally setting in.

She let him go outside to work and sit overlooking the water. She went into the bedroom, quietly meditating on her predicament, and opened the drapes to find her solace in the moonlight. Her ancestors had revered the sun and the moon, providing the balance humanity needed to thrive. Her body responded to the call of it. The glistening reflection off the water and in the sky comforted her, making the dark less dark. She laid down, letting the richness of their freshly laundered sheets with a hint of lavender and rosemary give her sensory rest. It was the scent of his shampoo, and as she closed her eyes, she caught a whiff of the shower. He was back inside, and she hoped he was coming to bed. Her heart clenched as she drifted off.

The mental gymnastics of the last few hours had drained her; she willed that scent to signal good fortune to come. She wanted his scent to be the beacon of hope and love she craved, but that worm of worry wiggled its way into her unconscious thoughts. When she felt him draw close behind her, cupping her legs with his, his hips with her and her back against his chest, she relaxed. His hand slid under her pajama top to rest on her lower belly, and his other arm moved under the pillow, supporting her head. He kissed her ear and said softly, "I'm sorry. You are right. Tomorrow we go and it all changes because we will do it together. The Light Bringer is going home."

They would either soar or fall, but they would do it together. Those thoughts colored her dreams.

***

The ground shook beneath her, unnaturally and in rapid succession.

She choked on the dust and ash in the air. Inira reached up, grasping her throat. She coughed, trying to expel the noxious sensation that made her feel air would never reach her lungs in time to keep her alive. She raced to the window, tearing at the drapes, the need to see what was happening overpowering her. She was in time to see the Temple fall. A millennia-old beacon of hope for those seeking a better life and a world imploding in on itself. She could hear the screams of those inside before the final silence swallowed their lives.

All around the horizon line from her bedroom window, Inira could see pillars of clouds that signaled massive destruction. Her first thought was of Tomas; where was he? Was he ok? What was happening? Then she thought of her sister, her mother, and, belatedly, the Ruling Counsel. She knew Tomas would have the answers. He'd been so strange the night before, edgy and keyed up. He was never like that, never short-tempered. But last night, he was, and she couldn't think of anything but getting to him. She felt paralyzed until a frenetic energy fueled by terror shook her loose.

She ran to the doors of her room, trying to yank them open, but they were locked. She started banging on the inside of her bedroom door for their House companion. "Mathilde! Mathilde!

What is happening? Where is Tomas? Where are my mother and sister?" She choked out her words, forcing her breath around the dust rapidly filling the air through the windows. She coughed again and began knocking harder on the door to draw the attention of the woman who was supposed to be getting her ready for the ceremony in the Temple.

It was the holiest day of the year. Tov, as the capital, was filled with pilgrims and residents alike. Her mother would preside with her two daughters standing with her. Inira, as the Heir, on her right, and Samira on her left. They would visually demonstrate the hope of the present and future, with the inscriptions of their ancestry representing the blessed past that brought them here and would see them through. Inira had, strangely, overslept. She never did that, but she'd been up late, trying to soothe and distract Tomas from his mood. She hadn't been successful, and he'd been gone long before she'd woken. That he wasn't here with her, like always, shot fear up and down her spine, making her feel like she was bent over a twisted train track. She was a wreck waiting to happen.

Her eardrums nearly burst as the next shockwave passed through the air. It knocked Inira to her knees, and she felt it before she heard it. The shaking of the house she was in, the personal residence of the High Priestess and her family, was so intense, Inira was sure a volcano was rising from the Aegean Sea in the Mediterranean like in the days their island was created. For a split second, Inira considered laying down in a fetal position, curling up while the building crashed down around her, letting it take her life. Instead, her body moved of its own volition, propelling her into the doorway until the shaking passed. Her body wanted to continue to live no matter what. And whatever this was, Inira knew it wasn't natural.

A loud voice rang out, "The attack is working! The Tower of Sophia has fallen! The Temple is crumbling!"

Inira didn't know who the voice belonged to. It wasn't Mathilde or their other house companion, Violet. It sounded male and distant, which was strange. So many of those who worked in this quarter of Tov were female. Who would be here now, and why were they so pleased AN ATTACK was happening to the most peaceful place on earth? That got her moving – overwhelmed with sick curiosity and massive confusion. She picked the lock on her bedroom door, something she had done a thousand times before to get out to see Tomas and explore the city at night. She dodged debris falling from the ceiling from the explosions, which she now realized were probably bombs going off.

What the fuck is happening, Tomas? Mother? What in the name of the FourFold God was going on? Did the Mother and Father even know? Were the Son and the Daughter asleep during all this destruction? Her thoughts were wild and frantic as she ran down the stairs and out to the front of the house.

When she exited the front door, she stopped in her tracks; destruction as far as her eyes could see. The skyline of Tov, which she knew better than the back of her hand, was decimated. To her left, the two-kilometer walkway to the Temple from the High Priestess' house was blooming with smoke. As she turned in a circle, even with her vision blocked by her house, trembling from the last blast, she could tell everything had been destroyed.

People were wailing, children screaming. Inira put her hands over her ears and could think of nothing but getting to Tomas, to her mother. She felt a tug in her gut towards the Temple, and she wanted to take off running. Her young, strong legs could cover the distance in a few minutes. As she began, she stepped wrong on a piece of concrete, having tried to avoid the rebar sticking out, and turned her ankle.

She felt like she was going to suffocate with the debris in the air. Instead, she screamed, "FUCK! WHAT THE FUCK IS HAPPENING??"

Frustrated and terrified, tears streaked tracks down her cheeks, now dirty from the dust falling from her hair. A small part of her knew she should probably go to the safe house, but she needed to find her mother and sister. She needed to get to Tomas.

The only place she could make herself go was towards the Temple. It was the only place that made sense, even as the capital was ruined. She saw a man in black, her brain registering his size, build, and the sigil on the arm of his jacket. He was medium height, had dark hair, and a full dark beard. She was taller than he was, and even with the twinge in her ankle, she knew she could catch him.

She'd seen that sigil a few times in her studies, two snakes entwined around a flourishing tree. A bastardization of the Goddess symbol, mixing it with the symbolism of the Tree of Knowledge. She couldn't see the words but knew they were there, in Latin.

Ego Solus Via

"Self is the only way." Their enemy, the Serpent's, ancient motto. This was an outdated version in Latin because their leadership had begun in the Roman era. The language had changed over the centuries, but the motto was always the same. Their goal was also the same: bring down Teleosis and get their hands on the Song of Creation. They'd used every world power to try and get it; the last attempt was the assignation of her father.

She knew it didn't pay to be the Heir and not know what they were against. Her mother put the fear of the FourFold God in her, but she never could catch the zealotry. She felt there was more than enough goodwill in the world to stop them by peaceful means. She had to believe that because that's what she knew. Still, the feeling of security in her country's defense had lulled her into a stupor. The Serpents had never stopped working to bring Teleosis down. Now they had, but how?

All of this passed through Inira's brain space in a millisecond as she ran towards the man. She reached him, running full force while he was at a jog. She grabbed that emblem and yanked him backward hard. He nearly fell.

She screamed in his face, "What the fuck are you doing here? What the fuck are you doing?"

The man quickly recovered from his shock and gave her an awful smile. She realized he had bars on his collar; he wasn't just a mere soldier, he was someone important. She also, belatedly, admitted he knew who she was.

"Good morning, Heir to nothing. I am glad to see your city; your mission burned down. We figured out how to do it from the inside.

You should thank your husband for that." He smiled again until her fist crashed into his poisonous, nonsensical mouth. Inira hit him so hard; this time, he did fall, blood spurting from his mouth with a few teeth flying. Her knuckles were bloody, but she didn't care. He hit the ground, and all the breath rushed out of him. He lay on the ground, on his back, trying to catch it again as Inira stood over him, screaming like the Goddess, Kahli, which is what she felt like.

"Where is my mother and sister? What have you done? What are you saying – Tomas is involved?"

Her brain couldn't catch up. Her left arm spiked in, shooting pain down to her wrist while her right hand throbbed. Part of her absently worried her heart would give out from the sheer force of adrenaline pumping through her. Didn't left arm pain signal a heart attack?

Instead of focusing on what was happening to her, she readied herself to beat the shit out of this man until he told her what was happening. She crouched down, and he held up his hands, now smiling through blood. One front tooth was missing, and another was hanging loose. "I will tell you, Heiress. It would be best to see so you understand your life is over. Now you will know *Ego Solus Via.*"

"Shut the fuck up, you maniac! Why are you here? How did you get here? We know how to keep you disgusting Serpents and your vile, ignorant ideology out. We have for millennia!"

"No longer, Heir. You've been in the dark. It was your husband who betrayed you, betrayed all of you. He knew self was the only way. He let us in. He made this glorious plan happen. He is a hero who will be remembered in eternity." He made a weird sign with his hand and touched his forehead. "Long will Tomas Nahas live in glory."

Inira thought she was going to be sick. She opted to kick the man several times, making sure to crack a few ribs. If she was going to die today, she was going to make sure someone felt her level of pain. It wasn't even close to her feelings, but it would do.

"Tell me where to find Tomas."

The man, now curled on his left side to shield himself from further harm, didn't answer immediately. She kicked him again, her panic streaming into violence. "Tell me!"

The man raised his left hand, holding something out to her. "You should thank him. You were not to be harmed. He wanted you alive. Now I see he was right, but not for the same reason. He did it because he loved you," the man spat the words like poison and continued. Inira was rooted to the spot, transfixed by what manic admission he would say next.

"I am Amin, his second. I am proud to have served his ends and to be the one you found. He wanted you to have it. Remember him, his sacrifice, and this day that the Serpents finally triumphed."

He opened his hand. Inira's eyes bugged out, and now she was sure she would vomit. This horrible little man was holding out Tomas' wedding band to her. It was designed as six thin platinum bands woven together, symbolizing the love they shared, crafted together in the love of the FourFold God. She looked down at her right hand to see its match on her finger. As she reached for the ring, her stomach heaved. She threw up all over the man. It splashed all over his chest and got into his eyes. She didn't even feel bad or embarrassed. He was the living symbol of what would make her sick for the next twenty years. She hoped he choked on it.

She wiped her mouth, grateful for his shock that she'd vomited on him, maybe a more fitting assault than another punch or kick. He was holding up the ring, his arm locked. She grabbed it and took off running. She couldn't hear any more of his noxious words. She had to get to the Temple to see for herself.

The man recovered enough to laugh and call after her, "Don't worry, Heir of nothing. I will see you again and make sure you pay for this insult in blood. Everything you have will be mine!"

Inira didn't feel her ankle anymore, closing the last meters towards the Temple. A large crowd had formed around the site, trying to clear any debris to free survivors. Inira knew there would be none. She heard gasps around her and smelled the fresh vomit on the nightshirt of her pajamas. She suddenly realized she had bolted out of the shaking house in nothing but a tank top and sleeping shorts.

It didn't matter now. She knew all was lost. That's when she saw him. The sight of half his body sticking out from under a slab of concrete wiped everything from her mind. She couldn't take in the light missing from his green eyes. She climbed over shifting debris to get to him, with people yelling at her to stop. She tried to lift the slab, and when she couldn't, she started to sob. She grabbed his arm with one hand and put the other on the part of his chest she could reach. She knelt over him, the smoking ruins of the Temple threatening to collapse further.

She didn't care if she died when he was gone. She knew her mother and sister, probably all of the Counsel, was too. Everyone who was anyone had been here early to prepare for the ceremonies. Only she was left. It was too much weight to bear, and she preferred to be crushed under concrete, like her lover's body now was than to live without him or them.

Countless lives were lost, and with only devastation around her, her tears fell on his broken body. She could barely see through the water streaming down her face. She sat in that dangerous shell of the Temple for what felt like hours until the rescue crew picked her up and moved her. The adrenaline cascade was coming to an end, her body sagging and ready to collapse.

It was then she saw it as her eyes continued to roam over what she could see of Tomas' body, his right arm lying limp above his head. It was a small brand, seared into the flesh on the uppermost part of the inside of his arm, so close to where his muscular arm met his torso. That arm that held her through the night, in the overwhelming tenderness of the last ten years. That brand said it all: two snakes surrounding a flourishing tree, the same symbol as that horrible man's uniform patch.

Her heart exploded. Truly, everything she knew was gone, and the last thing she remembered before the world went dark was the feel of Tomas' ring in the palm of her hand.

Chapter 38

Inira woke in the pitch darkness, the curtains drawn tightly. She was covered in sweat. Mattias was wrapped around her like a blanket, the sheets tangled between their legs. She was glad for the comfort, even if it was stifling. The panic-induced nightmare – the memory of the destruction of Tov – where he planned to take her left her more unsettled than when she'd fallen asleep. This was an open traumatic event in her mind, and she felt drained and emptier than before she'd fallen asleep.

Mattias had done his best, but he hadn't been able to comfort her, which she knew was why he left her to herself the night before. His instinct was to go to fix anything that hurt her. The irony was that he was part of the reason she'd experienced the trauma of the bombings in the first place. The revelation of his intention – the reason for this entire trip – brought all that back in the form of her nightmare. Her feelings for him – which she was beginning to realize were also colored by her feelings for Tomas – were so layered. This relationship was so complex.

Looking at him sleeping, she could see the crease between his brows. She felt restless, in need, soul hungry, and knew she needed to take her own space. She wasn't sure she could think clearly with Mattias wrapped around her like a spider monkey. Carefully, she extracted herself from his body. She loved his warmth, the hardness of his chiseled form. They were the perfect contrast. He was hard, and she was soft, and they fit together perfectly. But right now, in the middle of the night, she needed to find peace within herself.

She rose from the bed carefully. He didn't move. She watched his chest's steady rise and fall and couldn't help herself. She leaned over to kiss his full lips. She whispered, "I love you, and I'm scared. I'll be back." This time, he did move enough to shift his position. He mumbled something she could barely make out as he pulled a pillow to him as a substitute.

Then, in an anguished voice, he cried, "Don't leave."

She stilled, frozen in place. She knew he wasn't awake, but what he said carried such a desperate sound of loss. It hit her square in the chest. She felt the compulsion to climb back into the bed with him and care for him until she realized he was dreaming. He was not talking to her but a phantom woman, perhaps his mother. Mattias was wrestling with his own demons in his dreams.

Then, as clear as a bell, she heard her therapist's voice.

Inira, you have to learn how to reparent yourself. You can fill in the gaps, reassuring yourself of your safety. Use the tools and the resources we've worked on—practice when you feel triggered to take that pause and recenter. You can work through your trauma. It just means putting the effort into it. You are more than capable enough."

She'd heard those words from Lexi months ago. She knew they came back from the recesses of her mind now for this purpose. She finally moved away from the edge of the bed. As she'd done before, she decided to choose herself. She would have the opportunity to comfort and care for Mattias, to listen to more of his past – his own traumatic upbringing. He'd only been able to share so much with her, but she trusted they would have time for him to sort it all out. That would come later. She needed to tend to her own heart first.

She silently padded out of the room and closed the door without a sound. She went over to the balcony outside the lounging area. The open concept of their accommodations, as lux as they were, meant that everything flowed in the space like water. Only the door to the bedroom closed them off to the world. She quietly opened the French doors and felt the rush of the sea air hit her like an embrace from the Mother. Barely 20 feet separated them from the water. The Aegean was dark, almost black. The moon was to her left, just a sliver. She was glad she would not arrive in Teleosis on a full moon, with the highest holy days on full moons or eclipses. The energy portals were wide open during those times, and the rhythm of their worship mirrored a lunar schedule to take full advantage of that openness.

Inira let out a full breath. There was just enough light to see, and she let her shoulders drop from her ears. At this hour, the waves were gentle, providing a serene soundtrack. She sank into the plush loveseat. She hadn't spent as much time out here reading as she would have liked and wished they had more time to be together without the pressure of his plans looming over them. She would love to have a month to wake up to the slow, languid drag of the tip of Mattias' tongue and the feather-soft kisses that followed wherever he felt like starting. She wanted more time to watch the load lift from his shoulders as they talked. They needed more time for her to teach him how to be her Consort, her partner—the last five days had barely made a dent.

As she prepared herself for meditation, for the first time in a long time, she prayed to the FourFold God that They would grant her and Mattias more time together. She wasn't sure they would have it, but it seemed only fitting to ask in the wake of that dream. The revelation of returning to Tov came back to her, and she heard the clock ticking loud and clear.

She felt herself upset again, the restlessness rising like a hot air balloon inside her chest; she decided to make good on Lexi's months-old exhortation. It was time to remember how to soothe herself. She'd learned and had some practice, but with the af-ter-effects of her panicked memories resurfacing, it was time to speak to that much younger version of herself waiting inside her.

She put her hand on her bare chest. She'd gone to sleep in a but-ter-soft v-neck nightgown, a gorgeous cream color. Mattias knew her color preferences and had thought about what he wanted to see her in. He wasn't disappointed when she came out of the enormous walk-in closet for the first time. She felt the heat of her hand as her fingers spread out across her chest. Her palm rested on her sternum, just above the slow thud of her heart, a heart that had been through so much. She sat with her head bowed, and at once, the tears overflowed from her eyes, down her cheeks, and on her hand as it rested on the battered organ that still kept pumping.

As the tears slowed and dried, she knew she had to speak to her younger self. The words didn't come right at first. It was like they were stuck inside of her, and it wasn't until she pronounced her name that it began to feel natural.

"Inira, we are safe."

The gentle ocean breeze stopped stirring around her face. The sound of the water below her feet faded away. There was no movement, no sound. It was as if the universe held its breath to hear what she would say next. Her hand still resting on her heart, she gathered her courage to speak again against the emotion crowding into her thoughts at her own admission.

Minutes passed silently until she continued, "Inira, we are safe. Thank You. I love you. I'm sorry. Please forgive me.."

The truth of each phrase, a Hawaiian self-forgiveness practice Lexi had taught her, rang slightly hollow. She didn't know if something terrible awaited her in Tov or not. Mattias had made it sound like it was only a tour of their reconstruction work. She knew there was more to it than that, that he wanted something from her. She didn't know how far he would go to get it, but she felt more than she knew that his approach to her had drastically changed.

She braved her fear again. "Inira, no matter what happens, we are together and safe. Thank you. I love you. I'm sorry. Please forgive me."

She kept talking to her inner child and adolescent, saying the phrases intermingled with others that came to mind. She told herself about her years trying to numb the pain, but now she knew they were strong enough to face it without alcohol. She repeatedly repeated to her young adult self, who was so scared inside of her, how safe, cherished, and powerful she was. She admitted she didn't know what would come but that past didn't have to affect them in the present anymore.

With the solid weight of her own hand against her chest, warmth spread across her chest, down her stomach, arms, legs, and even up her shoulders, neck, and face. The secret whispers she gave herself had a lulling effect. She imagined her brain rewiring those terror-filled experiences like some divine editor was clipping, cutting, and anchoring those memories where they were supposed to be in her brain. As she finished speaking, she closed her eyes to envision what was happening inside herself. The moon and the stars were still in the sky. A glimmer of the heavenly light flared, and she saw, behind her closed eyelids, that light descend towards her. The light came closer and closer to her, appearing in front of where she sat. She remained at peace, feeling complete serenity and oneness with herself and everything around her. Then, the light moved towards her. This was cellular, generational healing. This was what she knew to be *shalom.*

The light settled on her skin, and she felt ancient magic move from her skin into her bones. It took root there, holding her in total security. She didn't move or speak, only watching the progression of the spiritual manifest on and into her physical body. It was hers by right and always had been. She was grounded in the knowledge that she was, in fact, safe and would always be kept that way, no matter what. Her fear of returning to Tov transformed into a new connection to herself. But it was more than that, she realized. She recognized this connection was eternal. The feelings of the dream she'd had in London, the Creation Song, the rightness of herself, in harmony with everything, came back. She moved her hand off her head and sat back of them in her lap, palms facing up. She recognized this position. It was the position of surrender and reception. It was a personal form of prayer, to sit with hands open, naturally curled and ready to receive. It had been years since she'd sat like this on purpose.

She sat, bathed in moonlight, wrapped in the serenity, in harmony with herself and the Divine presence of the God she was sure had forgotten her; she felt herself take a full breath. Her lungs were filling to their total capacity, and the oxygen infusion was heady and spreading through her body like she was new. She felt reborn, alive, centered, and, most importantly, safe.

She opened her eyes and caught the first glimpse of the coming dawn.

She remembered the last words her mother had ever written and entered into the catalog of the worship book of the High Priestess. Her mother had not been particularly gifted in creating their faith's worship songs and poems. She had the smallest number of writings recorded. That gifting ebbed and flowed down the generations. Inira had never written or gotten the chance to enter anything at all. But at this moment, she felt a click in her soul. Her mother's words healed a long-standing place full of verbal barbs and splinters. She felt as if the Divine were gently pulling those out, and as They did, it lessened the pain and impact. Those places where her mother had wounded her with her words and abusive treatment were so tender. She knew they probably always would be to some extent.

Yet now, as a grown woman herself, she could see her mother as she was: traumatized, scared, and doing her best. Her adolescent self curled up into the warmth of her adult self, and together, they recited the refrain from their mother's last poem:

We must cry out to Them.

We must return to Them.

We must seek out The FourFold One.

The Mother will Love us.

The Father will Guide us.

The Son will Save us.

The Daughter will Show us who we are.

We will find home.

***

Inira returned to the bed, and when they both woke, they were quiet. Her nightmare and subsequent time of prayer had stilled her emotions. When Mattias rolled over to her, he looked tired, like he'd barely slept. He took her face and whispered, "Good morning, Light Bringer. You look different today. More alive, if that is possible." Then he kissed her, and she could feel his longing, his need, and so she gave herself to him once more. She poured her love into where their bodies touched. She felt her heart more open than ever before. He took it all, and when they were complete in each other, both panting with a sheen of sweat over their bodies, Mattias looked more alive, and Inira didn't feel depleted at all.

The feeling she had of being fully alive continued to expand throughout their morning before they left for the airport for the one-hour flight to her home island.

He cooked a feast, and Inira ate everything he served. Their time together had been so fulfilling and physical that she was ravenous. She did feel the background hum of anxiety in her mind begin to ramp up, almost like a low noise, mysterious in its origins, but she knew it was there. Returning home never seemed possible, so despite how connected she felt to herself, the FourFold God, and Mattias, she wasn't surprised at the nervous energy threatening to distract her.

She was returning home to begin her calling anew. She was finally going to see her birthright fulfilled.

It had gotten cloudy, and the wind had picked up, a storm brewing over sea moving west towards them.

Perhaps a fitting omen, Inira thought as they walked to the car for the ride to the plane. She hoped the storm would break on Teleosis after they left. She didn't think they would stay the night, but she didn't know the accommodations. She hoped they would be there only long enough to take the tour and for the plane to be ready again. Mattias reached over and wrapped his large hand around hers as they sat beside each other. She turned to him and smiled. He smiled back, but she noticed the tightness around his eyes. She still felt the peace and solidity from the healing within her in the early morning. She was still connected to the Source of her power despite her nerves.

Mattias didn't have that connection. Maybe one day he would, but as of right now, he was still a novice in the ways of the FourFold God. She knew she had a lot to relearn and remember as well. Teaching him would remind her. She looked over at him for a long moment before she spoke. He looked back at her, right into her eyes. She knew they needed to be on the same page, so she opened the conversation.

"Alright, Mattias Nahas. My Consort, Billionaire, Visionary, and illustrious Deitas." He squeezed her hand at the first title and grinned sardonically at the last. She continued, "What's our plan to ensure we both emerge from this visit safe and sound together?

Chapter 39

min Ahmadi was rarely nervous, a luxury born of the conviction of purpose. The façade of his pleasure at seeing Charlotte was perfectly in place. Yet, Lukas Nahas had made him anxious twice in the last two days. He had the girl, which was at least partly following directions. However, Lukas also chose to bring the Charlotte woman along until he could ensure Emerie Boehme was on the plane. The boy did not follow directions as instructed. He hoped the boy didn't think he could keep both women. That was not in the plan, and he didn't think getting Emerie Boehme pregnant would happen if she thought he was also fucking Charlotte. Not that Ahmadi had any proof he was, but given the boy's playboy reputation, he wouldn't be surprised.

Still, his plan was in motion. He was ignoring Mattias' attempts to contact him. Mattias was no longer in charge anymore. Even if Mattias didn't know it, the rest of the Serpent leadership did. Ahmadi had ensured that when he sent the text log to the Heir of Nothing's worthless husband. The whole organization knew the Deitas had slipped, and with carefully placed covert gossip that couldn't be traced back to him, everyone was willing to put their support behind Ahmadi's bid to take power. If there were a few holdouts, Amin would take care of those in due time, especially with Lukas under his thumb.

Amin could handle Mattias; he always could. He had spent the last several years securing his power with those underneath them in the organization. Mattias was only a figurehead, and everyone but him knew it. Puppet master extraordinaire, it was Ahmadi pulling the strings all along, securing not fealty to Mattias so much as the vision of the Serpents. If it brought them glory, people would die for a cause, and Amin produced results. Nahas was none the wiser, especially now with his idiotic distraction with Inira Boehme.

Of course, Ahmadi had been worried that Inira would recognize him from that moment during the destruction of Tov. He had a beard then and had shaved it not long after to avoid any identification with the attack. He often woke up feeling her kicks and smelling her vomit on him all these years later. He'd hated her then and wanted to see everything around her burn. Nothing had changed. What she stood for was abhorrent to him. He'd spent the last twenty years laying the groundwork for what would happen.

He would possess the blood of both the Heirs, more than enough to unlock every secret of Teleosis. Ultimately, the greatest prize was someone to sing the Song of Creation at his command. If one refused, he would use the other to ensure their compliance. Whether it was mother or daughter, he would be the one to put the knife in her arm and draw more than enough blood. It was his birthright. His family had been in the Serpents for generations; his ancestry was almost as illustrious as hers.

The one thing Lukas had done right was playing his part with Emerie well. After their initial meeting, he sweet-talked her over several days. They'd started texting, which she'd kept a secret from her father. Lukas had convinced her to join him on the false quest to save her mother once he "found out where his father had taken her." It was all a ruse, but at least he had the magnetism of his father, and apparently, the Boehme women couldn't resist.

He didn't want a woman – or a man – for that matter, to have that kind of power over him. The touch of another repulsed him. Between his father's beatings and his mother's abuse, his goal had never been about the physical. His body was there to help him achieve only one end - overtake Teleosis and dominate the world with his limitless power. The mission was his lover, his legacy, and those he crafted in his image, populating the organization's ranks. He had a wealth of progeny.

He knew Mattias would fall for Inira. It was inevitable. He openly supported the Deitas partnering with her, even suggesting starting Nahas Helps to ensure they met. Mattias only ever wanted the best, and Triune was. He could appreciate what Inira had done for that tiny player. She guided it to be the force it was today. She had her uses, and no one knew that better than Amin Ahmadi. He hoped Lukas was stronger than his father and could resist the doe-eyed little girl. He hoped he would snuff out her spark if he had to. They needed warm blood to unlock the safe house on Tov, where all the records were kept. But he didn't need anyone conscious to make that happen.

He absently stroked the brand on the underside of his forearm. He rarely wore short sleeves as he needed to maintain the image of his professionalism and place in their movement to the outside world. He didn't enjoy doing the ceremonial things of their beliefs, preferring the operations. The divine right was what the Nahas line was for. The Boehme women might have the Priestess bloodline, but the Nahas men shined when they were in front of an altar. Mattias and Lukas had the looks and enough intelligence to play the part.

Ahmadi worked in the shadows and preferred to stay there, like a spider, until it was too late for the prey to escape his web. He was the snake no one ever saw, coiled in the grass, ready to strike.

His current concern about Lukas occupied his mind. The reconstruction was on schedule and would be ready for their arrival on the island later today. The Temple site was completely restored, with a few alterations that made it a sanctuary for the Serpents, not the Teleosian religion reborn.

His phone buzzed, and Lukas finally messaged him:

Is my father ready? Will he be there?

Ahmadi shook his head in annoyance as he typed his response:

Yes, of course, darling boy. Continue to woo your future bride and make a plan to send Charlotte back. We don't want to confuse your beloved.

He saw the three dots before he even finished typing:

Charlotte will not be a problem; I'll ensure she gets home safely, and I've already secured her intentions to tell no one what is happening. The only outlier is Francis Boehme. No one has seen him in more than twelve hours.

Ahmadi sighed again in annoyance:

Yes, that is concerning. However, we have enough trackers on him, so he will show up. Your only job now is to woo Emerie into going through with the ceremony. We don't need that sweet girl under stress.

He knew that would piss Lukas off. Lukas was just as possessive as his father, and he had been captivated by the young woman from the moment he saw her picture. There seemed to be a type of predestination, a touch of magic whenever a man of the Nahas bloodline saw a Boehme. Amin shook his hand in comprehension. He knew Lukas suspected him of something, so he continued to work the angle that always had success, comparing Lukas to Mattias. Once Lukas came to live with Mattias permanently after his gold-digging mother agreed to give him up to run off and party for the rest of her worthless life, it had been so easy. Ahmadi treated him as his own. Lukas never entirely warmed to him, but he was compliant enough.

Now that he was older, though, he was thinking for himself. Ahmadi knew he'd been asking questions, even recruiting his faction of support. He was glad that the boy finally learned self-sufficiency. He was too late, though. Now was the time to fulfill his purpose. He had the Heir and the spare. And soon, their Boehme women would give him the victory snatched from him after the bombings. They could do it the easy way or the hard way. Ahmadi was prepared for both. He had worked his whole life for this. His family had bled and died with this vision written on their hearts. He would have what he needed, and the world would be his.

Chapter 40

Lukas blew out a hot, incensed breath. It was one thing to work with Amin Ahmadi at his father's behest and with the pretense of making sure Ahmadi had eyes on him. It was another to talk to *and partner* with him, even if he was running a game on the man. He wasn't sure how his father had put up with the undercurrent of sniveling and backbiting; it was mindboggling that he hadn't noticed. He was plotting against Mattias. Lukas was sure his godfather's loyalty was to his agenda, to get his hands on any weapon that would allow him to control everyone.

Lukas would be glad to rid the world of the Serpents. It was a disgusting and diseased vision, just like Ahmadi and always had been. He discovered that early on after coming to live with his father. He hadn't known what to do about it for a long time, so he followed what he was told. As a result, his hands were dirty. For the first few years of being with his father and under the tutelage of Ahmadi, he had been prepared to do anything to win his father's affection. His mother was in no way or shape capable of raising a moral, productive child. The proof that she'd left Lukas to be raised by a long string of au pairs and tutors at his father's expense. Now, though, he had his opportunity to rid the world of madness. He hoped for enough change in his father so they could talk honestly. Lukas said a silent prayer to whatever god was listening that Mattias would see reason and turn the sinking ship of Nahas Industries into something that benefited humanity instead of endlessly taking from it.

Jessamine, an older Kenyan woman who was his last companion, planted the seed of change in his heart. She had lived near a Teleosian outpost, going to the school started in her village. She learned about the alternative history, courtesy of her Teleosisan teachers, whom she called missionaries. They weren't there to convert her and her village to a religion but to serve, educate, and assist. The attitude of love and service in the name of the FourFold God – and how much they invested in the success of every person in the village – cemented her beliefs. And when she was hired to be his companion, she told Lukas all about it.

It was a shocking dissonance to go from those stories of goodness and light to being soaked in the toxic masculinity of the Serpents. He was put into a group of men his age for training and "re-education." For the first time, Lukas had a group to belong to, and they became his brothers. Until he watched them gang-rape a woman as part of an initiation. They'd gone out to a pub in the seedier part of London. One of the guys slipped a roofie in her drink, and they took her back to their loft. They each took turns with her—all except for Lukas.

Lukas threw up and ran out. He ended up at his father's office penthouse under the guise of telling him he was ready to begin to learn from him directly. Mattias was flattened and ready as well. Lukas never told his father about the initiation ritual and never saw any of those men again. He had ensured they were all transferred to the ends of the Earth. That was five years ago when Lukas was 19. He did tell Amin Ahmadi, who said sympathetic words but ultimately told Lukas to accept it as the order of things. Lukas was repulsed because no one ever deserved to be treated that way.

He floundered for a while, trying to stick close to his father. They didn't get along until Ahmadi suggested starting Nahas Helps with Lukas heading it up. They hired Triune, with Inira Boehme at the helm. Then Lukas was briefed on her history – and shocked to learn his uncle was her first husband. All the stories of Teleosis Jessamine had told him came rushing back to him as he got deeper involved in the rebuild and formation of Nahas Helps, the cover for the Tov rebuild. Everything changed for him when, as part of his research, he saw the picture of Emerie, Inira's daughter.

Something in his mind clicked. It wasn't love at first sight. It was hope.

He knew Ahmadi wanted Emerie and Inira for the same reason, but it wasn't clear precisely what that was. Ahmadi was an expert at holding everyone in the dark. Lukas decided, looking at the picture of Emerie, that he wouldn't stand there and watch another woman be victimized by a man's bid for power and prestige. Lukas knew he was no saving angel but wanted to be a good man. And if helping the soon-to-be Heir of Teleosis was how he did it, he would.

Even if, at the moment, she wasn't being cooperative.

He'd tried to explain what he knew, but her distrust was still high. He liked her right away. He liked her spark and wisdom, even at her young age. He had a nagging urge to want to guide and protect her. It didn't make sense other than he wanted to see the hope she would bring to the world. That spark in this situation, though, was grating on his nerves. They had to board the plane to Teleosis, and she was having none of it. She was furious as she felt he'd been misleading her, preying on her need to go to her mother. He leaned down to look at her, his tall form nearly bending in half to see her in the limo's backseat they'd taken to the private airport. She had wedged herself against the opposite door, as far away from him as possible but not out of fear.

No, Emerie Boehme was not scared at all. She was enraged like a feral cat.

Lukas Nahas wasn't a nice guy through and through. He had a plan and was focused, and her refusal to get out of the car was hindering that.

"Lukas, you cannot do this."

The voice speaking, however, was like a glass of cold water on his head in the middle of an exquisite meal. He straightened up to his full height and inhaled to a count of ten. He held it for five beats, then exhaled to a count of twelve. He'd been a competitive swimmer in university. His height was a great asset in the sport and had taught him to maximize his lung capacity.

He turned to face the woman he'd been leading on for weeks. He knew he could have gone about all of this in a way much closer to integrity, but he was also trying to navigate the noxious politics within the Serpents and stay under Ahmadi's radar. None either of the women understood. Facing Charlotte, he changed his tone. It was the opposite of the friendly, flirty tone she was used to. It was dismissive, formal, and very business-like. He needed her to be repulsed by him and, in her pain of his rejection, clue Emerie's father into what was happening. He'd dropped more than a few hints that he'd hate it if Francis found out the plans,' secretly praying again to whatever god was listening to get Francis to Tov somehow. He needed the distraction to get at least Emerie, if not Inira and his father, away from whatever horrific end Ahmadi had planned.

"Charlotte, I no longer require your opinions. I don't need your presence either. You've exceeded your usefulness to me and Nahas International. You *will* get on the next plane to the States. You *will not* tell anyone anything about what has happened. If you do, we will bury you. You will never see your son again. I don't have to work hard to make that happen—just a few phone calls. I wouldn't say I like repeating the consequences I've stated multiple times. So here is your last warning: if you choose to act against me, it will not just be your career that is over."

Charlotte looked now as if she was going to scratch his eyes out. He had enjoyed their dalliances and their one night together. He had needed her to get close to Emerie. When he discovered her outside the hotel after the encounter with Inira in the lobby bar, and she Uber-ed over to his loft later, it had all been too easy. Amin had discovered Charlotte was the path of least resistance to Emerie. She had her agenda for fucking him, thinking it was going to advance her career. The chemistry between them made it all the sweeter. Inira had given him a suitable warning in the hotel lobby that night, but it hadn't derailed Charlotte.

The moment he'd finished, he'd felt sick. He had a reputation as a playboy, which was exaggerated for effect within the Serpent's ranks. His body count was much lower than was reported, and using a woman for an agenda, even as she used him too, wasn't who Lukas was. And now Emerie thought she knew who he was, and it grated just as much as her obstinance to get out of the car. Not a small part of him was greatly enjoying Emerie Boehme's challenge because he knew after all of this was over and he deposited her safely back at home, he would have done something good.

Charlotte glared at him, her thick, tight curls whipping around her face in the wind. Her arms were locked in a self-embrace over her chest, and she stood just out of reach. "I thought you were smarter than this, Lukas. There are always other ways to achieve your goals. You don't have to resort to criminal activity."

Lukas laughed loudly. In another world, she might have been right.

"Charlotte, sleeping with me one time doesn't give you insight into my psyche. I was playing a part, just as you were. And because I'm well-versed in 'criminal activity',he said, using his index fingers as quotation marks around the words, like Emerie was so fond of doing – "You would do well to remember just how far I will go to see my plan through."

He nodded to the other car's driver, who stalked towards Charlotte. Charlotte saw him coming out of the corner of those chocolatey brown eyes. Now, they were menacing, full of venom. "You will regret this! She is not a toy to be played with! You are a worthless piece of shit and could never measure up to her!"

Lukas didn't even bother with a reply. He waved her off, a final, condescending gesture. Charlotte screamed in fury as the bulky man grabbed her arms and dragged her away. He'd already blocked her number in the Nahas system. Nahas Helps was a well-played sham. They'd paid Stanley handsomely, allowing the old man enough time to put his affairs in order and give his employees a generous severance. He'd privately met with Lukas and Ahmadi during that first London trip and told them he had weeks to live. Lukas wasn't completely heartless.

He bent down again, reaching into the limo to offer Emerie his hand. He could have sworn he heard her hiss. "Emerie, please come on. We've been over this. I'm taking you to see your mother."

Emerie remained silent, turning her head away. With only her profile visible, Lukas was struck dumb. He'd known many beautiful women in his young life as they circled the rich and powerful like sharks out for blood. Hell, that was how Lukas came to be, after all. But there was a radiance to Emerie he couldn't get over. It was like sunshine. It could warm you or give you heatstroke if you weren't careful.

Lukas sighed a long, deep, wounded sound. He decided he would poke this cornered cat and see what happened. Emerie was easily provoked, and if it got her out of the car, it was a risk he was willing to take. "I know you are unhappy with my treatment of Charlotte. She's like a big sister to you. I get it. I also know your 'girl code.' You aren't supposed to sleep with a friend's ex."

Emerie's head snapped back around to face him so fast that her neck cracked. "Excuse me? The level of wrongness in everything you just said is overwhelming. Fuck all the way off, Lukas."

Lukas smiled big, with all his teeth showing. Yes, he liked flying too close to this sun. He was fairly sure she would melt his wings. The fall back to earth would be worth it. He continued as if she hadn't said anything.

"Look, I'm not expecting it to happen overnight; maybe you won't even want to wait till the wedding night. However, in case you didn't know, we are betrothed. We will have a formal engagement ceremony as part of what we do in Tov. I knew we had to work together when I discovered Ahmadi's plan. Charlotte was the easiest way to get to you. I don't like how this is playing out either, and I can understand why you are mad. I won't force you into anything after we are married, but if you decide to try me on for size, you won't regret it." He winked at her.

She turned a shade of red, which was unhealthy. "Lukas, how could you think I would ever be attracted to you? You tricked me! You used Charlotte! You won't 'make it worth my while.' What freaking century did you grow up in anyways? We are practically the same age! I will marry who I choose when I choose. You do not deserve me."

She was right, of course. She didn't understand the stakes or the kind of game being played. Still, the other thing he liked about Emerie Boehme, even at nineteen (she reminded him), she knew her worth and what she wanted in a man. Liking their banter too much, he leveraged her mother's history against her. "Your mother was engaged at your age. She was married at twenty to my uncle."

At that, Emerie's face fell. "I know all about Tomas, Lukas. I know he was my mother's first love. I also know that he was a mass murderer, betraying everything he stood for and everyone he loved, including my mother. He broke her. I'm not about to let a man do that to me."

He felt the twinge in his back from the position of his body and a hollowness in his gut at her words. He didn't want to put her in danger. He didn't want to set her up for a breaking. He wasn't his uncle or his father – and he certainly wasn't Ahmadi or like the other men in the Serpents. He didn't know how to get that through to make her feel safe with him. So, he tried a gentler approach. "Let's continue this conversation on the plane. We have about four hours. We can talk, and you can shower, eat, and rest. I want to be your friend, Emerie. I want to help you get your mother to safety. Will you let me help you?"

"I'm not going, Lukas. I keep saying that. That is not the basis for a healthy start to a marriage, FYI. Nor is insinuating I will sleep with you, especially considering how you played Charlotte. You disgust me."

Every conversation they'd had since the truth came out on the way to the airport in the States returned to Charlotte. Even in their texts, when Lukas tried to steer her away from those thoughts, Emerie always returned to his relationship with her mother's friend. Charlotte was her big sister in so many ways.

He sighed, growing tired of this argument. He did what he had to do, and did he regret it? From the second he entered the hotel room with her. "Look, Sunshine, I know what I did with Charlotte was below board. In your world, there are better ways of getting what you want. But in mine, sometimes things get ugly. And let's be clear, it was Charlotte's idea, which I hope you ask her about. I'd like not to manhandle you, but I will. Come willingly or not, I'm getting you out of this car."

Lukas stood up to stretch his back and immediately heard the sound of the door opening. Yep, she was going to make him do this the hard way.

He watched her sprint down the blacktop towards the air traffic control tower in a dress he'd bought her so she could change out of her school uniform. She'd let him, thinking it was just a fun afternoon of flirting before he started driving in the opposite direction of her house. He watched her long, lean legs, feeling the stir of how fun it would be to catch her. She held the door handle when he caught up to her. It would not have mattered if she'd gotten in; everyone at this airport was on the Nahas payroll.

He grabbed her elbow and flipped her around to face him. He caged her in with both hands on either side of her head, standing with an inch between them. He lowered his face to hers, noses touching. She was tall, but he still had some inches on her. He spoke in a whisper, breathless from the chase. "I liked that a lot. You can run from me all you want, Sunshine. Trust me, though, I will catch up. I meant what I said. I'm trying to help you. I don't want to throw you over my shoulder and board the plane with your delicious ass in the air for all to see. But I will."

She glowered at him through her lashes and licked her lips. His eyes tracked the movement, and she was close enough that her chest heaved, brushing his. He had liked her from the start and had tried to play the part of Prince Charming. He knew she'd figured out it was all an act, but despite how much she protested and claimed not to believe him, he could feel her attraction to him. It was like they had a string attached to their belly buttons, pulling her towards him, too.

She was going to be his wife, but it didn't have to be for long. He would let her go. He felt he didn't want to but knew how this started wasn't the foundation for a successful relationship. The least he could do was make it pleasant and keep her safe. The last thing he wanted was to end up like his parents. "I like being this close to you. As much as I know, I have told you the truth about what's going on. I want us to be friends, Emerie."

At that statement, she laughed right in his face. Her warm breath hit him, and a little spittle landed on his cheek. "You have no idea what it means to be friends. And I will run again the first chance I get. I'll go with you now because I want to get my mother out of whatever nefarious plot you and your father have cooked up. It's like boys playing at war."

Lukas sighed forcefully, pulled back to wipe his cheek, and bared his teeth. "Sunshine, they are not playing. And my Dad isn't the enemy. He and your mother are working together. They ARE together. It's a perilous game!"

She tilted her face so her eyes met his, looking into him like she could see everything on the inside lay bare. She probably could. She whispered, "How did you get like this?"

He stared at her for a long moment. He was deeply uncomfortable and desired to tell her about his life. Her youth and innocence contrasted with the darkness he'd witnessed, the darkness he felt creeping in on him. He knew he had holes in his soul, and now, face to face with someone so pure, he wasn't sure if it was his agenda he wanted – or for the chance to heal himself. He looked into her eyes and moved his hand towards her face. He stopped himself from cupping her cheek, as he didn't want to touch her without consent. So, he told her, "Come with me, and I'll tell you."

She continued to hold his gaze, her breathing slowing. She was so warm. He was too close to the sun. He could see the drop of sweat run down her neck, past her collarbone. Their attraction to each other was undeniable this close. For the hundredth time, he wished he hadn't muddied the waters with Charlotte. But now, looking at Emerie, all he felt was wrong.

Instead, she asked something that threw him off. "Lukas, will you be honest with me? That's the only way I can see how we could start a friendship. You kidnapped me, slept with my mom's best friend, and discarded her. You seem just like I expected you to be – a spoiled, alpha asshole. Will you let me know who you are?"

At that, Lukas wanted to kiss her senseless. The impulse to lean down and claim her mouth was so strong, and he would have with any other woman. But Emerie Boehme was not any other woman.

If he wanted her to come willingly, he would have to drop the asshole bit. He pushed off the door, the sensation of burning from being too close to her leaving him. He turned to the side, holding his arm out for her to take, like a Regency-era couple going for a stroll. "I'll do my best, Sunshine. Join me, please. It is my honor to escort you to your ancestral homeland."

She rolled her eyes, a frequent response because she wasn't coy. She was direct, and her intentions were good. He needed more of that in his life. She took his arm, her hand resting on his bicep. She dug her nails in, which made him suck in a breath as he looked down at her. He, however, could flirt and often did. "Sunshine, don't tease me."

She narrowed her eyes at him. "I'm not. I'm reminding you I have claws and won't hesitate to use them on you."

He chuckled, low in his throat. "Oh, I hope not. You will make my life that much more interesting. Now, come my little kitty cat. Let me tell you about my life as a swimmer since we have that in common. That's what friends do, right? Share their commonalities? Then, answer all the questions rattling in your big brain while we eat lunch."

Lukas let her ascend the steps of the G5 first. He was happy now they were moving forward, but more than that, happy his bride-to-be had a mind of her own. He couldn't wait to see what would happen between them.

Chapter 41

T ext from Charlotte to Francis, Friday, 1 pm London time.

I know where your wife and daughter are. They are on their way to Teleosis.

Francis:

WHAT THE FUCK? What is happening? I got a text from Emerie that said she was at a friend's house. Is she not there?

Charlotte to Francis:

No, she lied. Lukas Nahas convinced her to go with him to save Inira. They've been texting and she agreed to meet him after school yesterday. When she did, he kidnapped her, flew her to London and now they are on their way to Tov.

Francis to Charlotte:

Tell me how to get there.

Charlotte to Francis:

I'll help you make the arrangements. I'll have to charter a private plane and it will take you about 11 hours.

Francis to Charlotte:

I'll pay whatever I have to. Stanley fucking owes me, I'll get him to pay for it.

Charlotte to Francis:

I've got it. Plus, you can't reach Stanley anyway. He is in the ICU. He caught a C-Diff infection at his last infusion treatment, and they are pretty sure he won't make the weekend. He is leaving Triune and all his resources to Inira. His sons are livid. I just found out.

Francis to Charlotte:

Well, I'll have to deal with all that later. I'm going to pack. Text me where and when to go and I will get my girls.

Charlotte to Francis:

I'm so sorry about all of this, Francis. I'm so sorry for my part in it all. I didn't see what was right in front of my face.

Francis to Charlotte:

And your part is what, exactly? Wait, never mind. It doesn't matter now. All that counts is me getting to them. Inira may not want me but I will fucking destroy anyone who tries to harm her or Emerie. When will I have the details of my flight?

Charlotte to Francis:

Giselle will text you within in the next 30 minutes. I'm on a plane back from London.

Francis to Charlotte:

I hope whatever you did to put my family in this position was worth it, Charlotte.

Charlotte to Francis:

> *It wasn't. Just get to them. The Serpents have bad plans for both of them, I fear.*

Francis to Charlotte:

> *I'll kill them all if they touch a hair on their heads.*

***

Inira and Mattias held hands on the short plane ride the whole way. Inira texted Emerie one-handed, and Mattias reached out to Lukas as well. If they were involved, as Mattias now feared, they were from what he'd heard from those who still followed him in the Serpents. Ahmadi was indeed bidding for power; Lukas had confirmed that much.

Inira hated that Emerie was involved, but Mattias swore no harm would come to her; there was no reason for her to be on the island. Lukas said the same, not that she had any reason to trust him. When she read the email from Stanley's sons, she despaired. He was dying, and she wasn't there with him. Her heart ached. He had stood by her for so long and through so much. It couldn't be helped. When she returned, she would meet with his sons to determine Triune's future.

Charlotte had been silent, and that concerned Inira a bit. She wanted her friend's advice. She'd been such an anchoring gift, helping her as Inira had helped Charlotte learn and grow. For her friend to go silent could have been tied to the issues with Stanley's illness or her displeasure at Inira's choices. Still, Inira, when she thought of Charlotte, couldn't assign her silence to either of those two things. She wondered if there was much more going on than she knew.

She was brought back into the present when Mattias squeezed her hand. Looking at him, Inira wished more than once that the short, beautiful dream of them in their bubble on the beach hadn't ended. She had gotten her power back and had given Mattias some of it. Maybe they stood a chance, but returning to Teleosis and what awaited them there cast a long shadow. She felt that storm following them.

Inira trusted their plan. They had to understand what was happening and what Ahmadi's plans were. Then, they could act. She felt the danger, but there was something more profound. She'd always had insight, yet this level of understanding, perhaps from pulling back the curtain on her subconscious mind thanks to her nightmare and the healing after, was denser. It was as if a different kind of life awaited her on the other side of this trip home. She knew something was coming. She could feel it, and it would change everything.

She was deeply concerned Amin had an ace in the hole they were blind to. When it was revealed, she would not stay silent. She would use her voice. She always had, and she hoped Mattias knew that. "Mattias, *Ahava ostar*, are you ready for what might happen today?"

He turned his head from where he was looking out the jet window on the other side of the plane. Their attention had shifted from swallowed up in each other to the outside world once again. He held her gaze, looking into her for a long time. When he spoke, she was surprised at his answer.

"*Luz de Amor*, I am trying to pray. I know there are still depths I have yet to gain access to – within you and myself. I plead desperately for the time to know you completely and in peace. I do not know what will happen today. I fear the worst, but I am trying to trust what has awoken in you. I know I have been blind to Amin's greed. It served me so well for so long. I made a mistake in giving Amin so much autonomy. Now, we will both have to reckon with that."

Inira wasn't prepared for such a raw answer. She knew he felt betrayed. She had never seen him so vulnerable. That was a double-edged sword. If she'd not gotten involved with Mattias, she would still have her marriage; yet, 'what might have been' fueled her drinking for so long. She had lost critical trust and relationship by choosing Mattias, but she would finally have some closure and answers she never expected to receive.

She had the chance to be who she always knew she could be.

Mattias' face hardened as he thought about the potential outcomes of the interactions with Ahmadi as they toured the rebuilt capital of Teleosis and what would happen if he forced the issues of how to access their hidden technological secrets that would change the course of history in anyone other than Teleosian hands. "Inira, I love you. You are my future. I will not let anything happen to you."

"Mattias, I love you. We are in this together. That is where our strength comes from."

"I will not let him harm you or Emerie."

She leaned over to kiss him deeply. She couldn't agree with him because she wasn't sure how much control of anything he still had. They were walking into the dark. There was no sense of security, only trusting the FourFold God would hold them through it all. In this moment, she gave him what she could: her presence, her physicality. He took it desperately. He unbuckled their seat belts and pulled them to standing. He swept her into his arms and carried her towards the private jet cabin, never breaking the kiss. He was kissing her as if it was the last time.

He gently lowered her to the bed, only then breaking the kiss to look into her eyes. He didn't move to undress her, and she didn't offer any more than her open arms. They just needed full-body contact. He climbed on top of her, and while she could feel his readiness at her pubic bone, neither of them removed any clothing.

She felt his weight, relishing the solidness of him. They looked deep into each other's faces, lightly stroking hair, cheeks, and jawbones. They were both dedicating themselves to remembering who they were to each other, even with the overhanging feeling that soon they would wake from this beautiful dream. Neither spoke, just touched tenderly, intimately. His gentleness and focus brought tears to her eyes. He saw her, and she saw the sliver line his.

They were almost there. In Tov. Teleosis. Where her past and his future collided. She wished time would stop so they could stay in this reverie forever, just the two of them. She whispered her wish to him in his ear just above her heart as he listened to the steady beat. He was still for a long time; she wondered if he'd dozed off. But then he whispered, "We will live this dream, I swear."

A tear rolled down her cheek into her hair at his words. She deeply felt how much they both wanted them to be true. Then she felt him slip away from her as he rose to offer her his hand to stand. He straightened her dress, smoothing out the skirt. He fixed his suit that was cut to his form perfectly. They cut such a regal, gorgeous figure together, incredibly striking.

That was what she'd thought about her and Tomas as well.

This realization at that moment, as the pilot instructed them to buckle in for landing, shook her. As they took their seats, memories of Tomas before the bombing and just how much Mattias looked like him flooded her mind. She felt her body jar with the landing, and her soul shook with the effects of reliving those thoughts of Tomas. She had experienced so much healing this morning, but maybe there remained more to reconcile about her first husband and his choices.

As they exited the plane, Mattias leading her, fingers entwined, Inira became aware of two truths.

The first had been coming to her, maybe from when she was initially alone with Mattias. Their relationship was the start of something that redeemed what happened with his brother. Even if it ended, she knew that this love would do something magnificent in the world.

The second came to her as she looked at her homeland for the first time in two decades. Everything had changed, and yet everything was precisely the same.

Chapter 42

Amin Ahmadi had to fight the feeling of his world tipping on its axis. The power and ancientness of Mattias and Inira nearly made his heart stop. He could feel the unifying energy radiating off them both, making him want to fall to his knees. It was as if they embodied the Divine lifeforce, and it flowed between them. It was mesmerizing and terrifying all at once.

He had seen it once before, from afar. It was during a public appearance of the Boehme woman and Tomas a few weeks before the bombing. He'd come to Tov to make sure the plans for the attack were in motion. Even though Tomas was entrenched with her, he was flushing with youth and young love. Ahmadi had felt the same surge of energy watching them from a distance as they looked out over the crowd and waved after her mother introduced them as the Heir and the Consort. There was no denying how they felt about each other, and seeing Inira with Mattias – Tomas's reflection – and up close – Ahmadi knew this was no ordinary connection.

He'd never cared about what God thought or even if there was any god. He'd never really even considered it a possibility. He was fully bought into the Serpent's *self is the only way* from the beginning. He had plenty of personal data to prove that relying on yourself was the only trustworthy way to go. Amin was, at heart, a coward. He had been a young boy afraid of his own shadow because he'd been taught that to fear those in power over him was right.

Standing below them as they descended the jet stairway, he saw the light ripple off them like they were gods. For that split second of seeing them emanate otherwordly light and love, he had to blink rapidly to clear the vision. The past was overlapping in the present with the reality of the future. That moment gave him pause as he wondered if he was, in fact, up against supernatural power.

Mattias embodied the Divine Masculine, powerful, fierce, and dominating. Inira was the image of the Divine Feminine, soft, wise, sensual. Both were at peak levels of strength, terrible in their own right, and it made them shine like rulers they were. It was a spiritual experience for Amin to see them together in London, and it only confirmed they had been intimate. He could practically sense where their souls intertwined.

Mattias was full of purpose and focus. He could see it etched into every line of his body. The Boehme woman setting foot in her homeland sent a ripple through time and space. She was in her power seat, filled with all the potential and promise she had been denied. He could see her straight back, rising above what had happened to her to walk fully into who she was and always had been. Amin's nerves shifted into survival mode for the first time in years. He froze. He was rooted in his cellular feelings of insecurity. He had none of the majesty these two had in their physical beauty and bestowed birthright.

He felt small, like a mouse before two hungry lions.

He dove into himself back when he grew tired of living in fear and decided to become the one to be feared. He plotted, planned, and sweet-talked his way to this moment, and he would seize it. No matter the strength rising like waves of heat from Inira and Mattias at being unified, he would have his chance to take it all for himself. They could stay powerful.

He told himself: *It no longer matters what they had that I don't because I have what they both want and will force them to do anything to get it back.*

He plastered a reverent smile as his gut churned with nerves. He strangled that freeze response and stuffed it deep behind a locked door in his mind. He would not bow. He would not grovel.

He had to remember what he was here for to get the blood he needed. He was here to unite and control both the endgames of the Serpents and Teleosis. He would show Mattias Nahas who the real god of the Serpents was. He had put his plan into action decades ago, and it would now come to fruition. He had no other option and set everything up so that each move on the chessboard had a countermove. And his checkmate was just a few feet away, unbeknownst to Mattias or Inira.

"Deitas and Heir, I bow before you as appropriate for your station in this place. Welcome to Tov and the Teleosis of the future."

His oily smile and genuflection hit the Boehme woman exactly where he wanted it to. He saw her startle and eyes widen. Her eyes narrowed, and, impossibly, she stood a little taller. She towered over him and continued to hold Mattias' hand. He drew her closer to his side and greeted Amin, who he probably still thought was his loyal dog. He was so clueless as to what was right under his nose. Amin's smile grew wider at that thought.

"Amin. Thank you for meeting us. I know you have much to share and be proud of, so please show us all the progress."

Bowing even lower, Ahmadi said, "Oh, yes. Deitas. You will be so pleased. It is ready to be used for worship. All the changes to the original Temple we've planned have been completed. Only the seating remains to be put in."

He watched, fascinated, as the tension in the Deitas' body grew to impossible levels. He drew the Boehme Woman even closer. She still stood tall and strong. She looked down at Amin, and he could see the glow in her eyes. Her four gods were close to her; even Amin could feel it. It made him wonder how she had gone from that woman having a panic attack in the conference room in London to the vessel of light who stood before him.

Mattias cleared his throat, a tell Amin knew that gave away his nerves. He was acting his part, but there had been too much shift in him for Ahmadi to be unable to notice. Mattias spoke with authority, "Those plans have changed. We will not be moving our headquarters here, Amin. We will ensure this rebuild happens only to relaunch Teleosis under our guidance and with our support."

Amin nodded solemnly, already knowing this would happen. It didn't alter his plans in the least. He had ensured Nahas International was about to own every square inch of Teleosis. Once Mattias Nahas was out of the way, Amin would be free to continue with the subjugation of the land, using it for his own purposes as he always designed. He had to make sure Stanley signed on the dotted line. Or his sons did once Stanley passed out of this life, and his inheritance was settled.

That was the only loose end still hanging, which irked Amin, but he had faith his plan, anchored in layers of effort, would come through. He had to; self was the only way.

It was time to play tour guide, and he could not reveal his hand too early. He looked up to Mattias, respect lacing his tone. "Of course, Deitas, as you wish, whatever you wish. Those documents can be adjusted at any time. Please let us have some refreshments before we begin the tour. It is a decent walk to the Temple, as you may remember, Mrs. Boehme."

She stiffened at his use of 'Mrs.', knowing it was the slight he intended, even if he said it with the utmost dignity. Mattias stepped forward. The Boehme Woman kept a hand on him, holding him to her. She leaned over to whisper something in his ear, and the effect was instant. Nahas relaxed, and while his focus was still on Ahmadi, his eyes cleared.

"Yes, Amin, let's begin. I'm anxious to see what you've done with the place."

Interesting, Amin thought again. He recognized they had a plan and were working together. How she had managed to leash Mattias Nahas, Amin couldn't imagine. He had read the High Priestess's power in the bedroom was unmatched until the Courtesans of Paris. They could literally fuck a man back to life. But they were too earnest, eager, and soft, so none mattered. He had the upper hand and knew they both suspected him of working for his own ends. He would wipe the proud look off the Boehme woman's face the second she set foot in the Temple. He couldn't wait.

But first, he had to treat her like the queen she thought she was.

Chapter 43

E merie was restless for so many reasons. She had been trapped in this backroom of the Temple structure with Lukas for company for far too long. She was tired of fighting her dual repulsion and attraction to him. She was exhausted. She had been too tense to sleep more than an hour or so on the flight, which meant she had been up for over twenty-four hours.

She felt crazy around him. She knew there was more to him than this alpha dickhead persona he projected. She now knew that it wasn't him but a mask he wore. He had shared quite a lot about his belief set with her. She was floored when he told her about the college gang rape initiation ceremony. She was as shocked by it as she was by him telling her why he was working against Ahmadi. He wasn't exactly working with his father, which made her nervous. She wasn't sure if he was bidding for power in his own right and using her as bait to do it. She also didn't quite believe him when he said he would cut her loose after this whole thing was settled. She caught quite a few of his gazes, and they were hungry not just for sex, although that felt like it dripped from him. He was starving for companionship. She could see how lonely he was and how he never felt like he truly belonged anywhere.

Emerie Boehme had always belonged. First, at home with her parents, who loved her, she'd always had fun and lasting friendships to lean on. She'd had a core group, and while she wasn't the most popular girl in school, hanging with those on the outskirts of the in-crowd made for more exciting people to bond with. However, at this moment, she felt very alone. She knew her mother would know what to do. She always had a plan. Teleosis was where she grew up, after all. This was her home turf, and in a strange sense, Emerie also felt a connection to the land. She'd always wanted to see it and had pictured it in ruins in her mind. She'd done countless Google searches for what was on record, which wasn't a lot. Teleosis had done plenty to scrub online records, but there were always scholarly and historical records to read.

It was a shock to see it nearly rebuilt, with no ruins and the Temple standing erect and proud, like a beacon of hope. She could imagine how mind-boggling it would be for her mom. She knew it was also tainted too. Ahmadi had a plot; Lukas had a plan to stop him, and hopefully, her mother and Mattias had a plan. She didn't know exactly why she was here besides being Inira's daughter, which made her extremely anxious. She knew she would be involved in some ceremonial union between her and Lukas. He had told her that much. But he couldn't fill in the gaps for *why* other than saying it would give Ahmadi the power he needed to unlock the secrets of Teleosis.

He swore up and down he didn't know any details. Still, Emerie felt like a pawn to be used for someone else's end. She wanted to scream because it was exactly what her mother had taught her not to be. To now be controlled like a puppet made her want to howl. She'd tried to escape from Lukas once they landed. It was half-hearted, and she'd tripped, so he caught her easily. He wasn't mad. He was very gentle when he scooped her up, praising her for trying to save herself. He told her for the hundredth time that he would give her the freedom to do what she wanted once Ahmadi was stopped. He said he liked her fire and wanted them to be friends. He wasn't possessive, but something about him made her want to stop fighting.

She hoped she wasn't falling under the spell like a victim of Stockholm Syndrome because even though he had taken her, he wasn't violent. He was kind to her, and she felt like he was trying very hard to show her while being an asshole to everyone else. But he had slept with Charlotte. That was infuriating. Just such a dick move; she didn't know how to get over it. She knew Charlotte was no angel herself and had her reasons, but she couldn't reconcile how nice Lukas was being to her with the man who had treated the woman she looked up to like a toy that he was now done playing with.

Again, she wanted to scream in frustration.

She thought that if she could calm her mind down, she could tap into whatever spiritual force, magic, or divine Presence was still here. It was a pipe dream, but she wanted to try. The trouble was that she was only very calm when Lukas was in the room. She had to work very hard to stay defensive around him. Her body wanted to be calm and wanted his touch. She didn't want to be around him, but it made her feel peaceful when she was, even from the first time they met a few days ago. She'd acted like a total brat, which wasn't hard, but the more time she spent with him, the more she had to push herself to act that way.

And she didn't want to try any Teleosian summoning or magic around him. Not that she knew how to do that anyway.

She kept telling herself she would be free after all this was over. She and her mother would return to the States, and her parents would work things out. She might be forced to marry Lukas to fulfill whatever sick plans Ahmadi had, but she would never have to see him again. No matter what her body said. That was all chemical, and it would wear off. Surely, there was nothing redeemable about Lukas Nahas, even if he showed her otherwise. His father and Amin had twisted him; he was a bad guy.

Are you sure about that? Something inside her whispered the taunt.

Like any insane woman, she harbored the secret hope that maybe she could turn this fuckboy into a family man. She knew she was being truly mental. He was not worth her time, but her mother had changed Mattias. But no. No! It was best to look at him only as the guy who kidnapped her and planned to use her. They were not friends. No matter how he whispered, pleaded, and treated her with respect. They may not be enemies, but they weren't friends.

She was driving herself mad with these looping thoughts.

She heard the door open and promptly said, "Lukas, what the fuck are we waiting for?"

She addressed him directly as he came back into the room, trying to get him to show her his bad side to confirm for her one way or another how she should feel about him. He was serious, but when he saw her, he smiled. He always did that, smiled at her. She could tell it wasn't fake either. It was almost like she was his only friend, and everyone else in his life wanted something from him. Well, she wanted something from him – her freedom and she had every intention of making him remember to give it to her.

When he saw the look on her face and caught the tone in her voice, his smile wavered slightly. Was that because he was questioning himself or her? She knew they were here, in the belly of the rebuilt Temple on Tov, to *get married*. This wasn't just an arranged marriage but a forced one.

"Emerie, I don't like this any more than you do, but I want to make the best of it. I feel like a monster enough already, having kidnapped you and all."

His kindness made her so tired. God, she was tired. She felt all the fight drain out of her. She thought the mental games and social pitfalls in her private, super-privileged high school were tough enough to navigate. She'd had no clue. She decided she would tell the truth and see what happened. Trying to fight him was draining too much life from her, so maybe a different tactic would shift any power in her direction. She didn't want to partner with him, so she had to keep the upper hand. She knew he liked her. Maybe he'd never had someone be this authentic with him. After all, she was his sort-of captive, but he seemed to enjoy it when she acted like his equal.

She sighed and said, "Lukas, I'm no match for you. I'm tired. I've not spent my life trying to play the games of the rich. I saw enough in school to avoid social politics. I stuck to my team and my goals. Getting married at nineteen was not part of my plan. Why are you going through with this?"

He stared at her from across the room, wariness in his eyes. "Emerie, I don't have a choice. I've been a part of the Serpents, and this seems to be the only way to stop them." He scrubbed a hand down his face; he sounded as tired as she felt as he continued, "I've explained all of this to you. My father changed when he met your mother, and Ahmadi's bid to oust him is destabilizing everything."

She opened her hands in front of her, offering them to him. He took them as he set down the bundle he was carrying. It was a large box wrapped in a silk, purple bow. She was *very* curious about it but kept her eyes on him as she spoke, "Lukas, I know your agenda. What I want to know is about you, why this is so important for you. You say you didn't like taking me but have said – too often – you want to be my friend. You don't have any of your own, so why now, and why are you trusting me?"

He remained quiet, standing there looking at her. She realized that he had changed his clothes. He had been in more comfortable clothes but was now dressed formally. It was like a cross between a morning suit and dress robes students at European universities wear, neatly layered on each other. He had to be hot but looked as put together and at ease. He stood there, looking at her, and she felt the sweat start to crown at the top of her face. Her baby hairs curled in response. Her hair was not quite as dark as her mother's, and her curls always seemed to have a life of their own.

The longer Lukas stared at her, the more uncomfortable she grew. She didn't want to give in, but she did. She broke the long silence with another question, curiosity winning out. "What is that bundle?" She couldn't help it; she was not a patient person.

At this, his true smile returned, "I've noticed something about you, Sunshine. You are very demanding in your need for information. Is this why you have such good grades? You are like a dog with a bone, wearing it down till the answer is the shape and size you want. Do you do that to people too? Your mother has more finesse."

Emerie laughed, "Well, we are different people. Plus, propriety and social graces were practically beaten into her. She wields them as a weapon all the same, though."

Lukas started moving closer, closing the distance as he held her hands in his big ones. He moved into her space slowly, step by step, like he was approaching a wild creature. "She is more the rapier, and you are more the broadsword then? I see the Nahas men have been matched well by Fate."

"You mean to tell me you can wield a broadsword?"

"I did take fencing lessons. I was rubbish, though. No, I think I'm more likely to get my head cleaved in half than learn to use you as a weapon, Sunshine. Truthfully, I wouldn't dream of you being used at all. You are too rare a female to be a pawn in these sick games." He was close enough now that she could see the seriousness of his face and feel his warm breath.

She put a hand up, stilling his progression. She did not like the feeling in her midsection with him too close. "Answer my original question then, Lukas. Why trust me?"

He didn't move, but that assessing gaze never left her face. He reached up with one hand and wiped a tear of sweat from his brow, the first and only indication the heat was affecting him.

He noticed her noticing. "Sunshine brings heat with it."

"Duh, don't be coy. I know it is hot here; open a window if you are uncomfortable."

At that, he laughed aloud. "I'm not uncomfortable in the heat of the day, Darling. I'm uncomfortable around you. I've done bad things, but never before have I feared the consequences. I had to get involved and try to stop what was happening. I don't want to keep disappointing you in the process."

Emerie asked in confusion. "What do you mean disappointing me?"

Lukas sighed. "I will lay it out there because you will see it soon enough. I don't know what genetic power you and your mother carry, but it is enough to make Nahas men question their life plans. You do. I saw it the moment my father laid eyes on your mother. I went along with this whole change of plans at Ahmadi's suggestion because the first time I saw a picture of you, I thought, 'There's someone I can put some hope in for a better world.' Then I met you, and now know you are that better world. I don't think there will be room for me, but I'd like to help you get there to fulfill your purpose. You are light and heat, which I want to experience for as long as possible."

Her heart melted at his words as her brows knitted in confusion. "Lukas, I still don't understand."

"Yes, Sunshine, I know. You've never been a part of an organization like the Serpents. They were the only group I could call home. There could be no other path. But now, I realize I'm afraid there may be another path. I'm afraid of my choices, that I'll never get the chance to make a different one. I can't begin to imagine a world where our paths crossed differently, where I could have tried to make a real go with you, to be actual friends without the mess of history and this situation hanging over us—a path where I didn't use Charlotte or anyone else. I know I could have been brave and walked away from this life – that I should have the minute I was tasked with taking you and a thousand other times before. But I'm afraid that will never be, and you deserve so much more."

Emerie felt sick and elated at him sharing so much. She felt like a wall had come down between them, and maybe, just maybe, they could get out of this. She closed her eyes, breathing through her nose, taking in the first of several huge breaths. Eyes still closed, she smiled and only then realized Lukas had started moving again. That big, deep breath caught in her throat when she opened her eyes and saw that he was leaning down to her face, green eyes locked onto her light brown.

Before she could react, he pressed his lips softly to hers, and a strange electricity arced between them. They stayed like that, neither of them taking it any deeper. It was chaste and humble, something she never expected Lukas Nahas would ever be. When he pulled back, brushing sweaty curls off her face, she realized his eyes were lined in silver.

He whispered, "I would love to be the man you deserve, the man your father expects for you. But I am not, Emerie. I am afraid I will never deserve you so I won't offer you anything except for my friendship and loyalty."

She whispered, "That's not much, especially because I must compete with every gorgeous woman who crosses your path."

He smiled and leaned down to kiss her cheek. "No, Sunshine. There isn't a woman alive who could compare with your light and heat, and I want to bask in it. I would, if you will ever let me. If I can ever reverse the curse of how we started."

She looked at him and said sardonically, "That's a relief. To be my kidnapper, forced husband, and cheater would be too much to ask."

He smiled again, "I'm rogue enough already, so staying faithful is the least and the most I can give you."

"The least and the most?"

"Yes. Maybe friendship could turn into love, but I am not sure I would know how, not while I'm part of the Serpents. I can't keep putting you at risk. Even if I stop Ahmadi, getting out of the Serpents, the price is too high."

She pushed her lips together, still feeling the warmth of him being so close. "I think you expect me to be a hopeless romantic, Lukas. My mother might love the villain of her story, but I never will. I'll take my opportunity for escape when I see it."

He cupped her face with both hands. His green eyes sparkled as he stared down at her. "I like you so much, Emerie Boehme. Your fire is contagious. Lucky is the man who will get to burn in it. I have no doubt you will make your way. I swear to do whatever I can to help."

"Why don't you just call this ludicrous wedding off then?"

His face fell. He dropped his hands and stepped away from her, picking up the parcel he'd walked in with.

"Lukas, why don't you just call this whole thing off? Lukas?"

He was standing still, his back to her. He saw his shoulders lift at the sharp intake of breath. He turned back around, striding back over to her. He stopped before her and held the package out for her to take. As she did, he spoke definitively, although softly.

"Because Sunshine. They'll kill you if I don't go through with this wedding. They will kill your mother if you refuse. They are going to kill one of you either way. They need your blood and voice to access the Song of Creation, where all the genuine power is, to remake the world. That's why we are here. That's the ultimate piece of his plan. When we got here, it all clicked. You are an insurance policy for your mother's cooperation. Our marriage is to bind the legacy of Teleosis to the Serpents, to become the most powerful organization in the world, finally."

Emerie stared at him, slack-jawed. "What?" Her whisper was just barely audible.

"Only one Boehme woman is supposed to leave Tov alive today, but will give my life if I have to help save you both. I can't see another woman taken at the hands of greedy, vicious men. I knew my loyalty would shift to you as my wife, but then I met you. I will not allow your mother to be sacrificed if I can do anything about it, but trust me when I say you are my priority now. I feel my soul tethered to yours. Again, I don't know what power you Boehme women hold over us, but it is immense. I don't know how my uncle ever followed through on the bombings. You are worth more than world domination ever could be."

Emerie didn't know what to do. He placed his hands on hers and guided her to unwrap the bundle in her hands. Looking up at him, she saw the mask slide back over his face as if he were preparing for war. She felt dizzy and swayed on her feet. His hands came to her waist, stabilizing her and moving no farther. He pressed into her sides as if trying to convince himself to go through with the plans before them both. He stared into her eyes again. She could see the cool indifference he affected to convince Ahmadi of his compliance, but she could now see beyond it to the man who wanted to do something right for once rather than stand by and let terrible things happen.

She kept looking at him as he spoke one last apology to her. "I'm so sorry about all of this. I will get you out. But come, now, Sunshine. It's time for you to put on your wedding dress."

Chapter 44

Inira and Mattias continued their escorted walk towards the Temple. Inira let go of Mattias' arm to fall behind. He reached out, trying to pull her back, and she desperately desired to sink back into his side. Instead, she caught his eye and nodded, acknowledging him while, at the same time, silently communicating he needed to trust her. She had her part in their plan, especially as they knew it would unfold before them. She remembered the time before they left the Santorini house when they bared everything to each other and formulated their approach. When Mattias started to go too far in dictating her role, she stopped him.

"Mattias, *Ahava*. I know how good you are at strategy. You could not have built your empire without a vision that sees layers upon layers, the ways through, in and out. Yet, my love, you forget one crucial advantage in this."

He then looked into her face, and she saw the war raging on his. Those habits of control and absolute authority were hard to break. She knew she was pushing him into unchartered territory. His life motto had been about relying only on himself. However, hers had not. She knew the strength of the community. Her life had been built on it, and she knew it afresh through recovery. The legacy of Teleosis was always about a different way to live – together rather than as individuals. That had always been their power and what they had lost when they tried to do it their way. She fully intended to leverage that legacy now.

Drawing back into the present, she relished in the shift as his mind opened to a new possibility of her as a partner, a leader in her own right. She willed him to remember those feelings as she smiled at him now. She felt her spirit rush to the surface and asked the FourFold God to give him the peace and security she felt now. She saw her prayer answered as Mattias gave her the barest of nods, and the corners of his mouth turned up. He took a deep breath, and his shoulders came away from his ears by a few centimeters. She followed suit, breathing in courage and asking for mental clarity as she dropped back to play her part.

She fell back in step with Ahmadi as every cell in her body tensed in repulsion to his proximity. There was something so off about him like the skin he wore was a costume that was too loose. She could see the snake behind the mouse. Her goal was to gain information that would help her and Mattias anticipate what was coming. She realized he walked with a slight hitch as she was beside him. He gave off the air of someone so polished. To know about this chink in his armor might be useful, so she stored it up for later.

"Mr. Ahmadi, thank you personally for spearheading the rebuilding project here in Tov. I could have never imagined this possibility when we last spoke at that first meeting in London. I appreciate your hard work."

He looked at her side-eyed as they strolled along the main street that would end at the Temple. Inira could have walked there blindfolded, but she kept her serenity about her, letting Ahmadi lead. At least they'd kept the layout of the city the same.

She couldn't shake the feeling she'd met him before. She'd known it in London, but how evaded her like a mosquito. She kept her countenance as smooth as granite, a mirror of his.

He smiled in an ingratiating way. "Mrs. Boehme, it has been my honor to prepare this site. There are so many treasures here – imagine this ground's history! My only purpose is to make sure the Deitas can achieve his purpose and," he gave her a sly look, "I think we are united in that purpose, no?"

Inira nodded, giving him her most beaming smile, even as her heart iced over. What was it that seemed so revoltingly familiar about him? It was like a bad smell she couldn't shake as she replied, "Yes, Mattias has been quite open regarding how we are to partner to bring about a new life here and into the world."

Ahmadi sighed like a long-suffering servant, a surprising tell. It was supposed to sound relieved, but to her ears, she only heard annoyance.

"I'm so glad he has found you to stand by his side while he is elevated to new heights. May I call you Inira?" He asked as if they were old friends. She nodded her consent as he continued, regardless of what she said, "Inira, even though the Deitas will be far too busy to take vacations after today, I know your time with him has made him happy. We share that goal too, you know."

She smiled at him, putting her hand on his shoulder, even as if it felt like she was touching a cobra. She called his first name softly, and he stopped walking, somewhat shocked that she was touching him. He tried to pull away, which made her tighten her grip just slightly. They were almost to the Temple now, and she towered over him. Her memories were starting to drop in like rain, and she knew it was only a matter of seconds before she remembered how she had known him before. She held on firmly, using her height advantage to step closer and look down her nose at him.

It was her time to act.

Looking at him fully, she intended to draw him out as she spoke with prophetic intonation, "You might be here for another reason, but Mattias and I are here to see the vision of Teleosis, the hope of the FourFold God and the original purpose of humanity, resurrected. Only through a union of both the male and the female – that Divine wholeness and connection, can we truly experience what we all long for. A piece of you craves wholeness, attention, and safety. There is a better way to get it, though, than through violence and pushing others down. However, I know that it is only through a sacrifice that can happen. We must surrender ourselves to the better way. It's not too late to change, Amin. Our faith beliefs are not so far apart, you know, Amin."

His jaw worked as if he was chewing on a piece of gristle, with his eyes rounding as she spoke and his mouth parting in an "O." She could feel the power of hope flow into him. She could almost see the lines leave his face and his shoulders relax. But as peace started to take hold in his heart, it all went dark, like someone switching off the light. He would not receive her power; he would fight it at every turn.

In this split-second connection, the memory of their first meeting snapped into place. He was the man who had mocked her the day of the attacks, practically on the spot they were standing. He had shaved his beard, and it had been two decades, but she saw him as the maniacal zealot. She nearly laughed at the memory of throwing up on him; she was that free in her remembrance of the event that took everything from her. She was back now and could feel her purpose generating within her.

For those open to it, healing could happen, and vision could be caught.

Unfortunately, for people like Ahmadi, they would shut it down before it ever took root.

He started to stammer, then paused. He stepped back out of her reach and adopted a stiff tone. "Forgive me, Mrs. Boehme. You are uninformed. The Deitas is here to take ownership of Teleosis' power. I know you will gladly give it to him. You are of use, and that is all." He turned to go, but she stopped him, this time tugging hard enough on his arm to make him stumble, his toe catching on a rock in the road.

"Amin, you know what I realized the first time I met you." She stepped closer to him, his forehead level with the tip of her nose. She looked him up and down, from the top of his head to his toes and back up. She noticed the sweat beading on his forehead and his breath pumped out of his chest like a sprinter. She sighed, letting her warm, calm breath coast over his face. He made a face like her breath was sour, but she knew it was her proximity. She knew he hadn't let a woman get this close to him in years, if ever.

Inira continued, letting the force of her compassion try to infuse her words.

"I know who you are, Amin. I know what you have done. It is forgivable. You can still be saved from the darkness that eats you whole. You've just gotten too used to it. Let Mattias and I share what we both know: what is possible here on this holy ground. You don't have to feel so small anymore. Only this new community can save you from the isolation you've known. Will you join us, Amin?"

He took in her words, staring up at her. He did not cut a heroic figure, and he knew it. He had long ago decided that to be the hero of his own story; he would have to become the world's villain. She knew he was disgusted by how Mattias had quickly shifted in her presence, but it was because he had found something he had always longed for – acceptance. She saw all of him and still chose to offer him the same freedom from the trauma she had found from hers.

The air between them was charged. The tension rising with the heat of the sun above them. It was nearly midday, making the Temple appear as if it were on fire. Inira felt the sweat of anticipation, and her elevated nerves streamed down the channel of her spine. Then, before he answered her, she saw how his body shifted, and she knew the chance she'd taken had failed. He slid the mask of the faithful servant back in place, turning to greet Mattias as he approached them. He wobbled slightly on his feet as if recovering from a dizzy spell.

Speaking in a forced tone of joy, he said to Mattias, "How wonderful that you have this woman by your side, Deitas! She will ensure your legacy is secured. With a woman like this by your side, there is no way we can fail."

Mattias was practically standing between them now, green eyes boring holes into the other man's skull. He saw the shiftiness behind Ahmadi's eyes, and she, again, willed him to understand how broken this man truly was and have mercy. She didn't think Mattias was capable of mercy for the level of betrayal Amin had planned, but she tried to communicate it to him. She reached around with her other hand, brushing it along Mattias' back. He jolted as if she'd shocked him.

She didn't need Mattias to fight for her. She liked it but didn't need it. Ahmadi regained control over himself at this movement and said, "Come with me! We are about at the piece de la resistance. I know you will both be happy to see your children in their wedding finery. The ceremony is about to begin!"

Inira swayed in shock. "Emerie and Lukas are here?"

The oily smile returned to Amin's face, the same one from twenty years ago. "Yes, of course. I ensured she would join us so we could complete the ceremony. I'm sure you remember that's required from your history lessons."

***

Mattias got right in Amin's face. "Why is Emerie here, Amin? That was not part of the plan."

For the first time, Amin laughed, with a strange manic tilt to his head that began to give away his real intentions. She could feel the shift in her body as he finally ripped the mask off and threw it away. "Oh, there is so much you don't know, Deitas, about what is required for the Song of Creation to be sung and its power to be trapped. I would have shared it with you, but you were" – he paused to sneer around at Inira – "preoccupied."

Mattias had his hand around Amin's throat before Inira could move. The smaller man's face quickly turned purple because of the lack of air, but he kept smiling. He choked out, "The girl is here for insurance."

Inira pulled at Mattias' arm to get him to let go. She considered letting him finish Amin; maybe this ridiculous plan would end. That was until she felt the cold barrel of a gun pressed against the back of her head and saw another at the base of Mattias' skull. He let go of Ahmadi. The bodyguards, dressed in black with Serpent tattoos on their forearms, who had been with Ahmadi when they got off the plane but vanished when they started walking, reappeared to rescue the mouse.

Ahmadi breathed hard, still smiling. Mattias looked murderous, ready to take on the men once under his control. "It seems you were outplayed, finally, Mattias. Once the hunter, now the hunted. It was almost too easy to strip away your image. All it took was a few well-placed rumors, and you were so removed from your men they turned on you easily. It was almost as easy as sending all your text records to this whore's husband."

Inira felt the pit of her stomach drop out. They'd been outplayed indeed. Who else would have access to Mattias' phone records? She took Mattias's closed fist in hers. He opened his hand and interlocked their fingers painfully. It was just the two of them now, against the world.

She whispered, "Mattias, we must go with him to the Temple. I need to see Emerie."

Ahmadi listened like a hawk, "Yes, the girl is safe. Lukas is getting her ready for the wedding."

Both Inira and Mattias started, but Mattias got the words out first, demanding, "Amin, what in God's name do you mean wedding?"

Amin cackled with glee. "Yes, yes! The Binding! Your whore can tell you all about that."

Inira felt a pit open in her stomach. Yes, she knew all about the Binding. It was a ceremony they had discontinued because of the toll it takes – sometimes the life – of the High Priestess. A lot of blood is required to become one of the Song of Creation. And that blood has to be keyed into the genetic signature of the line of the High Priestess. When it was performed, it was used to strengthen Teleosis to the FourFold God, build up their fortifications, and release the inspired energy to the whole community that would ensure the mission would continue through the efforts of the faithful. It required the High Priestess to become the altar. She wasn't a sacrifice but a willing vessel for communicating the power needed to channel the Song of Creation into the world.

That Ahmadi knew about it meant he had found some ancient writings. He had done his research, and that wasn't good.

It was very, very bad.

Mattias looked at her, and she closed her eyes as the full extent of Ahmadi's plan bloomed in her mind. At that moment, she felt the gun press sharper into her head, urging her forward.

He cackled again and nearly danced with glee, "Whore lost her tongue? Then let me tell you as we walk."

Now that he had the upper hand, he meant to intimidate them. She could feel Mattias' barely restrained violence. She could feel the Truth of who she was rise in her to fight back against the insult, but now wasn't the time. She had to remain clear-headed for herself, Mattias, and Emerie.

Amin decided to detail the ceremony as they walked the last ten meters to the Temple entrance. "You see, Deitas, that is who you are for now until the ceremony is complete when the High Priestess here channels her power into me. The Binding is a ceremony where the High Priestess relinquishes her power to the Heir by giving her blood – almost all of it. Then, she can determine who gets that power by her touch. It is an act of sacrifice to pass along the mantle. Very clever to key it to the blood."

Inira interjected, "It hasn't been done in centuries because of what it requires. We stopped doing that because it no longer made sense. Plus, I can't give you the power. You don't have the DNA signature."

He cackled again, "Well, WHORE, that is where you and the other High Priestess WHORES made their mistake. If you'd kept passing along the power in your blood, we would not have been successful in bringing you down, but you stopped the ceremony. Now, the DNA signature is no longer required." He was spitting now, enunciating every syllable like she was a child.

"No, Ahmadi, you are wrong. The FourFold God demanded we stop the sacrifice. They spoke through the Heir during one of the ceremonies in the 3rd century. It was too much like the barbarism of the nations, especially Rome. Only the wedding portion of the ceremony took place after that."

He turned to face her, getting so close she thought he would strike at her. She narrowed her eyes, daring him. They both knew he needed her so he wouldn't harm her. He still chose violence.

He grabbed the gun from the man standing behind her, leveled it, and pulled the trigger. Mattias went down in a shriek of agony. Inira, horrified, dropped next to him. Amin had shot him clean through the kneecap.

Inira, bile rising, turned as Ahmadi said, "I may not be able to kill you yet, Whore, but I can kill him. I don't need him, so if you want him to live, you will do exactly as I tell you. Don't worry; I'll finish him when you are dead. May you both end up in hell where you belong." With that final wish, Ahmadi stormed the rest of the way to the Temple entrance, leaving them there.

Inira dropped to her knees beside Mattias, realizing she was crying, tears streaming down her cheeks and neck. Mattias was writhing on the ground, the guards surrounding them impassive. She scrambled to find a way to help him, panicking at this on-slaught of pain, never imagining the confrontation would end up in Mattias' torture. Through clenched teeth, Mattias looked up at her, a bloody hand reaching up to touch her face. He didn't scream or whimper in pain. He just looked at her, desperation in his eyes. He wanted to save her and saw that, for the first time in his life, he wouldn't be able to make what he wanted happen. Their plan was going to shit.

For Inira and those she loved, she would have to draw from a deeper well. Her tears for Mattias emptied her soul, preparing her for what would come.

"*Ahava ostar*," she whispered, horrified and stricken.

The men grabbed Mattias under his arms and hauled him to stand on his one good leg. They practically carried him as he hobbled the rest of the way to the entrance of the Temple.

Chapter 45

Service order for The Binding and enacting the power of the Song of Creation. From the Teleosian Archives, retired in the year 325 AD. Originally written in Sumerian by the High Priestess Senscha in 589 BCE. Subsequently, the Heir Redonda translated into Aramaic and Farsi in 69 BCE, with the final translation into Latin in 217 by High Priestess Isha. This version was used until this ceremony's replacement by the Marriage Covenant between the Heir and her Betrothed.**

To be performed on a Spring Solstice, ideally during a new moon or, for greater portal transference, during a lunar eclipse. The Temple will be set up with an altar table in the middle of the space, holding the sacred bowl and knife. The Community will stand in a circle surrounding the altar. The Community will form the circle first, and then the High Priestess and her Consort will enter. The High Priestess and Consort will circle around the Community from the North and the Heir and her Consort from the South. They will meet in the middle and take their places with the High Priestess in the East and the Heir on the West.

The High Priestess will take her place behind the altar, with her Consort behind her back. The Heir and her Consort will face them on the other side of the altar table.

Welcome by the High Priestess, who joins hands with the Consort

: Today, we are gathered as a community to witness the power of the Ancient of Days, Who always answers our call. From the beginning, we have been given the key to abundance. In partnership, in union, we gather and grow our strength. We will see the soil and sky united through our connection to all Creation that binds the Earth and Heaven together. In Unio, the FourFold God incarnates The Father, the Mother, the Son, and the Daughter, with the Divine Quadrant - both halves of feminine and masculine made whole.

The Binding

: The Heir and her consort are presented, facing the community. The Heir will wear a dress of sky blue with a veil over her face and a connected train that fans out behind her. This symbolizes her power after the Ascension. No sleeves shall cover her arms so she may be unhindered in reaching out to the world. No rings will cover her hands so they may be free to offer the gift of this vision of transformation meant for all.

The Consort shall assist the Heir, wearing robes of heavy, dark fabric that show his power and virility. He is the darkness to her light. Together, their mission is to create a Rule of Balance for the generation to come of shared experience that allows the Heir to serve and then rest in channeling the power of the FourFold God into the community.

Once presented, they will turn and face the High Priestess.

High Priestess: Heir and Consort, welcome to this most sacred of spaces! You will remember this day for the rest of your lives. Bow your heads as you now receive. Holiness is your crown, and determination is your insignia. If the FourFold God accepts you, you will be anointed to be the one who takes over the

S

ong of Creation.

High Priestess to the Consort: Will you be the support needed as the new High Priestess sings the Song over the community and into the world by ensuring her care and maintaining her strength to keep leading?

Consort to High Priestess: Till my very last breath.

High Priestess to the Consort: Consort, are you prepared to dedicate your life to the creation of the Rule of Balance, ensuring the Heir has a safe place to retreat so she may gain strength to continue to lead the world into the Divine Expression of Unio?

Consort to High Priestess: Till my very last breath.

High Priestess to the Heir: Heir of Light, are you prepared to take on this mantle and learn to sing the Song of the Ancient of Days?

Heir to High Priestess: Until the stars burn out.

High Priestess to Community: I now declare they have made their commitment and are prepared to embody

the of life everlasting

.

The High Priestess removes the veil from the Heir and asks her to present her arms. The High Priestess takes the right arm of the Heir and the left arm of the Consort, with their wrists facing up. The High Priestess shall take the ceremonial blade in her left hand and slice up both her forearms with the tip of the blade, ensuring unhindered blood flow. She will allow the force of her life to empty into the communion bowl as she becomes the altar on which the Song of Creation can be sung.

The Heir shall dip her finger into the bowl as the blood flows in, anointing her Consort with an "S" on his forehead. He then does the same to her. They offer their fingers to each other and then kiss to share the blood on their tongues with each other in an act that will seal their covenant.

High Priestess now joins her hand with her Consort, who then the hand of the Heir, who takes the hand of her Consort, who completes the circle by taking the open hand of the High Priestess. Then the High Priestess shall sing the

S

ong of Creation, letting the power flow first into her, then her Consort, then to the Heir, and finally her Consort. The two Consorts and the Heir will join in with the High Priestess during the second sacred singing, with the Community joining in on the third.

And they shall sing:

S

ing me a song of your sweetness.

Sing me a requiem without fear.

Sing to my soul in your goodness.

And let my body calm as you come near.

Help me hear up to Heaven,

A melody only my spirit knows.

Gift me a sense of your presence,

So I can remember how the chorus goes.

Give me your truth like a lullaby.

Sing a symphony in my flesh to sleep.

Send me courage like a battle hymn,

Where only in my dreams do I weep.

Tell my heart of your praise.

Teach me to worship by ancient form.

Where women ruled and reigned,

With unity and love with men was born.

Give me a legacy for my daughters,

And the daughter and sons to come along.

Help me witness the sounds of Creation,

As the world was before the first dawn.

Save my life on the altar.

Let me come home with you in bliss.

Let me be found between the angels,

Knowing nothing in my life was amiss.

Play the lyre, the harp, and the timbre.

Let them take me to a frenzied place.

Show me how to praise with my body,

Because nothing else can take its place.

Accent the song of my life with your power.

Let the crescendo of the song ring true.

Never let me question my own goodness.

Because I owe everything to you.

The lion and the lamb will unite.

Cheetah and gazelle follow through.

A whole new world is beginning,

A world where one becomes two.

Teach me the Song of Creation.

Root and anchor it in my bones.

Hold me tight in your presence,

And together, we will never be alone.

The ceremony is complete when the High Priestess, holding hands with her Consort, speaks these words as a concluding blessing over the land: *Unio canto. Unio canto. Unio canto. Ad Quad Deo Canimus.*

{This ceremony was discontinued because the blood loss often irrevocably impeded the High Priestess from continuing in her role so she was not able to train the Heir and Consort properly. Most never recovered and died on the pallet. As a result, the new High Priestess and Consort were left without full guidance to teach them to sing the Song of Creation and how to wield it's power to lead the people of Teleosis into their calling in the world.

The Song of Creation was then lost to history.}

Written by Consort Danarius in 1153 AD,

<u>The Written History of Teleosian Ceremonies</u>

Chapter 46

Lukas helped Emerie dress in the beautiful sky-blue sleeveless gown with a veil and overlong train and explained the Binding, which was the Teleosian version of the Marriage Covenant, as he deftly attached the gossamer veil, weaving it through her hair. His proximity made her head spin a bit.

To fight the dizziness, she asked, "Lukas, where do you learn to do this?"

Lukas paused with his left hand in her hair, lightly touching her scalp, and she could feel his smile. "I had practice when I was young. My mother made me help her dress for her nights out, and those outfits always involved intricate details and skinny straps."

"I like you like this," Emerie whispered.

"Behind you with my hands in your hair?" His voice dropped, with an edge to it that whispered promise. She giggled and rolled her eyes, "No, I meant, I like you vulnerable. I like it when you share your life. It's a much better version of Lukas than alpha asshole you seem to have to be with everyone else."

Lukas's hand dropped from her hair as he walked around to face her, veil drooping. "I told you, Sunshine, I want to be friends. I don't know exactly what the next few days will look like. Hell, I have no real idea what this ceremony will entail. Amin won't tell me much, but he says getting the information we need to complete our task in Teleosis is essential. I never intended to get married, but now that I am, I will take my obligation to you seriously. If we can be friends, so much the better."

She didn't respond as she looked at him. Everything she had picked up from him was that he felt he had no choice in his actions. Perhaps he knew more than he was letting on, but if he did, it wasn't enough to assure either one of them about what would happen today. This ceremony hadn't happened for thousands of years. Her mother probably knew about it – had studied and researched it as part of her education as Heir; she had told Emerie in her last text she and Mattias had their own plan. Her mother would have told her if this was part of it.

She looked into Lucas' beautiful green eyes as he stared down into her brown. She told him, "Well, I guess I didn't come to this willingly, but if we are going to be forced into something we don't know about, we might as well make the best of it. Just do a great job on my hair. This is the only wedding I plan to have, you know." She winked at him jokingly, but he didn't return her smile.

Lukas stared into her eyes like he couldn't decide what to say. Emerie let the smile fade from her face before she said, without really thinking, "I don't get you, Lukas. I can't figure you out. You pretend to be an asshole playboy, Daddy's good little helper, but all the time you are a spy and working against the organization you grew up in. Do you know who you are?"

Lukas continued to look into her eyes, and she felt like she would melt into his. Then he reached up and finished attaching the veil over her head. With both hands, he gently brought the shimmering fabric down over her head and neck. He paused, letting his hands softly cup her face. Emerie tensed, and her breath caught as he tilted his head and began to lean in ever so slowly.

He stopped as his lips touched the barrier between them. He held them both in a spell, and she met his eyes as he whispered against her lips, "Sunshine, I don't know who I am, but I know who I am not. I'm counting on you to help me answer your question. You may be the only one who can."

***

I've ruined my life. I've wrecked my family, crushed Francis' heart, got Emerie kidnapped, and now Mattias has been shot by a psychopath. I thought this would go so differently just an hour ago. Still, now, I'm here, in the Temple in Tov, about to officiate a ceremony that will probably kill me, bind my daughter to someone she doesn't want to be with, and give the ultimate power to my enemy.

Hell does exist, and this is it.

Inira thought all this as she sat on the front row of chairs, holding Mattias' hand, who clutched hers back just as strongly. He had a furious light in his eyes, as if getting shot was what he needed to clear his mind of any lingering doubts. She turned to assess the rest of him for the thousandth time. Ahmadi was nowhere in sight, nor was Emerie. Mattias' leg had been bandaged; the blood flow stopped. He was pale, bordering on ashen. His eyes were open, and he looked between her and the ceiling. He had been quiet so long that she was startled when he spoke.

"I always wanted to see this Temple. As much as I hated what Teleosis stood for, Tomas's pictures of the Temple, especially the stained-glass ceiling, captivated me. The colors communicate life in a way I've never felt before. Even through the photographs, I could feel the presence of something greater. At the time of the bombings, it seemed right to destroy it, like we were stopping the heart of our enemy. But I secretly regretted destroying this place, at least before I could see it."

The Temple was breathtaking and exactly as she remembered it. The domed ceiling depicted their origin story, the gift of the Song of Creation to humanity, with the First Man and Woman – Adan and Sophia – working in partnership with the FourFold God. The song was woven into her life – she could feel it reverberate through her bones in this place. Her grandmother had tried to teach her once. She had forgotten the tune, but the words she could feel now.

As the Song sang in her soul, she told her love, "Mattias, I wish things could be so different."

It was a paltry statement. It was one of the things she always longed to say to Tomas. Saying it to his brother made the ache in her middle, the pulsating pain in her heart, her longing for this not to have happened, ease just slightly, but it was a tangible, living thing inside her. There was no language for it, and all she wished was to let Mattias crawl inside her so he could feel what she was feeling. Then he spoke more words than since they'd landed.

"Inira, my *luz de amor*, I've been so wrong. All my life, driven by vengeance. Trying to fill a hole in my soul, like it could bring my mother and Tomas back so we could be a family. Like I could belong somewhere, somewhere good. I've made violence, death, and pain my legacy, and now there is no going back. I desire to try to control the flow of this situation so palpably. I deserve this pain. I deserved to be shot because I ignored the signs. I thought with you, I could be something. I could start a new life, one of integrity. But it is not to be, my sweet love. You are and always have been my light and my home. When you die, I will make sure I do as well, even if we are separated forever. You will ascend, and I will descend. This is a fitting punishment for my crimes."

Maybe he did understand what she was feeling.

Her tears were flowing freely. She held his hand and looked at his face. She leaned towards him and whispered, "I will ask the FourFold God to have mercy on us. We will be together in death, *Ahava ostar.*"

He cupped her face and looked up at the brilliance of the ceiling in the mid-day light. This ceremony was supposed to be done in the dark so the light could shine even brighter, but that didn't matter now. His eyes moved back and forth as the colors danced everywhere above them. Then he asked, "Will you tell me the story of the two up there? Could that be us?"

She smiled and said, "I hope so." Then she told him the origin of her civilization. When he would take a break from looking at the story expressed in the glass above them, he would look at her in wonder. She realized maybe he'd never heard it from someone who lived here. This story of Creation was embedded into her brain; from the moment she could listen, someone was telling it. It was so different than what the world typically heard, as the patriarchal powers had erased many of the other Creation myths from the lexicon of belief long ago in favor of the Jewish and then Christian adopted story.

Yet, Teleosis had remained and, for a long time, done its best to live into the reality that humanity, in partnership with the Divine, could be greater. We could live abundantly, freely, and in harmony with each other. They were proof, and by some magic still left, it would come to pass again.

She finished her recounting with, "Mattias, I've never read or heard our origin story where Sophia was without Adan. I never planned to be without my Consort, either. I even had designs on elevating him so we would be full partners. When it came to Tomas, I would live with him, or I would die with him. I didn't die when he chose to speed up the timeline. But now, I see that I must be the first High Priestess in history to have not one, not two, but *three* consorts. And I failed them all. I am glad I will die with you. I *deserve* that."

She smiled a sad, forgive-me-smile. Mattias looked at her – he looked *through her* – and spoke as if he were reading her mind. "You didn't bring me here, Light Bringer. You didn't set this all in motion. Please don't take that on because it is not yours to own. It is mine. That is why I will burn in hell. I am the one who brought the Light Bringer to be extinguished by the darkness."

She squeezed his hand and said sadly, "We must disagree on whose fault it is since we are in this now. Maybe we could blame it on Amin in the final accounting of it all, eh?"

He smiled a small smile and looked down. She could almost see the words in his mind: Yes, *but I created Amin.*

She put her fingers under his chin and lifted his head to speak directly into his eyes. "Mattias, some of our religious practice here believed the darkness was only a place to start. Many religions believe that a descent into hell, into the underworld, is necessary for us to find out who we truly are. We must be stripped of all adornment from this life to come back fully empowered to build a better world. Like Jesus, may we both be raised from the dead."

At this last statement, Mattias threw his head back and laughed, the sound bouncing off the walls of the otherwise silent structure. His body shook, and he replied, "Oh, my precious love light. Only you would bring up Jesus at a time like this."

They sat there smiling at each other until she could tell the pain returned to his body. She pulled him to her, resting his larger body on hers. She would support him as long as she could. He would be behind her during the ceremony if Ahmadi were going to follow the service order. She'd had to write a whole paper on the service once when her mother was furious at her. She wrote all the changes she would make. The first one is that the High Priestess wouldn't die.

It seemed like such a faraway thing now, such a silly memory to remember at a time like this, but it made her laugh. She thought about her teenage self, how sure she was of everything. She didn't fault her for that but loved her all the more for her certainty. Certainty in her disgust for her mother, certainty in her love for Tomas, certainty in the future they would have together. She was glad for the momentary reprieve and wanted to strangle Ahmadi with her own bare hands for masterminding all of this in such a sneaky way. She hadn't seen it. Mattias hadn't. She wondered if he'd pulled the wool over everyone's eyes. Maybe she would try and strangle him the first chance she got.

As if the thought of him conjured him, the doors swung open, and Ahmadi entered. He was followed closely by Lukas and Emerie, who wore a veil and a light blue dress. Inira stood to her feet, knowing this was the moment it all began. Inira started to move without thinking toward her daughter. Amin stopped her by pointing a gun directly in her face and spitting, "No, Whore. She is pure and untouched. You will not defile her. Your only role here is to bleed."

Mattias tried to stand, rage painting his handsome face. Inira noticed too that Lukas' free hand balled up, and Emerie, under her veil, stiffened with indignation. She'd had too many run-ins with Emerie's teenage self; she knew exactly what she looked like when offended and angry.

Inira put her hands up in surrender. "Well, if I can't speak to my daughter and you won't allow me to do anything but *bleed*," – she practically spat the word back at him, "what do we do now? We are all apparently at your mercy, Amin. Or should I say Deitas?"

At that, Amin Ahmadi smiled like a cat who'd caught the canary. "Now you are getting it. It took you long enough to see who was really in charge and how easily the Nahas men are disabled! Typical, it would just take one woman each to do it. I, however, am much better than them. I took care of that temptation a long time ago."

At this, Emerie spoke up. "That's because you cut your dick off, you sadomasochistic asshole."

Amin's face clouded over, turning cherry red. He spun to her and reached to grab her by the throat. Lukas got there first, grabbing his hand. The young man said smoothly. "No. You will not touch my bride, especially because you, of all people, would make her impure. If you come anywhere near her, I will break your neck. This is not the plan, Deitas. Get on with the service." His voice held such a hard edge that he looked at Inira at the last second.

She knew from that look that someone had seen the danger they were all in, and she'd been wrong about Lukas Nahas. He wasn't perfect, but he planned on protecting Emerie as best as possible. She was glad he could do what she could not. She gave him the barest of nods in understanding.

Amin, however, just smiled and put the gun between Lukas' eyebrows. "Stand in my way again, boy, and I will not hesitate to make a hole in your skull. She can still become the Heir with your brains splattered on her dress."

Inira held her hands up, and she broke the stalemate. She looked at Mattias as she spoke, "Amin, I know what you want, and I am ready. Mattias and I both are. The sooner we complete the ritual, the sooner our children will be free."

She looked at Lukas and then at Emerie, hoping they could read what she wanted them to do in her eyes. *Kill him the moment the ritual is complete.*

She knew she wouldn't live to see that new life in this world can only come through violence.

Chapter 47

Ahmadi moved them like puppets to where they would stand to perform the ritual. Inira was behind the expansive olive wood altar that gleamed, having been polished to a blinding shine, with Mattias standing behind her. She wasn't sure how long he could stand with his weight on only one leg, but the look on his face spoke of his determination. Lukas and Emerie stood across from her. They were not facing each other like in a Western wedding but facing her. They would be joined after they shared her blood, and then she would teach them the Song of Creation.

She suspected things would go downhill fast because she didn't know the melody.

Ahmadi explained the ceremony in his thin, reedy voice, all the while standing to Inira's right with the gun in her side. She could feel the cold metal pressing against her hip. She wanted to look back at Mattias, silent tears slipping down her face, but she knew it would enrage Ahmadi, and he would act out. She met her daughter's eyes behind the veil and mouthed *I'm so sorry.* Emerie nodded grimly with only what Inira could guess was a sad smile on her face. She noticed Lukas reach for Emerie's hand and lace their fingers together. Emerie leaned into his side, and Inira was glad her daughter could trust him. They didn't look at each other; they kept their eyes on Inira.

I'm glad at least Emerie isn't alone, she thought as Ahmadi intoned the liturgy of the ceremony as if he were the High Priestess. Inira had never heard this version of the ceremony spoken, even as she knew it by heart. The Binding hadn't joined her and Tomas before that long-ago day of destruction. She started to feel like she was floating, and that signaled to her that she was disassociating from her body. She closed her eyes and tried to recall the feeling of total peace from early this morning. It felt like a lifetime ago now. She called to that power, that strength, and that serenity she had felt. It was slow to come. Time was slowing, and reality was caving in on itself. She stood apart from it and felt like she was almost looking down on what was happening. She could see Mattias, eyes streaming, with the bodyguards sitting behind him to prevent him from trying to get to her.

She could see Emerie and Lukas standing as still as statues, eyes boring into hers, begging her to do something. She didn't even really hear the words Amin was speaking. She didn't even feel the cold metal leave her hip. She came violently back into herself when she felt the scalpel pierce her left arm and her warm blood swelling up and out. He repeated the motion on her other arm, cutting her from the base of her hand to the elbow. He wasn't taking any chances.

Her blood flowed quickly and freely into the rose quartz bowl. The wounds were so large that half of the blood leaked out and began to drip on the floor. As she lost blood, she began to disconnect again. She absently thought how slippery the floor would become with all this blood on it and hoped Mattias wouldn't slip. She didn't register the horror on Emerie's face and the revulsion on Lukas's. She guessed by the shade of green he was turning; he didn't like blood. She didn't hear a thing but the dripping.

Then the smell hit her, and she almost fainted. Copper tang filled her nose and mouth, overpowering any other scent. She started to sway; she could feel she was losing too much blood too fast. She didn't know how she was still on her feet. Ahmadi now had the gun pointed at Emerie's face to force Lukas to complete the ritual. They were hastily painting symbols on each other's forearms, both looking like they would vomit or pass out any second.

She hoped Emerie wouldn't break, and in her heart, she called out to the FourFold God to protect her daughter by any means necessary.

She realized then that Ahamadi was saying something to her, shouting in her face. His spittle landed across her nose, in her eyes, and on her mouth. She tried to reach up and wipe it off, but her arms wouldn't move. Her consciousness was fading, but she heard one word.

"SING!!!!!!!!!!!!!!"

He was screaming it, but she had told him she didn't know the song. She'd only heard it as a child and that one time in her dream back in her hotel bed in London, right before she met Mattias. She smiled and thought thinking of him before she died was right. She fell forward, trying to grab the altar to catch herself, but everything was too slippery. She slid down, barely conscious. Everything was a mess, but it didn't matter now. She felt her body being dragged and then cradled as Mattias held her against himself. He was so warm, and she was so cold. She didn't see a light; all she thought about was darkness. What she'd told Mattias before was true. It is the darkness that finds and claims us. Maybe the darkness would show her the way home, where the bright light shone.

She knew no more and missed all the chaos that erupted.

***

The heavy Temple doors slammed open with what sounded like a war cry. Every head turned, Lukas clutching Emerie's hand. He felt her mother's blood on his arms and tasted it in his mouth. He wanted to spit it out. They'd completed the ritual. Their first kiss as a married couple tasted like copper. He knew he was so far gone for her, but this kiss had done nothing for him, especially now that her mother's head was on his father's chest and she was dying, if not already dead. He knew he had to get his wife out of here to get her free. His need to do so was like an engine gearing up in his chest, propelling him forward. He reached for her, pulled her into his chest, and turned her away from the sound of the chaos at the entrance.

He couldn't see who was entering. He held onto Emerie until she heard him scream, "Daddy!" He released her from his grip, letting her move to his side, keeping an arm around her shoulders. Emerie's father had stormed the room, waving an assault rifle at a legion of bodyguards, some of whom were already wounded, hot on his heels.

Francis screamed, "Emerie!! Are you ok?" The veil was no longer over her head, the blood in the shape of an S leaking down the bridge of her nose. She was in stunned silence at seeing her father here. He screamed again, "Ahmadi! Nahas! What have you done to my wife and daughter??"

He looked insane. He had blood all over him, possibly not his own. There was a splatter pattern. Had he shot people? Lukas would never have expected that from this mild-mannered American lawyer. His hair was sticking up. He had more than a bit of scruff on his face and clothes. He looked like he had just emerged from the grave and was ready to enact his vengeance on those who dared to take what was his. Lukas nearly laughed. Instead, he looked at Emerie, grabbed her by the shoulders, and turned his new wife to face him. She was utterly shell-shocked. He leaned into her, resting his cheek against hers, knowing what he was about to tell her might save her life.

"When I tell you, run to your Dad. Get to him and get out of here. I promised to get you out. This wasn't the plan, but it's better than what I had. Blink if you understand me, Sunshine."

She looked at him fully, her milk chocolate eyes huge in her entrancing face. The blood was drying, and he wiped it off. He touched his other hand to her cupid's bow, pressing his thumb into the indentation. It activated her like an on-switch, and she finally blinked at him. It was all the sign he needed. He pushed her towards her father, who was halfway down the aisle with Serpent goon hot on his heels. Ahmadi, as Emerie had been, was rooted to the spot, shocked at the unplanned interruption and just as stunned that Inira's second husband was charging towards him. Lukas lunged for him, for the gun, and managed to grab it as Amin pulled the trigger. The shot went down into the floor, and Lukas wrested it out of the smaller man's hands.

He pointed the gun at Ahmadi's head as Francis shot a stuttered round up into the ceiling, stained glass shattering and falling all around them. Everyone took cover against the falling glass, and several shards landed squarely in the altar wood, with still more landing around where Mattias cradled Inira. Francis swung around and pointed the rifle at the guards rushing him as he grabbed his daughter. He started walking her backward towards the altar; gun pointed at the group. He stopped at the first pew where Lukas had Ahmadi now pinned.

His father was only looking at Inira. He hadn't noticed the commotion. He held her so tenderly. He looked wretched, and he saw his father mouth the words, "I'm ready."

He barely moved when Francis screamed his name. "Nahas! What have you done to my wife?? You fucking bastard!"

Emerie bent down, grabbed Mattias' arm, and shook it so hard it was a wonder Mattias didn't even look up. Lukas noticed Emerie was starting to shake herself, the shock of the last fifteen minutes setting in. His heart leaped out of his chest. He wanted to go to her so badly, but that would mean letting go of Ahmadi, and that wouldn't happen. He thought about putting a bullet to the man's head right that second to bring this whole farce to an end. As Francis leveled the assault rifle at his father, though, Lukas realized he had to keep Ahmadi alive for a few more minutes. His godfather was the trade for his father's life.

Emerie was practically convulsing when she finally got her father's attention. Her barely audible whisper carried in the acoustics of a room where even the softest sound was meant to be heard. "Daddy, look at her." She pointed her shaking finger, arm covered in bloody runes, to where her mother lay. Francis tensed, handed her the rifle, and ran to his dead wife. He slipped in the blood and fell to his knees like a worshipper. He tried to reach for her but stopped.

They were all under the altar, Inira unmoving, Mattias cradling her, and Francis frantically kneeling before her.

Lukas thought it was the saddest thing he had ever seen. Two men, in love with the same woman, who was now so very dead. It broke his heart, but he had committed to Emerie. She was his focus, so Lukas made something happen. He leaned forward and got in Ahmadi's face. Lukas smiled and must have looked like a maniac with the blood on his forehead that had dripped down his face. He felt like war paint. It was his job to take care of the Heir. He was the Consort. They didn't have the Song of Creation, but he didn't want it. He would not let so precious a gift – the song and the person who could sing it, his bride, be controlled by this murderer.

He spat in the man's face, "Ahmadi, you're a dead man. I'm taking over the situation. I'm taking over the company. I'm taking over control of this whole endeavor. Be glad I don't strangle you. I will not rest until you face the consequences of your mutiny against my father."

Amin only smiled. A smile so big it cracked his face in half. Then he began to laugh, doubling over, holding his belly. It was now Lukas' turn to be shell-shocked. Why was this insane motherfucker laughing?

He didn't have to wait long to find out. "You? Are you taking over? We aren't done here, boy! What we need is still yet to be obtained! We must have the Song! The Boehme woman is dead, but her Heir lives! We have a way to get it! Take your bride! Then we can have an Heir! Emerie will sing for her child!!"

Lukas was aghast. This crazy fuck-face thought he was going to *impregnate* Emerie, then hold her hostage until the baby was born so we could repeat this ridiculous farce? He had lost his senses so long ago. Best kill him now and get it over with. Lukas leveled the gun at Amin's head and wrapped a large hand around the smaller man's throat. He didn't hear Francis moaning. He didn't hear his father start keening as he cocked the gun back and prepared to fire.

All he heard was Emerie say, "Lukas, stop."

He stilled and looked at her. She was no longer shaking. She was clear-eyed and standing proud. Sunlight from the broken windows streamed in and bathed her in light. She looked like an angel. She looked like the personification of his nickname for her, which he spoke now, with not a small touch of awe and softness in his voice. "Sunshine, we need this to end. This is the only way."

Emerie shook her head, the veil swishing from side to side as she moved. The sunlight danced through her brown hair, making it shine. Her eyes had a strange fire behind them when she said the words that made him wonder if her mind had fractured.

"My Mother will come back to us. We must wait for her to return, and she will sing."

Lukas shivered. She wasn't crazy, she was a fucking oracle. With the way she looked at him and the truth of what was about to happen radiating through her face, he listened to someone other than himself for the first time in his whole life.

He cocked the safety on the gun, putting his index finger up on the side of it rather than directly on the trigger, but kept his hand on Ahmadi's neck. He looked at their story's villain and said, "The Consort serves the High Priestess. But if you so much do anything other than breathe, I will fucking end you and be happy about it. Then we will cut you up into little pieces, burn your body, and scatter your ashes to the wind. When I'm done with you, there will be nothing left. We will wait until The High Priestess directs me on what to do about you. She is in charge now; you have nothing."

Uncertainty flickered across his godfather's face for the first time Lukas had ever seen. He swallowed, and Lukas watched his throat move up and down with satisfaction. He liked seeing this man uneasy. It was about time.

He then looked at Emerie, into the sacred fire burning in her eyes, breathed out, and smiled at her before he said, "I wait for your direction alone, Wife."

Chapter 48

Inira didn't know where she was, but it wasn't any reality she was used to. She felt open, weightless, untethered, and it was a delicious feeling. She'd had a lesser version many times when she drank – that liminal space where everything is quiet before you tip over into really plastered. Yet, this was not just any altered state due to chemicals. She knew she was between what was, what is, and what could be. She didn't know if she was dead, even though, with the amount of blood she lost, that was a genuine possibility. Still, she hadn't ascended or descended yet.

Suddenly, she knew where she was. She was in the realm of the eternal soul, what the Ancients would call "The Great Below" or the "Great Unknown." She knew there was no return. And just like that, she knew her physical body was dead. Her consciousness had left, and this was what was next.

So be it.

Because she was used to it, she tried to open her eyes. They either weren't there or felt like they were sewn shut. The only sense she had at this point was hearing. So, she focused on what she heard. She had no sense of time in this state, but there wasn't silence. There was just absence, nothingness, only the dark around her, behind what could have been her eyelids. She felt like she was nothing but an ear, only able to listen, stripped of everything else that would define who she was.

She no longer had a husband, a daughter, a job, her calling as High Priestess. She'd lost her body and her voice. All she could do was try to hear.

Then she heard it, a barely there whisper, against what could have been the shell of her ear.

Come join us.

She didn't know where to go exactly. She felt a pull in the center of her body – if she had a body – like a string attached to her. She felt drawn with a sensation of going down, but she couldn't say the direction since she didn't know where she was. It felt *down*.

The pulling continued slowly at first but gradually began to pick up speed. She still couldn't see or feel anything, hear almost like a slight, dry wind rushing past her "ears." Then, she started to pick up notes or beats. She felt it more than she heard like the sound waves reverberated through her. She would have started to move with the music if she felt like she had a body. She continued with this *down* feeling. It accelerated and she began to hear more notes and beats, like there was music being tested out, similar to how an orchestra warms up. It wasn't discordant, but it wasn't cohesive either. She continued to listen, and hearing it became the focus of her entire existence.

She knew this song.

She reveled in the sound until it became all of her. She felt every energy particle syncing as the notes and beats came together. It was fast and swirling, nothing that was becoming something. The sound became a song she participated in, lending her energy and essence. She felt at one with it and tried to sing what she was hearing, maybe add words or feelings to it, but she couldn't. She could do nothing but hear it. She listened for what felt like forever, but she became impatient. She only longed to hear, experience, dance, and have a mouth to perhaps sing this everlasting song herself.

But she couldn't do anything but listen.

She was mute and blind, with hearing as the only sense allowed to her. As she remained there, she began to sense another with her. She began to feel an intense yet familiar presence. It wasn't menacing, just observant. She began to try and find, to feel where this presence was. She only felt it chuckle before she heard it say her name.

"Inira – Light Bringer, calm yourself. You must experience the Song of Creation before you can sing it."

Light exploded before Inira's eyes, which she did not have or got back that instant. She felt her bones reforming, her muscles coming together as if she were being rebuilt from the inside out. She felt the Voice, the Presence, chuckle and say, "Yes, healing happens from the inside out."

And it hurt – she hurt. She felt her pupils contract rapidly. She brought her hand up before her eyes when it dawned on her. She was in a body again – her body! She felt weirder than when she was untethered. Being at one with the song was more at home for her than standing here wherever that was. When her eyes adjusted to the light, although still bright, she stood before what could have been an ancient version of the Counsel room her mother and the Teleosis leaders used to meet to discuss matters of state. There were twelve seats, and all but two were filled. Then she heard the voice again, and it said,

"Welcome, Light Bringer, you have finally come to commune with us! Your journey has been arduous and lengthy, but you have made it. For your service, you have been remade. That is the power of the Song. Impressive, no?"

Inira didn't know what to say. As she looked around the room, her mouth dried up. Several of the beings around the table were clearly not human. Several had so many eyes it made her head hurt to look at them. Then there were the winged creatures. As she looked around, gaping at everything and everyone, her gaze finally settled on two human-looking creatures who shone brighter than any sunny day she'd ever seen. One glowed with pure, white light. The other with gold, shimmering light. As she looked at them further, she could see differences. The pure, white light seemed more male in form than the one with the gold shimmer. The golden shimmery One, Inira realized with a start, looked a lot like her reflection.

Inira's mind was empty. She had no skills for processing anything she was experiencing, so she asked an idiotic question.

"Where am I?"

The pure, white-lighted One seemed to chuckle. "No one ever knows what to say when they first get here." The golden shimmery one swatted a hand in the air towards him. "Don't pester the girl; she's been through a lot. Come, Inira. Daughter, come closer."

As Inira looked at "her," her soul felt the pull. Yet she stayed rooted to the spot. This "woman's" voice was so comforting, almost grandmotherly, and at odds with the radiance streaming off "her" in waves. Eventually, Inira felt like she was being encouraged to move, as that string still attached to her middle was yanked, and she was drawn in towards the golden shimmery grandmotherly type being.

She approached the table and immediately felt full of shame. She was unworthy to be here, unclean amongst the holiest beings in the universe. She had done great harm. She shouldn't be here and be among surely what were gods. She fell to her knees, feeling the crunch of bone against hard stone.

The pure, white-lighted One sighed. "It happens every time. Humans have their notions of worthy and holy. When will they learn that's not how we look at them?"

Suddenly, Inira was being raised to her feet and drawn into the orbit of the pure, white-lighted One. She felt safer, trusted, and cared for as she got closer. There was a purpose to her being here at this moment, in this time. She looked into the unusual but appealing face with its highbrow, strong chin, and singular depthless eyes. She felt at home and unafraid. She felt the kind of love she'd never experienced.

It was the love of the Father.

"Light Bringer, you have indeed been through so much. We never intended this for you or your daughter. We have seen the violence

– humanity's original sin – and e brought you here to undo it so that you may carry on what we started. You are the daughter of our daughters and sons. You must return to rebuild and restore what has been lost."

Inira blinked and continued to stare into "his" eyes. "Who are you? What are you?"

It was then the Golden, Shimmery One spoke. "We are You, Inira. We are the I am that I am. We are the God and the Goddess. We are the Mother and the Father. We are the Alpha and Omega, First and the Last. We are Sophia and Adan, your ancestors, and we were hoping you could return, or the Song of Creation will be lost. However, as always, it is Your Choice. The Great Creator gifted us with free will, and we will not take away yours."

Then the pure, white-lighted one – Adan – spoke again, a smile in "his" voice. "You will make an informed choice, of course. You will see what waits for you if you stay and what must be given to return. To make your choice, let's start with what waits for you if you stay."

Adan then gently turned her around, his "hands" warm and soothing on her shoulders. She drew strength from that warmth as she belonged, and he wanted her here. It was a delicious feeling. It reminded her of when her grandmother would pull her favorite treats out of the oven, making her wait just long enough not to burn the roof of her mouth. The tension she was carrying melted under his assuring touch, and she felt as if whatever happened, it would be okay. When she got all the way around and turned around, she saw him, and she dropped back to her knees like a stone.

Tomas stood before her. Not like he had been when she knew him, especially not the Tomas, whose soul had darkened in the months and weeks leading up to the attacks. No, this was Tomas, the *real* Tomas at his core. She saw his soul, and it was her undoing. She couldn't move. She couldn't breathe. She stayed so still and didn't look up in case this was a dream she would awaken from. She didn't even look at him for fear that he was a mirage and would evaporate.

She felt his warmth before her, and he took her hands. She could tell he had kneeled before her, and he turned her arms over, the pale skin of her underarm nearly gleaming. She heard the voice of the Golden Shimmery One – Sophia – speak to them both, "Now the Son and Daughter are One again." She could feel the pleasure, the smile in her voice, and the delight of reuniting her children.

It was then she noticed there were wounds on her forearms from the cuts Ahmadi had made during the ceremony. Tomas noticed, too. He looked so sad as he took his finger and traced the outside of the cuts. "I see the Serpents found you. I am so sorry, Inira. I never meant for any of this to happen. And I would trade my soul for eternal torment if I could go back in time and change the choices I made. I tried to do just that when I got here. But They wouldn't let me come back. They told me you had another who would help you along the way. They told me my twin, the one I share a soul with, would now be the one who helps you sing."

Tomas continued to look sad, even as he spoke of his brother. He paused as if remembering his time with Mattias, maybe knowing him better than he thought.

He reverently held her arms, supporting them from underneath. He looked up into her eyes, such the familiar and loving green she had dreamed of for so long. He spoke the words she longed to hear, "If I had known what I was doing, I would have chosen you, like I swore to. I would have chosen you like I said I always would. I would have been your consort, Protector, and guide. I would have been the home you had instead of the home I destroyed. You were my heart light, and I let that light go out. You were right, and you paid the price for my folly."

Warm, wet tears fell on her cuts. Tomas wept over her arms, and she felt a strange sizzling sensation on her skin. When Tomas sat back up, her scars were gone. There was nothing left of the damage Ahmadi had done to her.

Adan chuckled, but Sophia spoke, "There is nothing love cannot do, isn't that right, my darling? It can even heal the unhealable wounds of this world."

Inira looked up into Tomas' eyes and knew what one of her choices was. She told him, "We could be together again if I stay."

Tomas smiled a brilliant smile, similar to Mattias, yet so different because it was unencumbered by pain, loss, and shame over his chosen path. "Inira, you were always the smarter one of us. My brother knows that now."

Inira's breath hitched at the mention of Mattias from Tomas. "You never met him, did you?"

Tomas smiled sadly when he spoke, "Yes, once. We were identical but so vastly different. He was all fire and ice—such a complicated, driven man. Still, I knew you would bring out the goodness in him. Your love would heal his broken heart, and you did."

"What will happen to him if I stay?"

Tomas looked into her eyes for a long beat before saying, "It will break him completely. It will break everyone you love completely. There will be no one that can continue the legacy of Teleosis. Emerie doesn't know enough and won't have time to learn. Everyone's life span will be cut short if you don't return. That is the cost of staying here with me. You can choose for yourself, but you should know the world will pay the highest cost."

Inira felt like this was a grossly uneven bargain. If she stayed with Tomas, everyone else would suffer. If she went back to them, she would lose Tomas all over again. She didn't feel strong enough to do that. She felt whole here with him, with the Ancients. Her time serving Teleosis was complete, even if it had come to a horrific end. It didn't feel right to return; besides, there wasn't anything left to do now that Nahas International owned the island and everything and everyone connected to it.

"There is nothing more I can do, Tomas." She looked up and around the room at the members of the Heavenly Counsel. "How can you doom my family, Mattias, and Lukas, to die because of my choice?"

Sophia came and knelt beside her; Inira instantly felt like a light bulb turned on inside of her.

She felt infused with life and hope when Sophia spoke to her. "Light Bringer, it isn't our choice that they would perish. This results from many choices, and those consequences will go unchecked if you decide to stay. We would never want you not to know the cost of saying such things. You will return here, my Daughter. It is your destiny to sit with us. The High Priestess and her Consort always serve in the Great Unknown until the next pair is ready to take their place. It is one of the gifts of the Great Creator to let the work of the Song continue in us until your time of service is finished."

Sophia took her right hand from Tomas, and Inira turned to face her. The Mother explained, "If you go back, Teleosis and the mission will continue, and you will also be able to show the world. And the world will listen as you sing. You had the vision of equality, to show the world what women and men can do together in their strengths. You and Mattias will do that. You will have the resources to completely rebuild, completely restore the mission, and teach it so it will continue."

The golden eyes looked into hers as she said, "You will finally be able to do what you were created for, and it will come to pass. If you spend a few more years up there, you can do what no High Priestess ever accomplished: get people to listen to the potential as you sing the Song that lives in your heart."

Tomas held her one hand, but he now stood and brought her up with him. Sophia stood with them, and Adan moved to them, placing one hand on each of their shoulders. He spoke her name and said, "It doesn't seem like much of a choice, but the hero always makes it. The Great Creator designed us that way. We are powered by hope, Daughter. We are carried forth in love. Don't be sad to leave your love; he will be with you just as he has always been."

Then he smiled at Tomas and said, "He will have eternity to make it up to you."

Inira itched to hug and hold onto Tomas, as everyone already knew she was going back. It wasn't a fair choice, doing what she had to do, but it was what she was born for. Her journey felt so circular;

could she be the agent of light and healing the world needed? Hadn't she made too many mistakes?

Adan and Sophia moved away; it was just her and Tomas now. He held her just inside the span of his arms. He leaned forward to whisper to her, "It is exactly your past that makes you who you are and makes it possible for you to do this. Your wounds, mistakes, and rocky road led you to become the woman the world needs – the Daughter to reflect the Mother. The Wounded Healer is the one who brings the cure for what ails this world. Don't cling to me, my heart light. I have missed you and have been in agony witnessing all you've gone through. But you cannot cling to me. You have more than enough strength to stand on your own."

She looked at him, and as she gazed before turning to view what Sophia wanted to show her, she felt the lock on the secret box of her heart that she'd kept Tomas in for so long spring open. She felt fluttering wings carry him out of her heart. She knew then, just before she turned to the Counsel, she had let him go like she'd needed to all along, with the promise that those same wings would return her here to be with him one day.

So, she let the butterfly of her love for Tomas fly.

Chapter 49

"**Y**ou must face us now, Light Bringer," a deep, resonant voice spoke to her from the direction of one of the creatures full of eyes. Inira did as it beckoned, turning her body away from Tomas but staying connected to him. She would hold his hand until the last moment she had to let go.

"You will not be able to return the same as you were before. You have lost your scars. That is the first of what you will need to give up going back and help carry on the mission and legacy of Teleosis." The inhuman creature, full of eyes, spoke slowly and in a way that felt like it wasn't used to language or communicating at all. Inira felt a wave of giggles at the idea of a heavenly creature being out of practice, but she did not let it loose.

It continued to instruct her with its slow, sloth-like pace, all the eyes blinking simultaneously, which was incredibly distracting. "When you sing the Song of Creation, its power will flow through it. The Song's power comes from the Source, which is pure Love. Not the kind of love humans know but the full force of the Divine Love for all things. It is the most powerful force in the universe."

She wasn't sure if it paused for effect or was growing weary of using spoken language, but it felt like several minutes before it spoke again. Inira began to feel slightly anxious. She wasn't sure if it was nerves – she already felt the pull to return to the life above. Or if it was having to wait on the majestic being to finish it's thought. She knew more was coming, and the feeling of it started to build like a thunderhead in her chest.

She could feel Tomas, Adan, and Sophia waiting with her with bated breaths, almost as if they were collectively holding the air in their lungs.

Finally, the being spoke again, the rush of it pouring over her like a wave cresting. "Light Bringer, you must know that this power can be used – or misused. Love this pure is the force that created the Universe from nothing. You have the choice of how you will use it. You will be the one to control it, and who you give it to – how you give it to them – matters. The intention of your heart sets the effect of this power. Love always changes what it touches, but the wielder of that Love determines what kind of impact it will have."

As if it was the being's final parting blessing, it concluded with, "Use your inner wisdom to seek the best intention before you sing. We release you to go now, Light Bringer. Fulfill your name as you so choose, and let it be."

The being bowed its head, all eyes closing, and stepped back into the circle around the table.

The four of them, Father, Mother, Son, and Daughter released their breath in a furious exhale. It was Adan who spoke first. "Well, that was intense. I've never heard the Great Obisan speak. Not sure if They ever have before."

Inira almost laughed again. She felt giddy, like a little girl at a birthday party. She knew she had already decided to return, but it would not be forever. She would be restored to Tomas again, and somehow, the Divine would work everything else out with Francis and Mattias. However, that came about; she treasured her time in the living world as she was treasuring this time in the eternal realm.

She turned to Sophia and asked, "Can I keep this feeling of being here with you all?"

Sophia cocked her head and said, "Daughter, it's always been there inside of you. It is always with you. Just ask for it, and it will return. It's your connection to Source, to Love. When you reach deep inside, it will meet you; from that place, you sing. Heed Obisan's words, though. Ensure your intentions are from a place of blessing, not cursing. Because with whatever heart position you sing from, whether blessing or cursing, it will come to pass."

Inira nodded, taking this information into herself and storing it on the shelf of her heart right up front. She could see it when she closed her eyes. She knew she would reach for it when she returned to her mortal body.

Adan stepped up to her other side, Inira immediately feeling settled by him and Tomas on the other side of her. Sophia stood behind her, and Inira felt her wild strength flow in, filling her with a feeling like passion and urging her forward.

The creature next to the one full of eyes, with black wings and a terrifying canine face, spoke in a voice like the depths of the darkest ocean. "Light Bringer, to return, you must give each of us something of value. What do you have to offer?"

Inira was dumbfounded. She had nothing in her pockets. She wore no jewelry and wasn't sure she was wearing clothes.

She stuttered her response, "I-I-I-I h-h-h-h-ave n-n-n-nothing to give you. What could you possibly want?"

"Light Bringer, we will take from you what you do not need to return with. But first, make your choice. Do you stay with your great love or return to save the others?"

Inira knew the answer, as did everyone there, but they needed her words. It wasn't a foregone conclusion, but the choice was clear since they had seen her creation, and she knew the cost. She turned to Tomas all the same. With Adan now behind her, she felt rooted and grounded. With Sophia beside her, she let all the love flow from her heart wide open for the first time in her entire life.

She looked Tomas full in the face and said, "Tomas, I have never stopped loving you, longing for you. It has always been you and will always be until I return to you when it is time. I forgive you and know that you have learned what was needed. I feel it." She reached up and touched his chest, right above his heart.

Then she continued her goodbye, "We both know it isn't my time yet. I have to finish the work we would have done together, and I must return alone. I will use the Song to reestablish the mission and vision of Teleosis. I will not let life fall into the dark in the hands of Ahmadi and the Serpents. I will return to you when my time is full. Will you wait for me?"

Tomas smiled and leaned forward, touching his forehead to hers, "I've never stopped waiting for you, Noni. Don't rush back; I'll be here when you are ready to return to where you belong. We will sit together on the Counsel like we were always supposed to."

He kissed both cheeks and let go of her hands as she faced the frightening gazes of the Ancient Counsel. One by one, they went around and asked for her gift to them. One by one, they each took something from her. One by one, Inira felt herself growing lighter, taller. She realized they were stripping her of everything she'd carried that she believed made her herself. But it was only the pain she'd carried for far too long because of what had been done to her. Underneath everything they stripped away, she felt naked, but she was unashamed.

They took eight things from her, one for each member of the Counsel.

Her hatred of her mother.

Her pride.

Her buried rage.

Her shame.

Her sense of entitlement.

Her desire to please others.

Her desire to please only herself.

Her identity as a victim.

She felt drained but free at the end of this unraveling of who she thought she was. She was loosed from her trauma, liberated from who she thought she had to be. She felt fully open and available to use Love – to sing. She no longer harbored resentments, fears, or a sense of what the world owed her because of her birthright or what had happened to her – or even her addiction. The gifts she had given to the Ancients had been holding her back from becoming the person she was created to be.

Just before that string on her belly button took her in what felt like "up," Adan took her hands in his. White light streamed off of him in waves, yet his gaze was soft and tender. He said, "Daughter, remember that you will not be alone even if you return alone. We've worked out some unexpected help for you to aid your mission." He winked. "And when your time is full, you will return to us and your great love. Blessings, my Light Bringer."

He touched her forehead and made an "S" sign, redeeming the healing power of that sigil Ahmadi and the world had tried to corrupt.

She caught a glimpse of Sophia as she felt herself ascending, and she was blowing Inira a kiss. Then she felt it; power and energy surge through her. She closed her eyes and saw her body, from the crown of her head to the soles of her feet, full of a swirling mix of white and golden light. Every cell was full of it as she opened her eyes in the Temple and sat up.

Chapter 50

Francis screamed. Mattias clutched her to his chest, speaking in rapid Spanish, which went from soft to near shouting in a couple of breaths. Lukas' mouth dropped open. Amin grinned like a mad fool, and Emerie looked up from where she was sitting in the sun with her head in her hands. She breathed a sigh of relief.

"The FourFold God didn't lie to me," she whispered. Lukas, who sat next to her with his arm around her shoulder, looked like he'd seen a ghost, which had been made into flesh before him. Then he started laughing, sounding insane and leaned over to Emerie, who turned to him simultaneously. He kissed her soundly, and she responded wholeheartedly.

Inira smiled. She got to see their first real kiss, after all. She was filled with hope for the two of them, and her heart felt near to bursting. To see her daughter happy was one of her greatest desires. She knew there was still a fight before them, but she saw the future in them. Now, it was time to rectify all that was wrong. Inira tried to stand up but realized she was covered in her own dried blood, and Mattias held her in a vice grip. Francis had stopped screaming, but now he backed away from her like she was a zombie on all fours, and she giggled because he looked like a crab scurrying away.

They were under the altar, where she had fallen, and Mattias had cradled her with his body. He was also a mess, and when she turned to face him, smiling, his eyes widened, and he crossed himself. That made her giggle, too.

He whispered to her, "My love, how can this be? How are you alive? You were cold in my arms, and I was ready to end my life to join you. Now you are laughing at me?" He crossed himself again, and she put a hand to her mouth to cover it. She reached up to stroke his cheek but saw her hand. Everything was covered in blood, but she had no cuts or wounds. She took a moment to marvel at it, knowing what she experienced in the Great Unknown was not a dream, but still, it felt like a miracle to be back here.

"Mattias, look at my arm."

She showed him the underside of her forearm, turning it into his gaze. His eyes got impossibly wider, and he gently took her arm to his lips and kissed it. He was reverent and worshipful like she was a Goddess reborn. She liked the feeling and told him so.

He met her gaze and whispered, "I am yours for the rest of my life, my *luz de amor*."

She turned her head to kiss him, just a quick peck. Before she stood, she leaned up towards his ear and said, "Remind me to tell you about seeing Tomas. He sends his blessings."

Mattias grabbed his chest at the mention of his brother's name as she pushed up to stand. She turned around and pulled him up, sticky and stiff. It was like the set of a horror movie. Indeed, it had been a horrible ending to her first life.

Now, it was time for her second one to begin.

She helped Mattias to the front row pew, everyone just watching her. She knew Lukas and Emerie had stopped kissing to wait for her direction. Francis, however, was as white as a ghost. She moved towards him slowly and sat down next to him in the pew. He didn't scoot away from her, but looked like he might bolt at any sudden movement.

"Francis, it's me. It's Inira." She spoke in hushed tones, conscious of how scary things must be for him. She wondered how he got here, thinking he had arrived after she was gone. The empathy for his pain engulfed her. "I'm glad you are here. I need to apologize to you. I betrayed you. I hurt you. I broke up our family. I don't know if you can forgive me, but I hope you can work towards that."

He continued to stare at her, sitting stock still. He looked at her, finally breaking it to look her up and down. "How are you alive? You were just there, on the floor with no pulse because you bled out. And where are your wounds? Your arms are unmarked!" He was shaking now, his body and mind unable to process this information and what was happening.

She smiled at him and. "It's a long story. But I'd like to tell you soon. Would that be ok? I need to wrap things up here, and then I hope we can find a place to talk it out."

Francis looked unsure but didn't move. He looked down, and she realized that he, too, was covered in her blood. He started to shake uncontrollably. She put her hands on his shoulders, familiar with being his partner for 20 years. As she touched him, she spoke in soothing murmurs and hummed a little tune. She wanted so much for him to be okay, to not question or doubt himself due to her actions. She wanted him to be whole and restored – but more than that. She wanted him to be fully himself without fear. She wanted him to know his mind and find someone who could enhance his life the way she had been unable to. They had both failed each other, even though her failing weighed heavier on the scales. They had been right for each other for a long time, a safe place, but she didn't do her part when that changed. She felt so sad, and she pulled from the Source out of that sadness.

She could feel the pure, white energy leave her and flow into him.

As it did, he stopped shaking. He stood without leaning on the altar rail and stood taller and almost proud. His face relaxed, and his shoulders dropped. He smiled and looked at her, "I feel so much better. I feel like myself for the first time in a long time."

Inira, hands still on his shoulders, said, "You are your own man now, Francis. You are free to live into all you were meant for." He kept smiling at her in wonder and put his hand over his heart. "I look forward to our conversation."

Inira, with silver lining her eyes, laughed. It was such a Francis thing to say at a time like this.

They looked into each other's eyes for a few more beats, and then movement caught her eye. Ahmadi was making his way towards her, stalking. Mattias had moved behind her on the pew and tried to block him, but he couldn't do much. She heard his hiss of pain and knew they would have to get him to a doctor very soon. The bodyguards behind Mattias stood up to restrain her so Ahmadi could take what he wanted. Yet, before they could touch her, she heard her daughter's sharp voice command them, "Sit down, gentlemen."

Lukas laughed and softly said, "That's my wife you report to now motherfuckers. Take a seat and watch the show."

Yet, before Inira could turn to face Ahmadi, she heard the *click* of the trigger on an empty magazine being pulled.

Amin Ahmadi stood there, having retrieved his revolver in the melee, and had it pointed straight at Inira. Lukas growled at him, "The clip is empty, you moron. Your reign of terror is over. Time for you to die."

Francis said, "No, he is mine!" He stood up, grabbing an AR-15, which Inira could not fathom where he got or how he knew how to use it. It looked so odd in his hands, so out of place with the peace in his eyes, but maybe he thought revenge was part of his reward. Lukas went to stand at the same time as Francis, but Inira stopped them both by holding a hand up.

"I'll handle this, gentlemen." She turned to face Ahmadi, gun still pointed at her. Bullets or not, she was not afraid of him. She knew what she had to do. She prepared her heart, which took some effort as she took steps towards him. He started to back up, looking behind him for some way to escape. She was between him and the door, so he could go nowhere. He was trapped. But a trapped animal was the most dangerous kind.

With his back against the altar, he spit at her and said, "You will give me what I want, Whore."

Inira smiled at him; the power of Love was overshadowed by pure rage. Here was a man who sought to destroy her, and without the intervention of the FourFold God, she would be dead at his hands. He was evil and would use this power inside of her to enact horrible things on the earth. He wouldn't stop until he was dead, and millions would pay the price for it if she didn't stop him. His hatred for women – for everyone – including himself had driven him to mutilate his own body. He had tricked everyone into thinking he was harmless, but his was the most potent venom in the Serpents. She could feel what he desired, taking out his pain on the entire earth.

She was feeling his pain at even being born into such a life – and then all the choices he had made, including killing his mother. What he would do with the Song was atrocious, and she would never give it to him. She felt her rage as white hot, the energy of that need for justice to ensure he couldn't continue his malevolent plans surging through her. She could feel her skin heat up, and Ahmadi's eyes got huge. He saw her transform into a goddess of vengeance right before him. The white-hot heat that had been so nurturing and soft with Francis was now a torrent. The power within her begged her to be released. It whispered *he deserves this*.

She wanted to scream the Song at him and watch the flesh melt off his bones. She hated him. She hated all he stood for. She hated all he represented and what was wrong with the world. She would show him what hate felt like. Ahmadi was grinning like a mad fool, even as he looked like his bowels would release any second. He had lost his mind, only thinking his plan would finally work out in his favor now that Inira was back alive.

They were separated by a few feet when she stopped.

The words of the creature Obisan and Sophia came back to her. Like a counter surge of power within her, the words of the final, parting blessing he spoke over her were like an antidote to the poison of the hatred she felt. *Use your inner wisdom to seek the best intention before you sing—Light Bringer. Ensure your intentions are from a place of blessing, not cursing, because with whatever heart position you sing from, whether blessing or cursing, it will come to pass.*

She was one step from him when she stopped. She turned to look around at her family.

Lukas sat beside a serene Emerie and returned his arm to her shoulders. He practically pulled her onto his lap to protect her from anything that might come. Emerie didn't fight him; she only welcomed his touch and comfort. She'd found her safe place with him and him with her. Mattias was still in pain but was watching her, eyes full of love and trust that she would do what was right and necessary. Francis was sitting next to Mattias, watching her as well. He had no expectations in his eyes. He didn't look like he would advise, tell her what to do, or try to control the outcome. He just waited for her to do what she was born to do, now that he had made his peace with Inira becoming all she really was.

She knew what she had to do. As much as she would have liked to destroy Amin Ahmadi, and he did deserve that, it wouldn't be acting out of Love. It would set a curse in place, and that was not how they needed to restart Teleosis. She was meant to be a vessel of blessing, and it was only with her heart full of that intention that she could sing. Otherwise, she would be no better than her enemy. She would use the Song of Creation to sing Love into him, not Hate. He was already choking on hate. Love was the only way to stop him.

At the exact moment she reached out for him, he pulled the trigger again.

Click.

Inira smiled at him, gently this time, as she watched his eyes bug out as the energy within her shifted. Like a mother instructing a young child, she told him, "Amin, we have unfinished business. I told you I knew you. Now I know what you need. Don't worry; I will give you the Song of Creation, but it will not be like you wanted. Love does its own work in us, Amin. When you try to control it, it comes out distorted and wrong. I want you to know Love fully, and I hope it returns you to yourself."

Inira reached for him, and he'd stayed glued to the spot. The gun was now between them, the metal resting against her sternum. Right over her heart, she did not doubt that if there were any rounds left in the chamber, she would see Tomas sooner than anyone in heaven or earth had planned. But his plan had failed because she had gotten help, just like the Father had promised. She had gotten help from her great love, all five of them. Her love came from those who surrounded her and the ones who waited for her return: Mattias, Francis, Emerie, Lukas, and, of course, Tomas.

She could feel their love surround her as she took the Song of Creation off the shelf in her heart. She spoke out the words she never imagined she could say to someone like Amin Ahmadi, but the force of that Divine Love gave her the power to speak.

"The FourFold God blesses you with Their love, Amin."

Amin started to scream as she placed her hands on his shoulders and opened her mouth. She began to sing the Song of Songs.

His screaming was louder than her singing, but only momentarily. The Song of Creation eclipsed every sound. Inira felt it surge from her chest, from her womb, from the soles of her feet. She felt the pulse of the "S" Adan had anointed her within her forehead. Her entire body and soul were aligned with the Song as she poured it out and into Ahmadi.

This time, it wasn't the white but the golden energy. She felt it drawing up from the earth beneath her feet, from the land of Teleosis itself. It rained down into his eyes, ears, and body from where her hands made contact. They were both lit up, enveloped in this golden light energy. Every note she sang was filled with joy, delight, pleasure, and promise. She couldn't stop singing it and could feel how the world was being remade.

She closed her eyes and became only feeling, only the notes and sounds and vibrations that streamed from her. She was complete, in total alignment with all of Creation, and she could feel the smile of the Father and the Mother. She reveled in it and couldn't help herself. She started to sway.

From the outside, she and Amin were dancing in a golden mirror ball, shooting light out to the Earth's four corners and surrounding Cosmos. Amin had stopped making any sound. His eyes were still bugging out, and his mouth hanging open in a silent scream. He never had the chance to make another sound as the full force of the Divine Love slammed into his chest. Unchecked, raw Love invaded him. The place where she was touching his shoulders looked blackened and scalded, and the skin underneath his shirt was severely burned.

And that's when she saw it.

His shriveled, black, malformed heart. Every evil choice he had made had changed it, warped how he could receive love until he no longer could. His heart could only give out pain. He could only harm others and himself because it was all he knew. Inira felt a tear streak down her face as she envisioned what he had endured to make him this way. She sang the final notes and pulled her hands free from his shoulders. He fell backward over the altar. His body teetered, and he landed on his head with a loud *crack*. He was already dead before he hit the ground. His soul had been taken from his body by Love, and what happened to him was now up to Love.

Taking a breath and wiping her face, Inira felt something on the back of her head. Her knees buckled as the power of the Song left her and returned to the container on the shelf in her heart. She stayed there on her knees until she realized what she was feeling.

It was sunlight warming her. No stained glass was in the ceiling, so the sunlight poured in on her. She felt wrapped up in it as she knelt before the altar; Ahmadi's body was on the other side, prostrate as if finally in the worship of something other than himself. She knelt there for a long time, feeling empty and full simultaneously. She knew her family watched her, Francis sitting on the other side of Emerie, holding her other hand. He had his arm over the top of Lukas' and was tenderly cupping his shoulder like the father he was. Mattias was separate but not far away. They were waiting for her to decide what to do next. They were each giving her this moment, here in the Temple, alive and well, before rushing headlong into the future that awaited them.

Finally, Inira turned into the sunbeam that seemed to come from nowhere and everywhere. She heard the voice, just a whisper, but it echoed in the space designed to carry the smallest sound. It felt like the first moment of the rest of her now-second chance at life.

The Light Bringer has come home.

Epilogue

S *eptember 10th, 3 years later....*

Inira stood up, cracked her back that was aching, and wiped the sweat from her forehead with the linen cloth in her back pocket. She reached for her water bottle and looked up to see the progress in the garden she was tending. It was full of lavender, rosemary, and other herbs. Also, she still had a lot of weeds to pull. They'd had unexpected rain the last few weeks, and those suckers were staging a coup in the Mother's Garden. That was her title now, The Mother. Mattias was known as The Father. They knew the more formal names were required, but nothing about this rebuild was formal anymore. She would let future generations build in the formality.

They were just a family.

Emerie had laughingly suggested The Crone, which Inira shot down quickly. The Mother fit her better anyway.

Her grandmother would be proud of her efforts in the garden even if she would frown at the outcome. Her grandmother, Noni, would have weeded in the pouring rain, but Inira was not as committed. She had no official state role or responsibilities here in Tov now that Emerie and Lukas were well-installed and overseeing the rebuilding and repopulating.

Inira smiled at the baby sleeping in the pram in the shade. Her eleven-month-old grandson, Tomas, was just as handsome as his father. He was a big baby, too. He had the Nahas green eyes. Inira could stare into them all day and quite often did when she was feeding, playing, and changing him while Lukas and Emerie made sure the resettlement of Tov – and all of Teleosis – went smoothly. They would push as long as possible until Emerie needed to rest again.

Baby numbers two and three, twin girls, were on the way. Lukas and Emerie took their organic efforts to continue Teleosis's mission very seriously. They had never been happier but needed a break to escape their responsibilities. She and Mattias often took the baby so Lukas and Emerie could have long weekends at the Santorini House.

Mattias would be back soon. They had made a life here together. The first thing he did was build a house for the kids and then one for them. Mattias regularly flew between here and London. He was dismantling the Serpents as fast as he could with Lukas's help, which had led to the prosecution of many criminals hidden in the ranks. He was working with international agencies to make sure what Nahas did now was to feed the vision of Teleosis, all on the global stage Mattias had excelled on for decades.

And he was installing the new CEO of Nahas Helps to lead into the next generation. Charlotte was glad for the promotion. Giselle was her second in command, and they were handling the all-male board quite expertly, even as that would change soon, too.

Mattias was due back later today and would be delighted they had the baby. He had promised just a small recognition of the day of her birth, just the three of them. It couldn't be more perfect in her mind, especially with her grandson around. She had done a lot of healing these last three years and now no longer dreaded her birthday. She still wanted it small. When she and Mattias Facetimed last night, he said he had two gifts for her. He showed her the first one – he had gotten the Teleosian Crest tattooed over his heart.

He said the second one was a surprise. "A very expensive surprise that I've been dying to give you since I met you."

Emerie had already sent her a happy birthday text and promised to bake cupcakes when they returned. She laughed at that because baking was a new hobby for the young couple and usually ended up with one of them making a mess. When she said that to Emerie, she said, "Well, Lukas has quite the talent. It's just me that's the mess, so maybe I'll let him do it!"

That was fine with Inira. Her small but growing family around her made her feel encapsulated in love, and that was all she needed.

Having their grandson with them gave them a chance to care for a child together, as they were both past the age of trying for their own. They also loved it when his parents returned. That was a perk of being a grandparent, she thought. When Mattias was here, she often found him in the evening, dozing with the baby lying on his chest, both having worn themselves out from playing. She would gently put Tomas in his room in their house – a second nursery the twins would share. Then she would take Mattias to bed, ready to share their bodies in sacred union as always.

She expected nothing less for her birthday.

Mattias was always busy in Tov, too, overseeing the emigration of new residents, building houses for them, and ensuring their re-settlement was living into all the standards of abundance Teleosis imparted. His fortune made it happen, and the new headquarters of Nahas Helps was also on the island. Its new name was Triune.

When he traveled, she missed him. She also had her work to keep her occupied. She was teaching Emerie how to lead in real-time and instructing her on the history of their civilization. She was busy most days, reconnecting with world leaders and influencers who were curious about this ancient movement that had, once again, been reborn from the ruins. There was a great hunger in the world for a new way of living life to the fullest beyond the failed attempts by every other ideology. Teleosis was the last great hope. It was satisfying to be someone who could show people the vision of how humanity could thrive that was always in their midst.

The world was finally ready to pay attention. In that, Inira shined, and she was also teaching Emerie how to shine.

Francis was their Lead Counselor, with his expertise in the law expanding to include international legalities. They talked once a week. It usually started as a business call, but then, of course, they would inevitably talk about Emerie, Tomas, and the development of the twins. They'd officially divorced but committed to staying engaged as co-parents and grandparents. He came to Tov as often as he could now that he had a woman in his life. They were both moving on. He still wouldn't speak to or be in the same room with Mattias but said he was in therapy to get there. He was also the Teleosian Ambassador to the United States. They'd ensured he was safe in their brownstone because it was now an official residence, but it was his home, and that's where he wanted to be.

How Inira saw her life was now totally different; not only had her perspective changed, but what she'd always longed for was now her reality. She never imagined being able to return and live a fulfilling life here on Teleosis. She thought that dream was dead and gone. Stanley had ensured, though, that she would have gotten a chance, eventually.

As it turned out, she was the owner of the land all along. Amin had never secured the island's purchase because it wasn't for sale. It was written into Stanley's last will and testament. He had purchased the island for pennies on the dollar a year after the bombings. When 9/11 happened, no one cared who owned a tiny island in the middle of the Aegean, so he scooped it up. He bequeathed the land to her and his remaining assets to his sons. They fought it for about six months until Lukas had the idea to fly them out for a visit to see what they would "lose" by dropping their suit. They didn't think much of an island barely rebuilt in the middle of the Mediterranean, which housed a dead civilization. They were happy after seeing the place to sign it to Inira.

And she had promptly signed it over to Emerie, Lukas, and their descendants.

Inira's life had come full circle. She no longer had triggers and anxiety. They planned to transmit the Song of Creation to Emerie when she was ready. They didn't know how they would pull that off, but she felt there was something in the archives that would help them. She felt that string attached to her belly button, pulling her towards it, so she combed through dusty tomes whenever she had a break. She had been restored to peace in all her parts, fully integrated and established in her primary purpose after she gave everything she didn't need away in her time in the Great Unknown.

It was only deep in the night when she was lying next to Mattias; the scent of lavender would drift through the open windows, and she would feel the longing to return to the Ancients deep within her. She longed to return to Tomas, for their family to be complete with all made right. Somehow, the FourFold God would make it possible for her two great loves, Tomas and Mattias, and their twin-bound souls to serve into eternity with her. She felt Sophia would ensure her boys were reunited, as before the world's breaking.

It was all alright already.

She would see her children flourish before she knew it was time to go home. And all that is within her would be at peace.

Acknowledgements

There is no such thing as art created in isolation. Since I consider writing projects, like books, part of our collective lore and myth, they are worthy of the title of art. I am honored to be the one who partnered with the Divine to create this work of art – a story for our times and one that has brought me so much hope and vision, starting as an outlet for healing when I needed it.

Teleosis is a book that starts with a question: what would have happened if women had been at the table all along? It was quickly followed by the question: what would have happened if women didn't get the blame for the fall of humanity?

I began writing after leaving my career as a pastor and ministry leader in August of 2022. Much more contributed to these questions before August 2022; however, the Insurrection of January 6th, 2021; the murder of George Floyd; the global COVID pandemic; and Hurricane Harvey that hit my hometown of Houston in 2017. I've had a lot of questions brewing in my heart, mind, and soul since the election of Donald Trump in 2016.

As I began to think about writing again, I was grappling with the impact of patriarchy on my own life, on women as a whole, and the more extensive loss of the potential in our human history because of oppressive systems that keep the abundance promised in the Gospel of John from being realized.

John 10:10 has long been my vision for how the Divine seeks us to live, and I desire to see that made real. There are communities, pockets of the kind of life alluded to in this book, around the world where this vision is realized. Writing *Teleosis* was a large part of my struggle on how it doesn't seem to be happening on a massive scale, yet it is. There are always glimpses around the corner. This book was a way to work through my cognitive dissonance – through story – that had brought me out of my depression and burnout.

I've seen the promised land through connection and the out-rageous love we were created for and shared in the best and worst times.

Like I said, a project like this – art like this – doesn't emerge in isolation. Many people are to be thanked because they were critical to birthing this baby to take on her own life.

I want to thank my Alpha readers – Natalie (my oldest daughter who also picked the cover designer!) and Blair. Y'all saw this story was worth reading, and that encouragement kept me writing it. Reading and giving me feedback as I wrote it over nine months unlocked a new layer of gifting in me and helped me see a path forward that was right in front of me. I'm living my life now because you both believed in this project – and me.

Thank you to Lori – my therapist – and the first person I told about this project because it came to me on the way to an appointment. Thanks for letting me pay you to discuss this possibility instead of discussing my deep-seated issues.

Thank you to my friends who were willing to read early ver-sions. Thank you to my beta reader team – Linda, Amanda, Erika, Suzanne, and Carole (my Mom!), who provided invaluable feedback and made the final edits enjoyable. Thank you to my writer friends I've found through Instagram. We are all gonna make it, ladies!

Thank you to Adrienne Kusner, my editor. Between her exten-sive post-it converted notes, I could hear and see that I had something on my hands worth moving forward – and that I have a voice to keep using.

Thank you to Kelly Carter, my incredible cover designer who took my book description, made it beautiful, and told the whole story in just two images. Here's to the need to upgrade the license on those images. #iykyk

Thank you to Margie, my Author's Assistant, who brought so much to the table that I had no clue about and made it happen. The launch is a direct success because of your efforts, sister-friend!

Finally, thank you, READERS. Acknowledgments are hard to write because you don't want to forget anyone. But if you've read this book, you are who I thought of this whole time. I pray you take away the reality that you are seen and loved, and another way of life – in abundance – is possible when we do it TOGETHER.

ILY and am truly humbled by this life that has taught me only to expect the best,

Amy (W) V.

P.S. Your voice is important, too! As an independent author, reviews are critical to the success of a project (and career) like mine. I would be over the moon if you reviewed the book on Amazon, Goodreads and spoke about it on social media, which also helps others come in contact with this work of art. You are helping me help others, as I hope you were helped. Keep paying it forward, and we will get there – TOGETHER.

Also by the Author

Amy Vogel is an accomplished author, speaker, and story coach. She loves learning and sharing what she learns, especially in story form. Her passion is to help people understand their inherent worth and goodness, giving them a vision of wholeness meant for everyone, everywhere. She loves to help people discover who they were created to be, how to find their voice to tell their own stories, and find ways for all humans to thrive.

Get your free copy of a bonus chapter by signing up for her newsletter here: https://books.bookfunnel.com/readerschoiceb undle

Amy has written and published five books at the time of this printing. Her first two are spiritual nonfictional devotionals, Third Person, then Come to Me. Then came Teleosis, her fiction debut. In the Fall of 2024, she released The Assist, a sport romance and then Feminine Rising, a novella set in the world of Teleosis.

Find out all about her books, get signed copies, book her to speak and discover how she can help you tell your story through her coaching practice on her website: www.amywvogel.com.

Also, follow Amy on social media for serious depth and tons of nonsense: Tiktok: @amywvogel; Instagram: @awvogel; Facebook:@amywvogel; & Youtube:@amywvogel.